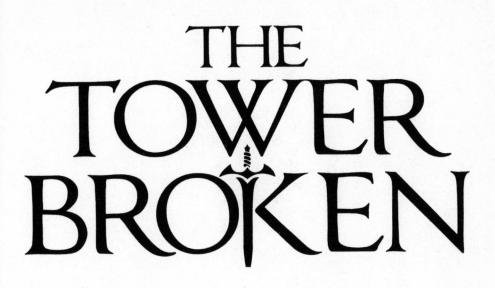

THE TOWER BROKEN

Also by Mazarkis Williams

The Emperor's Knife
Knife-Sworn

THE TOWER BROKEN

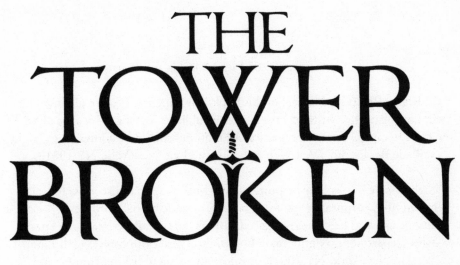

BOOK THREE OF THE TOWER AND KNIFE TRILOGY

MAZARKIS WILLIAMS

NIGHT SHADE BOOKS
NEW YORK

Night Shade books may be purchased in bulk at special discounts for sales promotion, corporate gifts, fund-raising, or educational purposes. Special editions can also be created to specifications. For details, contact the Special Sales Department, Night Shade Books, 307 West 36th Street, 11th Floor, New York, NY 10018 or info@skyhorsepublishing.com.

Night Shade Books® is a registered trademark of Skyhorse Publishing, Inc. ®, a Delaware corporation.

Visit our website at www.nightshadebooks.com.

10 9 8 7 6 5 4 3 2 1

Library of Congress Cataloging-in-Publication Data is available on file.

ISBN: 978-1-59780-526-1

Jacket art and design by Ghost
Map illustrated by Claudia Noble
Interior layout and design by Amy Popovich

Printed in the United States of America

For James

The Cerani Empire

To Vulcai and the unmapped West

KESH

FRYTH

GRASSLAND TRIBES

GULF of CERANA

COASTAL PROVINCE

The H... Ca...

N...

WESTERN PROVINCE

The River of a Hundred Names
The Blessing

C E R A

SOUTHERN

TO YRKMIR
YTHYCK
THE JAGGED SEA
EASTERN PROVINCE
A
INCE
DS '11

CHAPTER ONE

FARID

Farid's captors pushed him through the doorway. One moment he was standing in the alley, four hands holding him iron-tight at the shoulders, and the next, he was falling towards a pocked stone floor. He braced for the feel of cold granite against his cheek, the burn as it scraped his skin away, but then he flailed and righted himself. This was a small house—if it was a house—and a third of the space was taken by stairs rising up into darkness. The shadows beneath them held a man in dark robes, startled judging by his posture, a book held against his lap. Then strong hands took Farid again and steered him into the only other room, small and lined with shelves, stinking of foreigners' ale.

They shoved him against the far wall. He struggled to hear the words being murmured in the other room. The man from the shadows was asking questions—Farid could tell from the tone—but the words were too low for his ears. Just one captor stayed with him now. Farid sneaked a glance: he looked to be about his own age, and just as muscled. It would be a fair fight if it came to that. When his captor leaned over to pull on a length of fresh-smelling rope Farid got up to run, but with a casual movement of his foot the other man tripped him and he skidded against the hard floor.

While he was lying there stunned, jaw and arm smarting from the impact, his hands were tied behind him.

"Why are you doing this?" He did not expect an answer—from the time they grabbed him in the marketplace there had been no words. But they wanted something, otherwise he would be dead. The man half lifted, half pushed him into a wooden chair, then smiled, not a kind smile, though Farid sensed he could probably manage a semblance of such. He had smooth skin and regular features, not the sort one usually found in the Maze; more the sort you'd find in a comfortable position at a noble estate.

Or the palace. *The palace takes the best of us*, his father always said: the ones who showed unusual talent. The hardest workers. The strongest, the prettiest.

The palace would not have brought him to a tiny corner of the Maze, though. The palace would have taken him to a guard station in one of its outer walls, or worse, to the cold, dark cells hidden below its soaring towers. He had heard a person would do the unthinkable just to be free of them. Could this man have been in the prison dungeon, done something unthinkable?

Farid looked away, desperate to hide the current of his thoughts.

For months the Blue Shields had been in the Maze, hunting down the slave rebels and escaped prisoners, killing them in the streets and in the warrens where they hid. During this time the larger city had carried on with its usual business of exchanging goods for coin, and Farid with them. He had not considered the Maze and its outlaws his concern. Refugees from the north were a greater problem, crowding the streets and frightening his customers with rumours of deadly storms. He'd cursed them—too poor to pay for his fruit and too rich to disappear into the dark corners and alleys of the city and be out of his way.

But now that he was tied to a chair and at the rebels' mercy, he knew the refugees had been no more than a distraction.

The man laid a callused hand on Farid's cheek, the way his mother might. Startled, Farid looked back into his tea-coloured eyes.

"What did you see?"

Farid swallowed. "What happened back there? I heard—" *Nothing*. He'd heard nothing more than a chorus of gentle moans, drifting like ash on the wind.

"There was an attack." The man from the shadows stood in the doorway, lowering the hood of his red robe to reveal a shock of white-blond hair. Farid's pretty captor stood and lowered his head in deference.

"An attack?" Farid wiggled against his ropes. His hands felt numb. "It wasn't me. I was . . ." He had been looking down at the street-stones when they grabbed him.

The leader moved forwards, a look of sorrow on his face. "You saw them, didn't you?"

"Saw them? Who?" But at last Farid remembered. He had seen a glimmer in the afternoon light, had left his stall and squatted in the street to investigate. Shapes and lines, glimmering not on skin but on stone. He had thought it art, perhaps, or someone's idea of a joke. "The marks."

"The marks." This time it was the leader's turn to repeat.

"What do they mean?" Farid wiggled against his bonds again, looking from one man to the other. "Has the Pattern Master come back?" Part of him hoped they would not answer.

"No, this is not the pattern, not as you know it." The leader waved to the other man, who knelt to untie the ropes. Farid felt them loosen. "I apologise for the manner in which you were taken. Let's begin again. My name is Adam."

"I'm— My name is Farid." So this *was* about something they wanted. He relaxed a little. He knew how to barter and how to bluff.

"Farid." Adam held forth a flask. The old greeting, done with metal rather than skin.

The ropes slid away. Farid brought his hands forwards and rubbed them together before reaching for the flask. He said, "I don't know who you think I am. I sell fruit in the marketplace. Now my week's haul is left untended." He made his voice heavy with disappointment, emphasizing he'd already made a sacrifice. That would have to go into whatever deal these men had in mind. As he drank, he studied Adam. His build named him soldier; the robes named him priest. His bright hair spoke of the north, of Yrkmir. Of the enemy.

Adam showed his palms in a gesture of honesty. He knew the ways of Nooria, wherever he had come from. "Your fruit is gone, along with every living soul in that marketplace."

"What do you mean?" Farid grabbed the flask with both hands to keep from dropping it. There had been children there, old men, scrawny dogs, every one of them breathing and alive.

"Those marks destroy all that is or was alive. Once they surround a man he is already dead. But you saw them, and were saved."

Farid *had* seen them. He remembered leaving his stall, cautioning the boy who always sat on the barrels not to sneak an apple. He'd known the boy would do it anyway; he did it every time. It didn't matter. The boy kept good watch for him otherwise, from men and animals alike. Now Farid couldn't remember his name—he never forgot anything, and yet today, his memory failed him. *Gone.* Was the boy truly gone? It was impossible. He stood. "I want to see."

Adam pulled a piece of chalk from his robe and crouched. As he drew a white line against the stone Farid snapped, "No, not the marks." He had seen enough of the marks when the pattern took his mother. "I want to see the marketplace."

"It will not be a pleasant sight. In any case we can't let you go—not yet. The Tower will be searching for us." Adam said "the Tower" the way most people said "Yrkmir," hushed and wary. But then his hair, so bright, had already been a warning. These men were more than escaped prisoners. They were the worst of them: the very Mogyrks who had fomented rebellion in the first place.

"But I'm not one of you. I am a citizen of Nooria."

"And yet you see the marks."

"So you said. What does it matter?" Farid could not imagine what deal these Mogyrks might propose; he could not imagine why he still lived. It must have been they who attacked the marketplace, they who had killed everyone inside. Muad: he remembered the boy's name now. *Muad.*

"The patterns that lay a ward or an attack cannot be seen once they are set—not by anyone with normal eyes. You are blessed by Mogyrk to see them," said Adam, looking up at him from his position on the floor, sure and calm, though Farid towered over him. "The marks protect and strengthen those who are holy and hide from those who are not."

Farid had seen plenty of marks when the pattern ruled Nooria, when his mother had suffered and died, when Helmar had controlled half the city and sent the other half into hiding. "I'm not holy. I'm a fruit-seller. My father is coming upriver tomorrow with another load. He'll be expecting me to meet him."

Adam continued as if Farid had not spoken. "You are Cerani, but He has chosen from Nooria before. It is not for me to say why. You can see the pattern-marks."

"Again, what does it matter?" He wanted to punch the man. "What do you want?"

Adam looked up at him with eyes of the clearest blue. "You saw those pattern-marks. That means you can also use them."

CHAPTER TWO

MESEMA

Mesema unrolled a map of Nooria, laid it over the table engraved with the whole of Cerana and squinted. Nessaket had warned her that reading would take its toll on her eyesight, but maybe it was only the darkness of the library that made the lines swim under her gaze. The cartodome harboured a surprising number of shadows. She pushed the table towards the only window, where sunlight spilled in through the open screens.

"Majesty! Please, allow us." Willa took one corner of the table and Tarub the other.

"So you say with every turn of the glass. If it were up to the two of you, I would do nothing but sit in the bath all day until someone thought to take me out of it."

Tarub giggled as she set the table down under the window, then raised a hand to dispel the dust that danced in the sun like fireflies. Fewer hands cleaned the palace these days. Between the slave rebellion and the pale sickness, Azeem estimated they had lost a third of their workers, but Sarmin had put a hold on the buying and selling of slaves while he focused on a new code for their treatment. Mesema was never sure that words on parch-

6

ment could truly alter the way of things. She remembered hurrying past under the resentful glares of her father's Red Hoof captives, the hatred that guided their every word and posture. Even as a child she had understood they wanted to be free. Nessaket's injury and the kidnapping of Sarmin's brother Daveed had grown from such a legacy, and she was not certain Sarmin's code would bring it to any resolution.

Tarub and Willa showed no such concerns. Azeem said their happiness to serve came from being taken as children, that they knew no other life. He too, had once been a slave, and he thought it the way of things. For centuries slaves had kept the empire running and few who lived in it could imagine it any other way. Yet something in her said they must begin to do just that.

Tarub broke into her thoughts and pointed out the window, up into the sky. "Smoke, Your Majesty!" Dark plumes rose in the distance, drifting on the air. This had become the sign of unrest in the city as Mogyrk saboteurs took flame to guard posts and temples. Usually it stayed inside the Maze, but this smoke came very near, its ash drifting over the walls of the palace compound.

"That is the Festival of Meksha," said Willa, always the sensible one. "What you see are the smoke and ashes from the offerings, Your Majesty."

"Oh." Mesema had not been to a festival since she left the grass, but the celebration of a volcano-goddess did not appeal. One last glance out of the window, then she turned to her task, pulling five marble pieces from her belt, the kind used by soldiers to mark enemies on the field. One she placed over Beyon's tomb, once fallen to dust, and then repaired by Sarmin; this represented one of the blood-works Helmar Pattern Master had made to anchor his great spell. He had tricked Beyon into taking his own life and then used his blood to power the symbols hidden there.

She pushed the memory away and put a second piece along the river to the north, at the town of Migido, where Helmar had murdered the inhabitants and set their bodies into his design. Both the tomb and Migido had turned into great wounds, tainted by the death of the Mogyrk god and leaching colour and life from all they touched. Sarmin had healed the tomb, but still the emptiness in Migido crept ever south and east, towards Nooria and the river the Cerani called the Blessing.

The refugees from Migido had a name for it, borrowed from the nomads: the Great Storm.

Mesema took a deep breath. They had some time; the Storm in all its forms still remained distant. She placed a third marker to the northwest. The desert headman Notheen had spoken of a void in the reaches of the desert. That could be where Helmar's church had been—the church she had seen when first she came here, where she had learned a path through the pattern. Later Grada had killed the true body of the Pattern Master there.

She clicked the last two markers together in her palm. Five: that was always the number of Helmar's pattern; always groups of five carried out the Pattern Master's deeds. Five wounds: one healed and four remaining; four mouths to open and release the Storm, and nothing to stop them. In the eastern desert she placed a marker. This was where the Mogyrk god had died, and the scar he had left was larger than any wound made by Helmar. The eastern desert lay harsh and barren between Nooria and its farthest province; those who wished to travel in between sailed from the south rather than braving the sands. The eastern gate, called the Dawn Gate, but more widely known as the Dry Gate, had fallen into disuse and was now sealed.

She had placed four markers so far. The last she held in her palm, a mystery.

Sarmin said the pattern-skill had left him, that when he looked at a thing, the thing was all he saw—not the designs that made it what it was. "The pattern is a lie that is also true," he had said. Mesema felt she was just on the edge of understanding it. She had told many lies that felt true, such as framing a thought that was just beyond her, or telling a story the way she wished it had truly happened. The story she told herself today was that the Great Storm could be stopped with figures and a map.

"Your Majesty," said Tarub, her eyes cast humbly aside, "perhaps Pelar is hungry."

"He is sleeping." If she entered the room her son would know it and never rest until she held him in her arms. She smiled to think of his stubborn nature. He took after Beyon and her father both. Best to leave him in peace. Mesema traced the River Blessing on the map. It began in the mountains, ran past the fields that provided them with fruit and grain and down into the city of Nooria. She frowned, tracing the distance from the caravanserai of Migido to the river. The void had turned Beyon's tomb to dust; what might it do to Nooria's precious water?

"Perhaps the Empire Mother seeks you for a game of Tiles, Majesty," said Willa.

Mesema doubted it. Nessaket's injury had left her in great pain, and bouts of dizziness kept her bedridden much of the time. When she was able to visit Mesema, she carried her grief for Daveed along with her, bringing the shadow of his loss to all corners. Mesema would have done anything to fix the Empire Mother's pain, but she was powerless as anyone when it came to that. The royal guards and assassins still searched for Austere Adam and his followers, hoping Daveed was in their care, but in truth the babe could be as far away as Yrkmir. Sarmin spoke little of it, but she saw in the shadows of his eyes that it pained him too.

Mesema made a jest, hoping to lighten the mood. "You think my work is not ladylike and hope to distract me from it."

Willa leaned forwards, her expression serious. "Everything you do is most ladylike, my Empress. It cannot be otherwise."

"Hm." Mesema felt a rush of air over her skin and went still, one finger still poised over the blue line on the map. It had been long months since she had seen a message in the wind. The Hidden God did not live in the desert and must travel long miles to give her sight, but she watched and hoped as the breeze became a gust, carrying sand and ashes from Meksha's fires into the room. The map lifted from the table. For a moment it twisted, caught in the current, then landed on the floor, ashes circling it like bees around a hive. Their movements gained structure and purpose, finally gathering over the western quarter of the mapped city and forming a bright blue circle over the Holies. Then the wind blew again and scattered them to all four corners of the room.

"Did you see that?" asked Mesema, scrambling on her knees after the map.

"Your Majesty! You must let me—"

But Mesema already had it in her hand, seeking the building the pattern had indicated. "Here." She tapped the depiction of a large rectangular estate up on the Great Plateau. "That's the place. Tarub," she said, standing and brushing off her knees, "I need servant's garb and a pouch of water and—" She thought what normal townsfolk might carry. "A veil."

"Yes, Your Majesty," said Tarub, bowing. "But . . . why?"

"Because I am going into the city."

CHAPTER THREE

MESEMA

Mesema had known how to exit the palace by the Ways or servants' halls since the time she and Sarmin had hidden together in his room, but she had never before done it. She did not approach the Elephant Gate and its high teak doors but chose one of plain iron, used by slaves and delivery men, well-guarded nevertheless. She pulled the veil tight over her face as she stepped through. With her other hand she held tight to a bag of soiled linens, but nobody asked her business and she breathed a sigh of relief. A few feet outside the great walls she halted, heart beating fast.

No wife of the emperor was to travel unaccompanied. Her bodyguards and chaperones ensured her safety, chasteness and good behaviour. The women of the palace were never to set feet outside of it, lest they become sullied by the eyes of the common people. By the rules of the court she had already committed a crime. Tarub and Willa had cried and begged her to stay, and wisdom should have made her listen, but the Hidden God had pointed and she would follow.

And yet she paused, thinking of Sarmin. At this moment he was in his throne room, listening to petitions great and small, the lords and generals gathered around him like wolves. To keep their jaws from his flesh he required strength, and he gathered it from knowing she and Pelar were safe. Her absence could be devastating. Like all those born under the Scorpion's tail she had acted first and thought later. Mesema turned back, but one of the guards at the gate shook his fist at her, saying, "Stop lurking, you lazy get!" and she backed away. If he recognised her, it would be bad for him, for her and for Sarmin. After tossing her bag into a doorway she hurried down the palace road, a gentle slope that later turned into a steep incline approaching the river. The palace stood high above the city, overtopping all but the Tower.

The heat surprised her; this was the same sun that hung over the palace, but out here it reflected off the street and walls, bringing a sweat to her skin that soaked her robes. She walked along paths she had long watched from Nessaket's garden, jostled by petitioners, scribes, tailors, and money-counters. All were dressed in fine cloth, and the stones lay white and sparkling in the full day; but she would be walking on, through roads that were not so clean.

When she first arrived in Nooria, the air had smelled like char. Later she learned it had been the Carriers, turning to ash under the patient eyes of Blue Shields. Now as she left the palace compound the stench of rotting vegetables caught her nose and, as she walked further away, a urine-stink caught in her throat.

A marketplace set up along the road brought more welcome scents: roasting meat, incense, and cloves. Colourful fabric stretched from stall to stall, protecting customers from the harsh sun and casting a blue and yellow design over the streetstones. Mesema hurried across them as if the pattern chased her still. She recognised the young Tower mage Moreth buying a pastry from an old woman and she prayed to the Hidden God his gaze would not turn her way. To her relief his attention remained on his food; he waved the treat below his nose, smiling, as he turned back to the Tower. The common folk backed away from him, drawing circles with their fingers in the way of Mirra.

The house she sought would be on the other side of the Blessing, so she let her nose lead towards the smell of fish. She had often looked down upon the river, but from above it looked thin, a blue ribbon winding through a dry city. In fact it was wide enough for thirty pole-barges to float abreast, and for its high, arched bridges to hold hundreds of people, some standing still and watching the boats, others hurrying about their business. She took a lower path along the water, following the progress of the nearest barge, watching its poles push deep into the silt, their movements rippling along the Blessing's surface.

The next bridge loomed over her, an intricate work of red stone and copper, carvings of past emperors decorating each pointed arch. She climbed the steps to cross, dodging out of the way of one white-haired man carrying a sack of rice and another rolling a barrel; he clicked his tongue at her in irritation. Once on the other side she had a choice to climb the nine hundred great steps to the Holies, or to walk around the great rock to the western slope—not visible from the palace, but shown on maps to be a gentle, winding road to the great houses at the top. She had examined her route from the top of the palace before leaving, and she was glad of it, for the map was proving inexact. Now she embarked on a path her eyes had not explored, but upon turning west she saw with relief the carriage-road that led ever upwards towards the better neighbourhoods. This, the map had shown true.

She wondered whether Austere Adam might be in the house at the top of the plateau, hiding Daveed from the palace. Why else would the Hidden God have shown it to her? Nessaket admitted she had underestimated the Mogyrk priest, thinking him no more than a zealot, when in fact he had managed to organise a rebellion right under the noses of the palace guard. Mesema would have to think of a lie that would gain her entry to the great house. Though Austere Adam had great influence, she had fought the Pattern Master and watched Pelar struggle against the pale sickness; he did not frighten her. Sarmin would not think her actions wise; she knew this. Perhaps it was better he did not know.

On the plateau of the Holies she could see only streets and walls, interrupted by the occasional bench or statue. From the palace roof-garden Mesema had seen the graceful mansions and their lush enclosures filled with fruit-trees and jasmine, but at street level she saw only the dead leaves that had been blown over their high walls, dry offerings to the unwelcome. A breeze touched Mesema's cheek, tugging her southwest, and she found the house, marked by its walls of pink granite gleaming in the sun. Their long expanse spoke of the size of the building within, but still it was not as large as one wing of the palace. She walked along the stone, her fingers running over carved figures of Pomegra. The front gate she had seen, carved of iron and higher even than the walls, but servants would use the back.

The sharp cry of a baby pierced the stone. She stopped and listened, her heart beating in her throat. Perhaps Nessaket might have been able to say whether that was Daveed's cry; she could not. But she steeled herself and walked to the back gate, which was carved with a filigree pattern in the Fryth style that gave it a light and airy look. There a guard stood lazily sucking on a pipe, and when she approached, he lifted it from his mouth and stared.

"Please sir, blessings of the afternoon. I am looking for work. I was told to talk to the lord's steward."

The guard stood up straight, then brushed his moustache with a finger. "What kind of work?"

The lies came easily now she saw how embarrassed he looked. "I was nursemaid to the Lord Khouraf's babe, but it died, and they left the city in grief." The part about Lord Khouraf's babe dying was true—she had heard the story at court. She stepped forwards, an earnest expression on her face. "If I don't find another position soon, I—"

"Hold on, hold on," he grumbled, turning to the kitchen door. "I thought you smelled like a lady, is all." He left her at the gate and she lifted a wrist to her nose. Jasmine and musk. *Stupid.* Servants could never afford such a scent.

He remained in the house for some time as she waited in the quiet courtyard. Leggy roses grew against the wall, mostly neglected, but a lemon tree had been planted in a large pot and it gave off a fresh scent when the wind passed over. Beneath it sheltered a bench, and Mesema imagined the house's women sitting there, taking the morning air.

The guard returned and two men with him, rougher-looking, and big. "This her?" said one.

"That's her," said the guard without looking her way. His shoulders were hunched, like a beaten dog. *Danger.* She backed away towards the road.

"You asking questions?" The one to her right towered over her. He looked Cerani, but his eyes were blue.

"I was asking for work. If there is no work then I will leave." She held her shoulders straight, refusing to be afraid.

"Who told you there was work for a nursemaid?"

"I heard . . . people were talking . . ." She began to see the problems with her story.

"What people?"

"People at the church." She thought that would be enough to quiet them, but instead, they took more interest, stepping closer with new light in their eyes.

"What church?"

She swallowed, hoping her answer would hit the mark. "The church of the One God, the God of Everyone and Everything . . ." She recited what Eldra had told her, but the first man shook his head.

"She's one of those pretties, trained to spy. This is how they do it, Jafar."

Jafar took her right hand and turned it, examining the nails. "She is no servant, it's true." Then he dug his fingers into her elbow. "You'll come inside and tell us who sent you."

"I'm just a nursemaid," she insisted, digging in her heels. If they took her inside she did not think she would come out. Pelar's face flashed through her mind. It occurred to her that she might not see him again, and she felt as if she had swallowed all the emptiness in the world.

"You're—" The man's word ended in a wet sound.

Mesema felt a warm spray like summer rain on her shoulder—but this was the desert, and there was no rain. She turned, and the blood gushing from his neck hit her in the face.

"What—?" Jafar drew his sword and slashed at someone behind her.

Mesema had never been in a fight, but she had been in a war; she knew getting out of the way of a sword was more important than understanding why it was there. She dashed behind the lemon tree and now she saw it was Grada standing under the arch of the open gate, holding her twisted Knife while Jafar advanced upon her. He thrust and she ducked, spun, and came up inside his guard, putting her Knife to his neck. They stood nose to nose and her dark eyes locked upon his. The cold expression on Grada's face turned Mesema's stomach to ice.

Jafar's sword clattered against the flagstones when he dropped it.

"Tell me about the child," Grada hissed.

"Die, filth," he said, "or else kill me."

Grada was about to ask another question when her gaze flicked Mesema's way. At that moment Mesema felt the fabric press against the back of her shoulders and the cold of a blade against her neck. She had forgotten the first guard. "Let Jafar go," he said, "and I will not kill your little spy." He was not so awkward as she had believed, holding his dagger firmly where it would do the most damage. She stopped breathing.

"She is not my spy," said Grada, but nevertheless she stepped away from Jafar. Mesema saw something flash in Grada's hand just as her foot went out, connecting with Jafar's stomach. The blade touching Mesema's skin fell away and she heard a rattle as something hit the wall to her left.

The moustached guard crumpled behind her. Blood soaked both his shirt and her robes.

Jafar doubled over as if in pain, but really his hand sought the sword he had dropped. Grada stepped on it and brought her knee into his face. Another moment, and she was crouching over him, the Knife against his neck once more. "What does he look like?" she asked.

"Who?" Jafar was disoriented now, frightened and humiliated. Mesema watched, frozen in place.

"The baby you're hiding."

Jafar looked puzzled, and he moved his lips a few times before answering. "Some ugly get from the north. Don't—" Then he jerked, and gasped.

Grada's Knife had pierced his heart, but Mesema had not even seen her move.

Grada stood, wiping the blood from her twisted blade, and examined the house. "They have no windows facing the courtyard—probably to give their women privacy. Good for us." Grada sounded distant.

Mesema had seen much death during the Red Hoof War, even the clouded eyes of her own brother, and yet she could not move. Grada removed her knife-belt and drew off her grey robe, revealing a tunic and leggings beneath. "You're covered in blood. Wash your face and sandals at the pump, then wear this." She paused. "Your Majesty."

Mesema looked around for a water-pump, found it against the house and approached on shaking legs. Numbly she worked the handle and splashed water over her face and feet. "You killed them," she said, pulling on the grey robe.

"They laid hands upon my empress." Grada's gaze shifted from the house door to the gate as she replaced her belt.

Mesema frowned. The man who had come outside with Jafar had not touched her, but she decided to say nothing about that. "Hurry. We've taken too long." Grada retrieved the dagger she'd thrown at the moustached guard, who was now lying in a corner among some leaves, and walked out through the gate. "But there's something here. I saw—" In the map room she had seen blue in a shaft of sunlight, but perhaps it had been only her ring, caught in a beam from the window—a trick of the eye. Not a message from the Hidden God; nothing more than an excuse to leave the palace, to feel important. "Daveed is not here." She wiped at a tear.

"I was fairly certain he was not." Grada walked at a fast clip. "News of this will spread quickly among the Mogyrk rebels. A nursemaid comes calling and soon three guards are lying dead. If Daveed was anywhere near—"

"—he won't be any longer." Mesema made fists so tight her fingernails cut into the flesh of her palms. *Stupid, stupid.* And yet for a trick of the eye it had guided her true. Those men *had* been of Mogyrk.

"You should leave such things to me, Your Majesty." Grada's voice betrayed some impatience. A carriage passed them by, one bejewelled hand holding open the curtain, and Mesema pulled her scarf tight. Her wheaten hair could yet betray her to a courtier.

"That house is important." It had to be, else those deaths were for nothing.

"I have been watching it for some time. Lord Nessen's lands are on the northern border, and he has sympathy for the Fryth." Grada chose the steep stairs over the gentle road, and Mesema followed in her wake, picking a careful descent, looking in vain for handholds. "He's not in Nooria, but I think he soon will be. They have received several deliveries of food, as if they expect a large company."

The sun was beginning to set. How long had she been out in the city? "I was going to pretend to be a servant, since you cannot do such a thing," Mesema said. "They are prejudiced against your kind." Untouchable, Sarmin had called her. It was in her eyes.

"I am not the only spy the emperor commands, heaven bless him."

"I have made your work more difficult." Something compelled Mesema to continue talking, to wrap words around her actions until they came up clean. She had run out into the city, impulsive and arrogant, thinking to save Daveed with a map and blue light. Now men had paid for it with their lives.

Grada glanced over her shoulder and offered spare words of comfort. "They will be forced to play their hand sooner now, and that may help us."

"Their hand? Is there another Mogyrk conspiracy?" So focused had she been on Daveed that she had never thought there might be more at risk: another mistake she had made.

Grada quickened her pace without answering, almost skipping down the endless stairs, and Mesema had to hurry to keep up. She was no longer that girl who had run across the plains without tiring; now her lungs burned in her chest. "I will tell the emperor about this myself, may the gods bless him."

"It would be as well that you do, for I do not bother his Majesty with unimportant news."

Mesema's errand had not felt trivial. Anger flashed over her, renewing her pride. "You cannot speak to me this way. I am your empress."

Grada touched the Knife at her side. "In the city I am in control, so that I may keep you alive. In the palace you may do as you like." She had the right of it; the emperor's Knife was not just any member of the Grey Service. She could make decisions of life or death over any royal person, including Sarmin himelf. Grada served the empire, and in the way she saw fit. It was all in that ugly weapon.

They descended the rest of the way in silence, Mesema praying her legs did not give out on her.

At the bottom of the hill Grada stopped and listened, giving Mesema a chance to catch her breath. "There are rebels fighting around the edges of the Maze," she said. "We will take a different path."

Mesema could hear nothing but she followed Grada without a word, holding tightly to her veil. She had not realised the Maze was so close. They took a circular path to the bridge she had crossed before, where the crowds had thinned and a man dressed all in black pushed a broom over the stones. By the time they passed through the covered market the sun had settled beyond the river and vendors were packing up their stalls. They turned onto the broad avenue leading past the Tower and Mesema recalled the beginning of her day and the sense of rightness she had carried: it seemed distant. A man approached, stumbling, smelling of alcohol, and Grada put herself between him and Mesema until he had disappeared around the next corner.

"Thank you," she said, but Grada did not reply.

In the evening those who had failed to gain an audience filled the streets around the palace. Every sunset they could be seen from the roof, some well-dressed and moving with angry impatience, others in rags, stumbling. Occasionally a carriage, moving fast, entered the street and forced everyone to scatter, or a merchant's cart would move through, offering fruit or drink to the petitioners.

Mesema and Grada moved against the flow, coming towards the palace instead of leaving it. Then Grada took her arm and pulled her into the shadow of a doorway. "Soldiers," she said. "Best they don't see you."

At first Mesema could see only a disturbance, walkers and carts flowing to either side like water around a great stone, but as the group drew close she recognised the squad of Blue Shields, approaching the palace with brisk steps. They looked straight ahead, hands curled around the hilts of their swords. As a child in wartime Mesema had become accustomed to judging what sort of news a person had by their bearing. Stiff and nervous, these soldiers had come to report something bad. The two women waited for them to pass, and then a while longer, before following in their wake.

"What do you think happened?" Mesema looked up at Grada's expressionless face. "Is it about Daveed?"

"Probably not," said Grada, her fingers straying to the hilt of her Knife.

Mesema had seen enough of the Knife for one day. "Let's keep moving."

At the courtyard Grada held Mesema back while she checked for soldiers and guards, then waved her through. "Use the servants' entrance," she said. "Go and change."

"We're in the palace now," Mesema said with some relief. "You cannot tell me what to do." Nevertheless she went in by the servants' entrance and took the circuitous route to the women's wing. The guards looked at her grey robes with curiosity as they opened the doors. She ignored them as she passed through.

The new women's wing was white and spare, as plain as a Rider's longhouse, except for the mosaic of Mirra set into the floor. The peaceful room brought her calm and she smiled at the concubines who sat around the Great Room, embroidering their shawls.

Tarub, waiting by the mirror, jumped up when she entered her bedchamber. "Your Majesty! I was so worried—"

"Quickly," said Mesema, casting aside the assassin's robe. "I must stand with my husband the emperor in the throne room."

CHAPTER FOUR

SARMIN

S armin sat on the Petal Throne. His legs ached from too long in the metal seat. The morning had found the cushions missing once again, giving Sarmin a choice: to request them in the full presence of the council, or do without. He knew what Azeem would say—to ask for a pillow was a weakness before men who would eat the sharp, cold throne for supper if they could. And so he had said nothing. Now he remained on his throne as priests, generals, and merchant princes met in groups around the great room. Beyon had ruled through intimidation of the court and camaraderie with the soldiers; Tuvaini's short rule had been marked by arrogance. Since Marke Kavic's murder and the loss of his brother, Sarmin sat at a cold and furious remove, alone both in body and in mind.

The courtiers clustered into groups, some of them speaking loudly and hoping to be overheard, while others schemed in low voices. His own men, those he had elevated or done a favour, moved through the crowd, listening. Lord Jomla had betrayed the Petal Throne and paid with his life, but he had left behind his associates. Sarmin had brought each of them under his heel, and any who complained or whispered had met with Grada's skilled hand. It had been a month since last she cut a noble neck, and still he kept close watch.

Though the Great Storm was brewing in the desert, this evening the courtiers spoke of Fryth. General Arigu had invaded that outermost colony of Yrkmir, but the Felting horse tribes—Mesema's people—had shown treachery, attacking his army in the night and taking him captive. Those of Arigu's men who had survived the march home returned in rags, starving and ill. Much talk was devoted to revenge upon the north—beginning with the Felt. Sarmin's task was to prevent their bluster from turning into military action. Fryth had been Tuvaini's war and Sarmin had paid enough for it already. The new chief of Mesema's people had erred, but it was he who should pay, not all those she cared for. But as much as he tried to cool their anger, High Priest Dinar only fanned it again, for conflict was the realm of Herzu, and He would seek war whenever possible.

Lord Benna, Sarmin's man, passed by Satrap Kenneck and made two symbols with his hand: *War talk. North.* Sarmin moved his gaze across the room as if he had not seen, but he too could think of nothing else this evening. Herran, the master of Sarmin's spies and assassins, had received a new report, bringing dark rumours from those distant mountain valleys of Fryth. Most of the courtiers preferred to disbelieve them; their fantasies of revenge left no room for other possibilities.

Laughter and the clinking of glasses followed the arrival of the evening's libation. The courtiers began to circulate, winding around one another in an intricate dance of power. Only the guards, High Mage Govnan and the desert headman Notheen held an unmoving silence, rocks in a moving stream of finery and jewels. During the day lord and priest alike sat in their places, tiered according to birth and influence, but now the doors had been closed and all the reports read, they worked the invisible strings of empire.

Once he might have been able to see a pattern in it, but that kind of sight had left him.

Against the wall stood a harpist, plucking at his strings. He had been a gift from Lord Murti, governor of Gehinni Province. Sarmin did not like music; he neither understood nor anticipated how the notes were meant to come together. It came to his ears as a collection of tumbling noises, and it grated on his nerves when combined with other sounds. Azeem told him it was the latest fashion to have a musician hovering about, but he did not care. He waved a hand for the man to stop, and breathed a sigh of relief when the plinking ended.

Azeem gathered his work at the near table. "What did you think of the spy's report, Magnificence?" he asked, too low for anyone to overhear.

The report. Sarmin shifted and felt needles along his right leg. Herran's spy, a travelling merchant, claimed Yrkmir had destroyed Fryth not long after Arigu's men had retreated. And how . . . Sarmin remembered the way Marke Kavic had spoken of the empire, and he knew there was no great love between Fryth and the first austere—but no great nation destroyed one of its own colonies. What of tribute, men to work the land? It made no sense to punish Fryth so soon after its great victory against Cerana, their ancient enemy. Add to that the manner of its destruction . . .

Azeem busied himself with inks and signatures, his long fingers careful and precise, but Sarmin knew that he was waiting upon an answer. With the Many, he had held conflicting views, and a chorus had offered its wisdom, hatred, or fears. Now he was alone and could offer only his own belief, with no contravening whispers. At last the dark words found his voice. "I think it is true, and I think the Yrkmen's path will lead them to Nooria."

Azeem laid his hands upon the table a moment, saying nothing. Beyond him Satrap Honnecka and the gaunt General Merkel paused to chat; Sarmin watched their distorted reflections in the shining floor. It had been a long while since such men had encountered enemy soldiers. They liked to complain the White Hats had been humiliated when they left Fryth, and claimed they would relish a chance to restore Cerana's honour. But would they stand against Yrkmir, or flee to their comfortable homes in the provinces? Without Arigu, Sarmin felt less confident facing Yrkmir's army.

The time had come to send Pelar and Mesema to the safety of the southern province. Headman Notheen had long insisted the palace should leave the capital, and Sarmin would begin with its most precious inhabitants.

The herald's gong crashed and shimmered in the air, indicating a new arrival: someone too late to petition, but too important to turn away. Nevertheless he—or they—would wait. Sarmin raised a hand to stay the twelve men set to open the heavy doors, giving the courtiers time to finish their conversations and find their seats. *Never should a ruler act with urgency. His power is great: its shadow, eternal.* It was all within the *Book of Statehood.* With everyone settled, he motioned the doormen a second time. As the carved doors swung slowly on their hinges the smaller side door snapped open and Mesema slipped through. Sarmin took note, as always, of who bowed to his wife—High Priest Assar of Mirra, some minor lords, and his vizier, Azeem.

Dinar of Herzu stared at her with his dark eyes.

Mesema held her shoulders back and her head high as she walked towards the dais. She had defeated the Pattern Master—these men were nothing to her. Admiration rose up inside of him, warm and powerful. Before Mesema lowered herself into an obeisance she met Sarmin's gaze. Her cheeks were flushed, her hair in disarray. He would swear that every time he saw her she was more beautiful than before, her brightness sharp enough to cut him. He took the time she faced the floor to gather himself.

"Rise," Sarmin said. "Does all go well in the women's wing, my wife?" Some of the men glanced at one another, smirking at the absurdity that he should ask, and he marked each face. Mesema blushed and looked aside as if guilty. "Yes, Magnificence. The builders have made a beautiful home for us. I am grateful." As he puzzled over the space between her words and her expression, the God Doors reached their full extension.

Sarmin waved to the right side of the throne, and Mesema took her place there. His brother Beyon had never put his mother behind a screen, as much as he had hated her, and even if Sarmin had wished to keep Mesema from the court's view to protect her, he did not know where such a screen might be kept. Nor did he know how to keep Mesema away from the centre of things. Let the men of the council sneer; Mesema would stay. He motioned for the new arrivals to move forwards.

Blue-hatted soldiers approached over the long silken path, each looking more dour than the last. They came to the end of the runner and prostrated themselves.

Sarmin heard Mesema draw a long breath beside him. "Rise and report," he said into the silence.

"Your Majesty," said the man in front, a greying man with wide shoulders who held his plumed hat under an elbow. "Your Majesty, there has been an attack."

The rebels often started fires or threw rocks at Blue Shields in the Maze. Never had his soldiers reported about them with such ceremony. Had Austere Adam and his missing slave rebels made a move, done something more serious? Sarmin knew the attacks must stop, but at the same time each one brought hope, for violence left clues that could be traced, perhaps all the way to his brother Daveed.

Sarmin did not shift in his seat, careful to show calm. "Give me the details."

"An hour ago, we were called to the eastern fruit market, Magnificence. But we were too late: everyone there was dead." The soldier swallowed. "I don't know how many. We couldn't make out the men from the women, or the dogs from the children. They were . . . they were destroyed."

Icy fingers ran along Sarmin's spine. "Destroyed how?"

The soldier's skin paled and he glanced towards Mesema. "Bits of flesh everywhere, bones lying in the sun . . . just cooking there." He swallowed. "It was like they were turned the wrong way out. Your Majesty."

. . . *a wet fall of pulverised flesh, as if in one sharp moment the pattern shrank to a point and each line of it became a razor, slicing through skin and flesh to the bone* . . . Sarmin pushed away the memory that was not his. It was of Fryth, of a young boy named Gallar who had lived and died in those high and unforgiving places. Not here.

One of the soldiers swayed and held a hand to his mouth. Sarmin hoped he would not vomit on the dais; his men would take payment for such an infraction before he could raise a hand to stop them.

Sarmin's right hand wrapped around the carved roses of the throne, ridges and thorns pressing against his skin. He watched Govnan leave through the side door. The old man might move slowly, but he wasted no time.

"Keep the marketplace undisturbed until the Tower has completed its investigation."

"Yes, Your Majesty."

"Good work." Sarmin looked beyond the soldiers to where Grada leaned against the far wall. He had not seen her arrive, but he had felt her presence, like a cooling fountain at the height of the day. She shook her head at him, her way of telling him she had not found Daveed—not yet. Then she looked long at Mesema before making her exit. As she disappeared beyond the doors he felt a small tug, as if a string had been cut inside him. But that had happened long ago, and the familiar desolation touched him only briefly.

Sarmin turned his attention to the soldier. "You are dismissed."

The room held silent until the doors were closed once more, then erupted into chaos.

"The Mogyrks have done this!"

"We cannot stand for it, Magnificence!"

"We must raid their churches, slaughter all the rebels," said General Merkel, grabbing at the hilt of his sword as if a Yrkman stood before him. "Herran knows where they are—why does he not tell us?"

"Indeed, Herran . . . where is he?" Satrap Honnecka raised a finger to Azeem. "Call for the master spy at once!" At this Dinar of Herzu smiled, the only man in the room to take joy from the situation.

Mesema brushed Sarmin's shoulder, the briefest of touches, and he remembered himself, raising a hand. "I can hear all of you, even if you are not screaming."

General Hazran of the Blue Shields, always more measured, rubbed at his beard. "It is certainly possible the Mogyrks are responsible. It could be the prelude to something greater. Vizier Azeem, could you read once again the report from Fryth?"

Azeem shuffled his parchments, playing for time. It had disquieted him. The first time he had read the report, the courtiers had called it absurd. They had called into question Herran's wisdom in employing certain spies, who sent reports designed to deceive them about the state of their enemy. Such is the ability of many to forget all that has gone before.

At last Azeem lifted the missive and read in a clear, well-accented voice, "Word from traders who have passed through Fryth is beginning to filter into Nooria. The news is strange: reports of men reduced to flesh and broken bone, of a silent valley where no bird sings . . . and the rulers and generals who were there short months ago are nowhere to be found in the empty cities and farms. And everywhere, pennants fly the red and white emblem of Yrkmir."

CHAPTER FIVE

GOVNAN

Govnan made his way down the narrow street, his rock-sworn acolyte Moreth right behind. A butcher's-alley stench grew stronger with every step, and the dingy, windowless buildings rising high on either side blocked the moonlight and trapped the air at nose level. The guards had removed all citizens except for the witnesses, who waited in a coffee house nearby, so he and Moreth met nobody as they walked, heard nothing except the click of Govnan's staff against the stone. The houses at the end of the street tilted in so much their roofs met at odd angles, making the passage so narrow Govnan was forced to turn sideways in places.

"There's a step—be careful," murmured Moreth. The rocksworn occasionally helped him down the stairs, and had developed a protective air.

"My eyes are not so old they cannot see."

On the other side of the gap houses receded, leaving a rough open circle, a well in the centre, wide enough to set up three stalls and some barrels. Lantern-light revealed nothing tipped over or broken. The marketplace looked in order, except for the lumps of flesh on the ground and a dizzying odour of death.

Herran had provided them with cloths soaked in camphor and Govnan pressed one to his nose and mouth. A guardsman waited at attention beside a cart covered with dripping red paste.

As he approached the guardsman said, "This was pomegranate, High Mage."

"I see." Govnan turned to look at what lay on the ground—human, he thought, as shreds of clothing could be seen among the gore. Bones had snapped and turned out towards the sky, and the skin had either melted or turned inwards. Intestines slithered out onto the stone, glistening in the firelight. He choked back bile. He did not know whether a physician or a butcher would be better able to tell man from woman. And there were five more such deposits—two by the well, three scattered around the carts.

Sarmin had separated him from his flame-spirit Ashanagur and it sometimes felt as if he had lost half his intellect. Ashanagur might have identified the cause of death, though in Govnan's experience, the efreet did not always share information. Now he had Moreth. That would have to do. Govnan knelt, wincing at the pain in his knees and hips as he settled against the ground.

He looked down at a stretch of pink flesh, smooth as a mirror. "Your robes, High Mage!" cried Moreth. Indeed, blood had already soaked into the white cotton. "I have many," he said, and it was true, though there were few to wash them. The Tower had never kept slaves. When he was a young man the Tower had been teeming with mages and their apprentices, all sharing the work, but even that had been a decline from the days of Satreth the Reclaimer. In recent years they had been fewer yet. Now Mura had been lost to the Fryth war, to his unending sorrow, and only Moreth, Hashi the wind mage and the Megra remained. Of those not of the Tower, only Sarmin knew its emptiness, the cobwebs in every corner. Its potency had long kept Cerana safe from all enemies—that was, when High Mage Kobar had held the seat. There had not been a day Govnan had served as high mage when there was not some magical threat haunting the empire. And now this.

The destroyed flesh yielded little more information close up than it had at a distance. He was sure now the bones had not been cut with any weapon; the breaks were not smooth and he saw no scoring that would indicate a blade. He smelled nothing like poison or the sulphur used in casting certain illegal spells. Before replacing his camphor-soaked cloth he said a quick prayer to Mirra; though he had never been a believer, he hoped this poor soul had been lifted. He gripped his staff and stood. "I need samples from the flesh of each of these and"—he looked around at the positions of the dead—"I want a drawing, with distances. Get a draftsman from the Builders' Tower to do it."

"You think there might be a pattern here, High Mage?"

Govnan disliked revealing the path of his thoughts, so he ignored the question. "Find what the spirit Rorswan has to tell you."

Moreth knelt, pressed a hand to the ground and closed his eyes, becoming so still one might have thought him a statue.

The guardsman shifted nervously, looking at the stones beneath his feet. Most without talent did not realise the danger, but this one was clever.

The rock-sworn spoke in a grinding voice that crushed syllables as a millstone crushes wheat. "Magic here. Not the Tower. Pictures of light. A circle." He was silent again, and after a long while he stood, wiping sand from his lips. He met Govnan's gaze, eyes dark with what he had seen, but he would not share it in front of the alert guardsman.

The guardsman took a step to his left, where the market narrowed into yet another airless street. Doubtless he was eager to leave this place. "Will you interview the witnesses now?"

Govnan took one last look around. Nothing but death waited here, and all of it beyond the reach of man or elemental. "Lead us there," he said. He followed the man, his robe sticky with blood and rubbing against his knees. "Excellent work, soldier," he said, though he had no idea if that were true. He wanted only to put something kind into his day. The soldier stood a little straighter as he walked.

The coffee house nestled in a small courtyard off the street. Silken tent-cloth protected customers from the hot sun during the day, but it made the evening dark. Frightened and grieving residents clustered around candles at the wooden tables, guarded by impassive Blue Hats. The aroma of coffee hung over everyone, a scent Govnan usually disliked, but today he welcomed anything that could overpower the stench of the marketplace.

He eased himself into a seat, facing a man with a long beard and a copper ring on his finger. His clothes were of poor quality, but clean. "Blessings of the day. I am High Mage Govnan. What is your name, sir?"

"High Mage?" the man said, his voice sounding hollow. He did not raise his eyes to look. "My lord . . ."

"I am no lord, just an old man wanting to know what happened in the marketplace." As Govnan spoke, Moreth took his station behind his chair, casting a shadow over the table.

"We all saw it," the man said, turning his ring in a circle. "It was right after Farid left his stall."

Govnan waited, but the man only twisted his ring. A woman's sob punctuated the silence.

"They just fell," said the light-eyed girl at the next table, her gaze falling somewhere beyond Govnan. "I was buying a pomegranate from Thera, and it exploded in my hand. It felt hot. I heard a dripping . . . and then I saw her. She just . . . *wasn't.*"

"Did she fall and then die, or . . ." Govnan cleared his throat, "did she die and then fall?"

"They fell apart first," said the man with the ring. Several nodded their assent.

"And this Farid, who you say left the marketplace—do you think he had something to do with it?"

"Not Farid, no!" An old man with a goat's beard stood and tried to pace, but was blocked by chairs. "He saw something. That's why they took him."

"*They* took him? Who is 'they'?"

"This is what happened," said the old man, adopting a patient tone, though he looked anything but. "I saw Farid leave his stall and crouch down on the street. I thought he'd dropped a coin. Then Thera and the others just . . . they just died. When I looked up, I saw two men dragging Farid away."

"Not guardsmen?"

"No, but one of them was Cerani. The other was dark-haired and pale. Strong."

Govnan frowned. Pale sounded like the north. "Did they say anything?"

The old man waggled his head. "Nah."

"And where were you standing, that you could see both the marketplace and the street?"

The old man gave him a puzzled look. "I was in the marketplace."

The others nodded. "We all were," said the woman.

"So not everyone in the marketplace died." Govnan twisted his staff against the stone floor. Had the dead been targeted? But how?

"Only the ones . . ." The old man trailed off. Govnan looked at him, but nothing more was forthcoming.

"We were all part of the Many," said the woman, lifting up her sleeve to show faint scars, faded now with time: moon, circle, triangle. "Every one of us who lived. Not them, though. Those that died had been spared—if that's what you can call it now."

A hush fell over the group as Govnan studied her skin. Though the pattern had once been blue, it was a green glow that illuminated her scars now, flickering, growing brighter. He dropped her arm and looked up. Light shone through the silken roof.

"Torches," said Moreth, putting a protective arm out to Govnan. The high mage stepped away from the rock-sworn. Fire did not frighten him.

A voice called down to them, muffled by the fabric, "Taste what your gods Meksha and Herzu have to offer!" Govnan caught the stink of kerosene before the night exploded with orange light and heat.

The witnesses screamed and ran in confusion, smoke billowing in their wake, but Govnan stood firm. The runes he needed were simple enough to form, rough commands that had been Ashanagur's. His fingers moved to the task, splitting the air with radiance, each stroke bringing more intensity until the runes shone lightning-white, stretching their thready fingers into the air. The fire shrank away from them, towards the edges of the courtyard.

Again he commanded with the language of the efreet. Trails of light reached out to embrace the flames and the fire withdrew, leaving an empty space where the silk covering had been. Govnan looked up to the rooftops.

Moreth was already kneeling, hand to the ground. "Three men running," he said, "jumping down . . . on the street now." He closed his eyes, concentrating. His fingers sank into the stone floor as if it were sand. Behind them, a woman exclaimed in horror. "Tripped them," he said, his voice growing deeper, becoming the stone-spirit's. "I grow around them now."

Govnan bent over the rock-sworn, holding tight to his staff, speaking low enough that the witnesses who remained could not hear. "Have you killed them?"

Moreth—Rorswan—shuddered with pleasure. So they were dead.

"Moreth!"

Moreth withdrew his hand from the stone and shook himself as if waking. "One got away," he said. "His feet stopped touching the stone just as

Rorswan—" He turned to the Blue Shields. "They are three streets down, by the statue of Keleb. One of them climbed onto a cart or a ladder . . . Hurry!"

The men ran without questions.

"It is useless," Govnan muttered. "Two are dead, the other gone. Come. Let us see what Rorswan has wrought."

By the time they reached the statue of Keleb, Govnan's feet ached so that each step was an agony. He leaned on his staff, out of breath. Moreth glanced at him every few minutes, concern on his face. Govnan held back his impatience. The boy had only the barest control over his bound spirit, and yet he thought the high mage weak. He missed his children, Amalya and Mura, whom he had raised from childhood. Emperor Tahal had once told him that daughters were his greatest joy, and sending them away to be married his greatest sorrow. Though Govnan had no daughters of his own, the girls he had taken as children and trained in the Tower had indeed given him years of happiness. Now they were gone, and the grief rattled in his old bones.

The god of wisdom rose before them, carved from cold marble that looked every inch living flesh. His mouth was fierce, and one hand raised to the sky: Keleb's passion was not for war or revenge; those He left for lesser gods. Keleb's carved eyes were turned towards the palace, and He commanded those within it to adjudicate with balance and foresight. In His hands He held the books of law that even the emperor could not supersede. And at His feet, bloodstained stones told a story of death.

Govnan looked around the tiny square. "And so we do not even have the bodies."

Moreth sat on the edge of Keleb's pedestal and put his head in his hands. "It would appear that Rorswan has claimed them."

"It would appear? You do not remember?"

"I do remember. It was just . . ."

Govnan knew: the ecstasy the spirits felt when they took a life was contagious. It could overwhelm a mage if he was not careful. "You must be in control at all times."

"I am." Anger covered for shame on the mage's face. "If I were not, I would be stone."

Govnan considered Moreth: the future of the Tower. At Moreth's age Govnan had stood side by side with Kobar, Ansalom, and others, wielding fire and earth against wildings from the west. He had stood at the heights of the Tower and summoned spirits of flame to do his bidding and aided Kobar to build wonders of gem and stone. In those days the Tower had been filled with sworn mages, and bards had sung of their feats far beyond the mountains and the sea. But it was not Moreth's fault their power was waning; that had begun long ago—and Moreth had come to them after the pattern-sickness, already a man grown. His training had been both rushed and darkened by Govnan's grief. While most mages trained from child-hood, Moreth had accomplished much in one year. It was the best that anybody could have done.

He put a comforting hand on the rock-sworn's shoulder. "Come. It is time for me to report to the emperor."

CHAPTER SIX

SARMIN

"You are certain?" said Sarmin, sitting down behind his desk in his new, soft room decorated with tassels and bright pillows. His old room held nothing for him now, not since the Megra had drawn the last of its patterns away, and not since he had lost the ability to see them. Govnan and Notheen stood side by side before his desk, one small and hunched, the other tall and straight. The desert headman stood so still one might think him a stone, while the high mage seemed to shimmer, like the flame he had once held within him.

Govnan bowed his head. "Yes, Magnificence. Both strikes were at Mogyrk hands."

"What of this fruit-seller? Did he assist them?"

"By all accounts he was no more than a fruit-seller, and a devout follower of our gods."

Odd. Sarmin wondered whether these attacks came from Austere Adam, still hiding somewhere in the city, or if they heralded the arrival of Yrkmir as Hazran had suggested. He turned to Notheen. "What news of the desert? Does our enemy approach?"

Notheen took some time to speak, his eyes distant as stars. "No enemy has been seen, Magnificence, but nothing passes through the sand without a ripple. My people speak of something great that moves through the empty spaces."

All of the desert was an empty space to Sarmin. He riffled through old parchments, Helmar's writings. None of it made sense to him now. Kavic had been able to read the symbols, and he might have taught him, but Kavic had died. Helmar was gone, as were his Many. Of those who knew the pattern, only the Megra remained. "I must speak with the Megra."

"She is ill, Magnificence. I would hurry." Sorrow pulled Govnan's face.

Sarmin pushed the thought aside; he had no time to linger on the pain of losing the Megra. "And what of the sickness that creeps from Migido?"

"It does appear that the use of the pattern accelerates its growth." Govnan cleared his throat. "My wind-sworn Hashi reports the pattern attack in the marketplace has widened the void by one hundred feet. It now stands within a mile of the Blessing."

Sarmin met his gaze. After a moment Govnan looked away. "But it is still several miles from the north wall. We are exploring new methods to slow it."

Govnan's experiments had thus far gone nowhere. The wound coming from Migido threatened them now, but it was a pinprick in the world compared to the great scar left by the death of the Mogyrk god; he imagined that void as a night sky without any stars, enormous and heavy, too much to hold in one man's mind. If Sarmin could not heal that wound, there would be nothing left of his great city.

"Thank you, Govnan, Notheen. You are dismissed." The high mage looked about to speak, but he bowed his head and retreated. Notheen glided after him, his midnight robes whispering against the rug.

Sarmin stared at his hands. With these hands he had invaded the Pattern Master's work, opened Helmar's butterfly-stone and healed a god's wound. But he had been drained by it. He could do no more as a mage, only as an emperor. He stood and left his room.

Sword-sons trailed him as he walked to the women's wing. He did not know their names; he had not asked and did not mean to. He missed Ta-Sann. All the time he had been alone in his tower room he had never suffered a loss. Now that he was out of it, there had been too many.

The women's corridor stretched before him, plain and white. Here, con-cubines did not display themselves against colourful mosaics for his inspec-tion. They had their own rooms, and knew that he would not visit them. His time with Jenni had been a mistake, a trick played by the pattern. He stood in the empty corridor and knocked on Mesema's door. Her servant Tarub pulled it open, and set to trembling at the sight of him.

"Leave us." He was greeted by more plain white walls, glaring in the sun from the window-screen. Against the harshness Mesema appeared ever softer, her skin limned with light as she stretched across the bed, hair lit by honeyed fire. Sarmin knew she was no beauty by the standards of the palace, but she moved him nonetheless. Pelar slept beside her on a purple blanket, his eyelashes thick against his cheeks, and she played with his curls as she sang a Felting song. Though music did not move him, Sarmin paused to listen to her voice.

Mesema raised herself on one elbow and smiled; the line of her body beneath a thin layer of silk set his skin buzzing, but his mind explored it no further. Since the pale sickness had struck they had been no more than friends. He sat on the edge of the bed and touched Pelar's chubby foot. He was so healthy now that it was difficult to believe he had almost been drained of life.

Pelar was his son in every way that mattered. Though he had come from the joining of Mesema with his brother Beyon, he loved the boy with all his being. It was not so unusual in Mesema's culture to raise a boy this way; grass-children, they were called: the children a wife had given birth to before marrying her husband. He leaned over Pelar and smelled the baby-scent of him, soap and milk, and something sweeter. Daveed's face rose in his mind, in that moment sharper and more real than the boy who lay before him, and he feared the memory might cut him.

"Don't wake him up," whispered Mesema, "I just got him to be quiet."

"Not even for a moment?" He longed to see the boy smile, to wash Dav-eed from his mind's eye.

"If you can answer me a riddle," she answered, "perhaps I will let you rouse him."

"All right."

She sat up against the white cushions, slowly, so as not to jostle the baby. "The wound is spreading from Migido, is it not?"

So far this was not a riddle.

"And soon it will pass over the Blessing."

Again she was correct. He began to see the nature of her question. "So you want to know whether our river will turn to dust," he said.

She looked at him.

Govnan had told him there was only one mile to go before the Storm reached the Blessing. Then they would know for certain. "I do not know," he said, though his suspicions were dark.

That did not sit well with his wife. "The river . . ." She drew her knees up to her chin.

Sarmin leaned forwards, trying to find words of comfort. Nooria had wells that led to underground aquifers; there were glaciers in the mountains . . . but in truth it he did not know if the city could survive without the Blessing. It was time to send her away. In the end all he could conjure was, "Mesema."

She blushed and bit her lip. "So she told you."

"Who? No, this isn't about anything like that." He saw relief in her shoulders and wondered; she knew he did not care about the issues of the women's wing. "This is also about Migido—and the attack. Govnan is sure it was Mogyrk. Yrkmir approaches."

"Our scouts have seen the Yrkman army?"

"No . . . only, Notheen believes it is true." *They move through the empty spaces.* He thought about those words. Of course the desert was not an empty place to Notheen: it was his home, crisscrossed by his people, lived in and loved. The headman had meant something else. "In any case, it has become too dangerous here. It is time to send you two away, to my mother's people in the southern forests."

She wrapped her arms around her knees, and he longed to hold her as she held herself. "I understand why you ask. Once I thought nothing would be too dangerous for me, but now I know that I was wrong."

He breathed a sigh of relief. "So you will go."

"No. I will not." She met his gaze with her sky-blue eyes. "You know I will never leave you, not if there is a fight to be had. You promised we would work together."

"This isn't a game of cards!" He stood and paced to her window. "My mother must also go."

"She never will, not without Daveed." A slither of fabric as she left the bed. "Nor will I. Your Majesty."

"The skill that allowed me to best the Pattern Master has left me. I cannot fight for Daveed as I wish." He gripped the carved wood of the window-screen. "I cannot fight at all."

"Hush," she said, as if she were speaking to Pelar. "Listen. The pattern lies. Do you not think it can also lie through its absence?"

"It is not hiding; it is gone. And so must you be, or—" *Or I will lose you.* He could not say the last aloud. They did not speak to one another with such emotion.

She touched his shoulder and he turned to look down into her eyes, wide now with growing sadness. "You are a fine emperor without magic," she said, "and I will not leave you."

"But Pelar must."

She blinked back tears. "Yes, Pelar must."

"We will send him on with his nursemaids and guards. Gods willing, we will see him again." Sarmin stood, leaned over the bed and gathered the babe to his chest. Pelar stirred in his silk wrappings. His mouth was small and round, like Mesema's, but his dark hair and honeyed skin spoke of Beyon. The pattern had failed to capture Beyon; it had taken his memories and formed a cruel shell of what he had been. The true legacy of Sarmin's brother lay in his arms, so small a bundle to matter so very much. "Here is the true emperor," Sarmin said, watching the rise and fall of his little chest.

Mesema glanced towards the door and whispered, "Do not say such things, my husband."

"Sometimes I must speak the truth." It was impossible at court—complicated even with Mesema.

Mesema said nothing, only stared at Pelar with grief in her eyes.

Sarmin placed a kiss on Pelar's forehead. "What shall we do then, you and I?"

For once Mesema did not have an answer. Instead, she wrapped a bejewelled hand around his elbow and leaned over to give Pelar a slow kiss on the cheek. So the three of them stood, in an embrace of sorts, breathing in the baby's scent, in the plain white room: his family, surrounded by a deafening blankness. An emptiness. The idea took his breath and he stepped away,

Pelar still in his arms. Mesema's hand dropped down to her side and her eyes fell into shadow though the room was sunny.

"You should paint your room, I think. Trees, perhaps, like the last . . ."

But the tender moment had passed, taken by his sudden fear, and Mesema took Pelar from his arms. She turned to put him in his cradle and Sarmin did not know how to reach out, how to claim her, as Beyon might have done. The stark room served only to remind him that he was alone. The Many were gone, with Helmar, Ta-Sann, and his link to Grada. Mesema did not love him. Pelar was his brother's son, the true emperor, and he just a pretender. Wife, son, throne: it was all a lie, balanced on the thin edge of power to which he clung.

He turned to the door. "I will make the arrangements."

CHAPTER SEVEN

FARID

Farid spoke a few words of Frythian, having met some traders over the years, but his vocabulary was limited to numbers, weights, and thank-yous. Nevertheless the Mogyrk Adam spoke to him in that language, now drawing an elongated diamond on the floor and saying something like "hiss-nick." When Farid looked at these pattern-shapes he imagined them in blue, on his mother's skin. *They want to take what I am*, she had told him before she died. *I won't let them.*

Farid's gaze shifted to the two guards in the doorway. By their physiques he could see they had been called to fighting rather than trained to it—but then, he was no fighter himself. He had strength from lifting barrels and poling his father's boat, and he could count on some extra power from wanting his freedom—but against three men, he would not win. Adam himself had the bearing of a soldier and was enough of a match without counting the others.

"You are not listening," said Adam, speaking Cerani at last.

"Because I don't want to go to a marketplace and kill everyone."

Adam frowned as he wiped the symbol away. "Nor do I."

"Why then do you keep me prisoner? Surely there are others like you who want to learn these things?"

"There are not. They all were killed."

"Cerana kills all its enemies," said Farid with pride, making sure to speak loud enough for the men at the door to hear.

"So they do. Let's begin again." Adam drew another shape on the floor. "Shack-nuth."

"I don't know what that means." Farid stood, using his height as a form of protest.

Adam smiled. Farid could tell he was less than a threat to the man. "It is a Name. Shack-nuth."

"I won't remember it."

"I see." Adam put down his chalk. "How many fruits did you have to sell on the day of the attack?"

Farid remembered exactly. It was something he had always been able to do. "I started with fifty-two oranges and thirty-six pomegranates," he said, "twelve mangoes and just ten apples. I sold twenty apples the day before."

Adam raised his eyebrows. "How much money did you make, then? Don't check your pockets."

"I sold ten oranges at two bits a piece. Five pomegranates—I haggled a bit and got five bits for two of them. Three bits for the others. The mangoes were getting soft—I knocked them down to half a bit and sold five that way. Muad stole an apple—I count that as a loss of two-and-a-half bits. I sold four more for a total of four copper nine bits. But I have more than that in my pocket."

"Because of the apple."

"Right—but of course now all my fruit is lost because of you."

"And you can't remember this?" Adam drew on the floor with his chalk. Farid recognised it: *Hiss-nick*. But he shrugged.

Adam nodded to his men, who came into the room and picked up Farid by his elbows. "You may go to your room. Let us know when you are ready to begin again."

That night Farid tossed and turned on his pallet. The Mogyrks had put him in an airless closet. For obvious reasons they offered him no windows or outside doors, and yet he could still hear a baby crying in the house next door. As soon as the child quieted and Farid's eyes began to close, it started up wailing again. It was no good. He had prayed to Keleb for the air to cool, for the baby to quiet and for the Mogyrks to let him go, but nothing had any effect. He sat up and wiped the sweat from his forehead. "Hey," he called out to the guard he knew stood on the other side of the door, "is there any water?"

He heard the man's boots, then a silence that stretched until his sweat felt cold upon his skin. Then the door swung open and two hands laid a pitcher on the stained wood floor.

"Let me go," he said, but the man only placed a lit candle next to the pitcher and closed the door.

Farid held the pitcher to his lips, but he found it dry. Reaching inside, his fingers touched upon crumpled paper. "Mogyrk filth," he muttered, smoothing it open. A pattern had been drawn there, each shape flowing into the next, the web of lines suspending rather than connecting them. He frowned, turning it this way and that in his hands, trying to remember what he had seen in the marketplace. If he ever got free, the Blue Shields would want to know what these patterns looked like.

In the light of the candle he could now see another pattern scratched into the wall. He stood to look, but soon realised great spaces had been left empty, as if the carver had been interrupted. He held the paper up to it: these shapes formed a different spell. The finished one drew his eye, the lines having found their natural ends, the shapes having reached a pleasing balance.

Before she grew too old for such things, Farid's sister used to take their father's twine and wind it between her hands, her fingers spinning a complicated web. He would tease her by pulling on the lines, watching the empty spaces shrink and expand at his will, creating tension in her fingers until at last she cursed him and pulled free, leaving the twine a slack pile upon the floor. He ran his fingertips along the ink, remembering the feel of the rough string.

Adam had shown him some of these characters: *shack-nuth*, *hiss-nick*. Nonsense.

And yet, this design spoke of water to him. It waited somewhere in this collection of shapes and threads, caught like dew on a spider's web. He needed only to free it. He found the line he needed and *pulled*.

The pattern flashed, crescents and half-moons painting the ceiling in blue light, and a fiery glow wound his hands and arms in a design that reached further than the one in plain ink. It retreated into smaller and smaller lines upon his skin, so deep he thought he might fall into it, and a memory came to him of leaping off Asham Asherak's great bridge at full dark, the water an unknown black beneath him and the warm stone under his toes, before the light bled away, shimmering one last time in the distant reaches of the pattern before leaving him alone, bereft in the tiny room.

Water soaked the centre of the paper, spreading outwards. The pitcher! It was too late, but he caught some of it in his hands and slurped, ran his wet hands over his face and neck, then settled against the wall, his heart beating fast. *What had he done?* The light, the water . . . he ran a cool finger against his lips. He had used the pattern, the tool of the enemy, the poison that had killed his mother, and what he felt was . . . joy.

CHAPTER EIGHT

MESEMA

The men of the council spoke of the city as Tower and wall, palace and temple, landmarks of power that reflected their own standing in the world. Yet from where Mesema stood in Siri's rooftop garden, the city might have been two great hands cupping the life-giving river. Without the Blessing, there would be no Nooria, no palace, no great Cerani empire. It carved a path from the mountains to the southern province and fed the crops that in turn fed the city. From the roof of the palace the river looked like a wide blue ribbon laid between domed roofs and sand-coloured streets—but Sarmin had given her a great treasure: a tube, with glass on either end, that made all things look closer. It had been a gift from the astrologers of Kesh; now Mesema held it to her eye.

Three small fishing boats in flaking paint made their slow way downriver, pushed through the shallow passage by twelve royal guards disguised as polemen. She tried holding the astrologers' device even closer, but it did not further improve her view. Somewhere under stained tarpaulins her son Pelar was hidden, with his nursemaids and the wind mage Hashi. They would pass through the Low Gate to the south and continue towards the coast.

A flatboat passed by, going north towards the grain markets, its men too busy with the contrary flow to pay the royal hideaways any mind. But if Pelar should cry out, ask for his mother . . . She took a step towards the edge and imagined leaping from the roof garden, running down those narrow streets and swimming to the boats, imagined the look on his face when she gathered him in her arms. It was not too late to bring him back.

But she stayed where she was. After her trip into the city she knew her instincts were not to be trusted.

She and Sarmin had said their goodbyes in the private audience chamber, then handed Pelar to his nursemaid. He had been jolly, not knowing what was to come. At some point, on the road or in the boats, he must have realised she was not there, and it crushed her to think of it. But it would not have been wise to follow the prince and his entourage to the Blessing; they were travelling in secret, in boats secured from merchants fleeing Migido. It would not do for refugees of the Great Storm to learn their emperor was sending his own son south while they remained here with the god's wound inching forwards, ever closer to Nooria. Even so, she longed for one last good-bye.

The sun came around the mages' Tower and lit the river in shades of green. She turned the glass away from the boats; she had lost the strength to watch them go. Nor could she bear to see the Holies, where Grada had killed three men to defend her, and she jerked the glass away when its view landed there. Instead she traced the water's path north beyond the Worship Gate, so called because it faced Meksha's mountain. It had been barred, and travel north of the city had been forbidden. The Great Storm presented too great a danger.

She lifted the glass, hoping to catch sight of it.

"So he is gone." The voice came from behind her. Mesema lowered the astrologers' device and turned to see Nessaket standing over the roses, her shoulders stooped like an old woman's. Behind her stood the ever-present guards. No one came to the garden without them, not since Jenni—working for the treacherous Lord Jomla—had attacked them on the night of the fire, the same night rebels took Nessaket's son Daveed. Nessaket pointed towards the Blessing. "You should have gone with him, Empress." Since her injury she had taken to a plain way of speaking, like a Rider, though she would not have appreciated the comparison. The head blow she had suffered left her dizzy and prone to headaches, but her eyes remained clear.

"I will not leave you before Daveed is found," Mesema said.

"You should have gone," Nessaket repeated. "This city will turn to dust at last, and we with it."

"Sarmin halted the emptiness once before," Mesema said, too sharply, but then, Nessaket should have known better than to suggest failure. "He will halt it again, and we will find Daveed."

"It is better we do not."

Mesema took the Empire Mother's hand and guided her to the bench. "Come, Mother," she said, "your headaches tire you and you say things you do not mean. Sarmin will not leave his brother in Mogyrk hands."

Nessaket sat and did not speak again for a time. Mesema stretched out her legs, still aching from all those stairs.

"Perhaps he has a nursemaid who coos over him," said Nessaket. "Perhaps at this moment he is laughing, and reaching for a shiny toy. Perhaps he could grow to be a merchant or a priest and nobody will know who he truly is. But here . . . here he is one extra boy. It is easy to love a tiny child, but as he grows, Sarmin will watch him and wonder and begin to fear." She turned away, her eyes dark with memory. "No, he is safer elsewhere. And so are you."

"I listen, and I hear, my mother. But you do not know the future any better than I."

"Do you not know the future?" Nessaket glanced at her sidelong.

Mesema squeezed her hand. "The Hidden God is not always clear." She closed her eyes, remembering the events at Lord Nessen's house. "I must believe Daveed's safest place is with his mother." She looked out over the city: Sarmin's city. Those streets under the bright sun were filled with his people and he was responsible for all of them—merchant, beggar and prince—yet he had managed to save only his son so far.

It was not unusual at this time of day for a carriage to creak its way up the palace road, but it was unusual to see one with a painted roof. Mesema held the glass to her eye and studied the unique emblem, two pine branches enclosing a hammer. She had seen it once before, when the Fryth delegation had arrived bearing Marke Kavic. She tried to read the faces of the men who flanked this carriage, but the spyglass wavered in her hand.

Nessaket stood, her black hair tinted orange in the sunset. "Daveed." Her voice carried urgency and also hope, which Mesema found unexpected, considering all she had just said.

"You think . . .?" Mesema rose to her feet.

Nessaket did not reply but hurried towards the stairs, forcing her guards to dance out of her way. Mesema turned back towards the distant ships. *My son.* He was as safe as she could make him; she could do no more. She hurried after Nessaket, pinching the flesh of her palm to keep the tears away, letting one pain serve as a distraction from the other.

She followed Nessaket through the halls of the old women's wing, her breath harsh in her throat. The burnt sections had been taken down and removed, making the space feel hollow.

Once this wing had assaulted her eyes with its colourful walls and floors, its never-ending parade of luxury. Now the guards' boots echoed in the empty space.

They passed through the great doors and entered the palace proper, making their way down the curved steps and across the marble. Nessaket held her head high, but her shoulders were tense with fear. When Mesema had first met the Empire Mother, that day in Herzu's temple, she had never expected she would one day be sitting beside Nessaket and holding her hand, or sharing her deepest troubles. First they had become wary allies, and then something more.

Nessaket said not a word during the journey, and the men were silent as ghosts behind them, so that when two of Sarmin's personal guard threw open the newly carved God Doors, the bustle and movement inside the throne room took Mesema by surprise. The chattering of the courtiers carried to all corners, and beneath the lantern-lit dome, chin propped on his hand, sat Sarmin on his throne, a dozen men clustered below him on the dais. All were engaged with a petitioner, who held a number of scrolls. As Azeem took the first and began to unroll it, Sarmin caught her eye and offered a fleeting smile. Though he was becoming a cunning and fearsome emperor in the eyes of the court, for her he tried to be the prince she had first known.

Mesema began her way down the silk runner, matching steps with the Empire Mother. To her right, ragged petitioners stood in a long line, and on her left, nobles and wealthy merchants rested on cushions. She put a hand on Nessaket's elbow when she swayed: another dizzy spell. Sarmin waved them forwards and together they fell into obeisance, Mesema's head not a foot from the slippers of the men who sat on the lowest step. Sarmin concluded his business with a few words and the exchange of more scroll-tubes.

Then his voice grew softer. "Rise, my wife; rise, Empire Mother." As they stood he looked at Nessaket with a frown. "My mother is tired. She requires a cushion."

Azeem looked around, his mouth pinched beneath his long nose. Nessaket never sat, so the question of where to place her had never before been raised. The men on the bottom step muttered, not wishing to be displaced. With her head Mesema motioned to a stray cushion near the edge, apart from the others. Surely that would not be improper?

Azeem made a show of preparing it, then Mesema helped Nessaket to sit. For all of her weakness, Nessaket sank to the cushion as gracefully as ever and sat with her back straight, her eyes watchful.

With that settled, Sarmin turned his attention to his wife. "How is my son Pelar?" He had not been able to watch the boats as she had, for he had had to go directly from the private chamber to the throne room.

"He is very well, Magnificence." A flicker of sadness in his eyes, then he motioned for her to take her place behind him. She could not tell him about the carriage she had seen. In court she must always behave as if Sarmin knew everything already, but she pressed the back of his hand in passing, a warning.

Azeem spent some time organising the scrolls upon his table and marking his books. Petitioners shifted on their feet. Guards suppressed yawns. The noise among the courtiers had reduced to a murmur when Nessaket first sat among them, but as they waited, the volume increased until voices once again filled the room, calming only when the harpist began a tune upon his strings. Mesema watched the door.

At last the gong sounded, startling everyone except for herself, Nessaket and the emperor—Sarmin managed never to look startled by anything.

The music stopped with a sudden twang as the great doors parted for the immense herald. He walked along the runner without hurry, his steps evenly paced, his long years of practise ensuring he was always calm and reserved, no matter the situation.

"Captain Yulo of the White Hats, Magnificence, Mura of the Tower, and a prisoner." He bowed his way from the room, walking backwards.

Mura of the Tower! They had assumed her dead. Govnan had grieved for her as for a daughter—and yet, here she was, her white robes tied with a gleaming blue sash, approaching the Petal Throne. She was younger than Mesema had expected, and short, her head coming only to the captain's shoulder. Her eyes contained the brightness of the sky, and she did not focus on anything in the room but rather, seemed to look through it all into a world beyond.

Mesema was so intent on the mage that she noticed the prisoner only when the captain pushed him to the floor. His hands were tied behind his back and when he landed on one knee, the other leg pushed out awkwardly to his side. A burlap sack hid his face and draped over his sun-cracked leather jacket.

The mage and soldier came forth to make their obeisances. A grin danced over the captain's lips. He must have known this was a great opportunity.

"Rise, and speak," said Sarmin. Only his fingers, pressed into the petals on his armrests, betrayed his fierce interest.

"Your Majesty," said the captain, "I have recovered the mage Mura and captured the man who held her."

"Where did this blessed event occur?" asked Azeem, dislike heavy in his voice. Azeem valued humility over many other virtues.

"He was attempting to sneak into the city, Grand Vizier." With a wide smile Yulo returned to his captive. "It is the traitor, Majesty," he said, untying the sack. "The horse chief who betrayed us." As he lifted the man's head, Mesema saw a pointed chin, a scraggly beard, two eyes green as grass, and then a shock of golden curls. She took a step forwards and stopped herself. She must control her face and her beating heart, for it was Banreh on his knees before her.

CHAPTER NINE

SARMIN

S armin settled onto the throne in the private audience chamber. Removing the Windreader chief from the commotion of the throne room had been the only choice, but the council was seething at being refused immediate vengeance. "Let us kill him now, Magnificence," General Lurish had said, his sword out, and Dinar had crept behind the chief, a terrible grin on his face, as if he meant to claim his prize at once. But as much as Sarmin had loved his brother, this was not Beyon's court; he would not allow open violence. This had furthered the rift between himself and High Priest Dinar, but that was a matter for another day.

He signalled his sword-sons and they opened the doors. In spilled the smug Captain Yulo dragging the Felt captive, the wind-sworn mage, Azeem, the Empire Mother, and finally, Mesema. Of course his wife would not stay away, but for the first time he was tempted to dismiss her.

Sarmin turned his attention to Yulo. "You will be rewarded," he said. "And you are dismissed." He could stand no more of this peacock captain.

Yulo's mouth opened as if about to protest—he had expected to be allowed to tell his story, to receive public accolades. But he thought better of speaking and bowed low before retreating from the room.

Sarmin took a deep breath and watched the Felting man, the man who had taught Mesema to speak Cerani, who had won her heart, the crippled scribe who had humiliated the White Hat Army of Cerana. Chief Banreh met his gaze, horse-chief to emperor. The books called the Felt barbarians, there to serve the empire or be wiped out by it, and of little importance otherwise. But Mesema was important, and this man refused to be trivial either. Sarmin could not deny his curiosity.

Azeem leaned close. "I have called for Govnan, Magnificence."

Sarmin did not reply, his eyes locked with the prisoner's. At last he shifted his attention to Mura. "When last we heard of you, you were in Fryth. Could you not speak on the wind and tell us of your situation?"

Mura turned her face his way, showing blue eyes over high cheekbones. Her robes lifted around her as if blown. "I could not, Majesty. I was prevented."

"This man prevented a mage of the Tower from speaking on the wind?" Sarmin gestured at the chief, not granting him the use of his name.

"Not this man, Your Majesty."

"There is another?" So Captain Yulo had not done such an admirable job after all.

"I was held by this man and the Duke of Fryth himself, Your Majesty. We travelled with two dozen Felting warriors and Fryth guardsmen, hiding in the desert, always moving. And waiting."

"Waiting? For what?" *Yrkmir. They wait to join in the attack.* He was sure of it, but Chief Banreh spoke unbidden, correcting his thought.

"They await your word, Magnificence." He said no more, for six hachirahs now pointed at his throat.

Mesema gasped, and irritation stirred in Sarmin. If she expressed further unsuitable emotion he would have to send her from the room, though that would not sit well with her.

Sarmin motioned for the sword-sons to stay their hands. "Addressing me without invitation is a good way to lose your voice all together, Chief." And yet Banreh's words presented a mystery that he longed to unravel.

Govnan slipped in through a side door, showing the first joyful smile Sarmin had ever seen from him, his wrinkled lips spreading wide, showing missing teeth as he turned towards his young mage.

"Mage Mura, explain this man's words to me." Sarmin did not give her time to return the high mage's greeting.

"Your Majesty, when Marke Kavic . . . died . . ."

"A terrible sickness swept the palace," said Azeem, addressing the room more than the mage. "His death, though regrettable, was one of many we suffered at that time." Azeem was practised in statements that walked the line between truth and lie.

Mura looked at Azeem with a frown; she must have heard of Kavic's murder. Sarmin wondered how news of Kavic's death could have reached Fryth as quickly and accurately as it had, as evinced by the rapid deterioration of their relations and the ultimate defeat of his men.

"When Marke Kavic died, Your Majesty, and the Iron Duke after him," Mura said, "Marke Didryk became the duke. He captured General Arigu and me—"

"And killed our soldiers in their sleep."

"Yes, Magnificence. He did." Her robes fell flat against her legs and for a moment her eyes flashed brown. "But his victory was brief. Shortly after the Cerani army left Fryth, the city of Mondrath was attacked by Yrkmir. Those few of us who survived made our way into the grasslands, and then into the desert."

So the report had been true: Yrkmir had attacked Fryth. He sat a moment in silence, watching the mage. Her words did not condemn her Mogyrk captors—in fact, her voice was inflected with an uncomfortable sympathy. She fidgeted under his gaze, and at last he spoke. "You have not explained why you were unable to call to us."

"Your Majesty, Duke Didryk is a pattern mage."

Sarmin sat up on his throne.

"He drew designs on me that kept Yomawa, my wind-spirit, silent. But he promised that when I passed through the walls of Nooria I would sense him again—and that was the truth, Magnificence."

A breeze blew about the room, shaking the tapestries upon their hooks. Azeem put a hand over his parchments to stop them from blowing to the floor.

Govnan's joyful smile had faded and now he watched his student with a frown.

Sarmin let her admiring words float upon the moving air until she remembered herself. When she appeared properly disquieted, he asked, "What is the duke's business here?" Perhaps this pattern mage was turning his skill to the marketplaces of Nooria . . .

"Your Majesty, these men want peace."

Sarmin leaned forwards, and she shrank from the heaviness of his gaze. "Chief Banreh is a traitor and a breaker of alliances. You are a mage of the Tower, and have made a binding oath to serve the empire. Tell me why these men have come into Cerana, or suffer their fate."

The sword-sons shifted their weapons. Now three pointed at Chief Banreh's throat and three at the wind mage's.

Mura's eyes grew wide. She made to speak, but only moved her lips. He could see her arms shaking. He turned to Banreh instead. "Then tell me, Chief: why should I not kill you?"

The small room lay so quiet that Sarmin could hear Azeem's rapid breaths beside him, and the rustle of Mesema's dress as she clutched it. When he spoke, Banreh's low voice echoed against the walls. "Because if I die, the duke will know it and he will kill your General Arigu. Because he can help you. Because Yrkmir is coming."

So the general was still alive.

"Arigu . . ." Nessaket whispered to herself.

Sarmin leaned back in his throne. The chief's threat could not be allowed to pass without reprisal. It was lucky there were so few in the room; in the presence of the full court he would have had no choice but to have the man killed immediately, and that would not have gone well for Mesema—or Arigu, for that matter. Yet he dreaded the thought of sending any man to the dungeons—he had emptied them for a reason, and had kept them empty, since the slave revolt. The thought of the oubliette where he had found Helmar's stone filled him with a cold sickness. But he could not let Banreh go.

"My brother would have had your head by now," he told the man.

"Your brother had a chance at my head, Magnificence, and he let me live."

Sarmin stood, ignoring the familiar ache in his legs. "Is this true? You met my brother and he let you live?" Azeem looked up at him, a curious look on his face, as if he were seeing him for the first time. Mirrored in the grand vizier's eyes he saw not the emperor, but a lonely boy who had lost his brothers.

"It is true, my husband," said Mesema, touching his elbow. "Your brother let Banreh go, heaven and stars keep him now."

Anger stirred in Sarmin, for he remembered what she had told him of those times. "And then he came here, to work against Beyon further—is that not true?" He turned to the chief. "You came here to plot against the emperor, did you not?"

Banreh looked at the swords poised to cut him. "As did Arigu."

And there it was: a reminder of Arigu's double betrayal. Arigu had brought Mesema to the palace at the Empire Mother's request; he had been hoping to undermine Beyon, and then he had gone to war against Sarmin's wishes, ignoring his emperor's many messengers. To be reminded now, even before this small audience, was a humiliation to the throne—but Sarmin, in spite of all of this, did not want Arigu returned to a punishment; he wanted Arigu returned to his command.

Sarmin descended to the tiled floor and stood before Chief Banreh. He needed no tricks of steps and thrones to tower over the man. If the chief died here, in the dungeons or somewhere out in the desert, he was ready. Sarmin could see it in his eyes. What had Banreh lived through that three swords against his neck counted for so little? Curiosity won out over anger.

"So," Sarmin said, "how does this duke propose to help me?"

"He will teach your mages how to use the pattern to fight Yrkmir." From all corners of the room rose a startled murmur, and Sarmin struggled to disguise the visceral desire that rose in him.

"Govnan," he said, without moving his gaze from those steady green eyes, "I put Mura into your care. I trust she will remember herself once she is in the Tower."

"Majesty." The mages removed themselves and closed the doors behind them.

He had one last question for the chief. "Tell me, where is this duke who offers Cerana so much?"

"I do not know."

"A lie." Sarmin had no choice. "You, Chief, will go to the dungeon. You will tell us where your duke is hiding, and you will tell us anything else we want to know." He thought of the duke somewhere in the sands, the awesome power of the pattern at his fingertips, and wondered whether his offer could possibly have been honest. Perhaps it was, and the duke erred only in his choice of messenger.

Either way, it would not bring back Sarmin's pattern-sight. Gritting his teeth, he motioned to his sword-sons.

As the men lifted Banreh to his feet, the chief's gaze moved past Sarmin to where Mesema stood beside the throne and for the first time, his calm left him. Sarmin saw the emotion full on his face before the sword-sons turned and walked him from the room.

Sarmin stood on the shining tiles, watching the blue that reflected from his robes. He knew Mesema had been in love with Banreh; she had told him so. But that Banreh had loved Mesema—that had never occurred to him before. It should not matter, but it did, and now he was unsteadied by an unfamiliar sensation, as irrational as it was overwhelming. His hands curled into fists and he found he could not turn to look at his wife.

"Arigu is alive," said Nessaket, behind him. "It is a miracle."

"The man cannot be trusted," said Mesema. "Have you considered this could be one of Arigu's games?"

"He would not play games," said Azeem, "not now. Not after so many of his men have died."

"Are you certain? He was very happy to play with lives when I knew him."

"And what would he gain from it?" asked Nessaket.

"Power. Land. A pattern mage in his pocket." He could hear Mesema's dislike of Arigu in her voice. He knew well how deep it went.

"You should not speak so," said Nessaket. "You did not know the general, not truly."

They fell silent, but for the shuffling of Azeem's parchments.

"We are no closer to finding Daveed," said Nessaket with a long sigh.

Daveed. Sarmin's heart, already heavy, dropped to the floor. The Mogyrks had taken his only living brother, and this man—this *duke*, this enemy of the White Hat Army—now offered his aid. It could only be a trick, a distraction from his search for Daveed. Sense and history dictated he could not allow a pattern mage so close to Nooria. He must push aside his own desire for pattern-sight and see the situation with clear eyes. The answer was obvious.

"Chief Banreh will be put to the question," Sarmin said. "We will find this duke where he hides in the desert, kill him, and bring our General Arigu back to Nooria."

CHAPTER TEN

DIDRYK

"They will kill your pretty scribe. They will kill him, and come after you like the demons of Herzu's hell."

Didryk ignored General Arigu and poured himself another cup of water. Banreh had told him to keep drinking even when he did not feel thirsty, and keeping his hands busy prevented him from killing the man where he stood.

"What do you think Cerana does with traitors and oathbreakers?" Arigu took a step forwards, as close to Didryk as his ropes would allow. "They give them over to Priest Dinar. Your friend will be skinned alive."

"Is that what will happen to you? Aren't you also a traitor?"

Arigu smiled. The conversation was not new, but he took pleasure in it. "They will forgive me when I bring them your head."

The desert heat drove Didryk's anger. "I have done nothing to Cerana except defend my country, while you have betrayed and deceived the Petal Throne."

"Is that what your pretty toy told you? Did he whisper it upon the pillows, in the deep of night?"

It was an old accusation that missed the mark but it had an edge, nevertheless. Didryk forced a smile. "I prefer Settu to these discussions of ours."

"Your mind is not quick enough to offer me any challenge in the game."

Didryk replaced his empty cup and glanced at the general. Arigu had always seemed to him a bear, wide, strong and hairy, but his eyes were cunning. For hundreds of miles and under the threat of Yrkmir Didryk had kept him in chains, this great general of Cerana who had burned his city and slaughtered its austeres with such merciless focus. Now he needed to keep him alive, for just a while longer.

Banreh would have spoken with reason and patience. Didryk reminded himself the general never did or said anything without a reason either, and the constant needling was meant to shake him, to intimidate him and make him doubt—for if all went as planned, negotiations would soon be upon them and Arigu would do what he could to improve Cerana's position.

But events gave Didryk the advantage: Mogyrk's Scar in the eastern desert was growing. He stood closer now to the source of His power than ever before. He could feel His vitality in the sand and sky and in the very air that he breathed—but it was a temporary gift. The Scar consumed all it found, just like His wounds, and Yrkmir was coming to meet it.

Didryk had passed one of Mogyrk's wounds in the desert, an area where dunes large as cities had been swallowed whole, leaving neither sound nor colour, and all was covered with a blankness that nevertheless felt *hungry*— a place from which he had instinctively looked away, and ordered his men to do the same. This was the coming of Mogyrk foretold, the Great Storm, when His wounds, laid in the earth itself, spread, and rotted all they touched until every man joined Him in death.

It filled Didryk with a blank horror. Patterns fed the Storm. Yrkmir wielded patterns as other men wielded swords, and Yrkmir was coming.

But caught between Mogyrk and His followers, Cerana would look for an ally who could counter their magic. The emperor would never trust an austere like Adam; it was to Didryk he would turn—to Didryk he *must* turn.

He had been intended for the church, and raised among the novices. He had learned with them, eaten with them, drawn his first patterns with them, under Adam's less than tender care. Those dozen boys who slept in the cloister attic had been like brothers, but only Didryk remained. Arigu had tortured and burned the rest. When he closed his eyes Didryk still saw their charred corpses hanging from the city wall; he still choked on the stench of burning flesh.

Didryk set the pitcher and cup within the general's reach. "Drink." With that he pushed open the flap and stepped out into the desert, into the sun that fell so gracelessly upon every inch of sand, and the biting heat that came with it. It was no wonder the desert empire was known as unforgiving and ruthless, for its sky held no kindness. He gestured to his men who were gathered under tarps and drinking from waterskins, and began to climb the nearest dune. It was harder than he had expected, and the breath came harsh in his throat. Halfway up his calves and thighs began to strain, and the sun burnt the back of his neck as he zigzagged to the top. At last he looked out towards Nooria. Banreh was not yet returning—he would have sensed that—but soldiers could be seeking them instead. Didryk was prepared to die. One did not enter into such a plan as his without being so, but he would like to see it coming.

He looked east over the sands until a bright pain pierced his eyes, but saw no colours cut out from the unending brown, no plume of dust that would indicate movement from Nooria. A reluctant glance towards the north showed no sign of Yrkmir either. Would Yrkmir pass by the same wound, or would they be caught by it and torn apart, unravelled?

He looked down at his camp, blinking away the dark spots in his vision; it was surprisingly far below. Coming from the mountains as he did, he should be used to gauging heights, but these dunes tricked the eye.

"Didryk." A crimson-robed figure made the crest and ambled towards him as if this were a calm summer day in the courtyard at Mondrath. Didryk knew him for Adam even before the pointed hood fell back, revealing white-gold hair, and he backed away before thinking better of it.

"Adam." Didryk's instinct was to protect himself, but their talk would not go well with weapons in hand. "How did you find me?"

"You are my student," Adam said with a smile. "I will always be able to find you."

"I *was* your student," Didryk corrected, his mind racing. Adam must have marked and bound him long ago, when he was a child. Why had he never realised it?

Adam spoke with conspiratorial pleasure. "I felt your hand in the marketplace. I would not have recommended that, my Duke. Now the Blue

Shields are inspired to seek us everywhere—why do you look so surprised? Did you think I would not know your careful pattern-work?"

Didryk knew nothing of any marketplace, but he looked stonily at the man, willing him to stop, to leave, but Adam continued, still behaving as if they stood over his mother's rose bushes outside his long-lost home. "But now we shall have some assistance. I have a new student now. Of all the desperate and downtrodden Cerani I have brought into the light only one shows any promise. That is how weak I have found the stock of Nooria to be, and yet they enslave our people. Yes"—he nodded with emphasis as if Didryk did not believe him—"I saw Fryth slaves in the palace."

His mention of the palace brought only one thing to Didryk's mind. "Did you kill my cousin Kavic," he asked, "or was it the Cerani who killed him?"

Adam pressed a hand to his heart. "Of course I did not kill him. Why would you come to Cerana looking for me if you believed I had done such a thing?"

"Perhaps I was not looking for you." As ever, Didryk could not gauge whether the austere spoke true, but it did not matter. He had not wanted the peace and he had let Kavic die, and Didryk would have his revenge either way.

"Don't be embarrassed, child. Why else would you come so close to the lion's mouth, except to join with your old teacher? I heard what you did to the White Hats. The Cerani will turn the desert inside out looking for you, but I can offer protection. It was wise of you to find me."

"I play my own game." And a mad one at that: one that depended on gaining the trust of the emperor before turning all of his people against him, one that pitted him alone against the Tower, the priests, and all of Cerana's soldiers. But it was one he would rather try than join with the second austere.

Down in the camp, Didryk's men began to shout and point upwards towards Adam. Some of them began the torturous climb up the dune, not well-aided by the heavy swords they carried.

Adam ignored the soldiers. "You are still stubborn. Like the Cerani." He crouched over the sand and ran his fingers along the surface. "How stubborn a man must be, to make an empire of this. Yes, they have great pride, but their leader is weak, and he shrinks from fighting. The Tower has been drained of its talent. Yrkmir will soon come, and the first austere will bring us all into the light, as was foretold."

The first austere. Once those words had invoked awe, the image of a man close to a god on his high, cold throne, but now Didryk felt nothing but hatred. Adam remained faithful to Yrkmir, but if he were not such a prideful fool, he might have asked what had driven Didryk so far from home. Despite himself, anger coloured his next words. "As Mondrath was brought into the light?"

Adam looked up at him, his brows forming a question.

"You did not hear? Yrkmir set a pattern around our great city. We lost two-thirds of our people and the rest have scattered into the mountains. Mondrath is no more. Whatever their design, it does not include us, Adam."

Adam stilled, his gaze on the shifting sands of the dune. "What of your grandfather, the Iron Duke? Kavic's wife and their children?"

"Dead." He pushed the word from his mouth. It had not become easier to say.

"I see." The austere came as close to expressing regret as Didryk had ever seen, and did not speak for a long while. He did not meet Didryk's eyes as he asked, "What is your plan, then? Will you turn against your church?"

"It is your church. It was never mine."

"Mogyrk gifted you with His skill. Whatever Yrkmir has done, He has not abandoned us."

"Mogyrk is dead." He knew it was not true; the power he felt around him, shifting on the breeze, belied those words—but he would say them nonetheless.

Adam rose from his crouch. Sand trickled away from his feet, slithering down the dune the soldiers were struggling to climb. "How could he be dead when we may still draw our patterns? It is that attitude which killed your people. Now look at you, so full of rage, and there is no comfort for you, Didryk."

"Mogyrk offers no comfort." The apostate words caught in his throat.

"You cannot take on both Yrkmir and Cerana without our God. If I may offer a former student some advice, leave. Now. Go to the west."

"And the Great Storm?"

Adam held his arms wide. "It is destined to sweep Cerana from this world. We must save whom we can before that happens. Will you help me do that?"

"Do you think Cerana will satisfy the Storm, appease the Scar? That the God's wounds will not look north?" Didryk shook his head. "It is foretold He will take all of us into death with Him."

"You never understood the teachings of Mogyrk—you did not care enough to learn."

"You have no idea what I care about," Didryk said.

"Perhaps you are right. My old student would not have killed those souls in the marketplace before they had a chance to be saved."

Didryk covered his confusion by focusing on the pile of sand Adam had left on the dune. If neither he nor Adam had laid that pattern, then there was another austere. "Yrkmir must be very close."

Adam backed away. "There are souls to save before they get here. Don't lay another pattern." He slid downwards, putting the dune between himself and the soldiers, then called out, "You need a new outer ward. I have broken the one you set."

Didryk cursed to himself and waved his soldiers back down to the camp. "The prisoner!" he shouted, and his men began moving as he ran headlong down the steep incline and pounded across the sand, sweat flying from his skin. He pushed aside the tent-flap. Arigu sat in the centre, a cup held by both hands, surrounded by Fryth guardsmen.

The general took in the relief on his face and laughed. "Make no mistake, Duke. I will be free soon enough."

"But not today," said Didryk, "blessed Mogyrk, not today."

CHAPTER ELEVEN

SARMIN

In sketches and tapestries, the Tower appeared as a spike in the great city, casting a shadow on the domes below it, commanding a view far into the distance, all the way to its enemies. While it was the highest structure in Nooria, it overtopped the towers of the palace by only one storey, and its view might have swept the dunes, but it never advanced the mages' sight across the sea to icy Yrkmir. The legend of the Tower and its reality had grown even more distant in recent times. The stories told of a legion of mages, immortal and unconquerable, commanding all four elements. Now there were just three mages, one for rock, two for wind, and an old man who was their teacher.

Govnan met him at the first landing, looking flustered for the first time since Sarmin had met him. "Have you come to interview Mage Mura, Magnificence?"

"I came to see the Megra," said Sarmin, pausing for breath, "but I will speak with Mura, in time." He would need to learn from her what this duke could do, get a sense of whether his offer was in earnest. He dared not hope. All of him stirred at the idea of regaining his pattern-sight—though that was not part of the deal.

Relief broke over the high mage's face. "Of course. I will lead you to her room." After that he fell silent. They continued to climb, and Sarmin considered the carvings that lined the walls. They were not on the traditional themes of war and victory, but rather, showed men and women in poses of intense concentration and purpose. The carvings outnumbered the mages in the Tower by a factor of ten; that was why Sarmin must leave Mura's discipline to Govnan. They could not lose another mage. She had defended the traitor, but with the high mage's guidance she would soon remember her captivity with less emotion—and then he would speak with her again.

At last they reached a landing covered in thick carpet—the better to ease tired feet—and Govnan opened the door to a bright, sunny room. "Here she is, Magnificence." The window faced the river, and Sarmin's gaze followed the line of boats going south, hoping to catch sight of Pelar's. Failing, he sighed and turned back to the bed. The Megra lay there, looking older than he had remembered, all bones and onionskin and eyes looking out from deep hollows. But she recognised him.

"Sarmin." Just his name. He demanded no honorifics from her, no false respect, no obeisance. He sat on the edge of the bed and took her hand. "Megra."

"I have been waiting for you," she said, and then fell silent for a time, watching birds flutter past the window.

Sarmin said, "I have lost the pattern, Megra. I cannot see it any more."

She smiled and patted his hand. "You cannot change what you are."

"And what is that?"

"More than just one thing." She looked at the goblet of water by the side of the bed, and he held it to her lips. When she was satisfied, she leaned back on the pillow, momentarily spent. Then she said, "I've made a friend. Sahree. You know her?"

"I met her, yes." Mesema doted on the old servant—Sahree had brought her in from the desert, and then Beyon had thrown the old woman into the dungeon for the crime of knowing that. Now she was free and did as she wished, and mostly she wished to be in the Tower.

"She says what's coming is Mirra's work. I think she may be right."

"Mirra is a goddess of Cerana, but Helmar's work . . ." Helmar's work was of Yrkmir.

"Yes." She patted his hand once again. "But you should know . . . he was only a man." She closed her eyes. "Just a man . . ."

Of course Helmar was just a man, as was Duke Didryk. Two pattern mages, one dead, one living, and each holding a promise that ate at him. Sarmin fiddled with the butterfly-stone he still kept in his pocket. Megra stirred and opened her eyes again. "There was a wound in the Hollow," she said. "Helmar's making, turning men pale. That makes five."

For the fifth and final wound to be so far away in Fryth, beyond his reach, was a blow. "What should I do?" he asked, but she had drifted off to sleep. Sarmin adjusted her coverings and stared down into her face, the face that Helmar had loved.

Govnan was gone, most likely to his newly returned mage. Sarmin turned from the bed and left the room. As he began down the stairs, his Knife detached from the wall and fell in with him, giving no greeting or obeisance, as if she had been with him the entire time.

At the ground floor she said, "May I suggest the Ways, Your Majesty—it seems you left your sword-sons in the palace." Her tone reprimanded him.

As Grada worked the key to open the dark passages, Sarmin watched her dark, intelligent eyes, her agile hands. Since coming free from his own tower he had learned that women such as Grada were not thought to be desirable. Wide-shouldered and capable, arms strong after years of work, she was no delicate flower to wrap in silks and lay upon a cushion. But she drew him, flesh and bone: she drew him.

Guilty, he turned his mind to his wife. Mesema was insightful and kind, and he had come to depend on her standing at his elbow in the throne room, but she was impulsive and now he worried what would happen with her old love Banreh in the palace dungeon. He knew the chief would die, knew it as well as he knew every score and dent in the walls of his old room, and also that Mesema would do whatever she could to prevent it. That knowledge had hardened within him until it formed a hard, cruel point that he knew he might yet have to wield.

Since that first night when Tuvaini opened his secret door, Sarmin had been learning the art of influence. He took Tuvaini's dacarba that night and he wore it still, as a reminder that he ruled over every man and woman in Cerana. He had no qualms ruling over the court, but he shrank from doing

the same to his wife, even to protect her. With Mesema he did not want to
be the emperor—but nonetheless his weapon was sharp and ready.

They had walked a third of the way back to the palace in silence, the dark
of the Ways pressing against them, when he asked, "Why did you come to
see me, Grada?"

"Satrap Honnecka was nearly turned out of his carriage as he passed the
Maze today. His guards got him out safely. Now he prepares to flee to his
own lands." She thought a time. "There are seven times as many Mogyrks in
the Maze than came with Marke Kavic or escaped from the palace."

"Our citizens are converting."

"In all our searching we have not found Austere Adam, yet he has found
many Cerani. He looks for the hungry, the poor, the desperate, and turns
them to his purpose."

"Untouchables."

"Many like me, yes. For a time they contented themselves with starting
fires in the Maze, but now they turn their eyes to the wealthier citizens, and
the city entire. The attack in the marketplace frightened everyone. Eventually all will flee, except for the Mogyrks." She paused. "The Knife cannot
cut them all."

"What do you suggest, Grada?"

She walked for a time in silence. "I suggest you do not make them hate
you."

Twice the palace had been attacked in Sarmin's time, once by Helmar,
once by rebellious slaves led by Adam. Each time too many sacrifices had
been made. Now the workings of the government, the council's faith in his
ability to rule, the balance of his own mind—they all risked collapse under
the strain of a third attack. "Grada," he said, stopping to catch his breath,
one hand against the dark wall, "you must find Adam and bring him to
me."

"Yes, Your Majesty," she said. They had reached the door to his halls and
he drew Tuvaini's dacarba from his belt to work the lock. When it clicked
open, he turned back to her, to say goodbye, to hear her voice one last time,
to remember that bond that had once existed between them—but she had
already shuttered her lantern and slipped away into the dark.

CHAPTER TWELVE

FARID

F arid sat against the wall, watching the floor in the flickering candlelight. It had taken him a few days—he thought it was days—to realise the stains were blood, then another to begin to see shapes in the light and dark of them. He watched the stains as a child watches clouds. That one looked like a mango; that one, a monkey. And beneath them, the whorls and eyes of the wood itself, drawing him in.

It kept him from looking at the unfinished pattern scratched into the wall. That pattern left him wanting more, like a song with no ending or the touch of an apple's skin against his teeth. He had traced its shapes for many hours, followed its lines to their abrupt ends, and yet he had no sense of what it was supposed to contain. He had decided to ignore it. Adam had left him that puzzle, and to finish it would only please the austere. He was a Cerani fruit-seller. His father would have come up the river already, his boat full of mangoes and lemons. He would already have heard of what happened in the marketplace. He probably thought Farid dead.

There was a shuffling outside the door, and then a burst of sunlight that made him squint. So it was day; he had guessed night because the baby next door had gone quiet.

Adam squatted at the threshold, watching him, and it struck Farid that the man was always near to the ground, like a cat preparing to strike. Adam balanced his elbows on his knees and laced his fingers together. Farid noticed dark shadows under his eyes. "You have been calling water to yourself," he said.

"I had to. If I didn't, I would die."

"How did it feel?"

Farid did not reply. He did not want Adam to know how good it felt. He listened, trying to gauge how many men might be guarding the hallway.

"I showed you the pattern only once, but you built it again, with nothing but your fingers." Adam looked at the scratches on the wall. "Most of my students take weeks to memorise that pattern, and they are all chosen for their excellent recall."

"I'm not your student."

"No, no you are not." Adam sighed and looked at someone in the hallway, who handed him a platter of bread and cheese. "I think you must be hungry." He put the food down on the floor. "Though the end is near, we must take care of ourselves."

"The end?"

"Mogyrk comes to claim all of us, Farid. I have come nearer to the place where He died so that I may guide souls to His paradise."

"You mean to kill people."

"You do not understand. Here, eat." As Farid took a reluctant bite Adam said, "Everyone here will die no matter what I do. The Scar waits to the east and the Storm is coming. But it is foretold: Mogyrk will first shed light upon Nooria." He watched Farid eat. "You do not understand that, nor, does it appear, do my superiors."

Farid pushed his plate aside. "Why do you hold me prisoner here?"

"You can leave any time you wish. I want only for you to use what you have learned."

"By doing what? What will you make me do before I can leave?"

"You don't understand." Adam unfolded himself, standing to cast a shadow over the stains on the floor and the dirty pallet, and the shadows around his eyes deepened. "You *will* help me, but first you need to escape."

CHAPTER THIRTEEN

MESEMA

Mesema descended a dark staircase in the Ways, one hand on the wall to steady her, the other clutching her lantern. In the distance she saw two other lights, both above her, their owners set to different missions. If they did see her own descending flame, they did not care to investigate. By long tradition, one did not indulge curiosity in this dark place. This she had learned from the Old Wives. Those who travelled the bridges and stairs and passed through the hidden doors in the Ways respected the secrets of others.

The cold pressed against the bottoms of her feet, which were protected only by her dainty sandals. So far from the light and heat of the desert the air was chill, and a slow drip sounded against the stone. These wet and creeping fingers did not belong to the wide, shallow Blessing. The lifeblood that ran down the walls of the Ways like tears did not come from the river; this water came from a deeper and more secret source. She found it comforting.

Mesema reached the door to the dungeon and used the simple hook-twist lock, relieved to find the bar had not been dropped against her. Until recently there had been no prisoners to keep inside—there had been nothing to guard. She stepped through, listening. Someone cleared his throat, and she heard conversation—the guards talking amongst themselves. She covered her immodest top with a scarf, for it was not Felting custom to dress so, and eased around the corner. Six cells, three on each side, stood empty. She had heard they all were full when the Fryth prisoners had arrived and she tried to imagine how many people that had been, trapped here under the ground. It had been wrong, all of it had been wrong, but Sarmin could not say so; he could not admit any fault before the court. *Sometimes I need to say the truth,* he had said to her. But the greatest truths would remain forever hidden, eating away at the core of him.

Nothing had changed since the rebellion, not truly. Sarmin's *Code for the Moral Treatment of Royal Slaves* lay unfinished upon Azeem's table; the courtiers could not agree upon the merest detail. The fighting continued. The god's wound continued to bleed into the desert while austeres cast patterns in the city. And now Banreh was here, the worst place he could be, for this was the place where they would kill him.

Five cells further down she found him. He stood against the stones at the back of the small space, his arms crossed over his chest. She gripped the iron bars. She had not thought of what to say; she had only wanted to see him, to find out his purpose in returning to her, but now that she stood before him found her words missing.

He pushed away from the wall. "Your Majesty."

Something had changed. Banreh had been lame since Mesema was just a girl. It was part of who he was. Without his shattered leg, he never would have become her father's voiceand-hands. He had used his lameness to persuade Mesema to marry Sarmin, to convince her that something that looked like a tragedy could be a defining event. Now he moved with ease.

"Your leg," she said in her own language.

"I still have my limp." When she continued to stare he said, "The pattern has many uses." In all this he employed the respectful tone, one used by two equals who did not know one another. "The duke is a better bonesetter than a killer."

She matched his tone, though it brought a tear to her eye. "And yet the two of you killed those White Hats as they lay sleeping."

He did not shrink from her gaze. "Yes. As Marke Kavic died in *his* sleep."

"Are you Mogyrk now then?"

"No."

"So why?" She needed to understand his reasons. He had brought her to Cerana and then betrayed it. One or the other, she could accept, but not both things together.

He lifted his shoulders. "To show what we were capable of. For revenge. A play for the land and the iron it holds. Take your pick."

There was something he was not telling her. She looked around his bare cell. There were no parchments, no ink, no quills. He seemed naked without them, and without his pain. "I learned to read," she said, "Sarmin taught me." She had meant to write a letter to him in Fryth, to make him proud of her.

He looked at her as if she were mad. "Mesema—listen. Did the Felting slaves arrive in Nooria?"

"There were no Felting slaves."

His green eyes narrowed, gauging her truthfulness, and anger flashed within her that he would think her a liar for even a moment.

"There were," he said.

"No." For generations the people of the Grass had been exempt from the empire's tribute. Each chief promised to fight when called upon, which ensured no Felting parent ever sacrificed a child to the Cerani nobles.

Banreh stepped closer, and she watched the lines of his face as he spoke. He had always been handsome, even when his features were drawn with pain. "Arigu tells me they had converted to Mogyrk, that they had rebelled, but I know he just wanted them. Just as he waged his war after the emperor told him to turn back. This is a man who takes what he wants and afterwards provides a reason. You remember—he claimed you for Sarmin, though Beyon did not know."

"He lied to me," she admitted.

"You see." Banreh now stood so close that when he wrapped his hands around the iron, inches from her own, the warmth from his body washed over her. He switched to the intimate tone. "I knew the Felt would never be free unless I showed both empires what we can do."

"You think you have earned freedom? Every day the court asks Sarmin to invade the grass, to punish our people, to put them in chains for a hundred years—because of what you did."

"That is why I am here."

He was always calm. In the past it had given her comfort; now she wanted to hit him. Instead, she reached out towards his vest, grabbed a leather tie and gave it a sharp tug. "You always were a fool, Banreh." She laid her cheek against the cold, hard iron.

"Yes." And with that he leaned forwards and pressed his lips against hers. He smelled like grass and sunshine and outside spaces and she lingered against him, taking it in. "I should never have brought you to this place," he whispered. "We should have had grass-children."

With a jolt she remembered herself and let go the bars, putting a hand to her mouth. The guard station had gone quiet. "You cannot!" she hissed, looking down the dark corridor. "They will kill you."

He touched her cheek with a callused finger. "Not yet. They need Arigu."

"I cannot speak to you if you insist upon this foolishness." She backed away. She did not think it would be long before the guard returned.

He let go the bars and backed away into his cell. "Look for the slaves," he said. "You will find them. Then you'll know."

"I will." Her lips still felt warm from his touch. She turned from him and walked towards the Ways, but then thought of another question and turned back. "Will the Fryth duke truly help us?"

He stood mostly in the shadows now, the edges of his curls lit with gold in the light of her lantern, but then he shifted and she saw his eyes. Always they had reminded her of springtime. "Yes. He will."

She heard footsteps approaching and covered her lantern. She felt her way along the cells, moving quietly, but when the guard turned the corner and light spilled along the corridor she broke into a run, her sandals slapping against the stone.

"Hey!" the guard called out.

She whipped around the corner, hand on the stone, and pulled at the hook-twist for the door. *Hurry, hurry.* The guard's boots sounded against the floor but he was not as fast as she, even in her dainty sandals. She won through and ran halfway up the wet stairs before covering her lantern. She pressed her back against the wall.

The guard opened the door and looked into the Ways, holding his lantern aloft, but the darkness proved impenetrable. He craned his head towards where she hid and she held her breath as he stood listening. Surely he knew she was close by; it was only his laziness that prevented him climbing the stairs. His prisoner had not escaped; that was his main concern, and at last he grunted and retreated into the dungeon. She heard the bar fall on the other side of the door. That path was now closed to her.

She let out a breath, wondering what Sarmin would have said if the guard had caught her.

The Old Wives in the women's wing gossiped that Nessaket had kept many lovers over the years, but Mesema didn't see how that could be possible. There were rules for where a royal woman could go and with whom; for coming within the sight of a man, for speaking with him, and for touches both accidental and purposeful. While she knew a man's punishment was death in almost all cases, she did not know what consequences a woman might face.

She let her lantern shine over the steps and began her long climb. She would have to speak with many men, census-takers and taxmen and money-counters, for one of them would surely know about an influx of slaves from the north. One of them would have collected a portion of a sale, written down a name or noted the addition of slaves to an important household. She hoped it was so; she did not want to discover that Banreh had lied to her. He had been a traitor, but let him not be a traitor to her.

CHAPTER FOURTEEN

GOVNAN

Govnan lowered himself down the last step and faced the tower wall, taking a moment to catch his breath. At some point in the last month going down had become harder than going up. He placed his lantern behind him on a stair; it irked him, even now, that he required such a thing to light the dark. But he had lost Ashanagur that day in Sarmin's tower, when Sarmin had seen him and his elemental as nothing more than two interlocking patterns and pulled them apart. Though he was old, some experiences were new to him—the sensation of cold, the frustration of conjuring flame like a novice, the touch of a lantern's handle. The shock at seeing the crack in front of him.

It had grown since he first saw it two weeks before. Then, it had been about three hairs wide, looking as if someone might have drawn it there, and he had hoped that was the case. But now it had begun to yawn, showing teeth of crumbling stone, its throat a great rent in the Tower wall. He rubbed his finger along its rough edges. He knew an old building could crack; the rock-sworn always had fixed the foundations of old tombs and palace outbuildings. But the Tower had been created with the magic of

Meksha herself and blessed by Her, and it had always been impermeable to time and weather. Until now.

Though the light was poor he could see this was not the same kind of damage that had been done to Beyon's tomb; that also had begun as a crack, but it had spread out into . . . *nothing*. That had been without colour or form, a blankness that drew the eye and demanded payment. It had been the result of Helmar's work and the death of the Mogyrk god, and it had not yet ended; more wounds were growing. The one formed in Migido drew ever closer, called by the use of the pattern in the marketplace attack, and the place where the Mogyrk god had died loomed large in the east.

But this was something new.

Once it might have felt like a challenge, but today it served only to remind him of the failings of his tenure. The Tower had long been in decline: each generation produced fewer mages with less talent, and yet there had always been moments of greatness, of creation and brilliance. Govnan was beginning to fear he would be noted in the history of the Tower only for presiding over its end. And yet he could take joy in the time remaining him, for Mura had been returned.

He could still remember bringing her up the Blessing. She had been a tiny southern girl then, barely past his knee, clinging to a ragdoll. Her eyes, a deep brown before she was bound to Yomawa, had taken in everything—the crates and barrels tied to the boat, the mast and its sails, the poles tied carefully to the deck—and she had made him explain all of it. At every trade-town he bought her something new, here a pomegranate, there a tiny ring made of copper and agate. He always doted on the young recruits, for their lives would be utterly changed once they reached Nooria, where childish things would be put aside for ever. But Mura never outgrew her ragdoll; it rested on a shelf above her bed, guarding over her while she slept. She had left it behind when Sarmin sent her to Fryth, and Govnan had picked it up many times since and held it against his chest. He had never imagined giving it back to her as he had done the other day. A tear pricked his eye.

He wiped it away when he heard Moreth above him.

"You called for me, High Mage?" The rock-sworn took the stairs heavily, but with the ease of the young.

"Yes. I want you to see this. Bring the light closer."

Moreth held the lantern high as he approached. Govnan might have done the same, except that his shoulder would have complained. "You came down the stairs without calling me," Moreth scolded.

"I am your high mage," Govnan reminded him. "Now, look."

Moreth leaned so close to the wall that his nose nearly touched it. He closed his eyes and put a hand to the stone. After a moment he hissed and pulled back. "Rorswan cannot fix this," he said. "This crack does not come up from the earth, or by way of water, or through a flaw in the design."

"I did not think so. Did he say anything else?"

"No, but he does not always speak when there is a thing to say."

Govnan knew it well. Whether fire, water, rock, or wind, the claimed spirits rebelled. They did exactly what was mandatory as part of their binding and no more. A favour might sometimes be granted, but always at an extra cost—sometimes one a mage did not wish to pay. "Why did you jump away?"

Moreth hesitated, then looked to his feet in shame. "It was because of Rorswan."

"You are newly bound. Such problems arise. Do not be ashamed—tell me what happened."

"When I touched the crack," said Moreth, "I felt as if Rorswan was about to become free and turn me to stone, as happens with all rock-sworn."

"You lost control of him."

"No," said Moreth, meeting his eye. "I felt more that the crack tore us apart."

Govnan looked into the depths of the jagged tear. The power that went into the mages' elemental bindings was the same power that had built the Tower. When Uthman the Conqueror had come to this intersection of rock, sand, and stone and named it after Meksha's daughter, Nooria, the goddess granted his descendants the power to wield Her magic. Meksha's gift was laid by rune and incantation into every stone by Gehlan the Holy, and by her blessing the Tower had raised itself towards heaven. The mages today would never be able to recreate the spells that had been used—or even understand them. He had studied the fragments describing the building of the Tower and had touched only the edges of it, just enough to know how much he could not comprehend. His long years weighed on him, but his accomplishments were light in comparison.

"Has Meksha withdrawn Her grace from us?" he asked, more of the stone than of Moreth.

"Sometimes I—" Moreth frowned.

"What? Tell me, Moreth."

"Sometimes I wish I could go back to the time of Satreth."

"If you wish to fight Yrkmir, you need not go into the past."

The slaughter of mages in those times had devastated the Tower. *Let it not happen again.*

A rustling came to the top of the stairs. Mura, his returned child, stood looking down at them, and Govnan's heart lifted. "What is it, my child?"

She did not return his smile. "You must come."

"What has happened?" he asked, looking at all the steps he would need to climb if he obeyed her.

"The old woman Sahree sent me," she said. "The Megra has died."

CHAPTER FIFTEEN

SARMIN

Sarmin laid a hand upon the carved rosewood of the Megra's coffin. She had once called him Helmar's heir—not heir to the Pattern Master, but to the mage Helmar had been in his younger days, one who aspired to fix and to build, to make whole. In the end it had broken him. The Megra had shown him that Helmar was his brother, not by blood but by talent and experience. He and Helmar had shared the same imprisonment, the same victories, linked across time and by the designs that Helmar had laid across it—but Sarmin was not broken. Helmar had inflicted too much suffering upon himself, left too much behind, including the woman he had loved. The Megra would not be alone here; she would rest in Mirra's garden, its sweet scents a balm against the pains of her long life. "Goodbye, Megra," he whispered.

Priest Assar offered Sarmin a slight bow before motioning for his novices to bear the Megra away. A hush had fallen over Mirra's garden. The rosebuds and gardenia blossoms turned towards the sun in silent communion. Sahree sat upon a bench, out of tears, her eyes on the statue of Mirra.

Govnan stepped up to his side, staff clicking against the stones, and Sarmin willed him to honour the quiet. He did not. "There is something at the

Tower you must see, Magnificence." His voice had begun to lose the low rumble it had once contained, becoming high and thin, querulous.

Sarmin took his time before responding. He was not done mourning the Megra. "And what might that be?"

"I cannot speak of it here, Your Majesty."

"Very well." Sarmin gave a long bow to the statue of Mirra, closing his eyes and thinking of all the Megra had seen: Helmar, both young and old; Cerani soldiers ravaging her homeland; her young friend, Gallar, hanging from a tree. Somehow she had made sense of it all.

Straightening he laid a sympathetic hand upon Sahree's shoulder. "I must go."

He walked towards the exit, sword-sons trailing behind him, and found Dinar waiting in the doorway, a tower of muscle wrapped in elegant robes. It struck Sarmin that for all the gods in the pantheon, only two were worshipped in the palace. Women went to Mirra for comfort and men went to Herzu for power. Dinar stood straighter as Sarmin approached, holding a book against his chest, showing the tears tattooed on his hand.

"High Priest Dinar."

"Magnificence." Dinar barely dipped his head. "I had expected to perform the funeral myself. The old woman was not of our faith. By law"—he presented the book he held—"her soul belongs with Herzu."

"She was not of the palace, Dinar. Her law is not our law."

Dinar frowned, but he lowered the book. So bulky was he that it looked a toy in his hands. "I have another question, Your Majesty, if you would entertain it."

"Make it quick. I am on my way to the Tower."

"When should I expect the prisoner?" A smile of anticipation danced over the priest's lips.

Sarmin realised the full nature of his command in the private audience chamber. In the palace, no question was merely asked. There would be blood first, the removal of flesh, exquisite pain designed for Herzu's pleasure. He stepped away from the scent of Mirra's flowers, ashamed for Her to hear. "You will have him when I send him to you." *If I send him.*

Dinar's dark eyes flickered. "At that time I will be pleased to give him over to Herzu. He is one our god will cherish, though imperfect." With a slight bow he retreated.

Sharing the palace with Herzu's high priest required constant balance. Sarmin must be careful not to appear weak, to give the man everything he wanted, but neither must he leave him with nothing. Dinar had influence over at least half the court and must be kept content. Sarmin was not ready for a confrontation, covert or otherwise. Yet giving over *anything* to Dinar—the Megra's soul, Banreh's body—felt unnatural. He glanced down at Govnan, shrunken and silent at his side.

"Such is the way of the empire," said Govnan, as if Sarmin had spoken his thoughts aloud.

"We shall see." They began their slow walk, neither of them blessed with easy movement. Here the walls bore not mosaics or tapestries, but subtle carvings best seen in shadow. Pomegra studied her books, Ghesh stood upon a star and Keleb's finger pointed in judgement. Around them all spun the mass of the universe—planets, waters, and suns rendered in white marble, with no mind to scale. Beneath two clashing suns stood a bench for the comfort of worshippers journeying from temple to temple; there sat Nessaket, pale and gaunt. She should not look so; she should look well, and her child should be with her. His brother.

"Mother," he said, stopping, "you should not be walking about."

"We must speak." Nessaket tapped the stone at her side. He noticed the veins that stood out upon her hand, the wrinkles at her wrist. When Sarmin settled beside her, she said, "You must not give the prisoner to Dinar."

"Are you here to plead his case?"

"Not in the least. It is only that Dinar will take too long to kill him, and he must die."

Sarmin watched and listened.

"Arigu is not here—not yet—and without him the White Hats grow restive. They long to have their honour restored. The longer you keep the chief alive, the harder it will be to assure their loyalty to you."

"General Lurish—"

"General Lurish is a blustering old man. He cannot hold them to you. Only the public execution of the traitor will seal their faith."

Sarmin watched Govnan pretending to study the marble. "Only Banreh knows where this duke might be hiding."

"*You* are not afraid of the desert," said Nessaket, leaning forwards, her dark hair falling over his arm. "The desert made Uthman into a conqueror. The desert made ours the strongest empire in the world—and you lead it. This duke is a northerner who knows nothing of the sand. You will find him."

Sarmin laid a hand on her arm. It was true: all of this was his—the bench where they sat, the temple wing, the city, the whole empire, and all the history that came with it. And yet he was not so certain he commanded the desert as well. Mogyrk remained powerful there.

Nessaket pushed his hand away. "Now go."

Sarmin stood and motioned to the high mage. "Come," he said, "let us see what is so important at the Tower."

Sarmin ran his fingers along the length of the crack. "What does it mean?" he asked, more of himself than the high mage. The rock-sworn had felt a pull on his elemental when he touched it, but this was not the emptiness of the Great Storm. The Storm took more than magic—it took colour and memories. It *hollowed*. He remembered the question Mesema had asked of him. "Govnan, how long do you think it will be before the Storm reaches the Blessing?"

Govnan laid a hand upon the wall and patted it, as if it were his child. "We don't know that it will be altered by the storm, Magnificence. It was given us by Meksha Herself—a literal blessing. What is Mogyrk against Her?"

"I thought that fire was Her realm."

"She gave us this Tower, Your Majesty, and the ability to command all four elements. She commands Her fiery mountain, it's true—but there She might find not only rock and flame, but the winds upon its peaks and the water that runs down its surface." Sarmin considered this. "We know that rock turns to dust in the emptiness. The wind stops, the fire dies. Why would water be different?"

"Earthly elements are nothing against the Storm—but what of elements from another plane?"

The young mage Moreth spoke. "To learn such things, High Mage, we would require an unbound elemental spirit."

"Indeed," said Govnan, "since the bound are corrupted by our earthly bodies." He sighed. "In this world Meksha reigns over the elements. Over the years I spent with Ashanagur I felt a strong connection to Her. I felt Her power singing in the stones, beating in my heart, running in my fingers whenever I drew a rune upon the air." Govnan leaned on his staff, tracing the crack with his gaze. "Do you think Her power remains with us now?"

"I cannot sense such things," Sarmin said, disliking that it was true. "Can you no longer sense Her?" He was reminded that he had taken Ashanagur from the high mage, and for the first time wondered whether that had been the wisest course.

Govnan shook his head and directed them across the lowest floor of the Tower, a dark circular space, his staff tapping against the streaked marble beneath their feet. "Come. I have prepared a journey for us." He lifted a hand and the tip of his index finger began to glow, faintly at first, then with a rosy redness that showed the shadow of his bones through his old flesh. Perhaps some ember remained of the elemental fire once trapped within him. The glow increased and finally it shone with an incandescence that made Sarmin look away and threw their shadows black upon the walls. He wondered then what fed the fire now Ashanagur had gone.

"This is the key," Govnan said, and he started to trace runes into the air. His writing hung before them, as if he had cut through the fabric of the world into some bright place beyond. The archways changed in the moment Govnan set his last rune into the air. One opened now onto a white and endless sky. Opposite that entrance, natural bedrock replaced the tower's stones, granite shot through with glistening black veins. The third archway opened into blue depths, dark and unrevealing, a wall of water undulating across the entrance in defiance of reason. And opposite that archway fire rimmed a gateway into the hottest of Herzu's hells, an inferno landscape of molten lakes and trees of flame beneath a sun so large and close it left no room for sky.

"Doorways into the elemental realms," said Govnan placing a hand on Moreth's shoulder. No heat came from the flames, no sound or sensation from the other portals.

"Why are we here, High Mage?" Yet Sarmin stepped forwards.

Govnan pointed into the burning arch with a steady hand. "I need to go back, to revisit Lord Ashanagur in the City of Brass." Something flickered past the archway, something fast and large and trailing strands of fire like burning hair. "He will tell us something of Meksha."

Sarmin took another step. The place mesmerised him; every part of it was suffused with the fascination that burns in a dancing flame. "Will he?"

"Yes. Come." Govnan entered the realm of fire, and Sarmin followed.

No heat burned him; no smoke filled his lungs. Those were the by-products of combustion in his own world. Here all was pure flame, and he walked on it and through it. It licked his skin, touched his hair, slid against his lips in seductive caress.

Govnan led on without pause, seeming to know his way through intersecting rivers of liquid fire, blue and orange. At last he stopped near a vast expanse of molten rock, golden in colour but reflecting the sun's crimson across its rippling surface. Beyond it stood a great city, its walls shimmering with heat.

"The City of Brass," said Sarmin.

"And the Lake of Fire, Lord Ashanagur's home," Govnan replied, swinging his cane in a circular motion towards the centre of the lake. In seconds a pillar of flame rose from the depths. From it rose a churning ball, streaked with black and green, fire dancing along a surface twice Sarmin's height. It pulsed before the mammoth sun, spitting showers of sparks down into the liquid metal, before moving towards them, dragging behind it tendrils of white flame.

In Sarmin's tower room it had taken the form of a fiery man. Now Sarmin understood Ashanagur was no man.

"Ashanagur," said Govnan, his voice regaining some of the timbre Sarmin had thought lost to age.

The spirit's voice hissed and crackled. "You have returned, High Mage, old Flesh-and-bone. And you, who gave me my freedom. And this." It darted towards Moreth, who flinched. "Is this my payment for the crime of trespass?"

"No. I plan to offer you something greater than one man."

"What could be greater than a life?"

"Freedom."

Ashanagur rose up towards the great sun before swooping towards them again. "I have my freedom. Not one fire-sworn remains in your world."

"I could bind you, right now."

"You are frail. You diminish in the way of your kind, old Flesh-and-bone."

"I am stronger than I ever was." Govnan drew a rune upon the air and Ashanagur shrank away. "But I did not come to bind you. I came to ask a question."

Ashanagur drifted, fire spitting from its form, until it had reached the centre of the lake. There it remained, pulsing black and green, its colours reflected in the molten rock. Sarmin thought it would return to the depths, but in time it spun back towards them, trailing orange fire, until at last it settled before Sarmin. Even the white flame that trailed away from it was longer than Sarmin was tall. "I owe this one a favour," said Ashanagur. "I will answer the question for it."

"Very well." Govnan paused a moment, then asked, "It is about Meksha."

"I rule this plane, not some god of flesh!"

"Indeed, She could not power the heat of Her mountain without help from one so great as you."

Ashanagur gave a quick spin. "She does require my help."

"As She always has, from the beginning?" Govnan inched towards the question of Meksha's strength, but Ashanagur dismissed him with a bright shimmer.

"What is the beginning? She always has been in the Tower, as have I."

"One more," said Sarmin, stepping forwards, the toes of his slippers nearly in the rippling lake. "One more."

Ashanagur darted at him, stopping only a hair's width from his face. "For you," it said.

"Have you seen the emptiness of the Great Storm?"

"I have. It does not see me, just as you do not see it—Mogyrk blinded the Tower."

"How did Mogyrk blind the Tower?"

Ashanagur rose high above him and was silent. But at last it said, "Both of you creep around the same question." It hovered over Moreth, its tendrils caressing his face and shoulders as the rock-sworn cringed in horror. "You may ask it, if I may have this one as payment."

"No." Sarmin pulled Moreth away from the flames. "I thank you, Lord Ashanagur." He turned and walked a path of blue flame, his mind on Ashanagur's words, his feet cutting a path from memory. *It does not see me.* The pattern lied, but perhaps it could also be lied to—or tricked. Without his ability to see patterns, Sarmin lacked the skill to try. But it all had something to do with Meksha and the crack in the wall. To his surprise he passed through the gate and found himself standing once more at the base of the Tower, Moreth and Govnan beside him. Compared to the plane of fire, this world was drab and grey. He blinked, unable for the moment to differentiate wall from stair. "Your sight will improve in time, Your Majesty," said Govnan.

Sarmin barely acknowledged the high mage. "I must go," he said, starting towards the stairs and the sword-sons at the top. "I have much to do."

CHAPTER SIXTEEN

FARID

F arid woke from a dream. In it Adam stood over him, carving a pattern-shape into his cheeks, so when he opened his eyes he rubbed at his face and looked about the room until he was sure he was alone. Unable to return to sleep he stood and walked to the wall. He trailed his fingers over the design engraved there, following the lines with his eyes, trying to sense which felt unfinished or broken. He still had no sense of what the design might achieve when it was finished; the outlines of the shapes gave him no sense of their purpose. And yet, as with a cart half-empty, he longed to fill in the rest of it.

The baby began to wail in the house next door and he hissed with impatience. The noise made it difficult to concentrate.

You can leave any time you wish. That was what Adam had said to him, and since then he had been given no more food. He had come to believe—to hope—that the unfinished pattern was his escape route.

Whatever Adam thought, he was not going to help the man once he was free.

He was going at this all wrong. He was looking too closely. He stood away from it, the candle clutched in one hand. It was a question of balance, of full and empty spaces together. He looked until his eyes unfocused, shutting out the noise, the heat, the pain of his empty stomach. *Just see.*

He approached the wall again and placed the candle on the floor. He made a line with his fingernail in the soft wood, then another. *Yes.* Then, quicker, a circle here, a half-moon, line, two mirrored crescents, until he was working feverishly, using both hands. Sweat dripped down his back and thirst dried his tongue, but he did not pause. Hours passed, or minutes. Splinters tore at the flesh of his fingertips, marking the wall with blood. He knew what this design would do. It would reach into the grains and whorls of the wood, snake into the very fibres of the tree-flesh, and rip them asunder. The wall would cease to be. He made the last stroke and the scored lines disappeared, replaced by curves and angles of soft blue light. The design floated before his eyes, and behind it was the wall, whole, unscarred. He *pulled—*

—and stumbled into the night-time of the next room, coughing up the dust in his throat. This space was empty save for a table with a knife upon it. He knew as well as he knew the look of his own hands that Adam had put the weapon there for him. He lifted it and listened for the guards. He knew they had clubs and swords, but would they use them? After a moment he decided, yes, they would. Adam wanted him to *escape*; they could not merely let him go—even if they only played at fighting, he was weak with hunger and untrained with the knife.

And so he set to the next wall. The baby cried on the other side of it. No matter—he would run past the mother and the screaming child and then he would be in the Maze. That held its own dangers, but at least he was armed and that would be enough to keep most people at bay. He thrilled with each stroke of the weapon. Joy filled him, knowing where each shape belonged, sensing exactly where a line should stop, like a musician with his instrument. As a boy he had been given a broken harp and he had taken great joy in the meagre sound of it. This was far better.

He did not hear the guards or Adam as he worked. He thought of the pretty, cruel guard who first had held him. He would not mind fighting that one. Farid scored the last line, and *pulled.*

Darkness.

He stumbled and fell, sneezing; the baby screamed and someone coughed. He sat up, wiping snot from his nose. He could not see anything. His candle had been burnt down to a nub and must have flickered out at last. After a minute the baby quieted and he heard a girl whisper, "Where does that lead?"

"What?" He sat up, looking into the blackness.

"The hole you made. I can smell fresh air. Does it lead to the street?"

"No. It's another house. Don't go in there." He regretted opening the hole if it meant those men would now come through and cause trouble for her.

The girl was quiet a time, then said, "I need to find a way out of here."

You too? Farid wiped sawdust from his face. "I can't see you. Where are you?"

"In the corner."

He strained, but saw nothing. "Why don't you have a light?"

"I don't need light." So she was blind. "You must be careful. *He's* downstairs." The way she said it gave him pause. The house where he had been held was small. It made sense the Mogyrks might occupy all of the houses in this row. And if Adam were on the first floor . . . He gripped the knife in his hand.

"He pretends to be nice," she said. "When I first saw him I thought he was so kind—the sort of man you could really believe might bring you into a better place."

"Where's your family?" he asked. "Is there somebody who is looking for you? I can send them word."

He did not expect her to laugh, but she did. "You would not believe me."

"I'll tell the Blue Shields about you," he said. The confidence was more for himself than for her; he still had to get past whoever waited downstairs. "No: I'll bring you with me." He opened the door a crack and peeked out. A narrow landing led to a flight of stairs. No guard stood at this level. He crept out and paused on the first step, listening. He heard nothing, but Adam could be crouching there, waiting to pounce once he came into view.

He took another step, and another. No alarm was raised, from this house or the other, but now he heard murmurs and froze. There were two men, maybe three. He could not fight his way out. He would need to be clever. He returned to the girl's room and lifted her baby's cradle. "Are you ready to leave? Tonight?"

"Please," she said, "yes."

He paused. "What's your name?"

"Rushes."

Farid returned to the stairs and placed the cradle at the edge of the first step. Then he set to making his pattern for the third time. He wished he had learned more than two, but then he remembered they were the tool of the enemy and shuddered. He barely needed to think about the shapes now; his hands moved automatically, his sore, damaged fingers pressing against the knife. When he was ready he tipped the cradle down the stairs, making a great noise, and waited at the edge of his design.

Two men ran to the bottom of the steps and examined the contents of the spilled blankets. Whatever their purpose, they did seem to care about the child they had imprisoned. Not finding the babe they turned towards the stairs and as they rushed upwards, they caught sight of Farid and started shouting at one another to seize him.

He *pulled*, a smile coming to his face. He *would* get out, and once free, he would find his father. He thought of the old man's face, scored with wrinkles, his big hands as they lifted barrels full of pomegranates.

The men fell through, landing upon the barrels and crates that had been stacked below, still moving, but not rising to their feet. Their legs were broken. And he was not well either. He gripped the edge of the wood, fighting the blackness at the edge of his vision.

He gathered himself and returned to the room. "Come, hurry," he said, and when Rushes came closer he took the baby and clasped her hand. On the landing he guided her around the chasm and showed her where the steps began, all the while listening for Adam.

"They're not dead?" she asked.

"No, just hurt."

"Kill them."

Farid felt a pang of horror. He had never taken a life—he did not know how to thrust metal past bone and into living flesh. "No. Come on, let's hurry."

But she paused, then whispered, "I have to get to the palace."

With all the strange things that had happened to him he did not find this as unbelievable as he might have. "All right."

They made their way to the bottom and looked around the dark room. Someone was watching them: he knew it. Someone was there, in the shadows, but whoever it was made no effort to intervene. He opened the door and peered out, then cast one last look into the shadows before pushing Rushes through and stepping out into the Maze.

You will help me, but first you need to escape. The words hung over his victory as he ran towards the river, the babe in his arms and Rushes pounding after. Adam had let him go, but he wanted it to look like an escape. Everything so far had proceeded as Adam wished, and he did not know why, or what might come next. After they had run a few blocks he heard shouts, the clash of weapons and running feet. Were they being chased? But the tang of smoke carried on the air, suggesting another sort of conflict. He slowed, taking each step more carefully, listening to see which path might be safest.

"Mogyrk scum!" someone shouted, and the epithet was punctuated by a crash. Shortly afterwards cheers rang out, celebrating some small victory. A group of men ran Farid's way and he pressed himself against the wall, pushing Rushes behind him and the baby into her arms. They hurried past, too busy fleeing Blue Shields to pay them any mind. Farid got them all into a doorway just as the soldiers rounded the corner, pounding after the first group. He realised one second before the guards did that they had run into an ambush: stones and jeers pelted down from the rooftops as rebels entered the street from both ends. They were well-armed and smiling.

Farid pressed himself further into the shadows.

The guards were well trained and made of themselves a circle, using their shields to protect and defend, but the rebels were too many and soon the Blue Shields were bloody and limping. Farid still had his knife and he drew it from his belt, gripping the handle hard. If the rebels should notice his little group, come after the girl, Rushes . . . To defend her would mean certain death. He could take out one of the rebels, maybe two, before they overwhelmed him—but what choice did he have? He watched the fight, deciding how he would use his blade when they came, gathering his nerve. It was then more soldiers entered the fray, coming from the riverside, fresh and ready to fight, and he drew back into the shadows, feeling a fool. He was no fighter, nor a hero.

The rebels scattered and the Blue Shields gathered their wounded. Farid did not move. He held a finger to Rushes' lips, waiting for the road to clear. It was then one of the soldiers caught sight of him, and motioned to the rest of his men. "Look here, we got some more hiding."

"We weren't with them," Farid said.

"Look, it's a little family." The man looked past him to where Rushes sat, the baby in her arms.

"We were trying to get to—" Where? The marketplace and his apartments were the other way. Who would believe they were on their way to the palace? "—the guard station."

"The guard station's on fire. Did you light the match?"

"No," he said, "but there are Mogyrks in the Maze who likely did it."

"Listen to this man!" laughed the soldier. "He's a scholar!"

Farid approached him, palms turned out, knowing it was important to convince these soldiers, knowing Adam must be captured and quickly. "Look, I can show you where they are."

"You trying to draw us in? Get us surrounded like last time?"

"I told you, we're not with them."

Another soldier, older, came to stand beside the first, and Farid was struck by his eyes, blue beneath grey bushy eyebrows. "What's your name, son?"

"Farid."

The first soldier took a step back and hooted. "Not the Farid we're looking for? That would be some luck."

The older man stepped closer, squinting into the dark doorway at Rushes. "Were you in the marketplace?"

"Yes." When the soldiers looked at one another, he added, "I'm a fruit-seller."

"Come with me," said the old soldier, his blue eyes gone solemn, beckoning him with a gloved hand. "The Tower has business with you."

CHAPTER SEVENTEEN

MESEMA

Mesema lay where scented mountain beauty twisted around long blades of grass and the black summer soil warmed her skin. She twisted her hands in his curls as he kissed her, his cheeks rough, his chest smooth against her exploring hand. His lips wandered to her neck, his breath tickling the fine hairs and, further down, laying warm kisses between her breasts, one hand now between her legs. Her sister's voice carried over the distance, calling to someone, and laughter rang out around the fire, but they were all far away, and the two of them were alone . . . She rolled and put him beneath her. The moon was in her face and her need was so great, greater than she had ever felt it, so that the touch of him made her think she might burst, or dissolve into nothing, if she just lowered her hips.

Mesema woke with a start, her heart beating so fast she put a hand over her chest to slow it. She rolled to her side, then slipped out of her bed, glancing back at the pillows with horror as if the bed, not she, had been unfaithful. She stood in the middle of the room, the desert night cold against her skin.

Tarub stood in the doorway. "I heard a shout, Your Majesty. Are you well?"

"I am fine, Tarub. I need light."

Within seconds Tarub had given her enough light to make out the edges of the room, marked by Pelar's empty crib, the mirror with all of her Cerani makeup and jewellery laid out before it and the humble chest full of her Felting possessions. She fell to her knees before the chest and lifted the lid, gazing within as if peering into the Grass itself. She pushed aside the woollen blankets her mother had made for her and the wedding dress she and the others had embroidered by firelight and searched with her hands to the very bottom, where she had stuffed her old cloak when she came out of the mountains for good. Using secret methods, her mother had made the wool a bright white, so the flowers stitched across it in blue and red stood out even more. She gathered the cloak in her hands, ran her fingers along the hem. Once, Banreh had been writing in the carriage when it came to a sudden stop and his ink had splashed over the rim of its pot. She found the black spot and took a deep breath.

She pulled the cloak up around her shoulders and regarded herself in the polished silver, but she did not look like a plainsgirl. Her hair, the paint-stain lingering on her lips, even the way she stood spoke of the palace. She tore off the cloak and threw it on the floor.

She stood in the silence of her room, so empty without Pelar, and closed her eyes. He had gone south, so far from the Hidden God that she did not believe He would ever find him. She turned to the shadowed cradle and lifted Pelar's silks to her nose, filling her heart with his scent. Sarmin and Nessaket had been right: she should have gone south with her child.

"The Empire Mother to see you, Your Majesty," said Tarub from the doorway, and Mesema turned, dropping Pelar's wrappings. Nessaket entered and slid down upon a bench, rubbing her forehead with one hand. Pain had etched wrinkles around her eyes. She pretended not to notice the tears on Mesema's cheeks. "I heard you scream."

"A nightmare," Mesema lied.

Nessaket did not pursue it. "You spoke privately with the prisoner. What did he say?"

"How did you know?"

"I guessed. Now I know."

Mesema watched Nessaket's face, knowing she walked on uneven ground. "He said Arigu betrayed him."

The Empire Mother clicked her tongue in disbelief. "He will say nothing useful before he dies, then."

Mesema stared, afraid to ask what the Empire Mother knew of Banreh's death, but Nessaket read her face and said, "Don't worry yourself, Daughter. I have made sure he will die without pain, away from Dinar's knives."

"But—"

Nessaket motioned to the cloak on the rug. "Are you going somewhere in that? Back to the dungeon, perhaps? Or out into the city?"

Mesema picked it up, folded it and replaced it in the chest, blushing. So the Empire Mother knew of her adventure at Lord Nessen's estate. "No." She closed the lid, and once more had nothing for her hands to do. She kept them still at her sides.

"Good. When my son the emperor is dead, heaven and stars keep him, you may do as you like, but not before." When Mesema began to protest, she held up a hand. "You are young, and love can run you right through, hard as a spear. I remember that much. But do not risk this. You do not know what will arise should you take a wrong step."

"I love the emperor my husband," said Mesema, almost by rote. She sat on the bed and faced the Empire Mother. "Did you love Emperor Tahal?"

Nessaket gave a little shrug. "We of the palace should not be concerned with love." That might be true, but Mesema had seen Nessaket's face when she heard General Arigu was still alive.

"I don't know what I imagined when first I came here," said Mesema. "At first I thought I would lie on a couch all day, being fanned by slaves. But then the palace frightened me and I didn't know if I would survive it." The emptiness, she did not fear; she had faith in Sarmin to stop it. But Yrkmir was something new.

"You will survive, Mirra willing; you will. But I fear I will not. I survived my attack, but it drains me. Every day I feel a little less alive."

"It is because you are sad about Daveed." Mesema rushed forwards to take Nessaket's hand. "But we will find him."

"I know we will, for better or for worse. And my little servant Rushes, too. I miss her almost as much, though everyone else has forgotten her." Nessaket patted Mesema's cheek, then stood. "I must rest."

Nessaket left the room and Mesema clapped for Tarub; the girl would never forgive her if she dressed herself. A silk covering was chosen and wrapped around her. Willa drew a brush through her hair and pushed slippers onto her feet. To go before the emperor, a woman must bathe and paint her face—but that was a palace rule, not Sarmin's. He did not notice how she looked. She left her room and made her way towards the doors to the palace, hearing her guards behind her, soft on their feet. Once out of the new women's wing she squinted, for in the larger palace the lights, all lit, were harsh against her eyes.

Sarmin's room was further than it had been from the old women's wing, and she passed many slaves and administrators, who threw themselves down upon the floor at the sight of her. She began to feel embarrassed, wandering the halls late at night, and wondered at the impulse that had led her here.

Her guard Sendhil, the eldest of her men, said in a low voice, "Your Majesty, where are we going at this time of night? Protocol requires—"

"We go to see the emperor, Sendhil."

His hand went to his grey moustache. "Ah. But there have been days you disappeared, Your Majesty, and in all our searching of the palace and its grounds we could not find you."

"Do not fear. The emperor will not learn of your failure."

"I am not concerned about that, Your Majesty. I am concerned for you."

Mesema remembered her rescue at Grada's hands, and Banreh's illicit kiss through the iron bars. Sendhil was likely correct: she should never follow her instincts. "Thank you, Sendhil," she said, hoping that would be the end of it.

"Your Majesty," he went on, "remember, it is required that we be present whenever a woman of your stature is near a man who is not the emperor, or a woman of lesser status, or in the view of—"

Each word felt like another tether around her ankles. She took an authoritative tone. "I have told you it will not happen again. I have listened, Sendhil, and I hear, but you must know that what is improper in Nooria is not improper in my land. I will suffer no more instruction from you."

"Your Majesty." He slowed his steps and joined the men behind her.

Relief filled her at the sight of Sarmin's door and she entered, leaving his sword-sons and her guards doing an awkward dance in the corridor.

Sarmin sat at his desk conversing with Azeem, who stood with a scroll in his hands. Never did she catch sight of the grand vizier without scrolls or a ledger. Sarmin looked as if he had been running, bright spots of red colouring his cheeks, but Mesema knew better: he had become healthier in the last few months, but not so much as that. When she entered they both turned her way, Sarmin registering surprise and some pleasure, Azeem looking horrified. Indeed, the wife of the emperor should never enter his room without invitation.

But Sarmin smiled, strode to the doorway and took Mesema's hands in his. "I was hoping to see you. You're the first thing to look beautiful to me since I left the Tower."

It had been long since he had said anything of that nature, and she felt her cheeks go red. "Thank you, my husband." She had not known the Tower was so beautiful, to blind a man to the sights of the palace.

Azeem gave a stiff bow and gathered more scrolls into his arms. "I will retire, with your permission, Magnificence."

"Of course, Azeem."

Azeem left, the back of his robes as straight and unwrinkled as in the morning when he first donned them. Sarmin turned to Mesema. "Your question to me regarding the river has yielded some insight." He led her to a bench where they sat side by side.

She listened.

"I've had a thought. Do you remember how you and I slipped through the pattern, unseen?"

"Of course."

Sarmin gripped her hands more tightly. "Well, the same might be possible with the Great Storm."

"But when I slipped through the pattern, I followed a path. There is no path through the emptiness." Mesema sat up and looked into his copper eyes. The moment reminded her of an earlier time when they had shared the tower room as a hiding place, eating scraps stolen from the kitchen. "But perhaps it is not so empty. The pattern took memories and images. The emptiness also takes. It drains everything, even colour. I thought it the opposite of the pattern, but . . ."

"Maybe it is more closely linked to the pattern than we had believed." His enthusiasm was short-lived and he leaned back against the cushions, deflated. "But I cannot see patterns."

"Hush," she said, "you will." She thought how to broach the subject of Banreh and the Felting slaves, but just as she was about to speak, he caught her in an embrace.

"I am glad you stayed in the palace," he whispered into her hair.

Her heart burned when she remembered Banreh's lips against hers, and she closed her eyes to shut the memory from her mind.

Sarmin spoke again into her ear. "Do you think we will be husband and wife again, soon?" His breath fell upon her neck, and she was reminded then of her dream.

She blushed and pulled away. If she had not the courage to confess about Banreh, she would confess something else. "I require forgiveness, my husband, for motherhood has invested me with no more wisdom than I had as a child." She raised a hand to stop his protest. "I went out into the city. I had a vision from the Hidden God and I thought it showed me Daveed. I was foolish and tricked my guards. Grada brought me back."

His copper eyes went wide. "Why? Why would you go out there?"

"How much time have you spent with your mother since her injury, Sarmin? Listen, she suffers terrible headaches. At times she is so dizzy she can barely move, but when her body is well, grief fills her mind. She cannot sleep—and so neither can I. All day I dread the night, and all night I curse the Mogyrks who took your brother. I had to do something. But I chose the wrong path, Sarmin, and men died." She wiped away a tear.

Sarmin stood, his shoulders stiff. "You must leave such things to Grada. But I would hear of your vision, because none have been false so far."

"It showed me Lord Nessen's house—" The floor shook and the parchment on Sarmin's desk slid to the carpet. The room heaved, sending the bench through the air, its pillows streaming behind it, and throwing Mesema to the floor. A shower of plaster fell over her back and then at last the room stilled.

Mesema scrambled to her knees as Sarmin stood and looked about the room in horror. "What new manner of attack is this?" he breathed.

The Felting lived in the cradle of the mountains; the tribe had long suffered their complaints. "My husband," she said, "that was an earthquake."

CHAPTER EIGHTEEN

FARID

The Blue Shields led Farid across the Tower courtyard. Every citizen of Nooria was accustomed to its tallest structure rising over them as if to pierce the sky, and to the wailing of the wizards as they cast their runes under the moon, but Farid had never understood the true size of the Tower compound. Here was more space than lay between the Blessing and the fruit market, or from the market to his home—his entire range of movement for most of his life—and it was filled with statues of Meksha in various destructive poses, unsettling to look upon at night, with only lantern-fire to define them in a play of orange and shadow.

The soldiers looked at one another and shuddered.

The walk from the gate to the Tower door was not so long, and a female mage answered the call of the bell-pull, pushing open thick brass doors the size of a flatboat without any apparent strain. Her eyes held the open spaces of the sky, and black hair puffed around her face like dark clouds. She gestured at them with long, delicate fingers not decorated by any chains or rings. "Who calls upon the Tower?" She looked from one to the next. "Who interrupts our work?" Farid looked at his feet before she turned her haunting face to his.

The old soldier—Naru—bowed. It was he who had insisted on leaving Rushes behind—the Tower was no place for a child, he had said, so now she waited at the guardhouse, the squirming babe in her arms, for Farid's return. She would not tell the soldiers anything, for the only people she trusted were at the palace. It sounded like madness, but then here he was, at the Tower. Grand destinations did not seem so impossible any longer.

"I come here with questions of magic that are beyond the Blue Shields to answer," said Naru, his gaze still on the stones by his feet.

"All such questions are beyond the Blue Shields to answer," the mage replied. A breeze lifted the bottom of her robes, revealing fine sandals tied with beaded copper.

"This man," said Naru, indicating Farid, "was held captive by Mogyrks, and saw much of their workings."

Farid forced himself to raise his head and meet the mage's eyes. She watched him wordlessly, her eyes taking him deep into a realm of sky. Something moved within her, a creature of air and storm, and he felt its breath on his face, cold and curious. They stood in silence for such a long time the soldiers began to look at one another and make small noises in their throats. The mage paid them no mind, and turned to Naru only when she was satisfied. "I will take him from here. I am Mura."

Naru put an arm out in front of Farid. "I must bring him back to the guard-post. He has information—"

"I told you where to find the Mogyrk's house," said Farid, looking beyond the mage to where he could see a long, well-lit gallery lined with statues. "What else could I tell you?" The Tower pulled at him and he longed to enter it, to draw his patterns among its stones and curves.

"But what do we do with the girl?"

Farid looked to the mage. "I escaped with a girl and the child she cares for. Can she not come here?"

"Bring this girl. I will make a judgement then." Mura beckoned to Farid, and Naru dropped his arm and allowed him to pass. Farid knew the old guard had not expected him to be welcomed into the Tower. The Blue Shields turned and walked back towards the gate, whispering amongst themselves.

Farid took a final step that lifted him over the Tower threshold, bracing himself to see spirits strange and wondrous, men riding carpets or djinn standing upon piles of gold, but his feet met only stone and the corridor lay plain before him. Mura smiled at his confusion and pointed at the doors. They closed of their own accord, and Farid examined them, searching for a lever or spring.

"Yomawa." She offered no more, leaving him to wonder whether she had uttered an incantation or spoken to him in another language. He followed her through the gallery lined with statues, uncomfortable that he had been left alone with a woman of higher class. He did not wish to mar her reputation, and so he slowed to inspect the carvings, keeping a respectful distance between them. The artist had rendered the men and women so perfectly he could see their teeth, the fingernails on their hands, each hair upon their heads.

"These were our rock-sworn," she said, touching the last. "This was High Mage Kobar."

He drew back in alarm. "These were alive?"

"These were our mages. Their spirits claimed them, as all spirits will." She spoke without sadness.

She led him to a curving marble staircase and began the climb, her steps light and quick, and he followed, careful not to watch her from behind and to keep space between them.

At the first landing she spoke again. "I too was a prisoner of the Mogyrks, taken in Fryth. Only recently did he let me go."

"Why did he let you go?" Farid asked, hoping to understand why Adam had let him and Rushes escape. Perhaps Mura's tale would offer a clue.

"He hoped that I would bring a message of his good intent, but I cannot."

Farid thought about that a moment. Adam had not been bent towards helping, unless you counted the collection of souls for his god. "Your captor did not have good intent?"

She said nothing for several steps. "I do not know," she said at last, "and I will not say he did and become a traitor. Who held you?"

"His name was Adam."

She halted at the next landing; at first he believed her out of breath, but when she turned he saw it was Adam's name that had shocked her.

"My captor the Duke of Fryth spoke of this Adam," she said. "He is an austere, and ranks high in the Mogyrk church."

Farid held a hand to his mouth, suddenly realising the extent of the danger he had been in.

"Come," she said, and resumed their upwards journey with more haste.

When at last they reached the high mage's level, Farid leaned against the stair rails, catching his breath, though the mage looked as fresh as she had when first she opened the door. She looked at him, her eyes shifting with various shades of blue. "My name is Mura," she said, though she had already named herself in front of the soldiers.

"I am Farid." He wondered if there was an honorific for mages.

He had never heard of one, but it did not feel right to address a woman of such prestige with her given name.

"Wait here, Farid. I will call you when the high mage is ready."

He stood on the landing, his feet rooted to the ancient marble, worn by thousands of shoes and the passage of long years. This was no merchants' guild with wooden chairs to wait upon. Here one stood in respect, even to the stones themselves, and he, a mere fruit-seller, would give that respect willingly. He saw no one, felt no magical presence, and yet something in the stone itself spoke of its terrible power.

Below him came the heavy and regular thump of boots on marble: another mage was climbing the stairs, this one a muscled man, like a soldier. After a minute he stood beside Farid, revealing grey eyes veined like granite and dusty, pale skin. In a mournful voice he said, "The crack has grown larger."

"I see. I'm very sorry." Farid did not know what else to say.

The rock-sworn mage passed by, continuing upwards, his progress slow and steady. Just as his steps retreated into the distance above, Mura emerged and beckoned. "High Mage Govnan will see you now."

Farid followed her into another bare space, this one long and narrow, a window at the far end open to the night. Lanterns lit up lengths of blackened stone; a great fire had once burned here, leaving nothing but stains and the stink of char. In the centre a rusting iron chair curled its back like a great claw over the old man who sat within. Beneath a shock of white hair Farid saw a face crossed by wrinkles, punctuated by a large nose and two sharp brown eyes. He knew the great high mage carried fire, but he did not see it in the old man's gaze as he had seen the air in Mura's—but still there was a potency in Govnan that filled the air between them.

"So," said the high mage, balancing a staff on the arms of the chair, and Farid might have thought him someone's uncle or grandfather, but for the terror creeping up his spine.

Mura spoke, each word brushing against him like a breeze. "This is Farid, who escaped the Mogyrks and their austere, Adam."

"I see." Govnan looked from one to the other and waited.

Farid spoke nervously into the silence. "Last night, High Mage, there was too much fighting and the soldiers could not get to the austere. Today they will capture him, Keleb willing."

The high mage turned the staff in his fingers. "I do not expect so. He has had many hours to find another hiding place. But tell us of Adam and his dealings."

"He has a lot of men to do his bidding. As for himself, he's strong and acts like he's about to jump at you—but he never did." Farid remembered Adam's catlike stances as he spoke. "He liked telling me that we're all going to die, but whether he meant from a catastrophe or his own doing, I couldn't tell. He wants to save our souls for his god."

"And did he say what he wanted with you?"

Shame slowed Farid's words. "He said I was special. He showed me shapes and gave me their names, and I confess to working patterns. It was an evil thing, but it was the only way I could escape."

Mura turned to him in surprise. She had spoken earlier of treachery, and now she must look on him with hatred.

"He thinks I'm going to help him—but I'm not, I swear it, High Mage! The pattern killed my mother."

A long silence fell upon the room, and fear took root in Farid. Likely there was a harsh and eternal punishment for wielding the pattern. At last Govnan stirred and pointed towards him with the staff. Farid flinched, expecting lightning and heat to shoot from it, but the high mage only spoke. "Tell me."

"Yes, High Mage," he said, but then stopped. He might not get another chance to help Rushes before he expired in a pillar of flame and became nothing more than one of these dark spots on the floor. The girl was still waiting for him at the guardhouse. "But first, if I may, your Eminence, there was a blind girl with me. Her name was Rushes, and she had a baby with her. She needs help getting to the palace where her family lives. They must be servants, or— I'm a humble man, and I know I have no right to call upon your ai—"

The high mage had stood and was halfway across the room before Farid had even finished the word. "Where?" he demanded, the fire at last showing itself in his passion, "where is the child?"

Mura cleared her throat. "I asked the Blue Shields to bring them here, High Mage."

At that moment a bell rang out in the heights of the Tower, and Govnan's eyes rose to the ceiling, beyond which, Farid imagined, hung the great bell, worked by the rope outside the brass doors.

"Go and get him," he instructed Mura, his eyes sharp and bright. "Go and get the prince and bring him to me."

The prince—? But Farid had no time to ask, for no sooner had the high mage spoken than the Tower shuddered and swayed as if rocked by a great wind and Govnan stumbled and fell. His staff rolled across the room and came to rest under the window.

"Mura! Moreth!" the high mage cried, "all of you, get out of the Tower at once! The crack has widened!"

Farid looked at the curved stone wall in fear. The big mage had said the great Tower was cracked—could it really be so damaged that it would begin to fall?

Mura answered his thoughts in the negative. "No," she said, picking up the high mage's staff and looking out the window. "No, the whole city has been rocked."

Farid helped Govnan to stand and together they walked to the window. The Tower overlooked all, and from where he stood, Farid could see the empty courtyard and beyond it, the dark city spreading south towards the palace, lit here and there by torchlight, illuminating a piece of a wall, the curve of a turret, the edge of a guardhouse. He could not make out what Mura had seen; perhaps her bound spirit offered extra sight.

The high mage looked out into the night and gave a heavy sigh, though whether it was from relief or sorrow Farid could not tell. "Mura," said Govnan.

"Yes, high mage?"

"The bell has rung. Please go downstairs and let the young prince inside."

CHAPTER NINETEEN

SARMIN

The council table sat in a corner of the throne room, overlooked by most petitioners and unused on most days. Nobody knew its age. Its grain revealed the wood's origins in the southern forests, but it had grown dark over the intervening years, time, lantern-smoke, ink, and the hands of hundreds of men having marked it day by day. The table never would be sanded down and polished, though it showed dull and old against the bright cushions and fixtures of the room. Those scratches and dents upon the surface had been made by the great leaders of old, generals who had defeated powerful armies and priests who had called down the favour of the gods. They gave the men who settled around the table today a sense of purpose and distinction. General Hazran, with white hair surrounding a kind face, took his chair, while his opposite in the White Hat Army settled beside him, anxious and sharp. General Lurish glanced at the vacant chair meant for his second, General Arigu. High Priest Dinar, his eyes cold, sat across from Assar, High Priest of Mirra, whose fingernails were black with soil. Herran, head of the Grey Service, his face shadowed beneath his hood, took his place next to the silent, far-seeing desert headman Notheen. Above them stood Azeem at his writing-stand, hand poised over his stack of parchments. High Mage Govnan had not yet arrived.

"Report, Lord High Vizier." Sarmin watched the men's faces as Azeem spoke.

"The palace engineers have finished their assessment. The greatest damage is in the main hall, where the ceiling cracked and fell fifty feet to the floor. Those mosaics have been destroyed, but many of the tiles can be recovered. The staircase leading from the Great Hall to the second level is no longer safe for use. The west wing, where the scribes and money-counters are currently housed, shifted on its foundations. In the other wings there is naught but minor damage to the plaster."

"And what of the city?" asked Lurish, leaning forwards. Sarmin already knew the answer to that. From high on Qalamin's Deck, he had seen the devastation, the jagged paths of collapsed roofs reaching from the Blessing, where bridge-stones poked their heads from the surface, up into the Holies where noblemen stood stunned in the wreckage of their gardens. It continued down into the twisting alleys of the Maze, now filled with rubble and broken bodies, and all the way south to the Low Gate. The lines of destruction came to a sudden stop just short of the outer walls.

He had not yet been told how many were dead.

"There is extensive damage," Azeem answered.

The men muttered among themselves until Hazran's voice rose and silenced the others. "But was this an attack?"

"I have invited one of our palace scholars to speak on the possible cause." Azeem gestured to the guards and a balding man in worn velvet hurried down the silk runner with such haste Sarmin feared he might trip.

"Your Majesty!" The scholar knelt and touched his head to the floor.

Azeem said, "This is the palace scholar Rahim. He studies rocks and the earth." He made it sound a simple thing, but Sarmin sensed a lifetime of study could never encompass all the things there were to learn about stone. He wondered what other scholars the palace contained, and the worlds they explored on his behalf.

"Rise," Sarmin said, curious. "What news have you, Rahim?"

"Not news, Your Majesty, only the yield of my long studies. I have read of earthquakes in many other lands, and those studies have allowed me to collect information on them, as a doctor might collect symptoms of an illness he has never himself witnessed."

"Then what is your diagnosis, Scholar Rahim?"

Rahim frowned and rubbed an ink-stained hand through his hair. "Just as a doctor can never be certain, neither can I, Magnificence. However this quake seems to presage a volcanic eruption."

"What volcano?" asked Assar, looking from general to priest in confusion.

"He speaks of Meksha's holy mountain!" Lurish jerked up in his seat.

Rahim made a devout gesture. "My readings indicate Her mountain has not erupted since before the founding of Nooria, General. But these"—he produced three shiny black stones from his pocket—"these can be found around the Blessing, Majesty, and they show us that it *has* erupted in the past."

Sarmin took one of the smooth-faced stones and turned it in his hand. Its sharp edges put him in mind of the jewelled dacarba on his belt. "Meksha's mountain is a long journey from Nooria."

"It is, Magnificence—but we may nevertheless feel its effects." Rahim frowned. "There is much disagreement in the scholars' wing, but some of us believe that an offering of sulphur and bitumen, poured into the mouth of the volcano, may calm its great fires."

Sarmin returned the stone to the scholar. "And you, Scholar Rahim? Do you agree?"

"I do not, Your Majesty." Silence fell around the room.

"Well then, Rahim," said Hazran, "how long do we have?"

"Days, weeks, months—our estimates vary. If you would like to see—"

Lurish made a noise of disgust. "We would be better off rolling dice, Magnificence!"

Sarmin ignored him. Gesturing to Rahim he said, "You are dismissed."

As the scholar retreated, Hazran said, "I want to hear from someone who does not spend all his days among books and dust. What say you, Dinar?"

Dinar's ruthless face turned Sarmin's way. "I say Meksha has abandoned us. Uthman conquered this empire and earned Her blessing. Now we have become weak and She withdraws." He leaned back in his chair. "Your Majesty."

"There may be something to that." Lurish turned towards Hazran. "Think of our humiliation in Fryth. Our men came straggling back like beggars! Surely that was enough to anger the gods?"

"But now we have the traitor," said Dinar, his eyes still on Sarmin. "His painful death would go far to appease Them."

Sarmin met his cold eyes. The council might whine and object most of the day, but at the end of it, they listened to Sarmin. Through outright threats to the cutting of necks to gentle nudges, he had forced or eased them to his side—and yet Dinar could easily sway them away, for these were devout men who held Herzu in their hearts. He had to find a way to control the high priest.

Assar of Mirra held up his hands. "There is more than one way to please the gods, Magnificence."

Lurish snorted at that, and Hazran leaned back in his chair, looking pensive.

Sarmin looked at the desert headman. The others resented his presence at the table—Notheen was nothing more than a tribesman from the far reaches of the sand, a barbarian, in their eyes. But Sarmin knew he had wisdom and experience. "Notheen?"

Notheen looked at each man in turn, his dark eyes solemn. The words took a long time to come. "It is the end times, Magnificence. We live in the era of the Great Storm, which brings the desert to all of us."

Lurish barked a laugh. "Does your savage myth include earthquakes?"

"Earthquakes, fire, ash, and dust," answered Notheen in a steady voice.

An uncomfortable silence fell over the table.

Azeem cleared his throat. "There is more news, Your Majesty. We have suffered another attack, in another marketplace—this one a fish market."

Another use of pattern-magic meant that Mogyrk's wound would grow wider. Sarmin considered this with a cold dread as the other men spoke.

"The same? With the bodies . . . turned inside out?" asked Hazran.

"Yes." Azeem looked down at the parchment he held. "Seventeen men and five women."

Lurish hit his fist upon the table. "This is all Mogyrk! *All* of it! Why do we wait to burn their churches and slaughter them all?"

I suggest you do not make them hate you. Grada's words. For each Mogyrk worshipper he killed there would be five more to take their place. The struggle against the One God had failed. Sarmin saw Govnan enter through the side door and breathed a sigh of relief. "I will consider all that has been said here. You are dismissed."

Dinar lingered beside the table. "The traitor relaxes in his cell while we suffer earthquakes and Mogyrk attacks . . . surely this is not your wish, Majesty?"

He was correct: the Empire Mother's warning had been a good one. Sense told him the chief should die sooner rather than later, but he wanted to feel clean when that knife fell. He wanted to be able to look Mesema in the eye.

He showed none of this to Dinar. "My wishes are not your concern until I choose to make them known," he said. "You are dismissed."

Dinar's dark eyes narrowed, but he retreated, leaving Govnan alone at the table, Azeem beside him, scribbling on his parchments. Sarmin waited until the great doors had closed, then turned to the high vizier. "The priestess of Meksha who was here a few months ago . . . has she gone?" The priestess had brought him Helmar's writings, along with a warning.

Azeem looked flustered. "My apologies, Magnificence—I do not remember her. I can tell you there is no priestess of Meksha in the palace now."

Govnan approached the head of the table, his eyes shining with secret knowledge.

"How fares the Tower, High Mage?"

"The crack has widened, Magnificence, but Moreth says the structure remains sound." A smile played about his mouth, a strange reaction to their circumstance. Perhaps his joy at Mura's return continued to lift his spirits. "And the palace?"

"Some damage; the city is worse."

Govnan nodded. "Indeed. I saw the city from the Tower."

Sarmin watched him and waited.

"That was not my news, Your Majesty, which is of two parts. First, the fruit-seller who was taken from the marketplace has found his way to the Tower. He was kept with Austere Adam and has learned something of the pattern."

"He watched them draw patterns?"

"Austere Adam *taught* him patterns, Magnificence. I could not tell you why. An attempt at conversion, perhaps." He knocked his staff against the table. "Farid can call water and dissolve wood—the two spells he needed to survive and escape. But as far as I can tell, his skill is rote memorisation. He can draw the patterns that he has seen, but he does not appear to be a talented mage, not in the way we measure it in the Tower."

"The Megra said that about the austeres." *Their magic was a cruder kind, old and learned by rote, a blunt power that could be put in the hands of any fool with half a mind and ten years to study it.* "Are there no books about the Yrkmen incursions of old? Studies of their magics?" He could not forget what Ashanagur had said: *Mogyrk blinded the Tower.* What had the spirit meant?

"All of that knowledge was lost to us in the great fires built by the Mogyrks." Govnan sighed, and Sarmin considered whether that could have been Ashanagur's meaning. It seemed too simple, but sometimes answers were.

"If this Farid has some pattern-skill," Govnan said, "perhaps there is something we can learn from him."

"Mmm." What Sarmin needed was Helmar—what he needed was his own pattern-skill returned to him. He recalled Duke Didryk's offer and felt a tingling along his skin. The temptation to answer that call was growing strong, but perhaps that was the duke's intent: to make him feel desperate enough to agree to anything. Perhaps he was behind the marketplace attacks.

"There is something more," said Govnan, his smile growing wide. "Magnificence, there is good news—"

But before he could finish, the gong sounded and the herald approached. "Your Majesty," he called out in his sonorous voice, "Prince Daveed and his nursemaid, Rushes of Fryth."

CHAPTER TWENTY

MESEMA

Mesema found it difficult to sit still while Tarub applied paint to her face. Tarub did not want her to speak either, and pressed a finger over Mesema's lips whenever she attempted to do so. The concubine Banafrit sat sewing on the bench under the window, the blue silk in her hands making a fine contrast against her skin, and Mesema's fingers itched with their idleness. A distraction would be most welcome on this day, whether it be gossip about the Old Wives or news from Banafrit's island home. Her enquiries regarding the Felting slaves had yielded nothing so far. Either they were well hidden, or they were not in the city.

Banafrit dropped a needle and poked about on the floor, holding her place in the silk with two fingers. Her shoulder knocked Pelar's empty cradle, and Mesema looked away from the blankets inside it. Every time she was reminded of his absence she felt the loss anew. Banafrit continued to search until Mesema finally lifted an arm and pointed. "Take one of my needles, Frit."

"Your Majesty!" Tarub stepped away, paint in hand. "Please! Your whole face will be red."

Banafrit walked to Mesema's side table where needles were kept in a tiny bowl, but then she noticed a book there and ran her hand across the embossed leather cover. "What is this book about?"

"It's poems. You can't read the words on the cover? I can teach you, if you like, as my husband the emperor taught me." She remembered sitting with Sarmin during those long happy days after Helmar's defeat, learning the letters and the words, and wondered why Banreh, in all the years she had known him and their weeks together in that hot carriage, had never offered to do the same.

The concubine sat and pulled the heavy book onto her lap, turning the thick pages. "My father tried to teach me to read, but I can never seem to connect the letters with any meaning. It turns to a jumble in my head."

"Really? Well I could read it to you—"

"Your Majesty!" Tarub said again, picking up a cloth to wipe paint from Mesema's chin.

"But are you nearly done with my lips, Tarub? It has taken you a day and a night."

"It must be perfect, Your Majesty. If the emperor should see you—"

"Forget *seeing* me—if the emperor should kiss me he will end up with rosy lips. If he should do more than kiss me, he will be covered with paint from head to toe."

"Your Majesty!" Tarub covered her face with embarrassment as Banafrit giggled and shut the book. That encouraged Mesema to speak more wickedly. "I would have to give him a bath myself, as it wouldn't do for a slave to scrub him in those places."

"But Your Majesty"—Tarub's hand shook as she replaced the paint pot before the mirror—"surely the emperor, heaven bless him, is clean as the gods, and no corruption or stain ever touches him."

"Judging by his attention to the empress," said Banafrit with a smile, "I would call him well corrupted."

Mesema blushed, because she and Sarmin were not so close as that, not any longer. Banafrit for her part took on a stricken look and jumped from the bed, dropping the book to the floor, but before Mesema could ask why, the concubine had touched her forehead against the rug and Tarub had dropped also, looking pale as a ghost. Mesema froze, hoping it was not Sarmin behind her at the door.

"Rise." It was Nessaket's voice she heard, and she breathed a sigh of relief.

The Empire Mother strode into the room, dressed in bright gold, with all of her earrings and bracelets in place, looking for the moment almost as healthy as she had been before the uprising. It appeared that she was about to use that good health to put fear in all the women of the wing. She stopped at the bench and examined Banafrit's blue silk. "I have spoken to all of you about this sewing. It is slaves' work."

"But Your Majesty," said Banafrit, scrambling to her feet, "there are no slaves to do it."

"How dare you speak back to me! Not only do you act against my wishes but you draw the empress into your crimes."

"Crimes?" Mesema frowned at Nessaket's reflection. "It is only a dress."

"I cannot tolerate it." Nessaket waved at the concubine. "Go. Leave the work. I will have it burned." Banafrit ran from the room, Tarub right behind her. Nessaket sat on the edge of the bed and sighed.

"You scare them so. It's not fair." Mesema stood at last, shaking out her arms and legs.

"I am responsible for keeping this wing as it should be. We are not a wing of seamstresses and scrubbers—yes, I have seen you dusting your own window-screen. I would rather have you run out into the city again! It simply will not do."

Mesema clenched her fists when she remembered her visit to Lord Nessen's estate and the violence that had ensued, but still she longed to know if the Hidden God had truly sent her there. She knew Grada and others from the Grey Service were continuing to watch the manse of the Mogyrk sympathiser. She hoped that if Grada learned something, she would tell her.

Nessaket was watching her, awaiting a reply.

"So we have no one to do the work, Empire Mother. What do you suggest?"

At that Nessaket frowned. "In truth I do not know. A year ago I would have ordered more slaves." She touched her head where she had been injured. "Everything has changed."

Mesema sat next to the empire mother. "I have heard rumour of slaves taken from my own lands, Felting slaves, here in Nooria."

"I have heard nothing of that, and it seems unlikely. It would be a great insult to you, Empress, and few would risk it."

"Perhaps it was meant to be an insult."

"I suppose you speak of Arigu's alleged treachery, so let me offer you some advice." Nessaket folded her arms before her. "Arigu is far cleverer than you. If he did take these slaves, you will not find them so easily. And if you do find them, he will claim they came here by some other route."

"So you think I should not try."

"What do you think would happen if you did succeed? Do you think your husband will allow Banreh to live?"

No. I do not think that he will. Mesema blinked back tears. "I think he would let the slaves go home."

"We shall see about that. He is the emperor, and he does not think as we do."

A knock came at the door and the two women looked at each other, caution bringing silence. Then Sendhil called out, "Grada Knife-Sworn to see you, my Empress."

She could hear the concern in his voice, but Mesema knew the Knife would not ask politely had she come for royal blood. "Let her enter, Sendhil." She stood as Grada filled the doorway, her dark eyes moving past Mesema, deeper into the room, seeking the Empire Mother.

"You should come to the throne room, Your Majesty," Grada said, "for we believe your son has been found."

CHAPTER TWENTY-ONE

SARMIN

The doors swung on their hinges, heavy and slow, and Sarmin wanted to run forwards, to shout, make the men pull harder, faster, because he could not see his brother yet. Light spilled in from the corridor—he had not noticed he was standing in the dark—and he shielded his eyes for a moment. When he lowered his hand he saw a girl, her hair glowing crimson, carrying a bundle wrapped in silks. Her steps were hesitant and she cocked her head as if listening. A soldier took her arm and they walked the rest of the way.

Rushes. He remembered her now, remembered her fright when she gave him the butterfly-stone. He reached into his pocket and touched it with his finger. It had been larger then, before he broke it. And he could still see her through Beyon's eyes, his favourite child, running after a ball in the throne room. He smiled, for she had come home, and she had brought his brother to him. As she neared her eyes looked ahead, unfocused, blind, and her lips quivered. She was in the presence of the emperor and she could not see him and know that he was truly himself.

"Be easy, Rushes," he said. "It is me, Sarmin." Not the false emperor the pattern had created.

Her face turned his way. She was orchid-thin and pale as snow, save for her hair, which hung in tangles around her shoulders. "My Emperor!" She took another step and waited, trembling. Inside her arms the baby stirred and he wondered how she could carry him, for he had grown very big, one chubby leg kicking away from its coverings and a broad forehead strewn with dark curls turning his way.

"I will take my brother now," he said, so that she would not be startled by his touch. He lifted her burden and turned his back to the soldiers, taking in the smell of him, sweet like honey. This moment would be private. He lifted the silk from his brother's eyes, then tore it away further, revealing all of him from his chubby toes to his copper eyes. His heart caught and he ran a hand through the boy's hair, looking for the stubborn curl he remembered. He did not see it. The boy smelled wrong; his smile as he looked from the silks was wrong. The love that Sarmin had felt for Daveed failed to warm him. He looked at a stranger.

He turned back to Rushes. "Did you have the child with you all this time?"

She remembered her obeisance and threw herself upon the floor. When she spoke, silk muffled her voice. "The one called Mylo hit me very hard, my Emperor," she said, "and I did not wake up for days. When I came to myself, I could not see. But they gave Daveed to me then, for they said that he knew me and my presence would make him easy. I never let go of him after that—never, Your Majesty. They kept us in a little room and we never left it."

Govnan came forwards then and gazed down at the child in Sarmin's arms, twisting his cane into the floor as he did whenever his thoughts went in a dark direction. "We tested his blood, Magnificence, and found it true."

"But this is not my brother," said Sarmin, and the words took the life from him. He crumpled upon the stairs of the dais, the boy clutched in his arms.

Azeem took a halting step forwards. "At this age babies change very quickly, Magnificence. You have not seen him for many months."

"What do you know of babies, Azeem?" he asked, and spitefully, since the man had no wife and further, did not wish for one.

Azeem stepped back and said no more.

"They want me to embrace this strange child and call him brother." Sarmin leaned back upon the stair, speaking more to himself than anyone. "Where did they take Daveed, I wonder?"

"Your Majesty—" Govnan began, but at that moment Nessaket entered the room and cried out. She ran to Sarmin and fell to her knees, hands reaching for the child.

"It's not him." Sarmin felt as if he had looked into the Great Storm and let it take him whole.

"But it is." Nessaket lifted the boy and examined him, her voice hushed, reverent. "It is my son." Mesema came in from the side door and smiled at the scene. He frowned at her—why did her visions show her nothing? If she could not see this boy was a stranger had she been blinded, the way Ashanagur said Mogyrk blinded the Tower?

"There is some evil design in this," he warned as the women cooed over the child. Mesema looked up at him then, doubt crossing her eyes at last, but Nessaket touched her arm and murmured, and she turned away. Against all reason he felt it a betrayal.

His mother looked up at him, the false princeling wriggling in her grasp. Her face did not look joyful—only content—but she smiled as she spoke. "I will take him to the women's wing, with your permission, my Emperor."

"What else is there to be done with him?"

She reproved him with a shake of her ink-black hair. "This is happy news, my Emperor, the best we might have wished for." She gestured towards Rushes. "I will take my servant Rushes with me. She has ever served me well. I wish to discuss her reward at a time of your choosing, Magnificence."

"Of course." None of this was Rushes' fault.

Nessaket took her leave, taking the child who was not his brother with her. But Mesema stayed, smelling of jasmine, as she always did of late. When he first met her she smelled of the outdoors and horses and things he had experienced only through being Carried—but now she smelled of the palace. She knelt beside him as his mother had and took his hands in hers. "I am so happy for you, my husband. In all the trouble we have had there is a hole in the clouds where the sun can shine through."

He liked her metaphor, from another place where the sun did not beat down, where clouds changed the light and brought cool rain. But he must tell her the truth. "That was not my brother."

She looked at their joined hands, some thoughts warring within her, but then she looked up at him again and her eyes were clear as she spoke in a voice so low only Govnan, standing beside them, might hear it. "Your mother believes he is. The high mage believes he is."

"Some spell . . . some trickery . . ." Just as the pattern had created a false Beyon, so had it created this false Daveed. He looked to Azeem, squeezing Mesema's hands in his as he spoke. "The Blue Shields accomplish nothing in the Maze. Tell Herran to send his Grey Cloaks. Every house will be searched. My brother will be found."

"Very well, Magnificence." Azeem dipped a quill in his inkpot, his calm as cold and distant as mountain snow.

Mesema stared into his eyes. "My husband, if you find later that this child truly is Daveed, then only harm can come of this. The people of the Maze already suffer poverty and Mogyrk attacks, and now they will find assassins among them."

Startled, Sarmin glanced around the room. She had corrected him in court, where all must take him to be infallible—but his concern was for her, not himself. To his relief he saw that only the trusted high mage could have heard her. "I will not find that he is truly Daveed." As for the rest of what she had said, it reminded him of Grada's warning. *Do not make them hate you.*

Mesema pressed on, in a lower voice. "May I speak of another issue that may have some bearing on the Mogyrk situation?"

"You may always speak to me!" He glanced up at Govnan, who made a show of creating distance—but not enough. He meant to listen. With annoyance Sarmin turned back to his wife.

She cleared her throat. "I am working to find proof that General Arigu betrayed my people during the Fryth war."

He listened, though he knew it did not matter what new betrayal Arigu had committed. If the general ever returned, Sarmin would sit him in a place of honour, not disgrace. Arigu was the White Hat Army's favourite general, and he needed the White Hats, especially now. In laying out their gambit Chief Banreh and Duke Didryk appeared to understand that, while Mesema, with her guileless expression, did not.

"Arigu took Felting slaves, in violation of our ancient agreement." Her eyes spoke of urgency. "They are here, somewhere in the palace compound, or nearby. Once I find them, we can prove—"

The sharp thing inside Sarmin twisted. First she had not believed him about the boy and now she had sneaked away to Banreh. He cut across her with a harsh tone. "You spoke to the prisoner?"

She lifted her chin. "He is my countryman, and chief of my people."

Sarmin glanced again at Govnan. "You cannot think I will set him free, whatever you discover, especially now." In fact the chief would die, and Sarmin did not know how to tell her.

"Not free, my husband," she said, "only out of the dungeon. There is no limit to how many of your men you may send with him when you answer the duke's call. You can send the whole White Hat Army if you wish."

"I cannot," he said, "and you know it, for I have put them to search for my brother, and soon enough Yrkmir will be at our walls. This Didryk might be in league with our ancient enemy and hoping to ambush our men. He could be behind these marketplace attacks, and more." And yet Sarmin longed to meet this duke as a man in the desert thirsts for water.

"The duke wishes to help us."

"Do you know anything beyond the words of the traitor?" It was hard enough to quench his own longing; he could not quench hers as well. He dropped her hands.

She looked aside. "Arigu took Felting slaves, Sarmin."

"There were no Felting slaves. There have been no slaves at all." He glanced at his *Code*, abandoned on the table.

"They are here somewhere, my husband, and I will find them. I—" Her voice rose, and Sarmin glanced at Azeem, wondering how much he had heard of that last part.

"Yrkmir comes, Mesema," Sarmin warned, "and these slaves will not matter after that. We must look to protecting our family."

She stood, her blue eyes hard with condemnation, and he met them without apology.

Govnan stepped forwards, smoothing his beard with a veined hand. "If I may interrupt, Your Majesty," he said, "perhaps young Farid can be sent to this duke, with a small contingent? We may manage to retrieve Arigu. If they fail, and we lose them . . ."

Govnan meant to say the loss of Farid would not be great; but Sarmin was not sure that was true. While he might not have the talent to enter another realm and command its spirits, the Tower had no other mage who could work patterns.

A decision of empire, made on the great invisible scales, watched by heaven but weighted by men. Such decisions might leave one boy locked in a room and his brothers murdered, or kill thousands in the outer colony of another empire. A decision to weigh one life against many, and many against one: Beyon had gone mad with it and tipped the scales to excess, as if he would never feel a loss. But the death of his sword-son TaSann had shown Sarmin the difficulties of Beyon's way. It was not easy to send men into death.

But if the duke had some knowledge of Adam's plans, if he knew where Daveed might be kept . . . his grief twisted him again. For his brother he would spend lives; for his brother he would take the chance. "Very well," he told Govnan. "But we must act quickly. I cannot have half the army searching the desert for days. I will question Banreh myself."

"I will prepare young Farid for his trip." Govnan moved towards the side door.

Sarmin stood and spoke to Mesema, leaning in, voice low.

"Your chief will tell me what I need to know. If he will not tell me, then he will tell Dinar. You cannot return to him—do you understand?"

She backed away. "I wanted only to do the right thing."

"The right thing is for Cerana to survive."

"But what is it that will be surviving, Your Majesty?" He noted her formal tone, her physical distance. "I should get to Nessaket. She will need blankets and toys for—for the child."

She had not said *your brother*—because he was not. Sarmin knew it, because he felt no love for the child. "There are slaves—" He recalled Chief Banreh's accusation, and stopped.

"I must go." She turned and walked from him, her silks fluttering, her guards clustering around her.

"Azeem," Sarmin said, watching her go, "tell General Lurish we have need of a mediocre captain and six dozen average men." If this duke lured Sarmin's soldiers into a trap, they would not be his best ones.

.   Azeem hesitated only a moment. "I was just on my way to speak to him, Magnificence." He bowed and retreated.

Sarmin sat on the steps of the dais, surrounded by his nameless guards. What plan Austere Adam hoped to set in motion by sending the wrong child he could not fathom, nor why the Mogyrks had attacked with a pattern more foul than Sarmin could ever have imagined when Helmar lived. Each day the Great Storm crept closer to the Blessing; after that it would stand at the northern walls. The pale sickness would be upon Nooria soon enough, draining his citizens of colour and life until they were empty enough for the djinn to ride—if an earthquake or Yrkmir did not destroy them first. All of this while Govnan's Tower stood cracked, its mages few, and Mogyrk's Scar stood in the east. There had to be a solution; there was always a path through to preserving his empire, though it might be hidden. But this time there would be no messages from the past, no priestess or old woman to offer wisdom, no demons and angels to guide him.

The harpist chose that moment to begin plucking at his strings, a cacophony of twangs and vibrating sounds that served only to bring Sarmin's hands to his ears. "Who let him in? Get him out!" The series of clumsy notes came to an abrupt end, leaving a final orphaned chord hanging on the air. The sword-sons led the musician from the room and Sarmin followed after him. It was time to face Chief Banreh.

CHAPTER TWENTY-TWO

SARMIN

The Blue Shield guard opened Banreh's dark cell and Sarmin entered, leaving his men in the corridor. They stared through the bars, weapons ready. Mesema had been here before him and he looked around, seeing what she had seen—dirty stones, a slop-bucket, a ragged pallet on the floor with the chief stretched out on it—and wondering what she had made of it. Seeing the emperor and all his sword-sons, the prisoner struggled to a stand, levering himself with a hand against the wall rather than using his damaged leg. When at last the man was standing straight and they were staring at one another, Sarmin motioned to the Blue Shield, who said, "You did not touch the floor, prisoner."

At that Banreh lowered himself and made an awkward obeisance. Sarmin waited a minute, then another, the other man's obvious discomfort giving him a strange satisfaction. His dislike for the chief unsettled him. With Kavic, he had thought they could be friends; he had felt a fondness for the Fryth man that an emperor is not meant to feel. It had not been allowed in the end: Kavic had fallen victim to the games of empire. Over the last months Sarmin had wondered if there were other men in the world who might become his friends. Banreh, though, would never be one of them.

He held some part of Mesema that Sarmin could not reach, and he could not forget that.

"Rise," he said at last, and watched the chief go through the difficulty of standing for a second time. He waited. In the throne room he had learned his silence disquietened those who sought to deceive him. It gave them time to sweat, to wonder what he knew, to imagine punishments to come.

"Banreh," he said, discarding the honorific, "you will tell me where to find Duke Didryk."

"I cannot tell you, for I do not know, Your Majesty."

Sarmin drew out the time between questions, watching the man's drawn face. The chief felt pain from all the falling and rising, that was certain; but it was nothing compared to what Dinar could do. "I am confused, Windreader. You came to court to make an offer, and yet you give us no way to fulfil that offer."

Banreh glanced at the men in the corridor, every one of them tall and gleaming with muscle, each with a wide hachirah at his belt. "It is my understanding, Your Majesty, that one cannot correct the emperor, for he is never wrong."

"That is true."

"And so I find myself unable to explain, Your Majesty."

Anger drove Sarmin's words. "Are we playing games now, Banreh? For I think you are losing. I cannot think this is what you planned." He gestured to the stone walls. "You would have been better off staying in the Grass."

"Duke Didryk sent me as a messenger, Your Majesty. A messenger is protected by certain protocols."

"You are a messenger who has killed a great many Cerani."

"That number has grown with time and the telling. More died fighting the Fryth or in the desert than ever by my hand."

Sarmin gripped the hilt of Tuvaini's dacarba.

"Nevertheless." Banreh lowered his shoulders as if defeated.

"Tell me your plan, or you will end on Herzu's table."

The chief lifted his hands palm up, the Cerani gesture of honesty, but it looked false to Sarmin, too practised, too easily won. He was all guile and verbal tricks, utterly unlike Mesema. "Your Majesty, Duke Didryk knows he has few choices. He offers to train your mages in exchange for clemency. That is the beginning and the end of his plan."

"And your plan?"

Banreh held his palms out once again. "Only to help my people."

"Like Mesema?" He imagined her standing at the bars, within this man's reach. Had he touched her? Sarmin pulled Tuvaini's ruby-hilted weapon from his belt. When he killed Helmar, his dead brothers had shown him where to find a man's heart. He imagined running the steel between Banreh's ribs, feeling the warm blood run over his hand. Would he find it then, whatever was in him that Mesema loved?

The chief stood motionless, his eyes on the blade, and Sarmin lowered the weapon. That was not the man he wished to be.

By inches Banreh raised his left hand, careful not to excite the wrath of Sarmin's guards, and turned it out, exposing the wrist. On it Sarmin saw a diamond pattern circled with stars, and he knew what it was without asking. He and Grada had been linked by pattern-marks when she Carried him into the city and the desert: their thoughts had been shared that way during the long weeks when Helmar Pattern Master ruled Nooria.

"I do not know where the duke is," said Banreh, "but I can find him. With this."

Sarmin put away his dacarba, surprised to feel relief more than anything else. Banreh would go into the desert. He would not be killed—not yet. The day when Mesema would hear of Banreh's death at his hands or his word had been moved into the future. "Can the duke hear us?" he asked, drawn in by the unfamiliar shapes.

"No. He knows only where I am, and whether I am alive."

"Well, Chief," Sarmin said, turning away, "you shall live a bit longer. Do not become accustomed to it."

CHAPTER TWENTY-THREE

FARID

Govnan laid a fifth parchment before Farid. Each was covered with an inked pattern different to the last. "This was transcribed from a spell cast by Yrkmir invaders in the time of the great defeat," the high mage said, "when Helmar was taken from the palace."

"I told you, I don't recognise any of these." Farid slid back his chair and looked out of the window. They sat in an airy room near the top of the Tower, with a view spreading over the courtyard and the north quarter of Nooria. Between the Tower walls and the Worship Gate stretched long streets of houses and temples that crushed up against the Blessing, their dark alleys crisscrossing like the nets his sister once made with twine. The Blessing continued north, beyond the walls, towards the mountains. Farid had never been so high up. He felt like a bird soaring over the landscape and looking down—except that far in the distance, parts of the northlands were obscured from his sight; they were greyish, as if covered by mist. He squinted and tried to see what was there, but his gaze kept sliding away from it like oil from water.

When Emperor Beyon's tomb had collapsed, he had heard strange rumours about what had been inside: a nothingness, an impenetrable nothingness impossible to look at. And Govnan continued to glance out the window, his eyes returning again and again to the same spot.

With an uneasy feeling Farid turned back to the parchments. All of these patterns were much more complicated than those he had learned in Adam's cramped house.

Govnan was sending him to the desert, to a Fryth pattern mage. Farid knew the mage had offered to train him, but if he was anything like Adam, he expected to learn very little. Why the lofty Tower was showing interest in these witch-marks eluded him. Perhaps the Tower was sending him only because he was already stained by Mogyrk's hand. The thought sparked anger—it was not his fault he had seen the pattern that day in the market-place.

The high mage pointed at one of the shapes with a claw-like hand. "What does this shape mean?"

Farid folded his arms over his chest. "I don't know what it means."

"Marke Kavic suggested that each of these formations names something. Water, bird, wool—is it like that?" Govnan shifted the parchments. "If I could just learn the key to these patterns . . ."

Farid pointed at an elongated diamond near the centre. "That one I know: *Hiss-nick,*" he said. "Adam only gave me the Fryth words."

Govnan wrote down the word and placed a smaller parchment before him. This one was not so aged, and the design on it was thickly inked. "What about this?"

Farid turned it in his fingers. The shapes tickled his memory. "Where did this come from?" he asked.

"It was on our prisoner's wrist."

Farid turned it from left to right, but that was not the problem. He needed a mirror. "I don't know what it is, but I think it's only half of something."

"You are correct. It is a binding. But what are its properties?"

Farid stared, then shook his head. "Maybe the Fryth mage will teach me." He meant it sarcastically, but Govnan nodded in his patient way.

"How many symbols did Adam teach you?"

Farid could take no more of sitting. He stood and paced to the end of the table, feeling his new robes swirl around his feet. He felt naked in them, with the air brushing against his skin with every movement. He thought for a moment, then said, "Fifty-two, and I guess that wasn't even a tenth of them." When Govnan frowned, he said, "I never wanted to learn these evil things. I still don't. But words are not the key."

"What is the key?"

Farid turned it over in his mind. Finally he picked up one of the complicated designs drawn by the ancient Yrkmen. "It's the way they work together," he said, running a finger along a line of triangles. "No single part can hold the spell—they need to work together."

"Words have no meaning, then?" asked Govnan, frustrated, but Farid kept his eyes on the parchment. He had been looking at it wrong. These symbols were not meant to rest on a flat plane. Instead they ordered themselves above and below, forwards and backwards, into the storied ages of Nooria itself. The parchment set his fingers tingling and a longing to imitate the pattern on the stones around him almost overcame him, the need to surround himself with gleaming lines and interlocking shapes.

Feeling disgusted with himself, he dropped it.

Govnan took it as resignation and sighed. "We do not have much time, but you may visit your father. My mages usually have no family contact, but since you have lived in Nooria . . ."

Farid sighed with relief. "So he knows I'm alive." He picked up another parchment, and itched to draw its pattern.

"Of course he does," said Govnan, "he has been enquiring every hour if he may see you. He is in the courtyard."

Farid wanted to run towards his father, but he could not tear his eyes from the patterns. He touched one of the symbols with two fingers. "Fire, I think." *Shack-nuth.* He could give the old man that much. Before leaving he walked to the black basin where Govnan had built a sacrificial fire to Meksha. "*Shack-nuth,*" he said, but the flames did not alter. Of course it would not be so simple.

Mage Mura opened the door behind him. A breeze followed her into the room, brushing against Farid's cheeks, and he turned. She looked at him and the parchments with curiosity, and he looked back with no less. "Captain Ziggur is ready now," she said, and Govnan sighed.

"We are out of time," he said. "Hurry and say goodbye to your father."

Farid leaned closer to the old man. "Can Mura—can she fly?"

Govnan put a hand on his shoulder and gave a nostalgic smile. "No, my son," he said, "nobody can."

"What if she held more than one spirit? Could they lift her then?"

"Well, that has been done," said Govnan, "during the glorious past of our Tower. Controlling an elemental is a matter of will, and two are infinitely more difficult to control than one. In the time of Uthman and his descendants, we had many mages commanding two or more. But not today."

"Oh," said Farid with disappointment. "I thought one day I might fly, or swim in the ocean, like they do in the old tales."

"So did I, Farid," Govnan said. "So did I." He gave Farid's shoulder a pat and then pushed him on. "Hurry, now; they are waiting for you."

In the courtyard Farid met Captain Ziggur, a gruff man in his later years of soldiery who believed him a mage and treated him with deference he had not earned. Dozens of people stood around the statues, mostly soldiers, too many to greet, and so he did not—but he soon heard his father's voice.

"Farid!"

He turned and saw him, a plainly dressed man with rich brown eyes. "Farid," his father said again, holding his big hands in front of him as if in prayer.

"Father." He smiled. "I am so glad to see you."

His father looked away humbly, as if he were in the presence of a noble or a wealthy merchant. "I'm overjoyed you're alive. I know you have great things to do—Tower things—but perhaps we'll see each other again when you return. Sir."

"Father, you don't have to—"

But his father had bowed and turned away, leaving him shaken. Why did his father treat him like a stranger? His mother had died of the pattern-sickness—had he now lost his father too, because of the pattern? He hoped his sister would not shrink from him as well—and he started to wonder who Adam had lost during his long years as an austere. Had he become so alone, so emptied of love, that Mogyrk had filled every part of him?

Captain Ziggur spoke to him and handed him the reins of a horse, but Farid barely heard his words. He had gone from fruit-seller to Tower mage in a matter of days and perhaps he would be dead in a few more—but he would die as Farid, not as some mage his father did not know.

"Father!" he called, and the older man turned, showing his eyes at last, hope registering in the dark depths of them.

"I will be back."

Farid wobbled on his horse. The Blue Shields had given him an old mare, slow and gentle, but even so, staying seated took effort. The sun beat down on his unfamiliar mage's robes and put a thirst in his throat. The soldiers had asked him what sort of mage he was—whether he commanded rock or water, fire or air—to position him in their force for the greatest advantage. He had looked at them in frustration, until he finally remembered the word he was seeking was "novice," which meant he was useless to the soldiers, who put him in the centre like a child. That left him in a foul mood, and he found himself wishing he were back in the comfort of the Tower, examining old patterns.

The train did not move with speed, for the horse chief they were following had not been given a mount. The heat was taking its toll as he limped through the sand in his chains, and his fair skin burned red in the desert sun. From the soldiers' talk Farid gathered this chief had been responsible for the White Hat defeat. Though the Whites and Blues had an ancient rivalry, they joined together in hatred of their enemies. At midday, when they ate and rested, sheltered from the sun, these soldiers of the Shield boasted how they would knife their captive before sunset—but afterwards, they mounted and continued as they had begun, with the yellow-haired man in front, stumbling westwards between the dunes.

The soldiers threw water at him from time to time, and likely some of it ended in his mouth, but they jeered and shouted insults, threatening to kill him—though if he died, they would not find the Fryth mage they were looking for. To Farid they were small men, and not very clever, but at least they were confident in their mission. He was not so certain in his.

His legs ached from being in the unfamiliar saddle and his head ached from the sun. Some found the desert beautiful, but Farid's limited experience with the place was giving him a different opinion. He had heard stories of merchants who lost their way in the dunes and died of the heat within a day. He believed if the desert had to be dealt with, it should be done quickly, and he longed to return to the safety of Nooria and the cool relief of the Blessing. They had left the city through the Gate of Storms, the west-facing gate used by caravans and nomads, and he could not wait to see it again.

The long train slowed. In front, the captive had fallen to his knees, and thinking this the death of the horse chief Farid nudged his mare forwards. He might be the only man present who would look upon the event with any solemnity or pity. But the soldiers had not stopped for the chief's death; they had reached their goal, a camp in the lee of a great dune. Farid counted several dozen horses but only half as many men, some of them taller than any he had ever seen, long scabbards at their sides glowing orange in the setting sun. Brightly coloured tents rose from the sand, surrounded by a confusion of barrels and crates. Though the company was small, Farid worried that any group of armed men had been able to camp so close to Nooria.

As the Cerani paused, the tall soldiers in the camp gathered to look, hands hovering by their sword hilts—but then one of their number stepped forwards. Like the rest, his hair was black and his skin pale, but he wore a different garment, darkest blue, with epaulettes and bright buttons. Farid had never owned anything with a button, but this man had twelve, ten down his front and one on each shoulder. He looked like a captain of soldiers, not a mage, and yet the way he held himself, the way his eyes did one thing while his hands did another, suggested an uncommon awareness.

"I am Didryk." The mage spoke Cerani with a strong accent. He walked to where the chief had collapsed in the sand and helped him up before holding a waterskin to his lips. "Remove his chains," he said to the Cerani captain.

Captain Ziggur refused with a motion of his hand. "He comes back with us."

"But we have not even started our negotiations," said Didryk. He lifted his head and his blue eyes instantly picked Farid from the crowd. Farid felt a shock of recognition—like for like—before the mage backed up, pulling the captive with him. It was then Farid noticed a glimmer in the sand, and then another, spreading in an arc away from the mage's boots. "You are standing inside my pattern," said Didryk, "so you really should do as I ask."

"It's true." Shapes shone from the shifting ground, geometries of line and curve, all of it beyond Farid's ken but quickly saved to memory. He pointed. "Can you not see it, Captain?"

The captain ignored Farid and spat into the sand. "Putting a knife to our necks is not a good way to start, Duke Didryk."

"I take few risks," said Didryk.

Farid studied the mage with interest. He saw no pattern-marks, no totems or charms, no wind or fire behind his eyes, and neither was he muscled like Austere Adam. Even so, Farid did not intend to take him on.

The captain dismounted, pulled keys from his belt and leaned over the captive. All of the men watched in silence as he worked, until with a jangling the chains fell off to the side.

The duke said something in his own language then, and his tall soldiers took the blond man among them. "Now I will give you Arigu," he said, "and that will be a good start to our dealings."

"You are giving us no more than what's owed, Northerner, and taking our prisoner besides."

"We are trading, one man for one man." And as Didryk spoke, his men brought forth a Cerani, burly and soft in the way of muscled men who have taken to their chairs for too long, but this one was not lazy; his sharp eyes took in and measured their company. He could be none other than the fabled General Arigu, who wasted no time taking command. "Where is the Windreader chief? Give him to me."

"They took him." The captain motioned to the tents coloured by the setting sun.

"Fool!" Arigu struggled against the Fryth who held him. "Archers, kill them all!"

These were Blue Shields and they did not take orders from White Hat generals—yet the archers reached for their bows. No sooner had their fingers touched wood than a great concussion sounded over the assembly and Farid fell from his horse, holding his ears in pain. Other soldiers landed around him, eyes wide with fear, hands pressed full against their heads as their horses bolted from the circle. After a moment Farid found his feet and took in the size of the pattern. The duke had made it large enough for all of them, and for half again as many.

"Back up!" said the captain, waving at his men. "Get away from the Mogyrk camp!"

"Don't move!" the duke called out. "I will kill you before you take a step." He took a breath and Farid could see that he was trembling. "I want only to make a fair trade."

"All they have is that circle!" shouted Arigu. "Just some easy tricks! There are not so many of them—we can—" He stopped when a blade was put to his neck.

"See how brave he is when he stands outside my work," said the duke. A push, and the general stumbled forwards, landing beside the captain. "There you are. It is good to be rid of him. I trade you a man for a man."

Ziggur gave a respectful nod to the general before turning back to the Fryth leader. "And the help you offered, Duke?"

Didryk gestured at Farid. "You brought a mage with you. He will stay with me."

Farid stared, anticipation and dread together rushing over his skin. Everyone watched him, waiting, and so he took a step forwards, but General Arigu held out an arm to stop him.

"Do you think we will leave our mage with you? No. You will come with us."

To Farid's surprise Duke Didryk barely considered the proposal before giving his assent. "Very well—but give me the night. In the morning we will go to the city. I will not harm you if you leave the circle now, but try no tricks, for I warn you, our camp is well-protected."

Arigu turned upon the duke. Farid could see violence in the shape of the general's shoulders, the tightness of his fists, and it struck Farid how little more than a knife-edge separated blood from comfortable discourse. "You negotiate with *me* now, Duke. And we leave tonight."

The captain lowered his voice. "But General, my orders—"

Arigu took the man by the shoulders and dragged him aside, hissing, "You want to trust these men? You think to rest your bones by a comfortable fire, roast some meat, toast the emperor, heaven and stars protect him, and have a good night's sleep?" Arigu pointed at the mage. "This man is your enemy. The other one, the one you let go, slit at least twelve of my best men's throats while they slept—men better than you, Blue Shield. We leave tonight." With that he pushed the captain aside.

Ziggur rubbed at his beard, the cheeks above them bright red. "We leave tonight, Duke Didryk," he called out, but he was no longer in charge, and the duke was already bowing to Arigu, his former captive. "Allow me to gather my things, General." His eyes were calculating all the new possibilities.

"Do not take too long, Duke," said Arigu, "or I will come and find you."

"You may try. There are wards." The duke backed away. "Give me two hours."

"You have nothing left to bargain with, remember," said Arigu. "Be fast, now."

Didryk disappeared behind his men.

Arigu motioned to a group of soldiers. "Go around to the back of the camp. Make sure he doesn't leave us here holding our pricks."

At Arigu's command the Blue Shields galloped off through the sand. Ziggur stood rubbing his neck, looking a fool. Arigu ignored him and turned to Farid instead. They were of a height, but Arigu outweighed him; his shoulders were wider, his legs thicker. "What's your magic? I mean to capture the horse chief. Earth or air would be helpful."

"I have no magic."

"They sent me a decrepit captain and a mage with no talent." Arigu rubbed his beard and looked in the direction of Nooria. "I see. Our emperor, heaven bless him, has made a mistake."

Farid looked wide-eyed at the man's treasonous words, but Arigu had already turned away from him. "Where is the best horse?" he asked Ziggur. "I want the best horse you have." Ziggur indicated his own, and Arigu took a moment to remove the captain's things before mounting. "I will return to the palace when I have caught that lame bastard," he snarled, and with that, he kicked the horse and was gone.

Farid glanced at Ziggur before moving off to examine the pattern-marks. The duke had laid three concentric patterns on the sand, reds and yellows and blues glimmering under the sun. He followed the lines of them, walking the perimeter three times, one for each pattern. The inner two he could not fathom, but he shivered to look at the third. He did not understand the marks and he could not get a sense of their arrangement—the area being so large—but he knew it was there to cause harm. At intervals he crouched down and memorised what he could.

"Let's go!" shouted Ziggur, and Farid looked around to see the duke, dressed as before, except now with a satchel slung over one shoulder. He did not imagine mages required many possessions, their riches being of another kind, but this man was also a duke; he would have expected more in the way of baggage. Didryk whistled, and a fine grey horse, his coat gleaming, appeared, bearing a silver-trimmed saddle. Farid knew little of horses, but even so he could see this one spoke eloquently of the duke's station. His sense of social order satisfied, he found his own horse around the curve of a nearby dune. It took a few minutes to coax her into letting him mount, as awkward a rider as he was, and he guided her back to the column. With a shock, he found the duke was waiting for him, flanked by two guardsmen.

In the growing dark Didryk's eyes took on the colour of night and his pale skin stood out against the dunes. "You were with Second Austere Adam," he said.

Farid swallowed. He hated the thought of anyone overhearing that. "Yes," he muttered, and flinched when the duke raised a hand, but he meant only to touch a finger against Farid's forehead.

"Can you feel it?" he asked.

Farid grabbed at his reins. "Your finger? Of course I can."

"No; what Adam did." Didryk tilted his head in question. After a moment he said, "You do not know."

Farid remembered Adam's words: *You will help me.* His stomach twisted. "No. What is it?"

"I cannot tell." Didryk frowned. "Adam is good at disguising his marks. I think the word in your language is *sneaky.* He is neither a good teacher nor a good man."

"He taught you."

"No," said the duke, with a shake of his head, "I taught myself. I read the old books I found hidden away in the library. He whipped me for it, but I kept on."

"Because you needed to know," said Farid. He understood that desire.

"Yes." They rode on in silence for a time until at last the duke added, "But the pattern is not everything it promises. Its offerings are weak—it's all shadows in the mirror. And it lies."

"In the marketplace its offerings were not weak. It was not a lie that those people died."

Didryk turned to him, his face stern. "I will not be teaching you how to do that. Such things were never meant to be." With that his horse began to pull ahead.

"Why?" Farid awkwardly kicked his mare, struggling to keep up. "Adam taught me only two patterns. Will you teach me more?"

"What did he teach you?"

"How to call water, and how to destroy wood."

Didryk slowed his horse and looked back at Farid. "You learned them both? Already?"

"I did."

"Those are the only patterns most austeres need. They take most students years to master."

"Water and wood is all that I need?"

"Student," said Didryk, and Farid realised he had not introduced himself. "Student, you now have the ability to call and to destroy. That is all that is taught, besides warding, which anybody could do and I will teach you soon. All you need is to learn the correct symbols."

Those are the only two patterns most austeres need. It could not be that easy. It was *not* that easy. Farid lost control over the mare again and fell behind, and the nearby soldiers laughed at him. His cheeks red, he slowed even more and let them all pass. The duke had underestimated him. He was no scribe, to copy the same patterns over and over, replacing only the symbols inside. The patterns Govnan had shown him delved deep into time and history. The pattern could do more than call and destroy—the pattern could create, destroy, rearrange—and he would learn it. If the duke would not help him, he needed to go back to the Tower and teach himself.

CHAPTER TWENTY-FOUR

SARMIN

"The Great Storm has grown, Magnificence, as we feared."

Sarmin sat in his room, eyes on the wall, hoping to make out a pattern—a face, anything—from the curves of paint and play of light from the lanterns. To find his brother he required power, not the mundane sort he wielded with his spies and soldiers, but the arcane power he had lost to the god's wound.

Govnan sat down across from him. "I saw it from the Tower today and there can be no mistaking it. It darkens the sky and earth and crowds the mountains behind it from sight. We have a day, maybe less, before it reaches the Blessing, and three before it reaches the north walls of Nooria." He shifted. "Magnificence?"

"And the crack?" Sarmin asked at last, not shifting his gaze from among the brush-strokes. "The crack in the Tower?"

"It widens."

Azeem cleared his throat. Sarmin had forgotten him. "Our citizens flee south. There are so many leaving through the Low Gate that a carriage can barely move once it passes Asherak Bridge."

What had once been Asherak Bridge, Sarmin thought to himself, and now consisted of rubble sticking up from the water, threatening the hulls of the barges and other vessels plying the Blessing.

Azeem continued, "In better news, the scouts have not seen any signs of troops from Yrkmir."

"They are coming, nonetheless." *Through the empty spaces.* What did that mean? He would need to ask Notheen when next he saw him. Sarmin turned away from the wall; he would not be a pattern mage this night, nor any other. Govnan hunched in his chair, watching him with bright eyes, while Azeem stood to his left. The grand vizier held no parchments or ledgers; his elegant hands were folded over his robes.

"What of my brother? Has Grada come with a report?"

Azeem's face told Sarmin the answer. He wanted to knock the man to the floor.

"There is some good news," said the grand vizier. "Herran reports Ziggur's company is heading east towards Nooria. With luck, General Arigu will be among them."

"There was no ambush." Sarmin stood. That was indeed good news. "The empress was correct."

"Yes, Magnificence," said Azeem without inflection.

"But Arigu is only half of what we need to keep our walls safe. We also require a pattern mage."

"There is Farid," Govnan said, almost whispering. He drew two scroll-tubes from his robe. "I have brought the patterns he drew for me. He has an excellent memory."

Memory might be the only requirement for an austere. There were poets and there were scribes: the men who wrote soaring verse and metaphor, and the men who copied them from book to book. Farid might be no more than a man with a quill, but Sarmin would look at his work nevertheless. He gestured to the high mage. "Show me."

Govnan placed the first scroll upon the table and unrolled it to reveal a simple design more suited to mosaics than patternwork. "This calls water," he said, and Azeem too leaned over it, his face caught between curiosity and disgust; Helmar had left him with a lingering distaste for patterns.

The second pattern Govnan produced showed more complexity, but it was not at the level of Helmar's work. "In both of these patterns, the spell takes effect in the centre. That fits with the destruction in the market-place—only those within the circle were affected."

Sarmin picked up the second scroll. Each of these patterns existed on the parchment in only two dimensions. That had not been the case with Helmar. Helmar had made his pattern of the world, anchored among the dead and carried by the living, its threads whispering with the voices of the Many. Its breath had been the thoughts of the multitude, its sight their memories. What Sarmin looked at now was a mere drawing. He threw it on the desk. "I don't see how this could create anything." He would hold out hope for Duke Didryk's talent, now that he was on his way. "I will see Mura now."

Azeem glided to the door, silent as ever, and admitted the young mage. Sarmin knew the strangeness of the Tower was in part affected, allowing the ancient order to maintain its mystery and awe, but this mage did it well. Her eyes were focused far away and her robe moved absent of any wind. She fell into her obeisance, her spine straight, everything in her manner measured and perfect.

"Rise, Mura." He waited until she faced him again. "You were the duke's captive for many months."

"I was."

"What is your judgement of the man?"

She hesitated. She had been accused of treachery once already and knew better than to tempt it again. "He is passionate about his homeland, Magnificence. I overheard them talking from time to time—"

"The duke and the chief?"

"Yes, Your Majesty. They mostly spoke in Frythian, but I did understand some of it. They both hold Yrkmir and Austere Adam in contempt. As for Cerana . . . They were proud of their actions against the White Hats, but they spoke well of the empress and they appeared to have real hope of an alliance."

Sarmin leaned back and watched the mage's face. "And the duke's pattern-spells? What did you see?"

"I saw the duke cast only a few spells—the one that silenced Yomawa, and later, one calling water in the desert. I could not draw them for you. He is frugal with his talent, but I can tell you one thing: it frightens him."

Perhaps Duke Didryk understood the true cost, understood that every use of the pattern widened the god's wounds. While Adam encouraged catastrophe, perhaps the duke really did think better of it. His hopes rose at the thought. He stood at the window and looked out into the darkness beyond the courtyard, though if Ziggur were anywhere close he would know it. "You are dismissed, Mura," he said at last.

From the time of Uthman the Conqueror, Cerana had been a power beyond reach. The wide world feared its mages; its walls could not be breached; its army stood undefeated—except when it came to Yrkmir. And on that day when Yrkmen had sacked Nooria's palace, Helmar had been taken. From them he had learned the tools he used to become the Pattern Master—but it had not been Yrkmir that had twisted him; that had come from his neglect at the hands of his royal family, from becoming a prisoner, from being put aside against a future need. Sarmin understood that well. In every Cerani history Yrkmir was the enemy—and yet Sarmin was beginning to think Cerana could fashion destruction quite well enough on its own.

There had been no ambush in the desert; the duke had set his tiles on the board with no feint or trickery, and all had proceeded as he had promised. Sarmin should not be surprised; the man was Kavic's cousin, and Kavic had been a direct and honest man. The politician in him knew an alliance with a Mogyrk ruler could help to ease tensions in the city. He might even be able to bring into question Yrkmir's authority over the rebels and find his real brother at last.

When the wrong boy had been returned to Sarmin he had felt powerless, helpless; but now his strength had been restored by new hope, flowing into his limbs and fingers with sweet excitement, just as it had on that first night when Tuvaini had opened the secret door to his room.

I suggest you do not make them hate you. He remembered Grada's words and smiled.

"I will ally with this duke," he said into the dark.

"Your Majesty." Azeem fumbled for words. "This must go through the council. The priests—"

"That will take too long, Azeem. Begin the proclamation tonight. Heralds will announce it throughout the city in the morning."

In a rustle of silk the grand vizier was gone. Only Govnan remained, still in his seat. Sarmin could hear him breathing. "What do you think Ashanagur meant, High Mage, when he said Mogyrk blinds the Tower?"

"I do not know. Our power fades . . . but I do not see how that has anything to do with Mogyrk, or his wounds."

The Storm. Sarmin stared out into the night. "You must find a way to stop the Storm, Govnan. The emptiness cannot be allowed to destroy the Blessing or breach our walls while Yrkmir approaches. I cannot do it—I have lost the skill—but you command the Tower. The arcane secrets are open to you. You must find a way."

"Yes, Magnificence."

"If you cannot protect our Blessing and our walls, I will tear down the Tower and start a new one."

"There is no need to threaten, Your Majesty." There was a smile in his voice. "If I do not find a way to stop the Storm, the Tower will already be gone."

Sarmin turned to look at the old man. Govnan raised himself from the seat. "I am an old man, Magnificence, and sentimental. I have seen six emperors rule Nooria, and of all of them, you are my favourite." And now he did smile. "I will not fail you."

Sarmin found he could not speak, and so he bowed.

Govnan bowed in return and left the room, his staff gripped in one hand, his steps slow and determined. Sarmin watched him go, then left the room as well, heading east, towards the women's wing.

Willa opened the door to Mesema's room. With a motion, Sarmin was rid of her. His wife stood inside, alone, her eyes wide with surprise, her face free of paint, clothed in a wisp of blue silk. The air felt moist and he caught the scent of roses; she had been in the bath. He began to explain why he had interrupted her evening, the awkward words ready to twist his mouth and put distance between them, but instead he stopped speaking, crossed the room, and took her in his arms. "You were right," he said, whispering into the curls of her hair. "There was no ambush, and the duke is on his way to Nooria."

She raised her eyes to him and he looked down at her face in wonder. Cheekbones too broad, his mother said. Chin too pointed. And yet he could not stop looking. "And Arigu?" she asked.

"Perhaps Arigu also."

She did not ask about Banreh.

"You were angry with me," she said, laying a palm against his cheek. "And I with you."

"I do not wish for that. I wish . . . I wish for you."

She smiled as he kissed each of her fingers. "Today I remembered that you taught me to read. Now I can open any book and learn what is in it. Poor Banafrit cannot read. Willa and Tarub cannot read, and those worlds are closed to them."

"You also opened a world to me."

She stood on her toes and their lips met. Her scent, the touch of her soft hair and the warmth of her body overwhelmed him. He did not know how long he stood there holding her against him, his hands searching for a way through the silk, before they stumbled together onto the bed. He tore at her silk wrappings, breaking her free, each sensation coming lightning-quick, her skin soft beneath his hands, her scent surrounding him. Every touch brought an agony of pleasure. Their bodies flowed together, all soft flesh and taut muscle, until release came shimmering and trembling over them.

They pulled apart, smiling in the dark. "Mesema," he whispered, and she turned to him, her eyes lost in the shadows. "I think we will find our way through this."

She slid across the silk and kissed him. "My prince."

CHAPTER TWENTY-FIVE

MESEMA

Mesema woke to sunlight streaming through the windowscreen and stretched. She had not slept so well since the day Pelar left. She smiled, but rolling to her side she saw his cradle was gone—given to Nessaket for the child—and the emptiness of the room filled her mind. She sat up, rubbing tears from her eyes, and called for Tarub and Willa. Sarmin had already risen and returned to his own apartments, preparing to receive the duke and Arigu in the throne room.

Tarub entered first and brought her hands to her face. "Your hair, Majesty!"

"Quickly," said Mesema, swinging her legs to the floor. "Get me ready for court."

Willa put a plate of food beside her. "First you will need to eat, Majesty, and to bathe, so that we may pull those tangles from your curls."

Mesema turned to look at herself in the silver mirror. Hair rose in a stiff point from the right side of her head. She reached out to touch it. "Why are reflections always backwards?"

"To remind ourselves," said Nessaket from the doorway, "that we do not see the truth." Tarub and Willa threw themselves upon the floor and she waved a dismissive hand as she entered. "Get up and attend to the empress."

"Where is . . . Daveed?" asked Mesema, taking a morsel of cheese from the plate. Sarmin was certain the boy was not his brother, but she did not think it possible for a mother to confuse another boy with her own son. Pelar would continue to grow and change in the southern province—but his eyes, his hair, the shape of his nose were imprinted on Mesema's memory for ever. She wondered how much time Sarmin had spent with his brother, whether he truly knew the curve of his cheeks and the line of his forehead as well as Nessaket, who had borne him and birthed him. Perhaps his loss of the patternsight affected the way he saw the boy. She had also noticed that he could not understand music since closing the wound in Beyon's tomb.

"Daveed is with his nurses. I spent the morning questioning Rushes about Austere Adam, but she knows very little. He kept her in an attic room and she could not see." Nessaket wrapped a hand around the bedpost, looking at the state of the silks. "My other son has returned to your bed. That is well. Another few weeks and he might have started looking at the concubines."

"He wouldn't."

"He has before." Nessaket's voice brooked no argument. "You must keep him satisfied and diverted from conceiving more boys with his concubines. That is far more important than messing in politics."

"But *you* have messed in politics," Mesema argued. Willa entered carrying a heavy bucket of water and poured it into a wide copper bowl at her feet. Into this she threw rose-petals, soap, and a handful of salt.

"The Felt are your people and the traitor is their chief," Nessaket said firmly. "You must maintain a distance from him and his dealings, lest you be tarnished. I have warned you: this Fryth duke is part of Chief Banreh's story, for good or ill, but you must step away from it." Nessaket watched Willa working the sponge over Mesema's face and hair. "During Tahal's time, my own father was involved in a scandal. Over too much drink he was heard criticising the emperor's favourite general, and he was later implicated in a coup. I tried to defend him, and I nearly lost my place. Had I persisted, Beyon and Sarmin would never have been emperors. But I did not. I remained silent, as much as it hurt me, when my father was exiled from court."

Mesema kept a short silence out of respect for the story, then said, "But Empire Mother, no general of Cerana took your people as slaves." At this Willa started, and her elbow knocked Mesema's book of poetry from the side table. It landed upside down and Mesema looked at the words, unrecognisable to her in reverse. As it had been with Banafrit, they appeared as nothing more than a jumble.

As she studied the letters, an idea taking form in her, Nessaket answered. "You do not know that your people were taken slaves, either. You have found no evidence for it."

"I haven't spoken to all of the scribes yet." Tarub began working a comb through Mesema's hair and she winced. "Nessaket, Mother. Listen—I do hear you, but Sarmin would never displace me, or Pelar." She closed her eyes, remembering how Sarmin had kissed her the night before. "I think he loves me." No man, not Beyon, not Banreh, had ever been so open with her.

"You had better hope he does not love you," Nessaket said. "An emperor grants or withdraws his favour. He does not love, for that is a path to disaster." With that she stood, preparing to take her leave. "But since you have his favour at the moment, I have a request."

"Anything, Empire Mother."

"Will you help convince him that his brother has truly returned?"

"Of course." In her mind she resolved not to convince him, but to prove it—though she did not yet know how to do that. Govan's word and Nessaket's certainty had so far counted for nothing.

"Thank you, my Empress." Nessaket gave a formal bow and left the room. Distracted by her preparations, Mesema only watched the Empire Mother leave in the mirror.

Tarub stuck a pin into Mesema's hair. "I do not think you will be able to see the arrival of the duke, Your Majesty. Already the emperor has closed the doors and the first gong has sounded."

"Mm," said Mesema, "but I will try." Several minutes more, and her hair was finished, coiled around her head in an elaborate network of braids. Her face was carefully painted, and her skin carried the scent of jasmine. Willa slipped pretty sandals on her feet and at last she was released from the room. Sendhil and her other guards trailed after her.

"Come, Sendhil." Mesema hurried to the doors and out into the palace, taking the shortest path to the throne room, through the servants' halls and back stairways. At last she came to the landing overlooking the Great Hall and stopped, surprised to see so many gathered there. So recently the room had contained nothing but broken mosaics—the ceiling above her still showed unfinished timber joists and jagged bits of plaster—but the debris had been cleared away and the floor beneath the boots of the Blue Shields positioned below gleamed in the sunlight.

An old captain stood, with a dozen of his soldiers in formation behind him. Around them swarmed a few men of the court, the priests, generals and satraps who circled the throne like bees around honey. But one man stood out, taller even than Notheen, with skin as pale as the winter sky and a coat too heavy for Nooria's climate. The man bent his head towards a Tower mage Mesema did not recognise. So this could be no other than the Fryth duke, Didryk, Banreh's friend. As she stared down at him he looked up, and recognition flashed in his eyes. He gave a bow so slight that nobody in his vicinity noticed it, so engrossed were they in their own business.

She inclined her head in the way of her people and he returned the gesture as the crowd began to move, sweeping the Fryth, the Blue Shield captain and all the soldiers towards the throne room.

So that was Banreh's ally. Mesema was relieved the chief had been set free. She turned towards the servants' stair, but motion caught her eye and she looked back over the railing. In the corridor she saw a woman with long black hair walking towards the temple wing. "Your Majesty!" she called, thinking it was Nessaket, but the woman did not acknowledge her.

She hurried down the stairs and followed the black-haired woman into the corridor, but saw no one.

Sendhil asked, "You are not slipping away again, Your Majesty?" Always he worried. Her own father had never been so protective.

"Not at all. I hope to join my husband the emperor in the throne room," she said, re-entering the Great Hall, but right away she saw Grada.

"Mirra help us!" one of her guards said in a fearful voice. Those of the palace viewed the grey-robed, silent assassins as wraiths or demons, not men or women, and Mesema understood that. Once she had feared Eyul, but she had come to understand him. The Grey Service carried out their work with efficiency when called upon, but they were not ruthless killers. Eyul had borne the weight of his own deeds until his death.

Now his heir approached, her dark eyes taking in the men behind her, the broken stair and all corners of the room. She stopped a child's length away and looked her empress up and down, measuring. Though Mesema knew Grada intended her no harm, she felt spiders crawl over her skin. Nobody could—nobody would—stop the Knife if she decided to make a cut. "I came too late to meet with the emperor," Grada said at last.

"The Fryth duke has arrived to discuss an alliance," said Mesema. "You may speak to the emperor afterwards, heaven bless him, if you wait."

"I must go and watch Lord Nessen's manse." Grada's face betrayed that she thought herself of better use elsewhere. She held up a scroll, capped at both ends with shining brass. "This letter was taken from one of the lord's staff as he entered the city."

"Lord Nessen? So is he in Nooria, then?" She was pleased to know there was news about the Mogyrk sympathiser at last.

"No, he never arrived."

Mesema frowned. "And yet it appeared they were preparing for his arrival. You said great amounts of food had been carried inside."

"Just so." Grada tapped the scroll-end thoughtfully, and Mesema could not help but look at it, fingers itching.

"What does it say, Grada?"

Grada shrugged. "I cannot read it."

"I can read it for you." Mesema reached out for it, but Grada held up a hand. "No. This is for the emperor, heaven bless him."

"Well then, give it to me and I will make sure he receives it."

Grada hesitated, and Mesema sighed and added, "Unopened."

"Very well." Grada dropped it into her waiting palms.

A young Cerani man wearing white mages' robes stepped through the doorway. He blinked at the height of the Great Hall, then stopped in alarm at the sight of so many guards. He looked from Grada to Mesema as he spoke, his voice uncertain. "Has anybody seen the high mage?"

"I have not." The Knife assessed the man. "Perhaps he is in the Tower?"

"Of course!" His eyes went round when they fell on Mesema and her silks, and she smiled to herself, because he did not know her for the empress.

"I am very happy to see a new mage in the Tower," she said. "We have great need of you."

"Thank you, miss," he said with a bow. Over his head she and Grada shared a secret smile.

"I will walk with you," said Grada to the mage, "for the Tower is on my way to the Holies."

"The Holies! I never . . ."

As Knife and mage passed through the doorway to the temple wing, Mesema looked at the missive in her hand. She could not carry a secret letter into the full court; she would have to take it to Sarmin's apartments. Back up the stairs she went, Sendhil and the other men behind her, down one hall and then another, until Sarmin's guards bowed and opened his doors. She went through to the desk and set down the scroll, feeling relieved now it was out of her hands and the temptation to open it had passed.

She looked out of Sarmin's window. He had a better view than she, for his room faced the Blessing and beyond it, the plateau of the Holies, which was high enough to obscure her view of the Storm Gate and its path into the western desert. Directly below lay the courtyard where nobles and generals often arrived in their coaches, and as she looked down she saw the dark-haired woman again, walking towards the gate. Mesema gripped the window-screen. The woman would never hear her if she called out from up here. Instead she stared, trying to determine whether it was truly Nessaket. This woman had the same long hair and the same golden skin, but the white covering wrapped around her did not look like anything Nessaket owned. "What—?"

Mesema turned to Sarmin's desk and found the spyglass he had lent her the other day. Stretching it to its full extent she focused on the dark-haired woman and gasped. She was wearing her own white cloak, the one her mother had embroidered with red and blue flowers—the one she had thrown to the floor when Nessaket visited her room the other day.

The guards did not attempt to stop Nessaket as she passed through the gate—they did not appear to see her, and neither did Nessaket take any notice of them as she walked in a straight line, each movement measured and even. Outside the gate she turned and vanished from Mesema's view.

"No—!" Mesema folded the spyglass and ran to the corridor, pushing past Sarmin's guards, and for once Sendhil asked nothing; he only ran after her as she hurried to the old women's wing. Without a word he helped her to pull open the heavy doors, and once inside, she ran through the old bedrooms to the garden stairs. On the roof at last she put the spyglass to her eye and searched for the Empire Mother, but though she peered at one street after another, examining every person she saw, Nessaket was nowhere to be seen.

"No!" She sat on the bench and twisted the brass spyglass in her hands, wondering how long it would be before Sarmin was finished with court.

At last she gathered herself together and stood, looking out once again over the city, Sarmin's city, glinting in the full sun. The Blessing caught her eye, sparkling as it did at this time of day, and she followed it south, towards where Pelar had gone. And then she followed it north, to the Worship Gate and beyond, where the Great Storm threatened. Sarmin had told her that by staring at the emptiness too long she too would be emptied, but she could see nothing to the north but the gate and the wall.

She sat among Nessaket's flowers and looked at the statue of Mirra. "Where has she gone?" she asked the stone, but the stone did not answer.

CHAPTER TWENTY-SIX

SARMIN

Sarmin leaned back in the Petal Throne and looked out over the gathered court. The politicking of his lords and generals defined Cerana for those who lived and worked within the palace, but it was these meetings between himself and foreign rulers that defined Cerana for the outside world. It happened so rarely that it was of the utmost importance to get it right. Anticipation and dread together set his skin tingling. To strike the right balance, to be welcoming and yet demand the respect the Son of Heaven deserved, was to walk on a knife's edge. When Marke Kavic had arrived in the court, Govnan had been here to help him through a difficult moment in diplomacy, but he did not expect the high mage to be present today.

Within minutes or hours the Storm would touch against the Blessing, and all things hinged upon that moment, for if Govnan could not protect the river, they would have to leave their great city, just as Notheen had long recommended. The desert headman was also missing from the assembly, as were many others—the softer men who might talk of war but shivered at hardship. The earthquake had been the final straw for them, and he wished them well on their way downriver or across the sands. He and

Mesema might soon be joining them—but first he would find his brother, and to do that he needed Duke Didryk's help. His fingers wandered to the butterfly-stone he kept in his pocket to remind himself how much that seemed impossible was not.

General Merkel and Lord Benna remained, and with them an assortment of brave courtiers, all of them energised by the news that the Fryth duke had arrived. Some wore grim expressions—any alliance with Fryth would curtail their dreams of conquest—but others showed nothing but curiosity. Sarmin himself was looking forward to discovering who would be standing with him in the coming days, and who would oppose him. Dinar would be the man to watch as an alliance with the duke moved forwards. Now the high priest stood in the midst of a group of old warriors, his expression closed, his words few. Though he thirsted for power, the man was always careful; he chose both his allies and his battles well. He would not speak against the alliance unless he saw a better opportunity.

He watched the side door, but Mesema did not step through. He was surprised she would miss this. He remembered the feel of her, the way their bodies had joined together, and he pressed his palm against the carved metal roses of his throne to still his desire. He had always cared for Mesema and he had always wanted her, but something had changed, beginning with the day Chief Banreh had arrived and he was poisoned by jealousy. He knew his mother would not approve; in the *Histories* he had read many a tale of rulers thrown upon the rocks of their own passions. An emperor must always remain above such human foibles.

And yet still he looked at the door again, wondering where she could be, longing for the sight of her pointed face, the feel of her gentle hand against his shoulder.

The herald claimed Sarmin's attention, announcing the duke and his two noble guards in his sonorous voice. Courtiers gaped and whispered at the sight of the tall Fryth, and struck various poses of disapproval or acceptance, though Sarmin set no tone to guide them. He kept his own face blank, though Duke Didryk looked so like his cousin Marke Kavic that he found it difficult: the duke looked out from the same deep blue eyes.

Sarmin's last memory of Kavic was filled with blood, for it had been his own hand that killed the marke, though not his own mind.

Moreth had slipped in and stood now at the back, his grey eyes watchful. Sarmin did not see Grada but Herran stood in the shadows, his face betraying nothing. Other than Azeem, all of his closest advisors were absent. His mind went in a dark direction.

"Do you see General Arigu here?" he asked Azeem in a low voice. He did not know what the man looked like.

"No, Your Majesty, I do not. I was told Chief Banreh escaped and the general went after him."

"Yes—I was hoping he had returned." Sarmin hoped Arigu would be successful, and soon; if he could not retrieve Banreh there would be trouble between himself and the army. To the soldiers and the court the horse chief had come to represent all of Cerana's failings in Fryth; if Sarmin lost him, they would never be able to set those accounts to rights. And yet he did not like to think of what would have to happen to Banreh once he returned.

"I am sure the general—"

Azeem stopped when the duke drew near.

The Fryth had brought only two guards, the merest nod to his status, though both were taller than any other man in the room. Their metal armour was etched in complex designs and buffed to gleaming. They shone in the light cast down from the dome like moving god-statues, and Sarmin could see there were men among the cushions who watched them with awe.

The threesome approached the end of the silk runner and there stopped. They knelt into their obeisances as one, as if they had practised it. Unlike Marke Kavic and his austere, who had both waited too long to bend the knee, Didryk and his men performed on cue. The duke's fine coat stretched straight over his back and his long hands rested flat on the silk carpet. He wore one ring of office, a golden band set with carved ivory. In his elegant simplicity he reminded Sarmin of Azeem, but Tuvaini had been a simple man too, at least in clothing, and he knew that did not signify an elegant mind.

Sarmin waited, one minute and then the next, allowing the silence to settle in fully and for all minds to turn towards the expectation of his words. He had planned the same greeting he had given to Kavic, in honour of the fallen marke.

"Rise," he said at last, and a breath went through the crowd. "Duke Didryk, welcome to Nooria, and may the sand take only your sorrows."

"I thank you, Magnificence." Didryk bowed his head.

"As I told your cousin Kavic many months ago, heaven and stars keep him now"—he paused and allowed the duke to make his own devout gesture—"my cousin, Emperor Tuvaini, initiated an attack upon the Dukedom of Fryth in error, believing it to be the cause of a plague we had suffered. But the pattern-plague that appeared to have come from Mogyrk hands was in fact the work of Helmar, also my kin, and rooted in our long division. I feared the effects of our aggression would bring only further conflict through time. Now I know I was correct.

"Yrkmir approaches, having already ravaged your lands. In the aftermath of Helmar's work the wounds from your god fester within our empire. Our own great goddess Meksha threatens to release the fires of Her mountain, and we suffer strange attacks in our greatest city. But through all this you stretch out your hand in friendship, and we accept."

Duke Didryk bowed and said, "We are pleased to offer our hand in friendship, and to begin to heal the wounds caused by our enmity." So far all had passed as if he and the duke had practised it together, and the smoothness of their meeting gave Sarmin real hope. He longed to ask Didryk about his brother, but he could not do it here, before all the men of court. He raised his voice so that it would reach the furthest corners of the room.

"Ours will be the first alliance between Cerana and a Mogyrk ruler. To celebrate our new friendship I have prepared a proclamation." He motioned to Azeem, who produced a great scroll wound on mahogany rods. Amber glimmered from the rounded ends of the wood as he held it up before the eyes of the court. As Azeem unrolled the parchment and formally announced the alliance, Sarmin and the duke regarded one another. Kavic had been determined, but also curious and hopeful. Didryk's blue eyes, so much like the marke's, held more shadows; they carried the grief of the past war, as well as other sorrows Sarmin could not begin to guess. But he held the emperor's gaze and did not hide from it.

Sarmin was struck by a sudden inspiration, and when Azeem finished reading, he spoke. "On this day I dissolve the law making illegal the worship of Mogyrk. Mogyrk churches may now stand under the light of the sun, and its members will enjoy the protection of our guards and mages."

This time there were no indrawn breaths from the room, no gasps, no murmurs. A silence fell beneath the dome, and everyone sat so still that for a moment Sarmin wondered if a spell had been cast. Azeem's hands fell to his sides, the scroll forgotten, its furthest end touching the shining floor. General Merkel looked green, as if he might be sick. But it was Duke Didryk's face that concerned Sarmin the most: instead of looking pleased, he looked devastated. What secrets and grief did he carry, that a gesture towards peace brought him such desolation?

A private talk might clear the air. Sarmin stood, his loose robes giving the appearance of smooth movement and not a series of painful unbendings. "Duke Didryk, I am sure you are tired from your journey. Azeem will see you to a set of comfortable rooms, and my own sword-sons will watch over your safety. Please, be easy, and we will speak before long." He turned, ignoring the wide eyes of court, and exited through the side door. In that small chamber stood one of the low viziers, Azeem's functionary, who fell into an obeisance.

Sarmin washed his hands in the rose-petal water that had been prepared for him. His sword-sons crowded into the small space, careful not to step on the low vizier. No sooner had Sarmin thrown down the silk drying-cloth than the outer door opened and a burly man entered, turning sideways, for the doorframe was too narrow for his wide shoulders. He reeked of sweat and his leathers had long since worn out, but Sarmin knew him for an important man.

His sword-sons had rushed to stand in front of him, but he waved a dismissive hand. "The general, I believe?"

"Your Majesty." One of the man's arms had remained outside the door and now he entered the room fully, dragging Chief Banreh with him. The chief looked much the worse for wear.

He had been beaten and was badly sunburned. His hands were tied behind his back and when Arigu kicked him, he landed against the wall, one knee buckling beneath him, the other leg held out to his side—the one Mesema had said could not bend.

Looking down at the wreck, Sarmin regretted ever wanting to hurt the man.

General Arigu knelt before his emperor. It irked, but a proper obeisance was impossible in the small space. "Your Majesty, I have brought you a gift."

Sarmin looked to the low vizier, still face down on the floor. "Rise," he said at last, and the man stood and pressed himself against the wall, staring at the injured chief. Sarmin half wondered whether Banreh might be dead already. "You went against my word in Fryth, General. For that I should have your head. Instead, you offer me the head of the Windreader chief."

"His is prettier—or it was, Magnificence," said Arigu, standing to show a broad face and a friendly grin. "But it is also worth more than mine, for the time being. You have in your great wisdom entered into an alliance with the Duke of Fryth. Yrkmir approaches and a pattern mage will serve us well. But the man is passionate and unpredictable—the kind of man who, in the midst of peace negotiations, might take to cutting throats. But this one"—Arigu nudged Banreh with his foot—"will keep him in line."

Sarmin considered Arigu's description of the duke. He had not seemed like that kind of man at all. "How?"

"They are close, Magnificence, blood-brothers and more. The duke set Banreh to escape across the dunes, but I chased him down. The duke thinks his friend is free—but now here is Banreh to hold against his uncertain loyalties. If the duke should prove unreliable, hold a knife to this one's throat, or send him to the temple of Herzu—the nature of the threat does not matter. The duke will do as you wish."

"You are wrong about one thing, General."

Arigu raised his eyebrows. "Majesty?"

Sarmin turned Banreh's limp body so that his hands were visible and pointed at the mark on his wrist. "Didryk knows that Banreh is here."

Arigu's mouth twisted behind his beard as he studied the mark. "It will still work in your favour, Magnificence."

"Your army wants him dead."

"I can handle my army, Your Majesty," said Arigu with a conspiratorial grin, "if you can manage the duke."

"Walk with me." Before leaving the room Sarmin turned to the low vizier. "Have him taken to Mirra, but keep it secret."

"Yes, Magnificence."

Sarmin walked the gleaming floor towards the back stairs that led to his apartments. The spiral stair had been grander, but now it was broken, and in any case, Arigu had seen it before. Any awe Sarmin might have inspired by leading the general up that way had long since been used up by his father Tahal. "Yrkmir approaches, planning an attack upon our great city."

Arigu raised a hand to his beard but did not speak.

"You will command our defences."

"As you wish, Your Majesty. I will meet with Lurish immediately to coordinate our efforts. Except . . ."

"Spit it out, General."

"Except that Yrkmen attack like cowards. They cast their evil spells, then set their archers upon those who remain."

Sarmin looked down at the big man. "Were you in Mondrath then, General, when Yrkmir attacked?"

"I was."

"And how did you survive?"

For a moment Sarmin thought the general would not answer, but finally he said, "The duke had put a mark upon me, Your Majesty. I'd been cut and he meant to heal me, or so he said. It's a foul thing, wearing the marks, but it saved me."

"Well then, General, I am glad for it." Being marked had protected the general just as it had protected those in the marketplace attacks. At his door Sarmin said, "Azeem will arrange a room for you in the palace."

"With your permission, Your Majesty, I will sleep in the barracks." Arigu bowed and walked back the way he had come. He was the greatest general in Cerana, as well known for his political manoeuvring as for his battle strategy, and the man his scheming mother had favoured. There would be no private game between Sarmin and Didryk now. Arigu had thrown in his chips for a game between three, or four, if he counted Banreh.

Sarmin leaned against the doorjamb and spoke to his sword-sons for the first time in an age. "If Azeem comes, tell him that I need history books. I want to know about Satreth the Reclaimer." His own history book had been destroyed by the false Beyon, using his hands, and anyway, it had contained little of military history. He wanted to know exactly how the Yrkmen had attacked so many years ago, and how the Reclaimer had defeated them. The sword-sons nodded and he shut the door.

CHAPTER TWENTY-SEVEN

FARID

Grada had left Farid before the great doors of the Tower. He knew she expected him to be able to make his own way from here, but in truth he did not know whether to ring the bell or try to pull at the brass knobs. He was, after all, wearing the robes of a mage—but the doors were heavy and likely required real magic to open, and he had none of that. He turned back towards the unusual woman, only to see her disappear through the arched gate. He had never met a female like her, one who spoke frankly and carried herself more like a warrior than anything else.

The courtyard lay empty around him, his only company some slimy green pools and the statues of Meksha, and he felt as if the Tower's patron goddess was watching him with stony eyes, judging his worthiness. He ran his fingers along the brass surface of the door. If he knew the picture for metal, he could melt his way through . . . That made him smile, and when he turned back to look at Meksha's unmoving face he felt more proud than embarrassed. He rang the bell.

Mura answered with a smile. "You're home."

He would not have called it "home," though they had given him a room with a bed and a table. Home was his dingy apartment above the fruit market. Home was his father's boat, with the barrels of fruit he carried up the river. But more and more he was feeling that patterns were also his home: he longed to study their forms, to draw them with his fingers, to feel the delight of pulling the essence of a thing from a network of lines and shapes. And if patterns were his home, then perhaps the Tower was too. His father had believed it.

"Well, are you coming in?" Mura turned and walked away from him, between the lines of rock-sworn mage statues. "Govnan has some wonderful news, and some ideas of how to—" she stopped. "First, have you seen the Great Storm, to the north?" She was already halfway up the first flight of stairs and she turned to wave her hand at the brass portals.

Farid jogged after her to avoid them closing on him. "I've seen it—if you mean the greyness."

"It's grown. To the northwest it now takes up the whole horizon, like a real storm." She paused, her hands on the railing, her eyes far away, focused on a memory of a different place. Then she met his gaze with a directness that shocked him. "But this storm doesn't pass. It doesn't let the sun through. It just creeps closer."

Farid frowned. "I thought you said you had good news."

"Yes. Come." She turned back and ran up the stairs again and at last they reached the library. Mura threw the door wide. Inside, Govnan and Moreth were standing, looking over some parchments.

A tingling ran over Farid's skin: he could see some of those parchments had patterns written on them.

As they entered, Govnan looked up, his eyes bright, and beckoned them forwards. "Ah! Here he is. Did everything go well in the desert, then? Take a look."

Farid hurried to his side and identified the symbol in Govnan's hands. *Shack-nuth.* "Fire." He felt disappointed. They had been over this before.

"Do you know the one for water?"

Farid nodded. A quill lay on the table next to a pot of ink, so he found himself a blank piece of parchment and drew the symbol with bold, angry strokes. He wanted to see the ancient patterns Govnan had shown him before, though it made him ashamed, for he could not forget how his mother had died.

"Here is the good news," said Govnan, "and since you were not here, I will tell it again. The Great Storm has been approaching the Blessing for some time, and that has been a great concern to us, for all it touches turns to dust. We would not last long in the desert without the Blessing to feed and carry our crops."

Farid fell back in a chair and stared at the high mage. How could he not have known such threats existed? He had never even guessed at them . . . His hands curled into fists and he took a deep breath. "And now?"

"Now the day has come, and we find the river is indeed a blessing." Govnan handed him a brass tube with pieces of glass at each end. "Use the spyglass and look. The Storm touches the river, but it does not consume the water, and this tells us there is a way to stop the Storm from growing, even if we cannot heal it."

Farid stood and walked to the window. He held the glass to his eye, found the Blessing and followed it north past the Worship Gate, to where it rushed through the farmlands on its way down from the mountains. And then he saw it: a blank wall on the western side of the river, and behind that a colourless void that extended as far as the spyglass could reach, covering the world from sand to sky. It made his stomach turn and he had to look away.

But on the eastern side, all was as it ever had been. A strip of green led into the lushness of the pomegranate groves, dissolving into brush further east, and at last ended in the dunes, the start of Cerana's harshest desert. "I understand," he murmured. The Blessing was acting as a barrier against the Storm. "Is it possible to direct the river across the path of the Storm from east to west?" he asked, "as the farmers do in the fields?"

"There is no time for that," said Govnan, "but I am not without hope. If pure water—the water of the gods—can stop it, what of true fire?"

"Or true air," put in Mura, but Govnan waved her off. "Let us speak of fire first."

Mura folded her arms before her. Farid looked at Meksha's sacrificial flame which was burning in its black basin. "The goddess' fire?" he asked.

"No, fire from beyond our plane."

"The elements that are bound by this plane crumble," said Moreth in a mournful voice. "I raised many walls when Emperor Beyon's tomb was dissolving, but the emptiness ate every one of them. Hashi threw wind at the void, but it died and went still. Fire grew cold and flickered out. We know this."

"But what about an unbound elemental, as you mentioned before, when we spoke with the emperor?" Govnan leaned forwards. His eyes sparkled in the sunlight from the window.

Mura leaned in too. "How could we bring an unbound elemental into this plane? It would be bent on destruction, nothing more."

Govnan tapped the *Shack-nuth* symbol on the table. "There may be something here."

"You would use the pattern?" Farid asked, surprised. Surely that was anathema to the Tower?

The high mage smiled. "I cannot say yet. There are so many possibilities—too many, perhaps. But this is exciting news, is it not?" He studied Farid's face. "You look exhausted. When was the last time you slept?"

Farid remembered his dark closet room. Had he really not slept since escaping Adam? He should be more tired, shouldn't he? "I don't know."

"Then sleep." Govnan waved him off with an imperious hand. "I will not have a mage stumbling around making errors because he is too tired to think."

"I wanted to look at the patterns—"

"Now," said Govnan, his eyes narrowing in fury.

Farid backed off. This was the high mage, not his father; he would not test him. He bowed and withdrew.

In his little Tower room he found a pitcher of water and a silver mug, which he could not help but touch. This would have paid two years' rent for his little room above the market. He held it up to his face and watched the distorted reflection. He looked like a monster. He held it this way and that, looking at his forehead, but he could see no sign of any pattern there. Didryk had said the austere was sneaky. He put the mug down with a clang and threw himself onto the bed, where he tossed and turned sleeplessly.

Images of patterns and the Storm would not leave his mind, and at last he rose and settled himself against the window. His room faced south, towards the Low Gate, where the citizens were gathering to escape the city. The crowd looked like just a moving blur from this far distance, a more colourful stream than the river beside it. Farid focused on the Blessing. His father might be poling his little boat south at this very moment, taking himself to a safe place. He hoped so.

Do I belong here? Farid played with the belt of his mage's robe and thought about Austere Adam, the pattern, Duke Didryk, and the Great Storm. He was, it appeared, the only Cerani who could see the pattern-marks, the only pattern-worker whose loyalty to the emperor was unquestioned.

Yes.

CHAPTER TWENTY-EIGHT

DIDRYK

"**H**ere is your room, Duke." Azeem held the door open for Didryk. The grand vizier was long-limbed and lean, and he looked always to be in complete control, moving with a grace that spoke either of serenity or of long practise. "Is there anything else I or my staff may do for you before I take my leave?"

Didryk crossed the room and looked out the window. It faced a courtyard full of flowers similar to his own in Fryth and he closed his eyes a moment, for he would never see that one again. For an age his land had been caught between the wolf of Yrkmir and the lion of Cerana, and it had finally found ruin on the teeth of both—and yet his will for revenge had begun to falter. The emperor had made a grand and generous gesture towards his faith.

He reminded himself that no such generosity had been shown to Banreh. Didryk could feel his friend below him, in some dark place, his pain echoing in their shared marks. For most healers such a connection was useful, for it told them what patterns were needed; but on this night it was torture. Their bond was stronger than usual and he attributed that to the closeness of Mogyrk in the east. He leaned out, studying the wings and doors in his view, wondering, *Where are you?*

155

They had been through much, he and Banreh. Together they had uncovered Arigu's dishonesty, realising the impersonal cruelty of the empire
from which he came and pushing it aside. They had put their trust in each
other, and for a long while they had won. But there could be no saving his
friend now. Every day he thought of the Cerani invasion of his lands and
the destruction that came after and wished that he could have saved just
one person—his cousin's wife, his own sister, any loyal friend. But he had
not, and could not in the palace either; he could only follow the plan they
had made. That was all that remained for either of them. He looked down
on the courtyard, so far from his home, and told himself he could not turn
from his purpose.

First he must get the emperor to agree to use the pattern. It was a risk,
feeding the Storm with pattern-symbols; everything must be timed with care.

"Duke?" Azeem continued to wait in the doorway. "I asked whether there
was anything else I could do for you." Krys and Indri, Didryk's guards,
stood behind the vizier, peering in.

Didryk looked around the room, rubbing at his wrist. Wine and food had
been provided, the wine in a delicate glass, the food on a silver tray. He did
not think it would be poisoned. The emperor would not have gone through
so much pomp just to bury some pika seeds in his dinner—but perhaps
Kavic had thought the same thing before he died. "Azeem," he said, picking
up a fig from the tray though he lacked all hunger, "if I may ask, how did
my cousin die?"

Azeem stepped further into the room and folded his hands over his dark
robes. "A terrible sickness swept the palace at that time, Duke, a sickness
that turned men pale and robbed them of their wills. Many died."

"And my cousin Kavic, he went pale?"

The vizier bowed his head. "Many people did." His obfuscation was practised and perfect.

Didryk popped the fig into his mouth and motioned for Krys and Indri
to enter. The fruit had too many seeds; he choked it down. It was then he
noticed a Settu board on a low table. "Look," he said, "they have left me a
game to play. Do you know Settu, Lord High Vizier?"

"Of course—I did not expect that *you* would."

"Arigu taught me." Didryk gestured at the board and sat at the table,
pushing his chair back enough that his knees would not knock against

Azeem's. He was tall, even for his own people, and anyone who was not Fryth made him feel a giant.

Azeem settled across from him and began setting his own pieces on the board. "Arigu taught you? I thought he was your prisoner." Behind him Didryk's guards took up position at the door.

"He was, but of course we had no prison for him. We ate, played Settu, talked and drank all together." ·

"I see." Now the vizier would be imagining what kinds of things they had talked, about, especially during long nights when there was plenty of drink. He would look at Arigu and wonder if his ale-filled mouth had turned traitor. That pleased Didryk.

The game was set and it was Didryk's option to place the first tile. He put a soldier piece in front of Azeem's Tower.

"That is a bad move," said Azeem. "One soldier cannot hold against the Tower. Since the game is new to you, I will allow you to take it back."

Didryk smiled and withdrew the piece, putting down his River instead, creating an obstacle for Azeem's soldiers. "Better," said Azeem, placing a Pillar. "I wonder, did you ever win against the general? He is said to be one of Nooria's greatest players."

"I did not." Didryk pushed forward a Rock. "Though Chief Banreh won a match against him." Didryk had no sense of Banreh's fine mind at the moment, only the pain that roared along his nerves.

Azeem's nose twitched at the name.

"Have you ever won a game against the emperor?"

Azeem's hand hovered over his tile, then he pushed it forwards. "I have never played against the emperor, may the gods continue to shed their light upon him."

"Is it not allowed to play against the emperor?" Didryk moved his soldier piece again.

Azeem set out his first mage. "No one would gainsay the emperor, should he invite a person to play."

"So he does not play?"

Azeem reached for one tile, then changed his mind. "I have not seen him play Settu, Duke." He put a soldier into play and lifted his eyes to Didryk's face. "Are you well?"

"I am very well." Didryk touched his pattern-mark. Removing it would make everything easier, and yet he did not want to. He wanted to know when the pain stopped and Banreh died.

"I do not think you will win this game." Azeem surveyed the board.

Didryk shrugged. "I am learning." They played a time in silence, the tiles moving into place. He knew that if Azeem were to make his Push he would win, but he would not fell every tile—the grand vizier wanted to stretch out the game until he knew he could win them all.

"I think you are greedy," Didryk said, pouring himself another glass of wine.

"I am thorough," said Azeem, his brown eyes taking in Didryk's expression. "May I ask you something?"

Didryk motioned his permission.

"What is it like to worship a dead god?"

"I do not." Seeing Azeem's wrinkled brow he added, "That is a misunderstanding common to those who live outside the empire. I understand why you think He is dead—because He is not alive either."

"If he is not in this world then how can he help you? Mirra tends the wounded. Herzu aids our warriors. Meksha lights our fires and keeps us warm on desert nights. But your god leaves you to your own workings. Alone."

Didryk remembered it was his turn and moved a tile at random. "He gave us all the tools we needed when He left us, and He waits for us, in the place between life and death, a bridge to the light and peace on the other side." Through habit he described it as he had been taught.

"You mean that he is not alive and also not dead? That sounds like . . ." Azeem's dark fingers lingered over a tile, then he changed his mind and moved another. Didryk wondered why he still cared about a game he had clearly won.

"An abomination?" Didryk finished Azeem's question. He looked at the vizier's brown skin and eyes. "The first austere is an abomination too."

Azeem thought it a joke and smiled before motioning for Didryk to take his turn.

Didryk chose a soldier and said, "You are not from Cerana."

"I was taken from the Islands."

"A slave?" Didryk looked up in shock. "You are a slave?"

"I earned my freedom and rose far under Emperor Tuvaini, heaven and stars be with him now." He looked pointedly at the board—it was Didryk's turn once again—but Didryk leaned back in his chair. "On your Island, do you have the same gods as Cerana?"

"I learned of the true gods after I came here."

"So you have changed your mind once before," said Didryk.

Azeem smiled and made his Push. "I did not change my mind. I knew the greatest empire in the world must know the truth of it. Surely to reap so many benefits from heaven, Cerana must have the gods' favour. Who can live in the middle of the desert without the help of the gods?" Azeem's emperor caught the priest, the priest collapsed the Tower, and the Tower pushed all of Didryk's pieces from the board.

Didryk gulped the remainder of his wine and remembered what Banreh had said of Settu. "In this game both sides are Cerana, and so Cerana always wins."

"There is no foe that could win," said Azeem, rising. "The Felt with their horses? Yrkmen with their austeres? Westerners with their ships? Each have but one tile to play."

"Is that what your emperor thinks? That no foe can beat him?"

Azeem's friendly smile hardened. His gaze flickered over the fallen tiles. "Perhaps you are tired from your long journey."

"That is the second excuse you have made for me." Didryk stood, and Azeem was forced to raise his chin to keep eye-contact, though his gaze was no less steely for the difference in height.

"Will I have to make another," Azeem said, "or may I shortly return and bring you to your private audience with the emperor, heaven bless him?"

Didryk rubbed at the sand on his neck. "I will be ready." Azeem made a small bow, swept past Krys and Indri and disappeared into the rich colours of the hall.

"He was not so bad," Indri commented. Krys punched his arm.

Didryk returned to the window. The day was nearing its end at last, and the air was growing cool. He lifted his head and let it brush his cheeks. Below him, blossoms were waving in the breeze like flags and his heart twinged, remembering his home. Soon he would meet with the Emperor of Cerana, and somehow he must gain his trust. Something told him it would be harder to gain Azeem's. Whoever had laid the pattern in the marketplace had both helped and hindered him, increasing the emperor's desperation and at the same time reminding Cerana how dangerous the pattern could be. *Yrkmir*—but if they were here already, why did the first austere not order a full-on attack?

Servants arrived carrying a wide vessel filled with water and rose petals; when Didryk dipped his hand in, its warmth surprised him. He washed and shaved and ran wet fingers through his hair. After that he felt hungry at last and took a few bites of cheese, all he had time for before Azeem returned. He followed the vizier down gilded and over-decorated halls to the private apartments of the emperor, listening to a list of yet more rules and protocols, agreeing to all restrictions and demands.

CHAPTER TWENTY-NINE

SARMIN

Sarmin paced his room, twenty by thirty, twenty by thirty. Azeem did not arrive with the books he had requested, nor did Mesema take the notion to visit. He sat at his desk; a scroll lay there and idly he rolled it back and forth over the rosewood surface, thinking about Duke Didryk. He could not discard the idea that the duke had some deeper plan, some deception, in mind. And yet down to his bones Sarmin knew that he must try to repair that brief, broken friendship between Fryth and Cerana, to reach out, as he had done to Marke Kavic, and welcome another son of the cold mountains into the desert.

Finally he stood and looked out over the courtyard where the great men were taking their leave. His proclamation had caused a stir and he saw many aggressive postures in the crowd, turban-feathers bobbing, heavy rings glinting in the sunlight with every emphatic gesture. He wished he could hear their words. At last the courtiers climbed into their shining carriages, surrounded by more bodyguards than stood with Sarmin himself. They were frightened, and not without reason; between the rebels, the pattern attacks, and the approaching Storm, the city was no longer safe for them. Sarmin's window faced west, not north, but even so he could sense a darkness at the corner of his vision, a gathering cloud a thousand times larger than the one that had surrounded his brother's tomb.

When the last courtier passed through the Elephant Gate, his carriage of polished wood catching the afternoon sun, Sarmin turned from the window and summoned his sword-sons. One came forward, a tall man with a bit of vanity in his oiled ringlets, his beard shaped carefully below his lips.

"What are you called?" Sarmin at last pushed aside his fear of asking for a name. His death would be no less meaningful for the lack of it.

"Ne-Seth, Magnificence." The sword-sons kept the names given to them in their training—not Cerani names but names of power, telling who they had been and who they had become when born again into the service of empire.

"Ne-Seth." The name meant nothing to Sarmin. "Come." He left his apartments and made for Mesema's room. High above in the Great Hall workmen had already replastered the dome and were preparing for artists to press new legends upon it in gems and glass: Uthman versus the Parigol Army, Ghelen the Holy versus the southern sorcerer—perhaps even Sarmin the Saviour versus Helmar the Pattern Master. As he walked, it occurred to him that the new women's wing was too far from where he slept and conducted his business—or Mesema at least was too far.

Tarub answered the door, but quickly made her obeisance and disappeared into the corridor. Mesema paced in the room beyond, a spyglass clutched in her hand. When she saw him she cried out and rushed forwards, her arms wide, and he caught and held her, breathing in the scent of her hair.

"It's your mother," she said, pulling away, but he caught her hand, keeping her close. "She left the palace—I saw her from the spyglass. It was too far for me to call to her. I don't know where she could have gone, and there are fires in the city!"

Sarmin frowned and thought about the places his mother might go. "The White Hat barracks are outside the palace compound," he said. "Perhaps she has gone to her lover Arigu."

Mesema gasped. "She would be so bold? But she told me—" She faltered and turned away. "I did not think such a thing was allowed."

"It is not allowed, but my mother is twice widowed and nobody will take her to task as long as she's discreet." He turned her face back to his and pressed his lips against her forehead. "I will speak to her when she returns."

She pulled away again, frowning. "But are you certain? It was so strange—the guards did not see her . . ."

The more he thought of it, the more certain he was: his mother would want information about the duke, and Arigu would have it. He took the spyglass from her hand and set it on the cosmetics table, then lifted her up and set her beside it. The mirror wobbled as he leaned in for a kiss, and pots of paint and pieces of jewellery scattered to the floor. "I am certain."

And then she kissed him back, putting her hand in his hair, pulling him closer.

"I saw Duke Didryk before he went into the throne room," she said as he kissed her neck. "What was he like?"

Sarmin thought of the events in the throne room and afterwards, when Banreh's beaten body was thrown before him, and his passion cooled. He sat on the bench and faced the mirror. Beside the blue of Mesema's dress he saw his own face, thin and wide-mouthed. What did that face say about him? He remembered Duke Didryk's expression when he made his announcement about the Mogyrk faith. "His cousin Kavic was easier to read. I wish I knew for certain that he wanted peace."

Mesema slid down beside Sarmin and he watched her profile as she spoke. "Will he help us?"

"That is what he says." He looked at their reflections. It was just the two of them, with no ghosts and no brother looking out from behind his eyes. "Is that what I look like?"

She laid her head on his shoulder and watched him in the mirror. She answered him carefully. "I do not know what you see, my husband."

"My mother told me that Beyon looked like Tahal our father, fierce and powerful, while I have her delicate features." He turned his head to the side, caught up in the vanity of the mirror. "Delicate features look strange on a man."

"Nobody sees themselves the way others see them." She leaned in and kissed his cheek. "I do not see you as delicate."

"No?" He caught her mouth with his. "Come to the bed with me."

"I thought you liked the mirror." She gave him a sly look.

He glanced at his reflection. He did not want to watch that man with his wife. "No. I don't like it at all."

She stood and led him to the bed and the next long while was spent without thought. Afterwards, as they lay side by side under the light of the window, she said, "Don't you miss him?"

"I do." He turned his head to where Pelar's crib had once stood.

"I miss him terribly." She rolled onto her stomach and played with the silk. "It makes sense that your mother is only visiting Arigu. Of course she would not wander into the city and leave Daveed behind, not after missing him for so very long."

At the mention of his brother's name, the closeness he had felt to Mesema began to drift. He said nothing, but stood and gathered his robes.

She laid her head on her arm and watched him. "Have you seen the boy since the day he arrived?" she asked.

"I have not." There was no reason to see the child.

"How do you think Govnan could have made a mistake? Or Nessaket?"

"Some Mogyrk trick."

"A pattern-trick?" She wrinkled her nose in thought. "I don't think . . ."

"Austere Adam organised a rebellion under this roof while pretending to seek peace. If he is capable of that, he is capable of more deception." He tied his sash with a jerk. "You should know Arigu brought Chief Banreh back with him. He is with Assar in the temple of Mirra."

She sat up, pulling her covers around her. "Banreh's ill?"

"Hurt." He slipped his feet into his slippers. "Assar will tend to him. Do not go there, Mesema."

"He is the chief of my people. Is he dying?"

"I do not know." When she slid from the bed and picked up her dress from the floor, he added, "Do not make me forbid you, Mesema."

She paused in pulling on her silks, her eyes wide. "You would forbid me?"

They stared at one another long enough for the whiteness of the walls to begin to hurt his eyes. "No. I cannot forbid you anything. But I am asking you: do not go."

He turned towards the door, but she called out behind him, "Wait!"

"Mesema, we have said all there is—"

"Not that—look." She picked up the book of poetry he had given her, opened it and ripped out a page.

"Mesema!" Books were a rare and precious thing. In his time imprisoned in the tower room five of them had been his only friends. Ignoring his protest she took scissors from her sewing-kit and cut the page into twenty small pieces.

"I've been thinking about this," she said, laying them out on the bed, upside down and out of order. "Look. The words still mean something, but we can't read them now. Is this what the pattern looks like to you?"

"The pattern doesn't look like anything to me." He cocked his head and looked at the jumbled words.

"Maybe this is what the wounds are like: scattered images that we don't recognise."

"It felt empty." The emptiness had drained him, claiming his pattern-sight; of this he was certain. And yet her demonstration made sense. It reminded him of something the Megra had said before she died and he itched to recall what it was.

Mesema sighed, thinking he was rejecting her theory. "I didn't like that poem anyway." She gathered all the shreds of parchment and tucked them inside the book.

He smiled—he could not be angry with her for long. "I have a private meeting with the duke now, but we will talk about this later." She did not reply, and she stood on the other side of the bed, too far to touch, so he gave a slight bow before leaving.

As he walked back to his own apartments he resisted the urge to talk to Ne-Seth; it was enough to know his name. Ne-Seth did not require the friendship of an emperor; the relationship between sword-son and sword-son, forged in their harsh training and enforced through spellwork, far exceeded any other Ne-Seth could make. The sword-sons did not face their trials alone.

By the time he arrived at his own door his legs and knees were aching, but not as painfully as they had in the past. Every day his body grew stronger and became more accustomed to the demands he was placing on it.

Inside, Azeem and the duke were waiting together, making pleasant small-talk, the sort Sarmin did not have the experience to invent: weather, horses, travel, the things men saw and experienced when they lived in the world. When Sarmin entered both men ceased speaking and made their obeisances, but it was to Duke Didryk that he spoke. "So. We are allied, you and I. It was what I wanted when your cousin Kavic was alive. He let me know how strongly your people desired peace."

"We do," said the duke, and then, in a lower voice, "we did." Sweat shone on his forehead, but whether it was from the heat or from fear Sarmin could not tell.

"Kavic and I spoke briefly of reparations, Duke—the cost of rebuilding your capital city, Mondrath." Beside him, Azeem shut his ledger with a thump. Talking of money without council approval offended his sense of order.

Didryk opened his mouth twice before he could speak. "Reparations would be most generous, Your Majesty."

"If we all survive the coming Storm, we will discuss it—but let us now speak of surviving."

Didryk answered him with a curt nod, his blue eyes shifting through a range of emotions too fleeting for Sarmin to catch.

He sat down behind his desk and spread his hands across the cool wood, his reflection wavering up at him from the depths of the lacquer. "Do you know where Austere Adam is hiding?"

"No, Your Majesty. I have not been to Nooria before today."

Sarmin paused, frustrated. It would be foolish to ask Didryk about Daveed, to show his missing tiles so soon in the game, but the desire to do so nearly overwhelmed him. "What do you know of the marketplace attacks?"

"Your mage Farid told me," Didryk said, looking away. "I know what kind of pattern was used, and there are not many austeres who can make it."

"But of course it was Austere Adam," said Azeem.

To Sarmin's surprise, Didryk disagreed. "He would not kill anyone without giving them a chance to come into the light." He looked from Sarmin to Azeem. "To convert to Mogyrk."

"Then who?"

"I wondered the same." Didryk met his steady gaze. "If I knew, I would tell you."

Shock rooted Sarmin to his chair. "Are you suggesting that Yrkmir is already here?"

"It can be no one else, but it makes no sense. The first austere does not sneak."

Sarmin ran his hands through his hair. "But it fits with what General Arigu told me. He said they attack first with their austeres and then with their military. Do you not agree?"

"I do agree, but the austeres attacked my city all at once with a great spell, not like this, little by little, in marketplaces."

"Perhaps they mean to sow confusion?" said Azeem.

"Perhaps they are buying time, distracting us," said Didryk. "There is no way for Yrkmir to cast the spell they used in Fryth, not without surrounding Nooria. This is a large city, Magnificence, with many guards on the walls."

"If they tried to make a pattern right outside the city walls, yes—but they don't need to do that, do they? The pattern could be much larger, and written in the sands far out of our sight."

"Yes." Didryk leaned forwards, his hands clasped in front of him. "They could. It would take them a long time."

"Would it? How many austeres do they have?"

"In Yrkmir itself, hundreds—but I could not guess how many they have with them."

"So let's say they have hundreds: how long would it take for them to encircle us, even out in the desert?"

"Weeks only—less, perhaps."

Sarmin leaned back in his chair. "What do you know of the first austere?"

"I have never met him. Fryth is far from the centre of his empire." Didryk's fingers danced along his knuckles. "But the first austere is said to have a direct connection to Mogyrk, to understand his secrets in ways the rest of us do not. That he is capable of many feats . . ." He shrugged. "I always believed it a story to keep us in awe of the empire."

If the first austere had Helmar's skill, he would not be dabbling in marketplaces.

Sarmin turned to Azeem. "Did you find those books I requested about the Yrkmir incursions during the time of Satreth the Reclaimer?"

"Books?" Azeem scrambled to look at the notes he had written in his ledger.

"I asked the guards—never mind; I will find them myself. Meanwhile, our citizens are already leaving, but it is time to make it the law. We must order an evacuation."

"Yes, Your Majesty," said Azeem, picking up his quill and making a note as Sarmin watched him, puzzled. He would have thought an evacuation easy enough to remember.

When Azeem finished writing, Sarmin turned back to Didryk. "In the attacks we have seen, those who were patterned survived. This is also what General Arigu reported about the attack in Fryth."

Didryk blinked. "Yes, that is true. Patterns act as a ward."

"I think you speak truly." Sarmin fingered the hilt of his dacarba—Tuvaini's dacarba. "And so I see only one solution."

Didryk curled his hands around the arms of his chair, waiting. He *wanted* something, Sarmin could see the longing in his eyes. Already he had been offered an alliance, even reparations. Perhaps it was the return of his friend he wanted. Maybe it was something even greater; something related to that darkness Sarmin had seen in his eyes.

Azeem stepped forward, his quill held aloft, listening.

Sarmin looked from one man to the other. "We must mark everyone with the pattern. Beginning with the palace and our soldiers."

CHAPTER THIRTY

SARMIN

When Grada entered the room the next morning, Sarmin turned towards Ne-Seth. "Leave us, all of you."

"Magnificence," Ne-Seth intoned. The door shut behind the guards and Sarmin was left alone with his Knife. The tension that had kept him awake all night flowed out of him: he did not need to worry about appearances with Grada. He sat down at his desk and she sat opposite, though once they might have sat side by side. Grada stretched, lifting her muscled arms over her head. Her eyes were shadowed with fatigue. He did not ask her about his brother; if Daveed had been found she would have said so. The loss weighed against his heart.

"Notheen is gone," she said.

"He said nothing to me." Sarmin thought of the headman, his slow, steady voice and his calm.

"His first responsibility is to his people in the desert. The wounds spread, pushing them south."

"But I did not expect him to run with all the others." *I thought he was my friend.* But Sarmin knew that the emperor did not have friends.

Grada placed her hand on the table, close to his, then withdrew it. "Did you read the scroll I brought you? I have been watching Lord Nessen's house for some time. The empress had a vision—"

"Yes, yes, I know about that." Sarmin lifted it and unscrewed the wooden ends. "But I did not know this scroll concerned Nessen." The man was a Mogyrk sympathiser—he might be harbouring austeres, perhaps even the first austere himself.

Grada leaned back in her chair, her eyes on his face. She could not read; she would listen as he read it out loud. Sarmin unrolled the parchment and sighed when he saw the first few lines.

My darling Fatima,
How glad I am to have visited you in the time of your confinement. No greater happiness remains to me than to see my daughter in good health. Now that I have returned to our estate I see that the roses are in full bloom and blackberries grow in profusion among the rocky places . . .

It went on in that vein for ten more paragraphs and ended with an affectionate note. Sarmin was not familiar with handwritten letters. He was accustomed to reading those penned by talented scribes, and so the odd spellings and dots of black ink interested him. Out in the world, people wrote letters to one another that were not copied by a dozen trained men and scrutinised for accuracy and penmanship. A person could write a letter out of affection and make mistakes. Sarmin put it down. "It is a letter between a mother and her grown daughter. Flowers and berries. Lord Nessen did not write it. The Grey Service must continue to watch the house—or find a way into it." If the austeres were indeed hiding in the house, he could no longer wait for them to show themselves.

Grada examined the writing. "It is very long to be about flowers and berries only," she said.

"Have you ever heard the Old Wives talking? There is no end to it," said Sarmin, putting the scroll aside. He meant it as a joke, but Grada frowned at him.

"Speaking of Old Wives, I think my mother has gone to see Arigu in the barracks. If she is not returned yet, I think she will need a . . . discreet way back to the palace."

"I am your Knife," she reminded him with an ungentle tone. "Perhaps you could send one of her guards."

"A royal guard in full armour will attract attention. I need you, Grada." When she stood he felt regret. "But not yet," he said. "Please, sit with me a while longer."

She sat. "We have seen no one come in and out of Nessen's house save for his servants. We have been watching for weeks—we would not miss an austere."

"I do not think you would." He took a breath. His brief spurt of confidence had disappeared. Adam and his rebels had their run of the city. Yrkmen laid their patterns and he had not caught a single one of them. And now the first austere himself might be in Nooria. He had lost the counsel of Notheen and Govnan just when Dinar was taking a special interest in his decisions. The high priest would be angry to hear Banreh was not coming his way. If Sarmin made one false move, if his alliance with Duke Didryk did not fulfil their hopes quickly enough, there would be trouble with Herzu.

He let out a breath. "Stay, Grada, and tell me of the city."

Anyone who thought the Untouchables less intelligent, less loyal, or less able were speaking from a place of blindness. In particular, Azeem's prejudice against Grada had always irked Sarmin. The man was cleverer than that.

Grada's dark eyes moved as she spoke, taking everything in, from the papers on his desk to the sturdiness of the door, missing nothing. Finally they settled on his and he smiled. She paused in her speech, watching him with curiosity. Nothing she had said merited humour, and she was slow to read his emotions now they were no longer sharing minds as they once had—and of course he could not say that it made him happy just to hear her voice.

"Magnificence," said Ne-Seth from the door, his curls catching the morning sun, "General Arigu is here to see you."

Sarmin turned from Grada at last. "Let him in, Ne-Seth." His mother must have returned to the palace with him. He would see her after speaking with the general.

Arigu entered dressed in full ceremonial robes of thick white silk. The golden sash he wore over one shoulder housed an ornately hilted dagger, and at his hip hung a scabbard adorned with dozens of bright gems. His slippers were long and curled, stitched with gleaming thread. Despite these encumbrances, he dropped gracefully for a full obeisance.

Sarmin had wondered whether he would do so, given enough room and enough time, and he was pleased with the answer. "Rise, Arigu," he commanded as Grada stood and took her place behind his chair.

"Magnificence," said Arigu, "General Lurish and I have organised the defences. In truth, Lurish had already begun the work. War machines are in place, and we have bolstered the troops at every point along the walls. All that remains is to speak to Govnan—but he appears to be . . . occupied."

"I will arrange the placement of the mages," said Sarmin.

Arigu raised his eyebrows with curiosity. "Thank you, Your Majesty." He glanced at Grada. "I was sorry to hear of Eyul's death."

"He died bravely and rests with our greatest warriors."

"Mmm." Arigu had already forgotten Eyul. His gaze wandered around Sarmin's room. "If we may speak privately, Your Majesty?"

"My Knife can hear anything you wish to tell me."

"Very well." Arigu threw his shoulders back, presenting himself as Nooria knew him: the great and feared General of Cerana. "I have come to speak of a personal matter. Of marriage."

"Oh!" Sarmin covered his surprise. "You have likely spoken with the Empire Mother already." His cheeks reddened. "Of course I cannot object—"

"No, Magnificence, I have not seen her." Arigu tapped his fingers on the hilt of his ceremonial sword as he carefully prepared his next words.

Sarmin's stomach went cold. His mother had not been at the barracks after all—she had gone somewhere else. Mesema had been right to worry. *But where would she have gone?*

Arigu cleared his throat. "I have come to speak of my niece, Magnificence. She was too young when your brother was the emperor, heaven and stars be with him now, but I have received a letter from my sister. Now Armahan is a woman grown, and beautiful besides. I would be proud to give her to you, Your Majesty."

"I . . ." Sarmin squeezed the edge of the table between his fingers. "I did not expect such an offer. You do not know what my other courtiers already know, General, that I will have only one wife, Mesema of the Windreaders. I mean it as no insult to your niece."

Arigu frowned. "The Windreaders, my Emperor, were once an honour-able tribe and represented a great alliance for Cerana." He left it for Sarmin to put the rest together: that they were now considered traitors. "My sister's family is from Gehinni Province, which is well-versed in the ways of the water. That is the home of our navy, Magnificence."

Sarmin nodded, his mind still on his mother. "My grand vizier is yet unmarried. Perhaps you would consider offering Armahan to him."

Arigu's shock registered on his face, but it did not show in his words. "If that is your desire, Magnificence."

Sarmin realised he had given some offence. He glanced up at Grada, but she was no guide to the rules of the palace. "Well. I am honoured by your offer, Arigu. I will consider it."

Arigu bowed and withdrew, his face tight, and Sarmin leaned back in his chair.

Grada let out a sigh. "You cannot accept her, Your Majesty." Sarmin knew this, but he was curious about Grada's reasons.

"Why not?"

"Because that is not the agreement you made with the empress." Grada shifted on her feet, and then added, "It would upset her."

"Decisions of empire are not made on emotions," said Sarmin, though he did not believe that to be true.

"But you won't accept this Armahan." A question there. Even now, Grada needed the reassurance. She needed to know that if he took anyone besides Mesema it would be her.

"I wouldn't." He rubbed his eyes. "My mother was not with Arigu after all, Grada. She is missing, like Daveed . . ."

Grada came around the desk and faced him, hand on her Knife, ready.

"Will the Grey Service find her?" Sarmin realised he did not know how many agents the Grey Service had. The *Histories* had taught him that the emperor could rely on dozens of spies, but he had never thought to ask for an exact number. Now that he had given them so many tasks, he wondered.

Grada bowed. "We will do our best, Your Majesty."

"That is all I ask." He reached out a hand, but she did not take it. "That is all I ask."

She cocked her head, listening to noises in the hall. "A moment," she said, and stepped out. Sarmin did not move except to lower his hand and lay it flat upon the gleaming wood of his desk. It felt cool in the morning air.

Grada returned. "That was Meere, Your Majesty. He has caught the man who attacked the Empire Mother and stole Daveed. He has caught Mylo."

Sarmin did not even take a moment to think. "Take him directly to Dinar for questioning. He must find out about Adam's movements." That would satisfy Herzu's craving for blood and lead him closer to his brother at the same time.

Grada paused, meeting his gaze, but said nothing. She gave only a bow before retreating. It was not until she had gone that he realised what he had seen in her eyes. It had been disappointment.

CHAPTER THIRTY-ONE

SARMIN

Sarmin entered the temple of Herzu with Ne-Seth and the other guards at his back. He had forgotten how confusing it was here: statues and chairs covered the floor in no order at all and he had to pick his way through them in the near dark, the only available light resting at the foot of the great statue of the God on the far side of the temple. He squeezed between an eight-foot gryphon and an empty soapstone basin and found something of an aisle that ended at the feet of Herzu. There he paused, looking up at the terrible, cruel, fanged visage. Something glistening and bloody had been placed in its outstretched hand and Sarmin felt a wave of nausea. He looked away, not wanting to know whether they were teeth, fingernails, or something else. They had likely come from Mylo.

Dinar emerged from the private halls behind the altar, wiping his hands on a rag, leaving dark stains. "Your Majesty," he said, smiling, in a fine mood. "I have been questioning our Mogyrk prisoner."

"Indeed. I have come to find out what you have learned." Sarmin looked down at the rag and felt strong misgivings. He had heard no screams, no begging; he thought if he were being tortured he would not be so stoic.

The high priest sighed. "He speaks of nothing but going into the light, Magnificence. He says we will all be destroyed, and Mogyrk will take him to paradise. No matter how I cut him, he will say nothing of the austere, Adam."

"He is brave, then." So the man had one admirable quality. He had attacked his mother and stolen his brother away, but at least he had courage. That would not be enough to spare him, though. "I want to see him."

Dinar smiled and turned towards a dark hallway, saying, "This way, Magnificence."

Sarmin followed. At times the high priest looked like nothing more than a shadow among shadows, so dark was the corridor, but at last he opened a door into a well-lit room.

"The sacrifice," said Dinar.

Mylo lay naked upon a great golden hand. His head rested in the crook of the middle finger and the wide palm cupped his hips. His feet hung at odd angles over the edge where the broad wrist rose from the floor. Sarmin took that in quickly and made a point of not looking at what lay between those three points. Blood dripped from the hollow of the thumb onto the tiles, and Sarmin moved his feet away, his eyes taking in cuts, stripped muscle, and twisted fingers before he could turn his head to meet Mylo's gaze. Mylo looked back at him, his eyes calm.

"Where is Adam?" asked Sarmin.

Mylo looked at Dinar before he spoke. "Mogyrk will bring light to all of Nooria," he said.

At this Dinar made a sound of impatience and picked up a hammer. Mylo swallowed, but kept on, "There will be a rebirth. After the destruction—"

The high priest brought the hammer down on Mylo's foot but the man did not scream. He tensed, then turned his head to the side to allow thin yellow vomit to flow from his mouth. After several moments had passed he said, "After the destruction, we will go into the light."

Sarmin closed his eyes turned away, his own mouth filling with bile. "You are right—he will tell us nothing," he said. "There is no point in continuing to torture him."

Dinar led him into the hallway. "There is always a point to torture, Magnificence. These brave ones who last the longest—they come closest to Herzu before they die. Some even gain His favour. To offer two such men to the God in one month—this is a blessing." When Sarmin did not reply, he pressed him, saying, "When may I expect the other?"

Sarmin did not bother searching for Dinar's features in the darkness. By "the other" he meant Banreh. He swallowed the spittle that had collected in his mouth. "I have told you: when I deem it time."

"It will soon be time, I expect," Dinar said.

Sarmin wondered what he meant, but an emperor never asked such questions. He must never appear to lack knowledge. "High priest," he said, by way of goodbye.

But Dinar called after him, "Magnificence!" and he turned as the darkness shifted, revealing the vague, wide form of a man. "I would have found it preferable to kill the Mogyrks—to root them out of their hidden churches and hovels and sacrifice them all to Herzu."

Sarmin focused on where he thought the high priest's eyes might be. "I made the decision to call their worship legal." As he was the emperor, that meant it was the correct decision. He turned away and left Dinar in the shadows. Herzu had been the patron god of the palace for more than a century, their priests gathering power and influence, their hands stained with blood and their ears filled with screams. He found it difficult to believe no emperor had ever questioned their presence at court, or what benefits the empire had of such a cruel god.

Sarmin met his guards in the main temple. Anxious to leave Herzu's domain, he led them swiftly out into the corridor and through the entryway into the Great Hall. There on the floor sat the scholar Rahim, parchments spread around him. He dipped a quill into a pot of ink and looked upwards at the dome, where men on ladders were still working on the repairs. As Sarmin drew close he saw drawings of the beams that supported the ceiling.

When Rahim recognised the emperor he leapt to his feet, only to fall immediately to the floor again and prostrate himself, nearly knocking over his inkpot. "Your Majesty—"

"Rahim. What are you doing here?"

"Your Majesty, with the plaster and mosaics having fallen from the dome, it is an excellent time for me to study its construction. This dome and the one in the throne room are so wide and tall that they are true architectural wonders. It is not in my skill to build such things and so I thought I would come and take notes."

"How interesting." Sarmin had never wondered about the construction of the palace before. He had always lived in it, and so for him it had always just been here. Now he looked at the broken staircase, the doors leading off into various wings, and he realised that the palace could have been built in an entirely different way—maybe even several different ways. "Are there other scholars in the palace, Rahim?"

"Yes, Magnificence—many."

The presence of other men of learning caught Sarmin's imagination. "How many, Rahim? What do they study?"

"There are fifty of us, Magnificence, and our research encompasses the heaven and the earth. The movement of the heavens is as of much interest as the making of the human form. But lately we have been particularly interested in the construction of machines."

"I would like to see one of these machines."

Rahim bobbed his head. "Of course, Magnificence." He frowned, and then added, "But as yet they exist only on parchment, Your Majesty."

Of course. They would need workmen and materials and imperial permission to make any such works. Had his brother Beyon ever met with the scholars? "Send them to me," he ordered, and when Rahim had stammered his agreement, Sarmin smiled kindly on him and left him to his work.

The library was to be found in a forgotten corner of the palace. It was dusty, and filled with cobwebs. There were not as many volumes here as he had hoped. Perhaps over the years they had been borrowed or sent to scribes for copying and never been returned. He found several empty spaces. As for histories, he could find only two: one a recounting of Uthman's founding and the other a detailed log of his father Tahal's legal proclamations. He looked through it, curious about his father's relationship with the temple of Herzu, but nothing was mentioned about that. He put it down and continued to search. He found nothing about Satreth or the Yrkman incursions. He was still wondering what Ashanagur had meant by *Mogyrk blinds the Tower*. Was it something the Yrkmen had done in the past, or something the Storm was doing now?

His brother Beyon had obviously been no scholar—judging by the state of this room it had been used seldom in the last twenty years; he doubted it had ever been guarded. So the curious must have taken the books and scrolls that caught their interest and carried them off to the far corners of the palace to read in the comfort of their private chambers, then never returned them. The palace was large and whole wings that had once been inhabited now lay empty. Setting slaves to search every room for missing books was a demanding task, especially considering he did not have enough people even to meet the palace's basic needs.

Sarmin tapped his fingers on a shelf and looked out at the sun, which had moved from early morning to late morning. Duke Didryk waited on him in the throne room.

"Come," he said to Ne-Seth, but as he turned towards the door, a gilt-edged tome caught his eye. He picked it up and blew dust from the cover. *The Gods of Cerana.* He leafed through it. The gods painted upon the ceiling of his tower room had kept him company for so many years: Ghesh, walking between the vast spaces between the stars; Keleb, clutching His books of law; Mirra, watering a pomegranate tree, rendered in tiny sweeps of paint; Torlos, cutting down his enemies in bold, thick strokes. Herzu had been one of many looking down upon his bed, but here in the palace, he overpowered them all.

Mylo's pain still made Sarmin feel sick from shame. Death in itself was not the worst; compared to his short time on earth a man's time in heaven was endless, and a knife only brought it closer. But Herzu's ways did not reflect the empire Sarmin wanted to shape, the man Sarmin wished to be. He should not have allowed it.

But what would the courtiers say—what would the army say—if they thought him soft?

With the book in his hand and followed by his sword-sons he walked to the throne room.

CHAPTER THIRTY-TWO

DIDRYK

Didryk sat on the bottom step of the dais, blinking away his fatigue. His first day marking the palace workers was halfway done, and his second night in a high palace bed awaited him at the end of it, though he dreaded closing his eyes. His first night among those scented silks had brought him no sleep. Visions of his own burned city alongside a ruined Nooria kept him awake. In the dreams it was his own hand that sent the innocents screaming, his own hand that pulled down the stones of every building, and he could not blame Yrkmir or Cerana for the horror. He awakened with his heart pounding, unable to breathe.

In the cold light of the morning he did not know if he could follow through with his plan, but it was proceeding, whether he wanted it or not.

He had been prepared to manipulate the emperor, to nudge him towards his own goals—he had been raised in the court of the Iron Duke, taught from an early age that it was always better to let a man believe an idea his own. But it had not been necessary here: the emperor had taken all the clues and put them together in a fortunate way. The austeres responsible for the market attacks had helped his cause by showing the emperor how useful the pattern could be when it came to Yrkmir.

So now they were proceeding with the emperor's plan of marking every person in the palace. He had taught the Cerani mage Farid how to do a simple ward against harm—but each time Didryk formed one himself he added a tiny hook, a trick the newer pattern-worker was too inexperienced to recognise, that connected each person to himself. The power in each connection was so bright it surprised him. Nooria, so close to the Scar, brimmed with Mogyrk's power—and yet the Cerani were unbelievers.

With the god's strength in his fingers it would be a simple thing to turn these men and women to his will—but once again he wondered if he could bring himself to do it, to cause harm to the palace that had offered such an unexpected welcome. He did not need to remind himself that Banreh had not received the same generosity. The chief's pain ground against his mind at all times, flowing through the mark on his wrist. He had almost grown accustomed to it.

Farid had been sent to the Tower, not far from the palace, to mark the mages there; but Azeem had politely insisted Didryk remain in the throne room to do his work. Though he had spoken the words of alliance, he was not trusted away from the view of the emperor and his sword-sons; he had not been given the freedom to draw patterns throughout the palace. Considering his true motives, Didryk thought the grand vizier wise—though not wise enough. Not one of the men other than Farid could even identify a pattern-symbol, and Farid had been able to say only that the mark was a ward. Sarmin had examined it—though Didryk had been able to tell it meant nothing to him—and ordered the marking of his own Blue Shield soldiers.

The throne room held only a few courtiers, standing in small groups and whispering. Azeem had told him that on a normal day there would be a few dozen men sitting beneath the emperor, or positioned on the cushions under the dome, but the current unrest had them hiding in their manses or even fleeing the city. Those who remained were either battle-hardened, foolish, or too close to death to worry about the timing of its arrival, and it was these men who huddled in small groups and talked in low voices, often sending dark looks his way. Didryk sat on a cushion on the lowest step of the dais, and anyone who came to be marked sat on another cushion, directly opposite and slightly lower. It made it easy to reach foreheads, that was certain, but for much of the time he had his back to the emperor and his sword-sons and it made his neck itch.

Not that he would have been able to read the man's face. His grandfather, Malast Anteydies Griffon, the Iron Duke, had kept his face still as stone when sitting at court, and Emperor Sarmin was the same. In his private apartments Didryk had seen flashes of concern or curiosity in him, but here in public, sitting on the great Petal Throne, he neither moved nor spoke.

The grand vizier remained standing, his parchments before him, ticking off the names of every person marked by Didryk's design. He spoke for the emperor, each greeting as crisp and clear as the last, commanding the workers to rise, to move forwards, to accept the marks. From time to time he reassured the hesitant. The work of the Pattern Master Helmar was their chief concern; they remembered the Many and wanted no part of it. Didryk had explained to Azeem that such a thing was impossible for him to achieve; the kind of pattern built by Helmar was far beyond his ability, and that was true. He would be using a simpler, rougher force against them.

A young girl approached them now, and with surprise he noticed her red hair and deep blue eyes. She was Fryth—and as she drew closer, her feet hesitating over the runner, Didryk realised she was also blind.

At that same moment the emperor spoke for the first time, his voice kind, almost fatherly. "Just a few more steps, Rushes, and you will feel a cushion with your toes."

For this girl there would be no obeisance, Didryk realised. He watched her with interest.

Rushes smiled, stepped forwards and explored the floor in front of her with one small slippered foot.

"Just one step more." Azeem left his parchments to take the girl's elbow and helped her to sit. Didryk wondered who this young woman was, that she was treated with such consideration. Surely she could not be one of the Fryth slaves Adam had mentioned?

"Thank you," he said to the vizier once the girl was settled, and their eyes met over her bowed head.

"Of course," said Azeem, straightening. He walked back to his parchments and picked up his quill. "Rushes, also Rufynkarojna, nurse to the emperor's own brother," he intoned. There was a pause, during which Didryk could hear the emperor's robes rustling. "This man is of Fryth," Azeem said to her.

"You need not fear him. It will not hurt when he marks you, and you will not become one of the Many. This is done for your protection."

"I am not afraid," she said to Azeem in Cerani, and then to him, in heavily accented Frythian, she repeated, "I am not afraid."

Hearing his own language brought tears to his eyes. He knew so very few Fryth still alive. "Very good," he said. "Lift your head, child."

As she did so he laid a finger upon her forehead—then pulled it back with a hiss as he recognised the hand that had blinded her. "You were with Adam," he said, still speaking Frythian.

Tears welled in Rushes' sightless eyes as she nodded.

"It is best if you speak so that we all can understand, Duke," Azeem said, fingering his quill the way another man might finger the hilt of a sword.

"My apologies," he said quickly. "I told her that I could feel an evil hand in her blindness."

He heard the emperor's robes rustling again, and then Sarmin spoke for the second time that day. "Cure her, if it is within your ability."

Didryk took a deep breath and laid his palm flat against her brow. His ability had always leaned towards fixing broken bones and torn flesh, while Adam's went in the direction of harm. Now he delved into Adam's work and discovered a simple, malicious twisting of what lay behind the girl's eyes. Her sight was not ruined, but Adam had drawn a veil there, like pulling a curtain across a bright window. He knew Adam had also done something to the mage Farid, but that was something different, more of a compulsion—but for what, he could not tell. He had left it there, to his shame.

"Does anyone have a cloth to wind around her eyes?" he asked, speaking against a sudden swell of pain—not his, but Banreh's.

"I do." The empress, Mesema of the Windreaders, stood at the edge of the silk runner. Her voice lacked the harsh consonants and guttural sounds that marked Cerani speech. The men of the court watched her, whispering among themselves, disapproval on their faces, but the empress had her back to them and so was unaware. She wore an orange scarf around her neck and now she unwound it and presented it to Didryk. He had seen her before, standing above him in the Great Hall on the day he arrived, her eyes alert, her cheeks flushed. Today she looked more an empress: her face was careful, her movements measured. He believed Banreh loved the first Mesema more than the second, and wondered whether either version of her loved Banreh.

She had obviously not arranged for a doctor for him—if she had, he would not be sensing so much pain now.

"Thank you, Your Majesty," he said, trying not to sound gruff. She might not even know Banreh was in the palace—and in any case, her personal guard, six men with wide, heavy weapons, stood behind her, so it would not do to be rude. He looked away from them and wound the scarf around Rushes' eyes. "When she first starts to see again, the light will cause her pain. As time goes on, you may allow her more and more light." And then he drew away the pattern Adam had laid there.

Rushes gasped and clapped her hands together. "I can see shapes, even through the silk!" she said.

Didryk dipped his finger in the greasepaint that had been provided for him and drew a quick pattern-mark on her forehead. Though he could have done it with his fingers, the emperor liked to see what he was doing. Once finished, the shape faded into her skin, but Didryk could still see it, lit in shades of blue and yellow.

"I wish the Empire Mother was here," said Rushes. "She would be very happy that I can see now."

"She will be," the empress murmured with a guarded glance at Didryk. "Now, let's get you back to your work." She helped the girl to stand.

"A moment, Your Majesty," said Didryk, knowing this was his chance, before she left, to find a way to gain her aid. He might not get another opportunity. "May I ask if you were patterned?"

"I was," she said, turning her wrist his way. "It started with a half-moon, there."

"A half-moon?" He saw a faint mark, lighter than the fair skin around it, and to that he pressed his thumb. The men standing behind the empress drew their swords; he must be quick. With the slightest movement he drew a fingernail across her mark and imbued it with his will. *At least let him die without pain. At least that.* Right away he dropped her wrist and raised his hands. "I apologise—I have made offence by touching the empress."

"I took no offence," said Mesema, rubbing her wrist where he had scratched her. She would begin to feel Banreh's pain soon.

"One does not touch the empress." Azeem spoke without moving. The empress' men stood frozen too, and all their eyes were fixed on the emperor. Didryk stared at his pale, pinched reflection in the curved blade held by the nearest guard. Mesema held her wrist and watched her husband, and Didryk saw in her expression that he was safe. The outrage, the long pause: it was all a game of power the emperor had already won. He was reminded of Azeem, stacking his tiles. The silence stretched, a long wait meant to terrify, but Didryk relaxed and the tension in his reflected face smoothed away. If Sarmin meant to kill him, he would be dead already.

At last the emperor spoke. "Duke Didryk is a stranger to our lands. He can be forgiven this transgression. He must, after all, touch everyone if he is to ensure they are marked. Is that not so, Duke?"

"It is so. I was ensuring the empress' safety in the face of the Yrkmen threat, Magnificence."

The men behind the empress put away their swords. Their faces betrayed neither relief nor disappointment.

Mesema dropped her arms to her sides and curtseyed. "With your permission, Magnificence, I will return Rushes to her charge."

"You are dismissed." The emperor might as well have been talking to a floor-scrubber for all the love in his voice. He had shown more affection to the Fryth girl—but maybe that too was part of the act. Mesema took Rushes by the elbow and together they retreated from the room.

"That is enough work for the morning," said the emperor, and Didryk rubbed the heels of his hands against his eyes. Maybe he would sleep until it was time to return.

The men of court had been conversing all the while, in low tones and whispers, but now their voices gained energy as they discussed the pattern attacks in the city, the Mogyrk rebels, and Didryk himself. He shifted on his cushion, unsure whether protocol allowed him any movement, and watched the courtiers circle one another like sharks. One of them, a man in modest green robes, made signals to the throne with his fingers. The movements were so subtle that he doubted most people would notice— but Didryk's upbringing left him watching men's hands as much as their mouths. The man was obviously a spy.

After a moment Sarmin said to Azeem in a low voice, "Find out what Benna wants."

Azeem took his time organising his parchments, then he left the dais to speak with first one man, then another, taking an age to work his way round to the man in green as Didryk rolled his head to either side, trying to loosen the muscles. His spine hurt from holding the same position for so many hours and he needed a chamber-pot—but he wanted to see Azeem and the emperor at work.

"You must be tired, Duke," said Sarmin behind him.

Didryk turned to face the throne. Behind it stood the sword-sons, a wall of rippling muscle and biting steel. "It is not difficult work, Magnificence."

Sarmin's gaze followed his vizier's movements. "Pattern-work has been described to me as drawing from rote, like a child learning his letters. Is that so?"

"We draw upon the Names Mogyrk gave to us, which is very much like an alphabet."

"Do you have a symbol for every thing?"

Didryk frowned. "Mogyrk Named all things, but no one thing has meaning without all the others. Mogyrk pulled Himself apart to find His own essence, but even His Name by itself has no power."

"But Azeem told me that Mogyrk did not die."

"He both died and did not die." Didryk squirmed. He disliked speaking of Mogyrk. For him there were two gods: the one who helped him heal and the one who had destroyed his city.

Sarmin considered this a while. "And so you use His power and His Names to form commands?"

Something in the emperor's voice made Didryk shift again, his long legs in the way yet again as he attempted to settle on the step of the dais. His shoes were not suited to Cerani palace life either; they were stiff and hard, and did not allow for relaxing on cushions. "That is how most austeres imagine it, yes."

"But not you?" Sarmin leaned forwards, his eyes filling with a strange desire. "You imagine more?"

Didryk had said too much. He looked away, towards Azeem, who had already left the spy and was now circling back, pausing here and there to exchange more greetings. "I am no great talent." Sarmin's gaze had not left him, though. He could feel it against his back.

"I do have one question, Duke."

"I will answer whatever I am able."

"Why do your patterns disappear when you finish them? Helmar Pattern Master's never disappeared."

"Because Helmar did not finish his," said Didryk, turning to look at the emperor. "As I understand it, the pattern itself was his end: it had no other purpose—not to call or destroy, not to heal or to ward. He made no command, as you put it—not to the pattern."

Sarmin frowned, and leaned back in his throne. At last Azeem returned and spent a while shuffling his papers. Then he glanced up at Didryk, his eyes hard, before picking up his quill, leaning over to the emperor, and whispering. Didryk got the message that he was not to listen—and indeed, it was impossible to hear.

Sarmin was not so good at keeping quiet. "Arigu?" he said in a tone of disbelief.

Azeem said something else, and then Sarmin leaned towards him, saying, "Whatever rumours he is spreading . . ." Didryk heard no more, for the rest of the emperor's words had disappeared under the clash of a gong.

"What now?" said one of the courtiers, a gaunt man Sarmin had identified as General Merkel from the Jalan Hills, next to Fryth. Didryk had met him long ago, when he was just a child, but the general had not recognised him. Merkel's question was soon answered: a squad of Blue Shields entered, dust on their uniforms, their faces fatigued. They approached the dais and Didryk moved his feet out of the way as they prostrated themselves before their emperor.

"Rise and report to me," said Sarmin.

The soldiers stood and looked at one another, their eyes sad.

"Your Majesty, it is the temple of Meksha in the East Quarter," said their leader, marked out by a golden crest on the tall hat he clutched under one arm. "It has been reduced to dust."

"Dust!" General Merkel took a few steps forwards and halted, his eyes on the throne.

The emperor did not move. "Tell me."

Didryk looked at the gleaming floor. He knew it had been an austere—he knew exactly what spell had been used. He also knew it could not have been Adam. He was now certain the first austere and his men were in the city, but he did not understand why they played at petty destruction. They had given Fryth no warning, but here in Nooria they were teasing the emperor, giving him plenty of time to counter any major attack. Was it so they could play with the fragile alliances at court? He looked from one man to the other, wondering who supported the emperor and who did not.

The side door opened to allow a new courtier through. His robes left his muscled arms and calves bare, and tear-shaped tattoos marked his hands and the skin below his eyes, which flicked towards the throne with contempt. Here was one who could cause trouble for the emperor. He stalked towards the dais, and the men who had been listening to the soldiers turned to him instead.

With a start Didryk remembered that he had come here to destroy Sarmin, not to watch enemies on his behalf, and he dropped his gaze to the floor. He need only wait until enough people had been marked and Yrkmir defeated, then he would make his own move.

As the soldier and emperor continued to talk, Didryk shook off his thoughts enough to listen; he might yet learn something useful.

"—the people inside?" From time to time Didryk noted a childish, hopeful note in the emperor's voice.

"Suffocated, Magnificence." The soldier bit his lip. "We dug them out as quickly as we could, but we were not fast enough."

"Thank you. As usual, keep the area clear until the Tower can investigate."

"Magnificence." The soldiers bowed, backed away, and were gone.

The tattooed man had made his way to the dais and now he bowed. Clearly he held high status if he did not prostrate himself—or was this a power play?

"High Priest Dinar," said Sarmin, sounding bored.

"Magnificence—I heard the news about the temple of Meksha. Our patron goddess is under attack—no wonder She brews fire in Her holy mountain." The priest looked over his shoulder at the courtiers, who were watching with rapt attention, and gestured towards Didryk. "Mogyrk worship is now legal and so we resort to Yrkmir's ways, instead of traditions long established in Her Tower?"

"My decisions in this matter are not your concern."

"In this matter, perhaps not, Your Majesty. But I have been awaiting another decision concerning the prisoner. When may I expect him?"

With a jolt Didryk realised the priest was talking of Banreh.

"When I deem it time." The emperor's voice was cold.

The priest bowed and spoke in a low but urgent voice. "Your Majesty, destruction is nearly upon us. We cannot risk angering the gods further."

"I am the Light of Heaven, Dinar. The gods speak to and through me. You are dismissed."

Dinar straightened, turned, and walked out through the great doors, passing the small groups of courtiers. Their gazes followed him, their mouths stilled.

General Merkel turned back to the emperor, his eyes narrowed in accusation, before he bowed and followed the priest. His action created quite a murmur among those who remained. Even Azeem was not happy, jerking his quill and causing spots of black ink to fly across his parchments. He placed it in its box and pulled out a rag to wipe the splattered ink, his lips pinched together.

Emperor Sarmin spoke. "We will return to business this afternoon. You are all dismissed."

His cue at last. Didryk stood and bowed to the throne. "With your permission, Emperor." He could see Krys and Indri, standing behind the dais in the shadows between tapestries. In their heavy armour they must have been even more uncomfortable than he. They stepped forwards, relief on their faces.

"Of course, Duke." Sarmin waved an idle hand. "Azeem will see you to your chambers."

Azeem folded his rag and put it aside. "Of course. This way, Duke." He led him past the murmuring courtiers and through the great doors. Didryk had noticed the carvings when he had arrived, but closer attention now revealed the gods in the wood, and the way their faces turned towards the emperor. Following their gazes he saw the sunlight falling from the dome, bringing a bright glow to the Petal Throne and illuminating Sarmin's face. Surely most petitioners who approached him believed he was the Light of Heaven, as he had claimed. "It is quite a sight," he murmured.

"Yes," said Azeem, leading him on down a great corridor, "may the gods preserve it."

Didryk followed, an echo of Banreh's pain making him shiver though the palace was hot. *The gods can do what they like, but* I *will not preserve it.*

CHAPTER THIRTY-THREE

MESEMA

Didryk had done it to her. He had drawn his fingernail against her skin, quick as a rabbit, then dropped her arm as if he had done nothing. At first she had thought nothing of it, but now she recognised the feel of a binding-mark. Once she had been linked to Beyon, but he was gone forever. She remembered the desperate look Didryk had cast her from the Great Hall and knew he had been asking—was now asking—for her help. She knew where to find Banreh, even without the mark, for Sarmin had told her he was in the temple of Mirra. She longed to go to him, but instead she guided Rushes up the stairs towards the women's wing, her wrist thrumming. She would—she must—speak to Sarmin first.

"Do you think the Empire Mother will return today?" asked Rushes.

"I hope so. I wish I knew where she has gone." Nessaket had been so peculiar as she left, and the guards had also been strange, as if they could not even see the Empire Mother. When Sarmin had called Mesema to his room in the time of Beyon she had walked in a trance and the guards had not noticed her either. Sarmin had used the pattern to pull her there—and that raised a question in her mind and a fear in her heart. Had Austere Adam drawn Nessaket to him in the same way?

The doors to the women's wing stood before them and two guards heaved them open. Mesema led Rushes to Nessaket's rooms, where the babe was asleep in his crib. She patted his soft head. Without Pelar it was too quiet in her own rooms. This boy had brought some joy and comfort back to the wing, but Sarmin's words concerned her. She lifted the babe and studied his face. He had Beyon's fierce eyes.

A surge of pain roiled from Mesema's wrist, spreading over her skin, and her knees buckled. *Banreh!* "Rushes—take him." She spoke with urgency and as the girl took the boy into her arms, she doubled over, breathing heavily.

"Are you well, Your Majesty?"

"I am fine." She turned to go. "Take care of him, the poor child." What if Nessaket failed to return and Sarmin continued to reject him? She did not care to think of that. Sendhil supported her elbow as she made her way back to her room, and once inside she curled up on her bed.

After an hour twisted and turning in the sheets she at last fell into a fitful sleep, waking some time in the afternoon with her hair stuck to her clammy skin. She slid from the bed, touched her feet to a spinning floor and just made it to her chamber-pot before sickness overcame her.

Tarub ran into the room and placed a cool towel on her brow. "I saw you were ill as you slept, Majesty," she said. "Here, I will help you return to your bed."

"No," said Mesema, "I will go to High Priest Assar of Mirra." If this was how Banreh felt then she must see him. She could no longer wait for Sarmin.

"But you are not well enough, Majesty! Let me call him to you."

"No." Mesema clutched her stomach, but the second wave of nausea had passed. "Just make me look decent."

Tarub clucked her tongue, but she summoned Willa and together the two women washed the sweat from her skin, put her in a new gown, and combed her hair. Mesema looked in the mirror and found the result not beautiful—but that did not matter. She held the cool towel to her forehead one last time before exiting the room. Her guards followed, but not without question. "Willa said you were ill and not to be disturbed, Majesty," said Sendhil. "Are you certain it is safe to be walking through the palace?"

"It is never safe," she answered, "but I must speak with Assar in the temple of Mirra."

"I hear the prisoner is there." Sendhil's voice held a note of concern.

"Assar will be with me, Sendhil," said Mesema, "and in any case the prisoner is the chief of my people."

"With the Empire Mother missing, we must be extremely careful. The wife of the emperor should not—"

She sank her fingernails into the palms of her hands. "I told you, Sendhil, I will have none of your lessons."

They walked the remainder of the way in silence, though she could feel Sendhil's worry and disapproval with every step. At last they wound their way to the temple wing. Mesema glanced into the temple of Herzu as they passed and broke out in a new sweat. Whether it was from the god of pain or Banreh's sickness, she could not tell. Once in Assar's realm the peace and greenery comforted her, though the flower-scents caught in her throat.

Assar rushed around the fountain to greet her. He was not muscular like Dinar, but soft and well-covered; that combined with his large brown eyes to present a kindly image. She had always thought that if she were younger she would like to wrap her arms around him. "Empress –Your Majesty! It is an honour. Have you come to see the new roses?"

"No, Assar. I am ill."

"Then please, Majesty, sit, and I will examine you."

Though the bench looked tempting she kept on. "No; I will see the prisoner. I know he is here." Her wrist felt on fire, and it pulled to her left. She followed it, passing roses and tall grass growing in pots.

"I am not to allow visitors, Your Majesty."

"The emperor disallows even me?"

"Not the emperor, Majesty." Assar hastened to step in front of her. "High Priest Dinar."

She stopped, lest she bump into him and cause her guards to overreact. "*Dinar* gives orders to the High Priest of Mirra?"

"Not always, Your Majesty, but prisoners fall into his realm, and so—" Assar gestured helplessly towards the jasmine. "The flowers are mine and prisoners are his. Please let me tend to you, my Empress."

"No, do not tend to me: tend to the prisoner, for that is what ails me—his pain." A sudden anger overtook her. "Why, Assar? Why would you not treat an injured person in your temple?"

"Because the pain brings him closer to Herzu." Assar looked at his slippers and spoke in a low voice. "Herzu is the favoured god of this palace and always has been. He casts the illnesses and brings war to the men; I treat those who fall."

"But not all of them, I see." She stepped past him and continued, "Chief Banreh must at least have something for the pain. Dinar can speak to me personally if he does not like it." Assar and the guards followed behind her without speaking.

Banreh lay on a stone slab behind a wall of flowering vines—or at least her wrist told her it was him; his face was too swollen to recognise, mottled as it was with red and blue and too pale in the few places free of injury. He wore nothing but strips of white linen wrapped from his ribs to the tops of his bloodsmeared thighs. Her gaze went to where the bones in his leg were out of place. She had never seen his injury before, the old scars crisscrossing his knee and the shin bending the wrong way, for he had never swum in the spring streams or trained bare-legged in the summer. Now she saw the duke might have healed his leg, but not enough.

"Mesema." He raised his fingers. She had not thought him conscious, but now she hurried to the head of the slab. His curls were gone and his green eyes were nothing but narrow slits. His words were slurred when he spoke, and that bothered her more than his injuries. He had always been well-spoken, always the diplomat. "Do you remember what Great-Uncle said?" He spoke in their own language, in the affectionate tone.

Without thinking she took his hand, feeling the weakness of his grip. "That I was to create a new leader, and with him, more glory than we have ever seen."

"And did you?"

"Yes, I had my son. Pelar."

"You think he meant your son? I have wondered." He licked his lips and she looked around for water. "Because he did not say 'give birth,' only 'create.' Is it not odd—I thought it could even be me."

"You? I did not create you." She realised that in his presence she was free of his pain: that must be the purpose of the mark, to monitor his health when he was not in sight. Banreh had said Didryk was a healer.

"You had a hand in the man I became, just as you have had a hand in the man the emperor has become." He coughed, pink bubbles on his lips. "Or it could be you."

"Shush," she said, and looked to Assar. "I need water."

"Your Majesty," said Sendhil, his eyes on where her hands touched Banreh's, his voice a warning. She ignored him and accepted the flask of water from the high priest. She held it to Banreh's lips. "Assar will do what healing he can now."

"Your Majesty—" Both Sendhil and Assar spoke in unison.

Banreh moved his head from side to side. It looked a painful movement. "Don't worry about that. Mesema. Listen. Did you find the slaves?"

"No, I—"

"Empress." Dinar's voice resonated over the plants and fountains. He stood near the flowering vines, his broad shoulders blocking the view of the path behind him. "What an unexpected joy, Your Majesty." His dark eyes gleamed with triumph. "Are you catching up on family business?"

He mocked her, and so she made herself haughty. "I do not care for your tone. I am speaking with the chief of my people."

"You are speaking with the traitor." He turned to Assar, who shrank from his glare. "You allowed this tryst to occur?"

"I could not stop her," said Sendhil.

For a moment everyone stared at the guard who had spoken out of turn. Then Dinar continued as if Sendhil had said nothing, "She is touching that man. Assar, I trust you will testify to that."

"Testify?" Mesema's hand where she held the flask was sweaty, and she gripped it harder so as not to let it drop.

Dinar smiled. "Arigu could have chosen better, and at long last, he has."

"What are you—?" Mesema put it together. "Arigu will not prevail. Sarmin knows what kind of man he is."

"But he will also know what kind of woman you are."

At last her guards drew their swords, for the insults had become intolerable. Mesema met his smile. "What did you think would happen? My guards are sworn to protect my honour. I am the empress. When my husband hears—"

"When your husband hears that you were here, speaking with the traitor in secret words, holding his hand like a lover, he will have no choice but to cast you aside." Dinar spoke through a rigid smile. "Once they have heard the truth, the army will not have you. The priests will not have you. The Old Wives will not have you." He stepped forwards. "You, Mesema of the Grass Tribes, will be anathema."

Sendhil held his sword at the ready. "Your Majesty?"

At that moment Mesema knew the best course would be to cut the man down—as a man and as a witness he was better gone. But she could not kill Assar, too—and how would she explain the death of the most influential priest in the city to the soldiers and the generals? She held more sway over Sarmin, and he held more sway over the military, making them roughly equal. For many years she had watched her father and she knew an equal enemy must be neutralised before he could be killed.

She stepped back. "You should watch your words, Dinar."

The priest would not stop smiling: he knew she could not kill him. He gave a shallow bow. "Majesty." With a glance at Assar he was gone.

Banreh coughed and she held the water back to his lips. "You must find the slaves," he murmured. "You *must.*" His head fell back against the slab.

But Mesema was not so certain that would be enough.

While she and Dinar held equal power Arigu stood over them both, as the best strategist and the most well-liked general of the White Hat Army. Sarmin would forgive much from the man, especially with Yrkmir coming; this she knew. "I must go," she said, putting the flask of water beside him. "Assar, give him something for the pain." With that she turned and made her way from the temple, her men behind her, her thoughts running ahead, not even watching where she turned or climbed stairs. She did not even feel the pain of Banreh's wounds returning until she had opened the door to her room.

CHAPTER THIRTY-FOUR

GOVNAN

Govnan stood at the desk of the high Tower room and looked out over the god's wound, stretching from the river as far west as he could see and looming over the northern walls. A spyglass was no longer required to check its progress; anybody in the city could see it now, rising to the north as grey and featureless as fog. The attack on the temple of Meksha had been all that was needed to draw it closer. The pale sickness would be upon them soon, and with it the djinn who rode the emptied.

Emperor Sarmin had given him a command to stop the Storm, and he would do everything in his power to obey. If he did nothing else during his tenure as high mage, he must find a way to protect the city. Over the last few months he and Moreth had tried all of the knowledge they possessed—and some they did not, delving into the ancient spells they did not know how to work—and had achieved nothing. One thing Lord Ashanagur had said offered hope: *the Great Storm does not see me.* The hope had stood like a crack of light through a door, but he had not known how to push the door open—not until he had seen the Blessing, running unharmed along the edge of the Storm.

196

He looked over the parchments on the table. They understood so little about the Yrkmen, even after centuries of rivalry. He saw no similarities between Tower magic and the pattern. The runes he used were secret words of control. He did not need to arrange them—he used the word and his will, which was strong. But the Tower's strength was fading; even down to its cracked wall.

A copy of the binding-mark Sarmin had seen on Chief Banreh's wrist lay discarded on the table. Farid had not been able to identify that one, but he had identified another as "fire." Govnan examined them both. Could the magic of Yrkmir and Cerana together be his answer?

It was dangerous to fool with pattern-magic: the marketplace attacks had shown him that much. And yet he dipped his quill in the ink and made a bonding mark, replacing the original symbol with the one for fire. Nothing happened as he drew the last line—there was no flash of light or shaking of the earth—but Farid had warned him that no small part worked on its own. He lifted it, the ink still wet, and pressed it upon his skin, leaving a mirror image on his wrist. Night had fallen and the air around him turned cold. He shivered.

A loud crackle brought Govnan's attention to Meksha's flame in its black basin. It had grown brighter, louder, hotter, and he felt its heat from where he shivered by the window. With the night's cold a longing stirred inside him and he found himself beside the blaze. He passed a hand through it but he felt no warmth. Though it responded to the pattern-mark, this sacrificial flame gave only a dim reflection of true fire. Govnan knew true fire, and he desired it more than anything.

"Govnan," Mura called from the doorway. He turned to look at the young mage he considered a daughter, her dark hair and flowing robes, and felt proud. Beside her hulked Moreth, his face sculpted by worry.

"Come, come my children," he said, waving them in. "Where is Farid?"

Mura answered, "At the barracks, marking the soldiers."

The mages entered and sat together at the table, looking like children at class, and he laughed. Moreth was big as two men, yet he watched the high mage like a wide-eyed pupil.

"But you are grown now," he told them, "and the Tower will soon be yours. The two of you, and Hashi."

"And Farid," said Mura.

The cold still pressed around Govnan and he longed for the warmth an elemental would bring. "That will be for you to decide. I want to tell you both that I know you will succeed. Though our numbers are few, we have ever been wise and capable."

Moreth leaned forwards. If stone could burn, then it burned in his eyes. "What are you telling us, High Mage?"

"That unusual things are about to happen, and I do not know how they will end. But whatever occurs, I know my children will succeed. You will address the crack in the Tower and you will address the Storm as the emperor, heaven bless him, requires."

Mura blinked. "I just found my way home, Govnan—do not leave us."

Moreth took her hand.

"A mage of the Tower takes an oath to serve the empire, no matter the cost. That oath lies ten times as heavily on the man in that iron chair." He touched Mura's cheek. "You and Amalya were joys to me. And you, Moreth, you have come so far, in less than a year. My accomplishments are small, but not in this. Not in this."

Mura stood, a tear on her cheek, speechless.

"Where are you going?" Moreth's voice scraped with sorrow.

"To the realm of fire." Even speaking of it set a rush of desire rippling through his bones.

The rock-sworn stood. "Then I will go with you."

"No—it may not go well and I will not have you harmed." He put a hand on Moreth's shoulder. "You may help me down the stairs, though."

"Yes, High Mage." Moreth took Govnan's arm and together they stepped towards the door. Govnan stopped to put his hand on Mura's cheek. "My girl," he said. And then he left her.

He and the rock-sworn descended one storey after another, Moreth silent, Govnan brooding. He remembered Sarmin's threat to tear down the Tower, and thought to himself that something a bit wider and shorter might well suffice in its place. He smiled.

"What amuses you, High Mage?" asked Moreth, his granite eyes on the stairs.

"Only that everything ends, and that is not always a bad thing. Listen to me, Moreth. I *will* go into the portal alone."

Moreth's hand clenched around Govnan's elbow. "I have control of Ror-swan, High Mage."

"You do, but the power Meksha gave us may be weakening—thus the crack." In truth, it had been weakening for centuries, since the time of Satreth the Reclaimer, who had defeated the Yrkmen and driven them from Nooria the first time. "I will not risk you. Once I open the portal you must stay away from it."

Moreth was silent a long while, but at last agreed with a low grunt. They reached the lowest level and Moreth turned to him with a bow. "Thank you, High Mage, for all you have taught me. I will endeavour . . ."

"I know you will." Govnan patted his shoulder. "Now, Moreth," he said, beginning to draw his runes, "it is time for you to go." To his relief the rock-sworn made no complaints, and he heard his feet, heavy on the stairs. He continued his work, the runes glowing at first, then bursting with light.

He made his last stroke and the four portals stood before him in all their wonder. To the realms of water, rock, and air, he gave only a passing glance; he was not familiar with them. Fire, he knew; fire he wanted. He stepped through into a world of streaming colour. The great red sun burned low in the sky and rivulets of flame danced around his feet.

He took a step forwards, but a figure of molten brass rose before him, blocking his way. It had chosen the shape of a woman, well-formed and tall, hair streaming yellow threads of fire. Govnan recognised Amalya's form and knew the spirit mocked him, for it was the elemental that had consumed her. "I come to treat with Lord Ashanagur, Metrishet."

The mouth opened, dripping metal, showing teeth and a tongue that glowed coal-hot. "You will not."

"Step out of my way, fire-spirit, or I shall have you as my own."

"Old flesh-and-bone!" It grabbed its stomach in the imitation of laughter. "You have not the strength."

He drew a rune upon the air, the Cerani symbol of bonding. The spirit shuddered and gave a high scream, but Govnan did not end there. He added another, the same one inscribed on his own wrist, a symbol of the dead Mogyrk god. Molten brass shed from the spirit's form, pooling in the flames at their feet, and it shrieked and cried as its legs dripped to nothing and its chest cracked and shattered. At last only its head remained, and then Govnan saw nothing but its open mouth, glowing red, sounding its agony.

He reached out for it, saying the words, and they joined together. *Metrishet.*

Govnan at once remembered the feel of heat through his veins, the rush of power as he wrestled the spirit's will. He had been a young man the first time, but age had not weakened his determination.

"Metrishet, you will obey me and serve the Cerani Empire." Metrishet struggled and squirmed within him and he stumbled, falling to his knees. "You will obey me," he said again, and pressed the mark on his wrist . . .

. . . and fell into an alien world. All was dark, and need, and hatred. *I am stuck. I am stuck.* He struggled to get free, a wild fear driving him to thrash and claw against that which held him. *I will kill it.* Govnan lifted his arm and a plume of fire rose high against the sun, dancing blue across the red sky. He longed to devour his captor, to burn away the flesh and turn its bone to ash, for the fire was part of him now, its workings no matter of command but of instinct.

He fell upon his hands in the realm of fire. "No—!" He controlled the seething anger, the terror. *It is not mine,* not *mine.* "You will obey me in all things. You will serve Cerana."

Yes.

It was only one word, but the struggles ceased. It had been this way the first time with Ashanagur; once the fight was over, the elementals calmed and began their long wait for a sign of weakness, for the mage's control to slip. But this time it was different; this time the spirit could not hide its thoughts from him. He checked his wrist. The pattern-mark was still there.

Govnan stood, feeling ten years younger, and continued towards the lake of fire. Mages of his era did not take more than one elemental. It was difficult enough to control a single spirit, and the risk of being overcome was several times greater for each one beyond the first. And yet it had been done—by Ghelen the Holy, and by many who came after him. Those men had lived only six years, six months, six weeks—not the extended lifetime enjoyed by Tower mages today. But that no longer mattered.

At the edge of the lake he held out his staff and Ashanagur responded, leaping from the depths like a dolphin from the sea, aimed straight at Govnan. "Deceitful—"

"I made no oath," said Govnan, drawing the runes in the air, his staff adding power to the incantation. Ashanagur's glory, the midnight-blue and ebony-black of its flame, its train of orange light and the essence of its heat, shrank to a bright nimbus around the tip of his staff. He marked it with the pattern, standing fast against Ashanagur's complaints. The Lord of Fire knew Govnan well; it knew all the weaknesses that came upon him in the dead of night, and fought hard—but it could not overcome Cerana and Yrkmir together.

Blood running hot from his conquests, Govnan sought more: here, a lesser spirit, there a greater one, and joined all to his will, his mind, each one making him stronger against the next. He did not know how many hours he spent in Ashanagur's realm, raiding the lake of the lord contained within him, but at five, he could hold no more. Fire crawled from his nose and wound about his tongue; when he moved his hands, his fingers left a trail of white flame. He returned to the portal. In the Tower it was dark, but he lit the basement room with orange.

We go to the wall.

It does not know what we are.

It cannot see us.

Govnan turned to the stairs and began the climb.

CHAPTER THIRTY-FIVE

FARID

"There's nothing here." Farid looked around the abandoned marketplace that still carried the old smells of fish and vinegar. He felt more comfortable in the city, where he had never worried about his speech or his manners, than the Tower, but that also made him sad. He did not think he would ever return to his tiny apartment over the fruit-market. He tightened the belt over his robes—he was constantly worrying that they would fall open and reveal his nakedness, and he spent a lot of time arranging them carefully so they would not get tangled or caught in his sandals.

"Are you certain? Look more closely at the stones." Grada leaned against the wall, her eyes flicking over the few brave hold-outs who were still buying and selling in the tiny clearing between the buildings. Farid was not sure whether she was his guard or his boss, or something else entirely. She was clearly an Untouchable, but she had equally clearly been elevated by the emperor into a position of high prestige—her comfort in moving through the palace and the barracks told him that much. She had interrupted his work marking the soldiers to tell him about the destruction of Meksha's temple, and to pass on the emperor's order: that he look for patterns that might warn of another attack.

And so he looked.

"Look, I don't have to crawl around on the ground to know there's nothing here. I could see a pattern if it was all the way at the corner." He pointed. He had not slept yet, and she had dragged him around the empty streets for hours. Exhaustion set an edge on his every word. He wanted to return to the Tower and its promise of old patterns written on parchment, though that was beginning to feel like a distant dream.

"All right," she said, pushing off from the wall, "on we go."

"And what do we do if we find one?"

"You get rid of it."

"I don't know how."

Grada ignored him and walked off. He ran after her. "I can't undo one of those without . . . making it happen. If I can even do that."

"Stop worrying. We haven't found one yet."

Farid sighed. "I thought I would be taking lessons from the duke." More than that, he wanted the duke to undo whatever it was Adam had done to him. He felt healthy enough, and he certainly didn't feel controlled as the Patterned had once been, but it nagged at the back of his mind all the time, that Adam might still hold some part of him.

"There will be talks and more talks before that happens," Grada told him. "In the meantime, make yourself useful. I want you to check for patterns on a manse I've been watching."

He did not reply, but he kept his eyes open, looking at every street-stone and wall they passed for pattern-marks. In this part of the city the roads were narrow and every alley looked like night-time. He remarked on how empty the streets had become—without people to distract him he could see the cracks in the stones, the sand lining the edges of buildings.

As they approached the Blessing he saw fading paint, crooked doorways, leaning buildings. The whole city gave off an air of decay—his great city. He could not remember when that had started to happen.

"Stay near me," Grada ordered. "We'll have to cross the river to get to the Holies." They couldn't use the Asham Asherak Bridge, for it had fallen in the quake, but Farid's steps slowed as she turned and headed north.

The massive grey blur stood closer now, rising over the northern walls and stretching up towards the sky, and he could feel its pull, even from here.

Either through bravery or ignorance Grada paid it no mind as she made her way to the next bridge, Farid following reluctantly in her wake. She looked at the other side of the river, where they could see Blue Shields engaged in a battle with rebels, and stopped. He watched them, five soldiers against twice that number, but the five had the upper hand. Occasionally a shout carried over the water, but otherwise the swordplay was strangely silent, like a moving painting. One man lay on the bank, his head covered with blood.

"We'll have to go further north," said Grada.

She started to move off, but Farid remained where he was. "Can't we try south?" There were plenty of bridges there, five in all, between Asham Asherak and the Low Gate.

Grada said only, "Come, we cannot linger."

At the next bridge, she considered a luxurious boat drifting south. Its gunwales had been gilded, and instead of nets or fish buckets, plump silk cushions filled its length. Men in fine robes lay across them, sharing a bottle of wine. "One of them might recognise me," she said. "We will go further north."

Still Farid followed, though every part of him warned against it. The next bridge was barred for repairs and Grada slowed, looking around. They had reached the northernmost section of town, near the Worship Gate, and Farid felt a prickling along his skin: the void, that grey fog that his gaze could not hold, was near.

Grada must have known it too, for she glanced towards the wall and cursed under her breath.

Hiding his shock at her unwomanly language, he said, "Perhaps that boat has moved further south now and we can cross down there?"

She did not reply, so he occupied himself by looking for pattern-marks, first on the docks and then in the alleys leading east into the city. It was then he saw two bare legs, sticking out from a shadowed doorway. His unease deepened, but he motioned to Grada and said, "Someone's hurt."

"We do not have the time," said Grada, but she followed him when he went to investigate.

Even as he moved closer he was dreading what he might find, for he was no healer—he had been a mage for only six days.

Inside the doorway a woman was lying on her back, staring at the sky. She was not dead—not yet, at least—but had succumbed to a strange illness that drained all her colour. Her hair had turned white, as had her skin, which was nearly translucent under the sun. Blue veins tracked the curve of her cheeks like pattern-lines.

The woman moved her mouth as if to speak, but no sound came forth.

Grada took a step back. "It's the pale sickness," she said. "I have not seen this for some time." When Farid moved away too she added, "It is not caught from person to person, else everyone in the city would have died months ago."

Farid looked from one end of the street to the other: there must be a temple of Mirra somewhere nearby. He did not wish to stay near the emptiness for any longer than necessary, but he could not just leave this woman on the ground. "We need to take her—"

Before he had finished his sentence the pale woman arose, moving as if pulled by strings. She turned her face his way and a dreadful smile cracked her lips. Her eyes, which had been white, now shone icy-blue.

"A djinn," said Grada, drawing a knife from her belt. "The djinn take the empty bodies. Get back."

He obeyed at once, pressing himself against the opposite wall, and Grada faced the pale woman, slightly crouched, her strange, twisted knife at the ready. The woman laughed, a high, keening noise, and swiped at her with a claw-like hand. Grada ducked, then swung—and frowned when the knife made only a shallow cut. He got the impression she did not miss her mark very often.

"Stay back," she repeated, though he had no wish to get involved in this fight.

Farid watched in horror. The pale woman passed in and out of the sunlight swinging at Grada, and in the barrier between light and dark he made out a shimmer over her shoulders, a ghostly shape that was arching its back and crooning in ecstasy. "Higher, Grada," he murmured, not believing his eyes. "The djinn is above her."

The pale woman turned his way, fury in her eyes, and with a high shriek she rushed at him, brandishing clawed fingernails, her teeth bared.

Grada took aim and threw the knife over the woman's head. The blade caught in the air, scintillating with blue light, the djinn's form writhing around it. Grada grabbed the knife by the hilt and pulled upwards, slitting open the transparent creature. No blood fell to the ground, but a darkness showed along the edges of the cut as if she had sliced through to some lightless place beyond. The pale woman crumpled to the ground.

Farid blinked: the darkness was gone. Grada bent to pick her knife from the stone, then stood and looked towards the end of the alley. He followed her gaze and saw more colourless people, their mouths twisted into sadistic grins, their fingers curved forwards.

Grada backed up, pulling him with her. "Come; this way," she murmured, and they started moving eastwards now, away from the river and the bridges—and away from the Holies, where they had meant to go.

They reached another corner and took their bearings. Grada turned, but Farid pulled at her arm. "Not north," he said, "please." No sooner had he spoken than he saw three more people who had been emptied: a man in clothes so ragged they hung off him in shreds, a pale Blue Shield, and a young boy, all cackling, their own wills gone now, their bodies subject to the pleasures of the djinn who rode them. Grada pushed Farid back beneath a wooden stairway and ran to meet the attack.

The ragged man swung at Grada first, the soldier right behind him and both cawing with delight. Grada dodged out of their way, then jumped as the boy ran at her, pulling out her knife and spinning, cutting through the ragged man's neck. He fell in a spray of scarlet, his djinn detached now, rendered powerless, its face contorted with rage in the shadows where Farid could see it.

Grada backed off, glancing at the street behind, giving herself space.

The boy whooped and got on all fours like a sand-cat. His eyes had turned bright blue, like the pale woman's before him, but a crack ran down his irises, as if they were made of glass and had been broken. The boy ran at Grada at the same time the soldier took another swing; she crouched and extended her arm and her knife glowed blue as the boy slid limply to the stones. Without stopping, she pulled up on the soldier's leg, tripping him. When he fell she slid her blade through his ribs. Throughout the fight she moved with economy and precision, her body, which had once looked ungainly to him, now moving in a smooth dance.

Grada stood and examined her arms and stomach, as if looking for a wound.

"Are you well?" called Farid. He felt ashamed to have been hiding while the woman fought, though her skill was the greater. He stepped out from where she had shoved him.

Grada nodded, holding a finger to her lips.

He looked down the street and saw them, fifteen or twenty pale men and women. "How—?" But he stopped, the question unasked. He knew that the "how" never counted for anything. When his mother had died there was no understanding how blue marks could have taken her. There was no understanding this either.

Grada took his arm and pulled him up the street, further north, and he stumbled. Her callused hand was hard enough over his forearm to make a bruise. "I can't fight all of them," she said, her voice urgent. "We'll need to hide." They passed tall buildings, a shrine to Ghesh and a plaza with marble benches. As they approached the Worship Gate he stalled, the hair rising on his arms. "Over here," she said, and gestured to a small building designed for storing crates and barrels that came south on the Blessing—little used of late.

But they did not go inside. Instead, she hoisted herself up to the roof and held down a hand for him. It was only when he'd scrambled up on the roof next to her that he realised they were the only people on this street who had not been emptied of colour and mind. Everyone else had fled.

The pale folk came at the storage shed, their mouths wide, their eyes fierce with unwholesome pleasure. The first three riders Grada dispatched with throwing daggers, her aim as remarkable as it was deadly. That done, she patted herself as if looking for further weapons. "I don't have my bow," she said. Her voice always held that same tone of regret, no matter the situation.

"I can do nothing," he said, ashamed again, but his eyes caught smoke and he pointed. "Look."

The fire had attracted the eyes of the pale folk too and now they lost interest in Grada and Farid. They turned from the building and headed towards the flames as if drawn by the warmth and colour.

"What is it?" asked Farid, but Grada only shook her head.

A ball of blue flame hit one of the pale women. She shrieked and flung open her arms as the blaze rose up to consume her. Only now did Farid realise the fire was not an accidental one, a spill of flame from hearth or candle that shifted as the wind carried it. No, this fire was moving deliberately, with purpose. An emptied man was taken next, the outline of his body lost in a bolt of yellow shot with blue—and then another went, and the next, each figure dissolving in an impossible tide of heat.

And behind the wall of heat was a man. Fire roiled from him like water from a fountain; it licked against his skin and spread blue fingers beneath his feet. White-hot flame shot from his fingers and tendrils of light played over his gleaming scalp.

Over each shoulder was spinning a ball of flame both terrible and lovely to behold; it was black cracked with crimson on his right and on his left, blue streaked with the brightest orange. Behind him followed a woman made of liquid brass, her hair yellow fire, heat shimmering from her nakedness. Wherever they stepped the stones turned red-hot beneath their feet. On either side of the street buildings crackled and caught, then roared into white-hot infernos. The man kept on towards the wall and the Worship Gate, consuming one pale person after another, until at last he sent a wave of liquid flame sizzling over the stones and the road lay empty and char-black.

It was then the fire-mage turned their way, his coal-bright eyes searching, his hand raised to take them in a pillar of flame. Grada pulled him back behind the peak of the roof, but Farid could not look away, for he recognised Govnan, taken by his magic, caught in a world of power and destruction. He had a sense of how sweet that might taste, and he wondered if the high mage would soon be consumed himself, just like those statues at the base of the Tower.

But after a moment the high mage lowered his hand and turned away to continue his march to the wall. So he had recognised them; somewhere inside the living flame, Govnan remained.

Govnan reached the Worship Gate and held out a hand to the chain. Red-hot metal ran down the iron bars, which warped and gave under the intense heat.

"He is going to stop the Storm," said Farid.

"Time to leave," said Grada, pulling him down on the far side of the structure, "before we burn too."

Farid's feet hit the street-stones, warm beneath his shoes, and he kicked at them, wondering at the heat. The Tower of Cerana was indeed powerful. A great honour had been bestowed on him along with these uncomfortable robes. He smiled and tightened his belt before letting Grada pull him along again. He would find a way to make himself useful. Those ancient patterns were the key.

CHAPTER THIRTY-SIX

FARID

F arid ran his fingers along the brass surface of the Tower door. Everything seemed malleable now, destructible—even the Tower. The thought both shocked and excited him. He rang the bell.

Mura opened the door and when she saw him, her mouth curled into a sad smile. "You came back." She waved him through into the statue-lined corridor.

This time he studied the rocky faces with more interest and respect. "Tell me about Kobar."

"Pratnetun took him a few years ago." She ran a finger down the former high mage's shoulder. "Moreth reminds me of him: slow to action, slow to thought, but steady. He missed very little."

Farid studied Kobar's face. He looked as if he might have been kind. "And Govnan?"

"You are so solemn." She bowed her head. "Is he dead, then?"

"No. I saw him at the north wall, trailing spirits of fire. You might have seen the smoke from one of the high windows."

"I did." Her eyes went past him to the door and it swung closed.

Farid raised his hand, intending to touch her shoulder, but then he thought better of it.

Mura turned for the stairs, saying, "He will give his life to stop the Storm."

"He is nearly there. He had reached the wall when I saw him."

"The Storm is further away than it appears." She took a breath. "It is so large that it becomes difficult to gauge its distance. But you must be tired. Your bed does not look slept in."

"I don't want to sleep." He followed after her, taking the steps at a jog. "I want to look at the patterns Govnan was showing me."

"You have done too much," she said. "You've been out in the desert and the palace, and then into the city, and now, instead of sleeping you want to look at patterns."

"I forgot that I did so much," he admitted.

"You will sleep first." She continued up the stairs and before long Farid's legs were aching and he had to slow his pace. Mura was right: he did need to sleep. At last she opened the door to his high, stone-walled room with its narrow window overlooking the river. Days ago the river had been crowded with boats; now he could see only one raft, filled with desperate citizens fleeing south.

"It is for the best," Mura said, peering past his elbow. "They will be safer in the southern province."

He turned, blushing, for Mura stood between him and his bed and she had no chaperone. "You should go," he said. "I wouldn't want anyone to think that you—"

She gave a brief smile. "In the Tower we are not men and women but comrades and fellow mages. As children, Hashi and I slept in the same room."

He had not been raised that way, and he wondered whether he could live among women without noticing them. He looked again at Mura and that quick glance told him he could not. "Hashi?" He had met only Moreth and Mura so far.

"He's not here any more." She walked out into the corridor, then turned back. "He went south too. Sleep well." With that she closed his door and was gone.

Farid sat on the edge of his bed. He could not help but admit he was tired, but the patterns called to him. Govnan had shown them to him so briefly but still he remembered them, their depth and their complexity. He lay on his back and watched the ceiling. A vision of Mura rose in his mind, teasing him, but he pushed it away. "Stupid," he told himself. They were meant to be comrades, like two soldiers on the wall—and soldiers they would be if Govnan died. The business of the Tower would be left to Mura, Moreth, and himself. He could not even guess what Tower business might be besides what Govnan already endeavoured.

He dreamed of gleaming pattern-shapes and a road lit in bright lines. He walked over white stones, never tiring, as the sun blazed down over a hushed and sparkling world. He travelled as far as he could, never reaching the end, and when he woke, crumpled against a wall in Govnan's library, he opened his eyes to an arcane geometry. Across the floor and upon every wall half-moons, circles, and diamonds blinked and spun, each piece leading into the next, every one in its place. He stood and stumbled, catching himself on a chair and then wincing, because his fingers had been rubbed raw. He examined his hands in the light of the pattern and saw blood.

"I made this," he said, looking around at the pattern. "I made you."

A shimmer passed through the linked shapes of the pattern.

He wondered what it might do if he *pulled* it. "Or was it Adam?" he asked of the wall.

It did not answer.

CHAPTER THIRTY-SEVEN

SARMIN

Sarmin waited on his throne. The great doors had opened for Azeem and the duke, and they walked along the silk runner now, preparing for their obeisance, but he was impatient. Protections were not going into place swiftly enough, while Yrkmir seemed to be picking up speed. They had attacked the temple of Meksha, the patron goddess of Cerana. Mura and Moreth had already reported the results of their investigation to him, but there had been nothing to describe besides destruction. What could Tower mages, born into the elements, understand of pattern-work? What could a Cerani understand of a Yrkman's mindless destruction? He watched the duke fall into his obeisance and wondered what kind of man persisted in his faith despite evidence of such evil. But then he remembered what Dinar had been doing in the temple of Herzu.

Azeem climbed the steps of the dais and leaned close. "Your Majesty, the Blue Shields are reporting that the rebels have ceased their attacks, in the Maze and elsewhere."

"They have left the city to these pattern attacks," Sarmin murmured.

"They are ragged souls, Magnificence. Refugees and . . . Untouchables." Azeem fought to keep from glancing at Grada.

Sarmin cleared his throat and spoke to the duke. "Rise."

Azeem fell silent and took his place at his table with his quills and ink, but Didryk continued to face the throne. It looked like he had sent his guards upstairs without him—not that they would be much use in the face of Sarmin's swordsons. The duke looked as if he had not slept in a week. Grief—or guilt—was keeping him awake.

"Are you well?" Sarmin asked. "I can send for Farid to assist you this afternoon."

Didryk gave him a bow. "That will not be necessary." In his fatigue his accent had become stronger.

Sarmin focused on Didryk's blue eyes. "What can you tell me about the pattern used at the temple?"

"Without having seen it, I would assume it was a simple destructive pattern, Your Majesty, set to destroy stone."

Sarmin gestured for him to take his seat at the bottom step of the dais. The way Didryk had said *simple* interested him. A slip of the tongue caused by his exhaustion. If he had to distinguish one pattern as simple, it meant there were others that were not. He tapped the arms of his chair. He knew Didryk was more skilled with the pattern than he admitted.

The stream of slaves and administrators began, with Azeem calling out each name and Didryk formally marking each person. Sarmin clenched his hands on the arms of the throne, feeling the metal edges bite into his fingertips. His visit with Mesema this morning had been too brief. She had told him of her encounter with Dinar, leaving out no detail, which could not have been easy for her. It was no surprise to him that Dinar and Arigu were working together, that they planned to install the general's niece in Mesema's place. While that would never happen, he worried what else the two men might be planning.

They had also discussed Govnan's mission. With Mesema he did not need to hide his sorrow. The high mage's efforts could soon mean his death—he had known that in the way the old man had said goodbye—and yet it still pulled at his heart. The Megra had already passed beyond; he was not ready to lose Govnan, not yet.

He ran a hand over his eyes. He could not wallow in his grief, not while Mogyrks drew their patterns in the city, the Storm approached and Daveed and his mother had yet to be found. He knew now that Adam had blinded

Rushes so that she could not see Daveed had been switched with another boy. *What would he do to my mother?* he wondered.

He waited, wanting to end it, to take Didryk aside and ask questions about the austere who had taught him, but he could not; he needed to protect his people as much as he needed answers, and to protect them he needed to be sure they were marked. He waited the long hours until all the people on Azeem's list had been marked and the dome had grown dark above him. Most of the nobles had not stayed, not even Lord Benna—after the initial shock of seeing a Mogyrk sitting on the dais, there was nothing interesting about watching a man draw on foreheads.

Azeem put away his ledger and his ink and straightened his desk while Didryk stood and bowed.

"With your permission, Magnificence."

Out of the corner of his eye Sarmin saw a Blue Shield slip through the side door and approach his fellows against the wall.

"But first I—"

Before Didryk could finish, the soldier who had entered drew his sword. "For Mogyrk!" he cried, and pierced his fellow through the heart. As two of the sword-sons ran from the dais, their own weapons drawn, the man turned, smiling, and Sarmin shuddered at the sight of his eyes: they had turned completely black. The Blue Shield raised his sword in a feeble attempt to stop the two hachirahs coming at him, but he could do nothing; Ne-Seth's huge blade cut through his neck and thudded against the wall behind him.

Sarmin stood. "What manner of attack was that?" It felt too close to an attack by the Many.

Ne-Seth turned to him and made a gesture of confusion. Behind him, blood ran down the wall and along the edges of the tile. Sarmin remembered Mylo's blood in the temple of Herzu and he felt a weight upon him. He looked away.

"He knows," said Didryk, his eyes on the redness creeping across the floor. "The first austere knows we are protecting ourselves and he is trying something new."

"But how?"

Didryk spread his hands wide, empty of explanations.

Azeem cleared his throat. "We have overlooked something, Your Majesty."

Didryk looked at the vizier, fear passing over his face. *Strange.* Sarmin watched them both and said, "Have you, Azeem?"

"Yes, Your Majesty: it is your own glorious person. You have not been marked. Nor have I, or the child upstairs." He did not say *your brother* or *the false prince.* Only *the child.*

"I am not marked?" Sarmin tried to remember the time of Helmar, of his binding to Grada, of all the things that happened afterwards. He looked at his arms.

"I think you had best take the mark, Magnificence." There was urgency in the grand vizier's voice as he looked at the bodies on the floor.

"I . . ." He watched the duke's expression change from fearful to curious. "Will it protect me against that?" He motioned to the two dead men.

"I do not think so," said Didryk. He looked shaken. "But it would protect you against other attacks by lesser austeres."

"I will go first," Azeem offered, and stepped before the Fryth duke, who stood almost a head taller. Didryk looked down at Azeem, and after a pause he bent down to pick up his pot of greasepaint, dipped his finger in it and marked Azeem's forehead.

As Sarmin watched the black marks disappear into his grand vizier's skin he felt uneasy.

"If you are prepared, Your Majesty?" Didryk asked, turning his way.

Sarmin waved him forward and Didryk touched his forehead with the cold grease. "Just a line here, and this one . . . There—finished, Your Majesty." Didryk stepped back and the world changed.

Sarmin blinked and the room came into focus, altered and beautiful. Tangled shapes and skewed lines revealed themselves to him, resolving in his vision, shifting into place with a flash of blue. Symbols shone from each guard's forehead, bright and clean, finished with twists that led into tendrils of light, and beyond all that, the world itself, tangible and real but also defined by twists and curves, formations, structures.

Sarmin took a breath. The touch of the warding symbol against his forehead had woken his eyes to the pattern. He saw the mark gleaming on Didryk's wrist and the sickly green that was Banreh's health, weighing it down, and the duke's wide, knowing eyes.

Now Sarmin knew what Didryk had wanted—why he had come here. All those tendrils of light led back to him. This was what he had hoped for, to be allowed to mark everyone, to link each person to himself. But what he had meant to do with it—whether he had Helmar's strength to twist each person's will to his own—that Sarmin could not tell. Was Didryk responsible for the attack that had just occurred?

He raised a hand, intending to cut those tendrils away, to leave Didryk isolated—but he found he lacked the power to do so. To his dismay he found not everything had been returned to him. He could see the designs, but he could not alter them. He needed Didryk as much as he had before.

Sarmin stood, disguising both his new knowledge and his powerlessness. "Join me," he said. "I would show you something." With that he turned and led the Fryth from the throne room, Ne-Seth and the other sword-sons falling in behind them as Sarmin began the long walk to his old tower. He offered no explanation to the duke as they travelled through the palace, and his own mind wandered along other paths, including to Mesema. She had been right about this—the pattern had returned to him—but she had been wrong about trusting Didryk.

The damage done by the earthquake was not noticeable where they walked unless one knew where to look: here, a patched wall, there, a new pillar, carved with images of Mirra, set to right the floor above.

At the base of Sarmin's old tower Didryk hesitated, looking at the charred steps and the gathered sword-sons, perhaps wishing he had not left his guards behind. "Where are we going, Your Majesty?"

"I want to show you my room, where I met your cousin the marke." Sarmin waved the sword-sons off. "Wait here."

"Your Majesty," interjected Ne-Seth, tugging at his well-shaped beard, "at least let me ensure the room is safe. After what just happened—"

"Of course." Sarmin waved Ne-Seth ahead and he ran up the stairs. Very soon he was out of sight above them and Sarmin began his own climb.

Didryk followed him up the long, curving stair. Sarmin paused to rest from time to time, looking out of the narrow windows set into the curved walls. Each turn lent him a different glimpse of courtyard, wall or city, with no context in which to place the brief views. He thought that even when his view was constant and of wide breadth it did not give him any context either.

At last he reached the top, where Ne-Seth opened the door to him, letting him know the room was safe. He stepped in and looked about at the dusty carpet, the ruined walls, bare of gods, and the bed-ropes now hanging slack. Didryk followed him in, looking around curiously, and he shut the latch.

"This is where I was imprisoned during the time of my brother's rule. On the night of my father's death they brought me here, and from this window I saw my other brothers die in the courtyard." He stood at the still-bare window lined with pieces of jagged alabaster. Grada had broken this window more than a year ago, but he never had it repaired.

Didryk said nothing.

This was Sarmin's moment to Push and hope the tiles fell in his favour. There was no more time. "When my brother died, my cousin Tuvaini became emperor and after him, Helmar, the Pattern Master. It was he I killed to take the throne for myself." Sarmin turned to face the duke. "But this was my room: it was where I was formed, where I became Sarmin the Saviour, where I first met my bride. And here I remained until the demands of the palace forced me elsewhere. It was here I spoke with your cousin Marke Kavic, and hoped to become his friend. But he died before those hopes could grow into truth."

Didryk blinked. "Azeem said that my cousin fell to the pale sickness that swept your palace."

"Kavic was murdered," said Sarmin, and the duke made a noise in his throat, his hand held open at his side as if readying for the touch of a weapon. Sarmin continued, "I thought that by killing Helmar I had vanquished the pattern, but it was not so. It used my hand to kill your cousin, and it opened a wound in the city that threatened to destroy us all."

"*You* . . . killed my cousin?"

"Not me. One of the Many." *My false brother.*

Didryk let out a breath and seemed to waver, his right hand still hovering near his empty sword-sheath, the left pressed over his heart. "Why are you telling me this?"

"Because I do not wish to lie to you. Because I want you to understand the dangers we have faced—the dangers we still face. Yrkmir approaches, but we are threatened by much more now. I stretch out my hand to you in friendship, knowing that you may bite." He held out Tuvaini's dacarba, hilt-first: an offering. "If you are going to bite, then bite now."

Didryk took the weapon. First he laid it in his palm, then he flipped it in the air and caught it with a fighter's expertise. "For a long time I have dreamed of carving open the Cerani emperor," he said, his blue eyes far away. "When my austeres were tortured to death, I imagined this. When my city burned, I imagined this."

Sarmin stepped up to him and pushed his chest against the three-sided tip of the blade. He looked up at Didryk. "I must fix the god's wounds. They spread through my empire like open sores. I must find Austere Adam and those he has taken from me. I must hold off Yrkmir, protect the Tower and create a lasting peace so that my people—my wife, my son—may live. And to do so I must put all of my tiles on the board right now and make my Push. If I cannot succeed, if you will not help me, I might as well die, and at your hand as any."

Didryk held the weapon against Sarmin's chest, his gaze on the place where the metal pressed against skin. "This is not what I had planned."

Sarmin did not move, did not back away from the sharp end of the blade. "What did you plan, Duke? You have all those people tethered to you— what would you have had them do? Was that attack in the throne room yours?"

Didryk looked into his eyes. "It was not. My plan was to destroy your city after you had destroyed Yrkmir," he said. "I would have had your people tear down every brick and stone with their bare hands."

"As Yrkmir did to Fryth after the defeat of the Iron Duke." It made sense. "Your cousin Kavic told me. Here in this room."

"Did he?" Didryk's breath whispered against Sarmin's face. Sarmin nodded, and Didryk lowered the dacarba. "As soon as I met you, I knew—if you had been like Arigu, I never would have hesitated, but once I met you I knew that I would—hesitate." He flipped the dacarba, grasped it by the blade, and held it out to Sarmin hilt-first. "Your turn."

"I would not kill you." Sarmin tucked the blade into its sheath. "I will not even pretend to that."

Didryk fell to his knees, his hands over his eyes.

"Will you help me?" asked Sarmin.

"Will you release Chief Banreh?"

"I cannot—but he will remain alive for now; Arigu and I are in agreement on that."

Didryk leaned back on his heels and lowered his hands to his sides. Sarmin had thought him in tears, but his eyes were dry. "When you were imprisoned here, you must have felt that your world had been lost—one day you were a boy, playing with your brothers, and the next, here you were, trapped in this room."

"And when I came out, everything was different."

"I have lost my world, too," said Didryk, "and my brothers. Even if I go back, it will never be the same."

"You meant to die for this."

"That was what I expected."

A slight—though important—difference in meaning. Sarmin noticed Didryk's black hair shone in the sunlight the same way as Nessaket's did.

"I never wanted a war—any war." Sarmin stepped forwards. "Are we allies, then?"

Didryk held out his right hand in a gesture Sarmin did not understand, but after a moment he grasped it in both of his.

"We are allies," said Didryk. Then his eyes went towards the window and he frowned.

"What is it?" asked Sarmin, following his gaze but seeing nothing other than sky.

Didryk kept very still as if listening to a distant conversation. At last he turned back to Sarmin and pulled his hand away. "You do not sense the patterns moving? Yrkmir has arrived."

CHAPTER THIRTY-EIGHT

SARMIN

S armin stood on the outer wall, the second pillar of empire, a guarantee the ancients had built for themselves with stone and prayer. These ramparts gave the empire the time and leverage to outwait any threat. With the river inside and the enemy out on the sands, Cerana had time to hide, to call for aid, to pick off soldiers with arrow or catapult. Only one army had ever breached the walls and looted Nooria, and that enemy was Yrkmir.

But now the Great Storm threatened too; the northwest horizon had gone, replaced with a blankness that he could look at only from the corner of his eye. He felt its hunger even from this distance.

Sarmin had been out of the palace only a few times since his release from the tower room, and each time had brought sorrow: Beyon's tomb, dissolving; Pelar growing pale on Qalamin's deck; the crack in the Tower. Now he stood on the wall and waited for Yrkmir. His gaze fell beyond the market-stalls and the last well, beyond the rise of the great dunes, all casting dark shadows. On his left Moreth crouched, using Rorswan's senses, and on his right, Mura reached out her arms, her windspirit Yomawa seeking any disturbance in the air. Behind him stood Grada. He was never without her now, not since the first austere had shown he could turn anyone, even a Blue Shield, to his will.

Moreth spoke in a voice like tumbling stone. "Movement in the sands."

"Where?" Around him the archers readied their bows and soldiers stood by their loaded catapults; everywhere he looked he could see men ready for a fight, their hands set, their eyes carefully turned away from the north. Didryk's protective wards gleamed from their foreheads. And yet the desert lay smooth and undisturbed before them. Sarmin squinted against the afternoon sun, but still he saw only sand.

Where was Yrkmir?

Mura made a noise in her throat and he lowered the glass. Rivers of blue light ran before the walls, flowing together, dividing and rejoining once again, retreating towards the distant dunes. Shapes of green and red lit and died beneath the sun, and the desert shifted and wove into the shapes of a thousand men with eyes, mouths and noses formed of sand. At first Sarmin thought them golems, but they stepped forwards, shedding their earthly veil and revealed themselves to be men of flesh, wearing uniforms and brandishing weapons.

"They moved through the sand," said Moreth, "but they came from the Storm." From all parts of the wall Sarmin heard murmurs, his soldiers losing their nerve in the face of Yrkmir's magic, but he heard their officers too, their voices strict and calm, showing themselves unafraid.

"Moreth," said Sarmin, keeping his voice low, "can they travel through our walls that way?"

"No; they can only move through the desert that way because the sand moves. Stone will not part for them as it will for me." He was still speaking with the voice of Rorswan.

And yet they had travelled through the Storm: that meant he knew for certain now that it was possible for a human—not just water or fire—to enter the Storm and not be harmed by it. An austere stepped out from a line of red-clad soldiers. He was all white—white hair, white robes, white skin—and he took a long look at the walls, considered the men who pointed their arrows his way and turned his face to Sarmin. The moment stretched. The archers' arms began to tremble. Finally the austere lifted a white flag that had been hidden among the folds of his pristine robes.

"He wants to talk." Sarmin breathed a silent sigh of relief for the delay in fighting, but the strange austere worried him. Adam had looked like a warrior; Didryk looked like a duke. This man looked a full mage—perhaps he was *the* mage: the first austere.

He motioned to Mura. "Come. You will protect me from arrows."

"We need Farid, Magnificence," she said. "He will know if they cast a pattern against you."

In truth he did not require Farid for that now, but it would look well to have two mages standing behind him. The Tower had not lost its reputation yet, and the gesture would not be lost on the white-clad austere below him. The young pattern mage appeared, breathing hard as he came running up the steps to the wall. He looked as if he had not slept for days.

Seeing Sarmin, he fell on his knees, pressing his forehead to a stair.

"Rise. You are late," Sarmin said, "but not too late to join me and watch for patterns."

"Magnificence," said Farid, and fell in behind him with Grada and the wind-sworn. Sarmin looked back at the wall where Moreth stood. He had three mages left and he was about to take two of them outside the wall, leaving the inexperienced rock-sworn as the sole guardian of the Tower should anything go amiss.

Let us hope it does not come to that.

At the base of the wall stood the great Western Gates—three doors in all, with murder-holes above the paths between them—but Sarmin knew from the *Book of War* that more than thick stone protected the city. Ancient and powerful spells guarded the wall. It took some time to pass through the gate, walking through the shadows, with the desert ahead of him, the sun, sitting low in the west, blinding.

At last Sarmin stepped out into the light and found the austere waiting there. Even the man's eyes were pale. There were no wards on him that Sarmin could discern, no patterns in the sand.

"Emperor Sarmin." He bowed. "I am Second Austere Harrol." Behind him, a host of archers held their bows at the ready. Sarmin could see no other austeres; either they crouched beyond his sight, drawing patterns in the sand, or the Yrkmen had not brought them. He thought it unlikely they had been left behind.

"Second Austere? Not the First?"

Harrol smiled, his thin lips stretching over white teeth. "The First is concerned with things greater than earth and sky and men. I am the one sent to speak to you."

"So speak. What is the meaning of this aggression?"

"We assail you? What did Cerana mean when it burned Mondrath to the ground?" Harrol's eyes focused somewhere beyond Sarmin, as if there were a truth more compelling, a world more appealing, than the one that stood before him. "Let us not play those games, Emperor. I come to make you an offer."

"Make it, then."

Behind him Farid was silent; he must not see any patterns either. Grada was also silent, but that was her way. If she had to cut someone down she would do it with little noise.

The second austere gave a bow. "We offer you a chance at paradise: to accept Mogyrk's path. You have three days."

Sarmin did not reply.

"We know you are keeping Second Austere Adam prisoner. We want him returned, and our Duke of Fryth also."

"You are mistaken; Second Austere Adam is not my prisoner." Sarmin wondered what it meant that Yrkmir did not know the man's whereabouts, but he used his words to make them wonder even more, throw them into confusion if possible. "Nor is the duke. If they prefer to join you, of course I will allow it."

"We will expect them," said Harrol with a slight bow. "Three days, Emperor."

"You will have my answer in two," Sarmin replied. With that he turned and made his way through the dark passage back into Nooria. The mages said nothing as they walked.

Suddenly he remembered Ashanagur's words: *Mogyrk blinds the Tower.* Was there something here the mages could not see? He wished Mesema were with him.

Arigu fell in with him and Grada as they walked to the carriage. "My recommendation, Magnificence," he said.

"Speak."

"We wait until night, and then attack them."

"We are in a three-day truce," said Sarmin.

"Why do you think they want three days? Never give the enemy all the time they ask for. They will move south, try to cross the river and surround us. I say we take them off-guard now. We're ready for it. All my soldiers are marked and protected."

It was dishonourable, but such attacks were discussed thoroughly in the *Book of War,* along with full consideration of the ethics and benefits. The question was what Yrkmir might do in those three days.

Arigu waited for an answer. Sarmin was disinclined to take the man's advice, but he knew it to be sound—that was why he had wanted the general returned to him in the first place.

"I will consider it." He climbed into his carriage and looked out at the general, who put on a diffident air.

"And the other thing, Your Majesty. Have you considered my offer?" Grada climbed into the carriage and sat next to Sarmin, but the general paid her no heed.

"That was only yesterday, General. I have hardly had the time."

"But I—"

Impatience overcame him. "If you must have an answer now, then it is no."

The general bowed with a grim expression. "Magnificence."

Sarmin closed his carriage door and the horses began to move. He had never been in a carriage before, more of a hot box that swayed and made him ill. He should have been more politic with the general; he needed Arigu more now than ever before. But he had said he would never raise another woman to Mesema's position. She was Pelar's mother, his princess, the woman he loved. But he remembered that his mother had warned him of love, and the air inside the carriage stuck in his throat. Would he be an emperor tossed aside by his own emotions, left alone on the rocks like Satreth II or Kamrak, Uthman's son? He had no choice but to wait and see.

CHAPTER THIRTY-NINE

GOVNAN

Govnan had been walking towards the Storm, not quickly, for his old legs did not allow that. With every step he had to consider Metrishet, Ashanagur, and the others; he had to control them, watch their movements. He had estimated that he would reach the void in another half-day, but while the sun was high in the sky the emptiness rushed forwards as if answering the call of a great pattern-work. He froze, expecting to be consumed by the Storm and for his efreet be loosed upon the world, but it stopped several lengths away. He faced west, not looking at the vast Storm, which would fill his vision and empty his mind if he turned his eyes north—but he could feel it, against his skin and deep in his bones.

It *wanted*—it *craved*—it *searched*. The blankness begged for colour, form, vitality.

The elementals would survive as Meksha's water did, unseen and un-claimed by the Storm. Metrishet, Ashanagur, and the others would form a barrier between the god's wound and Nooria, their flames spinning a net of heat and colour. Govnan presented the image to the fire-spirits and willed them to make it so. They would need to spread their fire both wide and high, standing between the Storm, the northern wall, and the river road that led down to the Storm Gate. Govnan set his will against theirs, and reluctantly, the spirits complied, weaving threads of fire so bright against the dullness that Govnan was forced to keep his eyes closed. He did not know whether the work took an hour, a day, or an entire week; his own senses, joined with the efreet's, had become alien to him.

The wound met the first fiery web-piece and probed, searching for something to deconstruct, to undo—but it found nothing, as if it had reached the end of the world. In fact, it had only reached something the god did not recognise, so the fire worked only as a barrier. To heal the wound would require something more.

Govnan's legs shook. It felt a year since he had bound Ashanagur for the second time, though he knew it could not be that long. The sun was so distant and yet its power so close, warming his shoulders, hot on the skin of his face, and he knew what he controlled now was only a small part of what fire promised and threatened; so small was man against the forces of earth and sky.

His mind had wandered, and already Ashanagur moved—only a finger-span, a test of Govnan's will—but it had abandoned its work on the net and the emptiness flowed through the space like water through a broken dam.

We must not be distracted. The web must be unbroken. He spoke for all of them, his voice foremost, but not alone.

Metrishet answered, *We are hungry. To the west there is flesh.*

Govnan explored the sense of his bound spirits, not with sight, smell, or hearing, but an inner one that rushed along the sands, picking up on love-charms buried deep within the dunes, pattern-marks and old wards. As he reached out, the city's wall flared to life, its ancient spells gleaming with power. The efreet sensed magic above all else besides fuel: anything combustible they perceived with a yearning, and during his many years with Ashanagur he had developed the ability to sniff out the many forms of its food. Now Govnan sensed the meat Metrishet desired to the south and west: row upon row of soldiers, a thousand and a thousand more. *Yrkmir.* And beneath them were patterns, not one great design, but a thousand small marks and circles, lighting his mind with the full force of the One God. He gasped, at last realising why the Storm had shifted so rapidly.

It is not Cerani flesh, Metrishet continued. *You will not mind if we eat it.* Not a question.

Govnan could not allow it; there would be no Nooria to protect if he allowed the void to flow past the Worship Gate. Sarmin had been clear with his orders, and so Govnan sent a negative along his bond to Metrishet. *We stay here.* But he wondered whether the emperor had a plan, and what magical defences he had managed. Helmar had come close to destroying them once before; now all of Yrkmir's power stood in the desert outside the western wall. He shivered, though the late afternoon sun beat down on him. He had made his choice. He would remain at his station.

He lingered on his sorrow for only an instant, for one of the smaller spirits now attempted to flit from his grasp. Kirilatat was its name. Govnan thought of Kirilatat as a woman though it was Metrishet who wore a woman's form. He wrestled with its will. *Stay in place.* But he grew weak, falling to his knees. Yrkmir's presence unnerved and frightened him. He could do nothing for the young mages, for the Tower, for all that the Tower stood to protect. He could do only as Sarmin had commanded. He geared all of his focus to the building of the net.

We are hungry.

He ignored the chorus of the efreet; he knew they could exist for years without eating. Ashanagur had eaten only five times in all the time Govnan held him before. It was a matter of will. *Stay.* He lifted his waterskin. An instant later he threw it to the ground. The liquid burned against his lips and left a trail that sizzled like burning oil as it dribbled down his chin. He was more fire than man now; water would no longer strengthen him. He untied a sack holding bread and cheese and wrinkled his nose in disgust. His own mind turned to the Yrkmen—so many of them, all that flesh living and unburned.

Ashanagur expanded again, its flames licking against Govnan's face, and Govnan lifted his chin, allowing it to heat his cheeks like the sun. When they had been joined before it had not been as two separate entities, and over the years he had forgotten Ashanagur's beauty and power. *So we eat?* Ashanagur asked, low and seductive.

Desire overwhelmed Govnan, so deep that his bones hummed with it and his throat hollowed. *No.* He struggled to master himself as well as the efreet. *No. We build this net.*

Soon. Ashanagur mocked him. *Soon.*

CHAPTER FORTY

FARID

"There you are." Moreth shuffled into the library, walking past the pattern that shifted bright upon the wall and looked over the table, his eyes stony but showing grief nevertheless. The warding-symbol Farid had drawn on his forehead glowed blue and yellow. "Mura has been in your rooms and up and down the stairs looking for you."

Farid had been searching the ancient patterns for anything they could use against Yrkmir, but his understanding of them was coming too slowly. He put his work aside and looked up at the rock-sworn. "I am always in the library. Hasn't she noticed?"

"Always? You have not been here so long as that," Moreth said. "Rock and wind measure time on a different scale, and even on the human one, you are new." He went to the window and looked out over the northern quarter. "Have you seen Govnan's fires?"

"How could I not?" Farid had watched them all night: Govnan had not slept, and neither had he. Both of them bore magic requiring more control than dreams allowed. His greatest fear was waking to find he had cast a spell upon the Tower.

He cleared his throat. "If you see the fires it means the high mage is still alive and the northern wall stands safe." *We will see about the western wall.* Farid felt a cold dread. The truce had yet two more days, but the Yrkmen soldiers and their pale austere filled his mind. He did not believe the truce would end peacefully—the emperor would not convert to Mogyrk; that was unthinkable.

And that meant only one thing: war, blood, death. He spoke to Moreth again, speaking bravely for himself as much as for the rock-sworn. "The way I see it, we're all soldiers, of a magical kind, and we have to work together to keep the city safe. I think Govnan knew this."

Moreth turned his head away. "Yes. He did. He *does.*"

Farid stood. "Why were you looking for me?"

"Your magic is different from ours. We have a problem our elementals cannot fix. Will you look?"

"Of course." Before leaving the room he stopped and said, "Can you see anything different in this room?"

Farid could see the colourful pattern on the wall, but Moreth looked around and shrugged. "Only the normal things." They left the library and began a slow descent. Moreth's steps were solid and sure but Farid held on to the wall with one hand, noticing the cracks between the carvings, the cobwebs in the corners, the dust that lay over everything. They reached the rock-sworn statues and Moreth showed him yet another stairway, this one going below. Here Mura joined them. She smelled of roses, and he could see her own warding symbol glowing from her skin.

This new stairway was underground and unlit. Moreth lifted a lantern from a hook on the wall and lit it before proceeding. Farid took the first step downwards and felt a prickling along his arms. He peered down past the lantern but saw only darkness. He willed himself to be patient as they continued, Moreth moving with consistent, plodding steps, Farid struggling with his robes and Mura coming up behind them, too fast to follow comfortably, always needing to stop and wait for them to move ahead.

At last they reached the bottom, and Farid drew in his breath. He had a sense of great distance, as if he had dived from a great height and was still falling. This was how he had felt in his dream, walking upon the endless road, and he knew that he could remain in freefall or keep walking for twenty years and never reach whatever it was at the end of it. As in the dream, he kept moving, reaching out with his hand, no longer caring about his robes tangling around his feet. The wall consisted of smooth, magic-worked stone that curved into a perfect circle, but here it parted, allowing magic to seep into the Tower like water through a crack. He pushed his fingers into the rent and felt a frisson of excitement.

"Can you fix it?" asked Moreth.

"Why do you want to fix it?" Farid's hands played over the jagged edges. He now had a sense of what it was that he would never reach, and it was sweet and bright.

"Because if it continues to spread, the whole Tower will fall!" Moreth exclaimed in impatience. "And it's letting the magic out."

"It's letting the magic *in*," Farid corrected him. "Can't you feel it?"

"I did feel it and I almost lost control of Rorswan."

"Maybe it gave him too much strength—that's what it does." Farid could feel the magic against his fingers. If only he could widen the rent and allow more of it through, he was sure it could help them fight Yrkmir. He glanced at Mura. "Touch it—you'll see."

"I will not, if it means Yomawa—"

The great bell sounded high above them and Mura made a sound of impatience. "I will get the door," she said. "I am faster than either of you."

She left them, and Farid let go of the wall at last and looked around the lowest floor of the Tower. Something else was pulling at him here—not another rent, but a doorway. He could feel it, but he looked at the curved stone and saw nothing.

"The portals to the other realms are here," said Moreth. "Can you sense them?"

"Yes." Farid turned towards the stairs. He could have stayed next to the crack all day, like a drunk with a bottle of wine, but he did not want Mura answering the door alone. Too many things were possible in Nooria now. He took the stairs at a run and realised the magic had invigorated him. Though he had not slept, he no longer felt tired. His muscles were not fatigued. He hurried after Mura and reached the hall of statues just as she opened the door. He slowed, knowing that the dignity of the Tower did not allow for mages rushing about in the entryway. More soldiers stood at the door—not the same men who had brought him here.

Mura finished talking to them and turned around, a scroll-tube in one hand. She raised her eyebrows at him. "A communication from the grand vizier."

Farid was gratified to know that even someone who had been at the Tower for years could still feel impressed and honoured by the palace.

To Farid's surprise Moreth spoke behind him. He had not known the rock-sworn could move so fast. "Open it."

They gathered around the scroll-tube like children around cake on a festival day. Mura removed the gleaming cap and pulled out the parchment. She unrolled it and said, "Ah. We are called to guard the wall, in shifts." She frowned. Perhaps she had not expected such a simple and obvious order.

"Of course." He should have thought of that himself. Govnan would have instructed them to do so, but the high mage was gone. With a shock he realised he was the eldest mage remaining.

"I will be first." Mura rolled the scroll back up and looked for a place to deposit the scroll-case, but found nothing and ended up holding it awkwardly in her left hand.

"I'll walk with you." It was a long way to the western wall. Farid looked down at his robes; he carried no weapon. If they met with any Mogyrks—

"Our reputation protects us." Mura must have sensed his disquiet. "Our reputation, and the spirits we carry. But of course the grand vizier has sent a carriage."

"Oh," said Farid, embarrassed because he had no bound spirit, and also because he had not thought of a carriage. Mura handed the scroll to Moreth and Yomawa opened the door for her. Farid squinted into the bright sunlight. The courtyard was empty today—no stray mages being delivered, and no soldiers preparing for a desert expedition. They passed two statues of Meksha, and Farid wondered what the courtyard had looked like two hundred years ago when the Tower was full of mages who could tend to it. Had there been gardens? Fish in these greenish ponds?

His foot fell on a glimmering path-stone and he stopped, lifting his foot. "Mura." To either side of his shoe pattern-shapes arced away, tracing a circle around the courtyard. "Get Moreth," he told Mura, "*hurry*." He crouched to examine the pattern lines. It was a destruction spell, but a symbol he did not understand. *Hiss-nick.* Adam had taught it to him—likely it meant stone. *Did I do this?*

"There's a pattern here," he said when the mages rejoined him. He showed them where to step in order to remain safe. "It's of Mogyrk."

Moreth knelt and put a hand to the ground. "There are five people close by," he said, "two with the carriage and . . ." He fell silent, then whispered, "Two more just jumped down from a wall. Running—"

"Can you catch them?" Mura laid a hand on Moreth's shoulder, her eyes wide.

"—away from us."

Farid jerked his head up and looked around the courtyard. "Where?"

"To my right." The stone buckled around Moreth's hand and rippled away in a liquid, shifting stream of sand and pebble. It flowed against the high wall, which billowed like a sail in the wind, shimmering a moment before returning to its rigid form. "Caught them," he said through gritted teeth.

Mura was already running towards the gate and Farid followed. Though the stone had caught them, they might still have weapons that could put her in danger. As he passed the carriage, not looking at the drivers who turned and called after him, he realised *he* was the one at risk—he had neither bound spirit nor weapons. He would be useless in a fight, while Mura had her wind. He was a fool to think he could protect her—neither would he have been able to protect Rushes had those Mogyrks attacked them in the alley. He remembered how Grada had fought the pale folk and his feet slowed. If he was not useful in a fight, he would be useful in some other way. To begin with, he could try to keep a level head.

Moreth's captives were further away than he expected and by the time he got there he was tired again. He bent, held his knees, and caught his breath. The two men wore dark cloaks; they were struggling against the stone which had risen over their feet, trapping them where they stood. Mura stood a man's length away and raised her hands. A strong wind blew along the wall and forced back their cloak-hoods, revealing Cerani faces, dark hair.

"Men of Yrkmir," said Mura, her voice loud and threatening, "you do not belong here."

The men looked at one another. "'Men of Yrkmir'?" said one. "We were just running—" The other one punched his arm and he stopped talking.

"Rebels, then." Mura faced them, her arms held wide, ready to counter any attack.

But Farid frowned. This did not seem right. The men were too well-dressed for Mogyrk rebels and not well-dressed enough to be austeres—at least, he imagined all austeres dressed as well as Adam. He would guess these men were thieves, successful thieves. Who else would have remained in the city this long? Only someone who wanted to loot the empty houses.

Moreth ran up beside him, balancing himself against the wall as if he felt dizzy. When he saw the two men he fell to his knees. "No, no, no . . ." His hands went to the ground.

"It's all right, Moreth. Let them go; they're not our men."

Mura turned and frowned at him. "You're sure?"

But Moreth made a high, keening noise and arched his back, then rolled to his side and curled into a ball, gasping.

"Moreth—Moreth, are you well?" Farid put a hand on his shoulder.

Mura screamed and he jumped up, his hands in fists, but she was not under attack. She was looking at the spot where the two men had been, but nothing remained there other than a pool of blood on the stone, reflecting the light of the sun.

Farid looked up and down the street, but he could not see the men, either dead or alive. He turned to Moreth, his hands shaking. "What happened? Where did they go?"

"Moreth is newly sworn," said Mura, breathing hard. "He lost control of Rorswan and let him swallow those men. He never should have been—"

Farid looked at Moreth. "You *murdered* them?"

"His spirit took them. Govnan trained him too quickly; he does not yet have enough control." She walked towards Moreth, her eyes on the stone beneath her feet. Farid realised the danger and stepped back, though he too was still standing on the paving.

Mura put a hand on the rock-sworn's shoulder and spoke in a calming tone. "Do you have control now?"

Moreth nodded and Mura rubbed her forehead, leaving a red mark beneath her ward. "There is nothing to be done about it. Moreth, I cannot leave you alone. You and I will go to the wall together. Farid will go to the palace and report about the pattern."

"I will need help to get rid of it." Farid could not take his eyes from the pool of blood in the street.

"Then do that." Mura tried to pull Moreth to standing, but he was twice her height and weight. As she struggled with the rock-sworn she glanced back at Farid. "Well, go!"

Farid ran.

CHAPTER FORTY-ONE

SARMIN

Sarmin stood on Qalamin's Deck, the early morning cool against his skin. Grada, as always, waited beside him. "This is my city," Sarmin said, waving a hand from the darkened Low Gate all the way north to the Worship Gate, nearly obscured by the fog of the Great Storm. In between stood the Storm Gate, where Yrkmen and White Hats stared at one another across the great wall. A month ago he might have seen colour and movement below him, heard the shouts of citizens as they passed through the streets, but this dawn the city lay empty, its wounds from the earthquake open to the sky, and the only smoke rose from the distant camps of the Yrkmen.

Sarmin raised his spyglass and focused on the Maze, where the rebels' knives and rocks had gone still. Somewhere amongst those twisting alleys and piled rubble Adam must be crouched, giving orders, planning his coordination with the Yrkman army. He might have Sarmin's mother with him, held against her will. But even the walls and stone defied Sarmin, for he could see nothing there. He turned the glass towards the northern quarter, lying in the shadow of the Storm, and then moved to the ruined marketplaces to the south. He saw nothing so clear and easy to define as an austere laying patterns or Yrkmen soldiers marching down the street; all looked calm, like the quiet before a storm. The Holies were spread out in front of him, clean and sparking in the dawn, and to his right, the Mages' Tower and the Tower of the Knife raised their proud domes towards heaven.

A buzzing beat around his ears and he shook his head in annoyance. He turned his spyglass east. Mogyrk's Scar was there, and if they beat Yrkmir then he would have to go to it. There would be no ending the wounds unless the Scar was ended first. But what the lens showed him brought out a cold sweat against his forehead. He saw a churning wall of light and movement, like a sandstorm without any sand, where objects flickered in and out of his sight. He saw a tree rise and disappear; a lake evaporated. This was not a wound, not a void, but something else—something *more*. He lowered the spyglass and Grada moved closer, curious for the first time. "What is it, Your Majesty?"

"It's the Scar. It has drawn close." He ran his hands down the silk of his robes, as he had seen Azeem do many times. He found it comforting. "Very close."

Movement caught his eye. At last he saw people in the streets—but these were not his ordinary citizens, running back and forth to the market or carrying rice from flatboats on the river. Through the glass he could see that these men wore torn, ragged clothes that showed the filth of the Maze. Most of them were cut or bruised; only half wore shoes. But their faces showed a determination and a clarity that made him wonder. In their midst stood a man in red robes, his yellow hair gleaming in the soft light of the dawn. This man stood perfectly still, his arms by his sides, and he stared up at Qalamin's Deck as if he knew Sarmin was standing there, staring down at him. Austere Adam. Nessaket was not with him.

"He surrenders," said Grada, looking over the edge, and he resisted the urge to pull her back, away from the fall. Far beneath them, Blue Shields surrounded the man and his ragged crew.

He snapped his spyglass shut. "Come. We have been too long away from the throne room."

"We must kill him, Your Majesty," said General Merkel, waving his thin arm at the great doors. "As punishment for the deaths he has caused, the damage to our buildings and the consternation of our citizens."

"The emperor, heaven bless him and keep him," said Dinar to the general, "does not make decisions that quickly. The first prisoner we took remains in the temple of Mirra." A smile played over his lips as Grada's hand moved towards the hilt of her Knife.

"The duke is well enough under your thumb, Magnificence," Lurish said. "It is time to show the troops that vengeance will be had upon their enemies."

Dinar smiled again. "Indeed. The duke has finished the wardings we needed. The Yrkmen want him and Adam both—why not throw both men's heads into their midst?"

Assar shook his head. "Why not return them both alive, as was requested? Perhaps that way we can avert any more deaths."

This led to open laughter, but before anybody spoke again Sarmin whispered to Azeem, "Make sure the duke stays safely away from these men until I have rendered my decision." He would not lose his second ally from Fryth in less than a year. It was not just his court watching; the whole world was watching. Beyond his borders lived kings and emperors and chieftains with whom he would one day need to negotiate; killing envoys was not the reputation he desired to cultivate.

In any case, he liked the duke.

Azeem stepped from the dais and spoke quietly to Herran just as the gong sounded. The herald crept down the aisle, his smooth expression betraying none of the excitement of the moment. "Austere Adam, Your Majesty."

The austere walked down the silk runner, and despite their earlier threats the men of court backed away from his path. He had an air of dignity and physical prowess, the sort of man most people were not brave enough to confront without significant preparation. He walked all the way to the end, his chin held high, and Sarmin started to worry, for the last time Austere Adam had come to this room he had refused to bend his knee until Govnan took action with his staff. If Adam would not kneel today he would likely die for the infraction before Sarmin could say a word about it—and then he might never find his mother or his brother.

To his relief Adam knelt without prompting and touched his forehead to the purple silk.

A collective sigh, felt rather than heard, rose from the assembly.

Sarmin waited a long while, and another long while after that, and the men of the court started to fiddle with their robes, to cough, to sneak looks at one another. The door shut behind Azeem and Herran and Sarmin felt the same buzzing in his ears that he had felt on Qalamin's Deck, but now he recognised it as the noise of the Scar, a clattering of things, the whispers of all the life that flowered and died there, over and over, in a confusion of sound and motion.

He cleared his throat. "Rise, Austere."

Adam rose to his feet. Dinar stood just behind him. Though Dinar was the bigger of the two, they were of similar build, and Sarmin wondered what it was in the life of a priest that lent itself to such muscle.

"What brings you here, my enemy, in this time of war?"

"Your Majesty," said Adam, meeting his gaze with eyes of indigo, deeper in colour than even Didryk's, "I hope that we will be allies, not enemies, once we have finished talking. I have commanded my men to lay down their arms."

"That is nothing to me. They have already done enough harm to warrant their executions."

Adam shrugged. "My men know that they are going to paradise, and soon."

Sarmin regarded him in surprise. If he did not care for the lives of his men, what then did he care about—and why had he come? He went directly to his own concern. "Where are my mother and brother?" At this the courtiers looked to one another, startled, for they did not know the Empire Mother was gone.

Adam looked surprised. "I do not know where your mother is, Magnificence. I have not seen her. I had your brother and I let him go."

Lies and more lies. "Why? Why did you let him go?" Sarmin leaned forwards, anxious to hear whatever reason Adam might offer. The austere had switched his brother with another boy, and Sarmin would get the truth out of the man eventually.

"Because I could not send him to Yrkmir. The first austere is mad, Your Majesty. The child would not learn about Mogyrk, not the way children are meant to learn of him, in his light and love. So I allowed Rushes to escape."

"Blinded."

Adam looked chastened, but Sarmin was sure he was only pretending.

"I did that early on so that she could not escape—or if she did, she could not tell anyone where we were."

"Not so that you could change my brother for another boy?" Again the courtiers murmured, and Adam looked at him wide-eyed. "No, Your Majesty! The boy who escaped with Rushes and Farid was the same boy I took from the palace."

"We can have no alliance if you continue to lie." Despite his words, a certainty took hold in him: he feared the austere spoke the truth. *Mother, Daveed, where are you?* He motioned to the Blue Shields and ordered, "Take him to the dungeon." With Adam safely in a cell he would have time to think—but he would need to send more than Blue Shields if he was to ensure the man did not die before he reached the dungeon. Herran had left with Azeem, so he turned and gestured to Ne-Seth and another of the sword-sons. "Go with him. Ensure his safety."

Adam struggled against the arms of the Blue Shields who held him. "Your Majesty! I come to offer you salvation. Death is near! You must bring yourself and your brother into the light before Mogyrk—"

The doors closed behind him and Sarmin heard no more. The courtiers stood in silence for a time. At last Dinar spoke.

"Would we truly seek an alliance with a Mogyrk austere?"

Sarmin leaned back in his throne. "If I wish it." Didryk had never met the first austere; Adam clearly had. There was information there.

"Magnificence," Dinar said, picking his words, "the gods have been very clear. The earthquake, the wound that grows to the north . . . I worry we may anger them further with our actions—or inaction."

"Which gods? I would think Herzu might enjoy the Storm." Did it not sow fear and kill indiscriminately?

"He cannot exist there." Dinar blinked, and for the first time Sarmin saw fear in those dark eyes. For decades the high priest had been one of the most powerful men in Nooria. Now Mogyrk's wound threatened to take that power away from him.

Sarmin stood. Herran, Azeem, and two of his sword-sons were not in the room and though Grada stood behind him, he felt outnumbered. "I will consider your words as I retire."

As he swept from the room, his nameless sword-sons close behind him, he heard the doubts of the courtiers in their murmurs and their shuffling feet. Something must be done to reassure them of the right of his ways, to affirm that enemies were punished and the empire, embodied in himself, was strong enough to prevail. Perhaps it was finally time for Banreh to die.

CHAPTER FORTY-TWO

FARID

F arid hurried to the palace, though once again every inch of him called out for sleep. His muscles screamed when he moved them, his eyes stung, and a dizziness pervaded his mind, but he had to find the duke—the duke would know how to destroy the pattern around the Tower. Adam had impressed many things upon him in their short time together, but he had not given him any clue about how to get rid of a design already laid. He frowned, remembering Adam's words: *You will help me, but first you need to escape.* When would he unwittingly aid the austere? Had he already done it, when he drew the ancient pattern on the walls of Govnan's library?

Or it was me who drew that pattern in the courtyard, me who tried to destroy the Tower?

He must put his hopes in the duke. He remembered Didryk teaching him the warding pattern he had since put on five hundred foreheads. The duke had taught him as much as he needed to know and nothing more: a line here, a circle, another line, and a triangle to hold it all inside. *Pull.* Farid had hoped to learn more from the man after that adventurous trip to the desert, but either the duke had been too busy, or he had no intention of upholding his end of the deal.

Farid's mage robes granted him instant access to the palace; the Blue Shields standing at the gate took one glance at him and stood aside. Govnan had given him this Tower uniform as a prop for his mission into the desert, but it gave him a power and access that he never would have dreamed possible when he was selling apples and pomegranates in the tiny market off Ashem Street. The distinctive weave of white cotton and linen threads set him apart, and the belt of shimmering blue silk could have only come from Govnan's own chest. They were impossible to imitate and harder to obtain, and they labelled him a mage of the Tower even if he carried no bound spirit.

In the Great Hall he paused, orienting himself. Men were still working to restore the dome high above, plastering around the exposed beams. In a few months it would be covered with mosaics of scenes from Cerana's great past; Uthman's founding, the defeat of the Parigols, and the blessing of Meksha would take up a large part of it, but Farid wondered what else they might paint. The defeat of Helmar Pattern Master, perhaps.

He took his eyes from the dome to find a grey man staring at him—grey-cloaked, grey-haired, grey-eyed. He stood so still that at first Farid had thought him a pillar against the wall. Now he backed away. This man must be a member of the legendary Grey Service, the emperor's spies and assassins. They watched one another for a moment, and finally Farid said, "I did not see you." A stupid thing to say to a man who likely sees everything.

The assassin inclined his head. "What brings you to the palace, Mage?"

"The duke." Not even the assassin's eyes moved, so he babbled, "I need to find the duke on a question of magic—a threat to the Tower."

Now the assassin stood away from the wall and glanced up at the workers as he walked forwards. Farid made himself not shrink away. "Be careful what you say in open spaces," the man said to him. He now stood very close, close enough to slit Farid's throat, but he only took his arm and pulled him down a corridor lined with tapestries. The grey man said, "You are the new mage Grada told me about."

So Grada was Grey Service too? Of course she was. Because she was a woman it had not occurred to him, but she wore the robes and she wielded her knife with experience. "Yes, I am."

"It is gratifying to see devotion from a mage not one week in his robes." Somehow Farid felt the old assassin was mocking him. "I am Herran."

"Farid."

"Farid of the fruit-market."

Again Farid sensed some joke was being made at his expense, but he realised that compared with the threat against the Tower, such insults did not matter. A week ago he might have made some retort, but today he was focused on his mission. "Yes. Do you know where to find Duke Didryk?"

"The duke has retired to his rooms."

"May he come to the Tower?"

Herran did not reply but continued to steer Farid towards a set of stairs set behind the broken ones in the Great Hall. Farid followed him down elegant hallways where the doorknobs glowed in the lantern light and the highly polished wood shone. In Farid's rented rooms above the marketplace, the wood that lined the walls had been roughly hewn and dull. Running his hands along the windowsill had been enough to give him splinters. Thinking about his old place made him remember the creaking bed and the threadbare old blankets, and he realised how much he would have loved to return, even if just long enough to get some sleep.

At last they stood in front of one of those elegant doors. It looked just like every other they had passed, but Herran walked straight to it with no hesitation.

Farid pulled the sash tighter around his waist. He wanted these men to respect him, to believe he was worthy to be a mage of the Tower. He swallowed as he faced the door. Duke Didryk held all the secrets he wanted to know—how to break a pattern; the meaning of the design he had drawn on the walls of the library; why he had been called by Mogyrk instead of Meksha or Keleb, gods he had worshipped all his life.

Herran knocked, and the door was opened a crack by a redhaired Fryth who towered over Farid and the assassin both, but who was still not as tall as Didryk. He looked from one to the other and finally said in a rough accent, "No Cerani."

"Didryk," said Herran, motioning past the door.

Someone spoke from within the room and the red-haired man opened the door the rest of the way. Farid had thought his Tower room luxurious, with its silver mug and high window, but the room he looked into now showed not one uncovered surface. Tapestries hung on every wall. A carpet covered the floor. Everywhere there were scattered cushions embroidered with golden threads.

A dark-skinned man dressed in elegant robes stood to greet them. He glanced at Herran only long enough for recognition, but his gaze lingered on Farid for several seconds. Farid looked back at him, then with a shock realised he might be standing before someone royal. He prepared to go into an obeisance, but before he could lower himself the man gave a slight bow and motioned them forwards. "Come."

Duke Didryk was sitting before a Settu board, studying the placement of the tiles. From the look of it, they had just begun a game. When he saw Farid he stood, knocking the table, and the pieces scattered. "What is it, Farid?"

Farid looked at the red-haired guard and the other, blond and threatening, and his words came out in a tumble. "A pattern was laid around the Tower, Duke. It's destructive, but beyond that I can't tell what it is. We caught some men but they—they died." He did not mention they probably had been innocent. He pushed aside the memory of their blood, and of Moreth, rolling in the ecstasy of killing, and swallowed; this was not the time, with everyone watching him. He continued, "We can't go back until the pattern is destroyed—but I don't know how."

The duke said, "I will accompany you back to the Tower."

"We had hoped you would, Duke." The "we" came from his mouth as easily as "four bits for this mango." He pressed his lips together. He had to remember his humility.

The assassin, Herran, still standing by his side, gestured at the man in elegant robes. "Lord High Vizier Azeem, perhaps you should come too."

So that elegant man was the grand vizier. He felt a fool.

Azeem closed the shining door with care and turned down the corridor. "This way," he said, and everyone followed him without a word. Farid thought Rushes must be somewhere in the palace and wished he had time to look for her. He hoped she and the baby were well—or even better, not in the palace at all but travelling down the river, far from the Yrkmen.

They travelled along simpler halls where the servants walked, warding-patterns bright on their skin, past the kitchen where he smelled baking bread and roasting meats and out into a courtyard filled with barrels and crates. On one side laundresses plied long sticks to stir the palace linens in great coppers; on the other an old man sat on a chair twisting the necks of chickens. At the sight of Azeem many of the workers gasped and hurried to drop to the floor, but he paid them no notice and glided to an iron gate which led to a yet more elaborate gate, which led to an even larger and more impressive one. There Azeem stopped to speak with an officer, a captain, and twelve more men joined their party, all dressed in the blue uniform of the royal guard, proud feathers rising from their hats.

Finally they reached the street. It felt hotter outside the palace gates. Sweat trickled down Farid's back. They moved with haste to the Tower.

Almost no one else walked the streets. Once a noble's carriage passed by, and a lone man stood holding skewers of cooked lamb as if he meant to sell them to nonexistent passersby. When he saw them, with the soldiers marching behind, he skittered away like a thief, reminding Farid of the men who had died. Finally he saw the Tower rising above them, casting a shadow from east to south, and felt a moment of hope replace his worry: it had not been destroyed. *He* had not destroyed it.

The duke stopped at the edge of the pattern and held out an arm to keep anyone else from moving forwards. "It is here," he said to those who were blind to it, crouching and running his finger along the stone. "Farid, here: let me show you."

Herran, standing by his side, looked around as if puzzled by what he could not see. The grand vizier did not look puzzled. His careful eyes were fixed on the duke.

Farid crouched next to Didryk. The duke gestured at the shapes. "You know when you put yourself into a pattern, it is as if you are opening a bag and letting everything inside come out."

"Ripping a cord."

"Ripping a cord: yes, good. But when you want to ruin a pattern you must close it tight, so it cannot open. Try."

"What if I—?" He glanced up at the Tower.

"I will not let you 'rip the cord,' as you say. Now, try." The duke sounded angry.

Was he upset at his fellow Mogyrks who had laid the pattern, Farid wondered, or was he more upset that he had to help save the Tower? He wondered if he would be as forthcoming as the duke if his city had been destroyed.

But for now he had to put wondering aside and focus on the glimmering shapes below him. He thought again of his sister's twine, strung between her fingers in an intricate web. Instead of pulling so the string fell, could he pull so the string drew tight? He gritted his teeth. If he got it wrong . . .

He took a long look at the Tower. Inside stood the statues of the former rock-sworn. He could not allow it to turn to dust.

"Trust me," said the duke.

Farid stared at the shapes again, focusing on the symbol he thought meant stone. *I will pull you out.* As he stared, the shapes shifted and the lines around them bent as if melted by the sun. Again he looked up at the gleaming Tower, standing white against the blue of the sky, and breathed a sigh of relief.

"You see?" The duke stood and scuffed at the stone. "You did it."

"I broke it—but can another person fix it?"

"I think it is good that there are guards," said the duke by way of answering.

Farid lowered his voice. "When first we met, you said Adam had put a mark on my forehead, but that you couldn't tell what it was for. Can you tell me now?"

Didryk frowned and touched his finger to Farid's skin. "It is a compulsion—he has twisted the symbols so much that . . ." He paused, then drew his finger away. "I think I can remove it for you."

"Yes, please."

As he touched Farid's forehead once more, Didryk said, "Such a small mark cannot be specific. It can only urge you upon a path—for example, a malicious mark could drive a man to drink, but not to drink any particular brew."

"Could it drive me to use the pattern?"

Didryk said nothing, but he glanced over to where Azeem and Herran stood side by side, watching them. Then he pushed hard against Farid's skin and Farid had to steady himself so as not to stumble backwards. He felt a sensation of unravelling, of falling apart, and a bright pain bloomed in his mind. Didryk lowered his finger and stepped away.

"Thank you."

Didryk nodded.

"There are other patterns in the library," said Farid, "ancient patterns drawn on parchment, from the time of the First Yrkman War." *And I put one of them all over the walls while I slept.* "Govnan did not know what they were. I hoped you could tell me."

But when they stepped towards the Tower, Herran held out an arm, stopping the duke. "The emperor must give permission for anyone to enter the Tower."

"Perhaps another time," Azeem said.

"Another time, then." The duke agreed so easily that Farid became frustrated with him.

"But I will need to know," said Farid, speaking more loudly, "I will need to know all the symbols and their meanings if I am to be of any help at all."

Didryk regarded him a moment. "I will teach you, if the Emperor is willing. I will ask for his leave."

Farid frowned as Grand Vizier Azeem, Duke Didryk, and the two Fryth guards turned away, but Herran paused, his grey gaze moving from fountain to statue to courtyard wall. "I will arrange for the Grey Service to watch the Tower compound along with the Blue Shields," he said to Farid.

"Thank you."

"It is not the custom," said Herran, and Farid could not help but hear the accusation in his voice. *Before I came, there was no need to guard the Tower.* And Herran did not even know the whole of it. The assassin turned away and followed the vizier. At the gate the Blue Shields had already taken up their stations.

Farid settled on the stone of the Tower steps. He was still not able to open the door.

CHAPTER FORTY-THREE

DIDRYK

Back in the palace, Azeem directed Didryk down a different path, towards the temples he had visited when he had first arrived. "Where are we going, Lord High Vizier?" he asked. Sarmin had taken him to a new place and ruined his life—or else saved it. Now Azeem meant to take him somewhere new. He did not know if he could face it.

"The emperor bade me take you to your friend." Azeem did not pause as he spoke.

They passed the dark temple of Herzu, the god of pain, famine, and fear—the patron god of the palace, he had been told. He felt eyes watching him from the darkness; as he passed he resisted the urge to stop, turn, and protect his retreat. Krys and Indri walked stiffly beside him, staring straight ahead.

The scents of blooming flowers met them at the entrance to Mirra's temple. Her high priest kept a lush and green space. "This way," said Azeem, breaking his silence, and led Didryk and his men down paths lined with tall decorative grasses and rose bushes. They passed a gurgling fountain and Didryk could not help but pause and watch his own wavering reflection in the surface. Water had been so rare in the last few months.

Azeem stopped before a curtain of flowering vines and remained there, gesturing for Didryk to step behind.

Banreh was lying on a stone slab, a pillow made of his own folded clothes resting beneath his head. He had been cleaned and bandaged, but otherwise Didryk could not see that his injuries had been treated. His breathing came shallow—that was thanks to the queenflower drug, most likely.

Krys breathed a sigh of relief. "He is alive!"

"Mogyrk be praised, my lord," said Indri.

Didryk placed a hand on Banreh's chest and tried to evaluate what had been broken in him. He had no physician's skill, only what he had gleaned from the books in Adam's library and the injuries he had seen when Arigu attacked his city. His ribs, he thought, and maybe one of his lungs, and there was slow bleeding, somewhere inside. Quickly he traced the patterns that would show his friend's body how to heal. Such things did not work immediately. Sometimes they did not work at all, so Didryk was surprised to see the strength and power of his commands. Already bruises were fading, cuts changing from angry red to pink. He knew that Mogyrk's Scar was near, but every time he was reminded, it surprised him.

He knew he might be healing his friend only to see him hanged—or worse. For his part, Banreh did not stir. Didryk had hoped to speak with him, but what could they say? Azeem would hear it all—and in any case, they had already said everything they needed to tell each other that day in the desert.

Banreh had insisted that Arigu would bring him to the palace. He had refused to try escaping, and he had refused the queenflower drug that would have eased his pain if they beat him. The man was too stubborn, and there had not been enough time. Didryk knew why: Banreh had only this one chance to save the enslaved Windreaders. But was this the only way—to turn himself over to be beaten and tortured? Who then would lead the freed slaves back to the Grass?

Didryk was certain a trip to the dungeons or that dark temple of Herzu was next for Banreh and he trembled with rage and helplessness. Yrkmir stood outside the gates of Nooria and the Storm grew near. Soon they would all die—and there would never be any reason to it. Once again nobody would be saved.

Low voices drifted over the humid air of the temple: They were no longer alone. Didryk clasped Banreh's hand and let it go. He could not stay any longer.

Azeem led, sweeping past a group of priests without a word, and Didryk and his men followed once again. The temple wing showed beauty in every corner, from fountains and mosaics to tapestries and friezes. Didryk's own home bore some simple decorations of polished wood and amber, but the emperor's palace never seemed to tire of ingredients for its walls, ceilings, and floors—gems, gold, paint, tapestries, on and on, until his eyes saw nothing but a blur. So much richness. Why had they wanted Fryth as well?

But it had not been Sarmin who wanted Fryth, he reminded himself. It had been Emperor Tuvaini, who had sat on the Petal Throne for mere weeks.

And how long will Sarmin last? Who will take his place?

They passed into a plainer corridor and Didryk realised Azeem was taking a longer route—buying time? What was happening in the throne room? He knew he would never get anything out of the man, who was unflappable in his ability to give every kind of polite answer except for the one Didryk sought. He gritted his teeth.

A group of Blue Shields approached and he saw a prisoner in their midst, wrapped in the red robes of an austere.

Adam.

At last his rage found a focus. He had found it impossible to hate Sarmin in all his strange nobility, or Azeem and his calm diplomacy, the guards, with their firm commitment to duty—he had been unable to dislike even the earnest young mage, who remained so determined to defend his city, as Didryk himself once had been . . . but the second austere stood before him now—Adam, who had so calmly accepted the ravages of Yrkmir and its first austere; Adam who had stood by and let Kavic be slaughtered; Adam who had once been his teacher. Now he turned his face towards Didryk, perhaps sensing the fury rolling from him, and their eyes met.

"Didryk." Adam spoke in rapid Frythian, "You were right about Yrkmir. They want to start it all again—" A Blue Shield hit him in the gut with the hilt of his sword. "The first austere is mad. I let the boy go—the emperor must believe me!" Another blow and he fell silent, drooping in the arms of the soldiers. They dragged him down a set of stairs that led to a heavy door. The dungeon.

Through it all Didryk said not a word, and his men stood still and silent behind him.

Adam was a zealot, blind to all but his own mission, never seeing the damage he did, and yet always ready to judge, to punish. But his instinct was to save souls, not destroy them.

After all your grand plans you will end up beneath the palace in a dark cell, my teacher. Didryk did not feel the satisfaction he had expected.

Azeem led him on without expression. "I will take you to your quarters."

Didryk had no choice but to continue on the path he had begun, to help the emperor against Yrkmir. "If I may request parchments and ink—I could make the mage Farid a guide for Mogyrk's symbols and their meanings."

"Of course: parchment and ink will be delivered to your rooms shortly." Azeem's shoulders relaxed.

"Thank you, Lord High Vizier."

As they moved through the door to the Great Hall, High Priest Dinar entered on the other side, coming from the throne room. Didryk's feet slowed and stopped as he came under the focus of the priest's snakelike eyes. They faced one another for some time, unmoving. Dinar meant to unnerve him, to frighten and intimidate, but Didryk did not flinch or look away; he poured all of his frustration into their unspoken battle, and at last Dinar laughed and turned away.

Didryk called it a small victory.

"Give us the word, my lord, and we will cut him down," Indri said.

"There will be no cutting down of anyone." That was why he had got in the habit of leaving his guards in the room. They were too prone to think of honour before sense.

They passed through the vestibule and made for a back stairway.

"Did you enjoy the visit with your friend, Duke Didryk?"

Surely the vizier only meant to be polite, but the question was out of tune and it hit Didryk where he was sore. "It was as I expected." Then he asked in a cutting way, "Do you have friends, Lord High Vizier?"

Azeem paused. "In my position one does not have friends. Perhaps when I retire, I will play Settu with the other old men."

"Perhaps." Didryk took the steps two and three at a time.

Azeem, being shorter, had to hurry to keep up. When they reached the corridor Didryk continued to outpace him until he arrived at his room.

As Krys and Indri went inside he turned back and asked the grand vizier a question. "Who is your patron god, Azeem?"

Azeem froze and looked down the length of the corridor at him.

"Is it Herzu, god of war and famine? The patron god of this palace?" He expected the man to say yes; then he could tell him exactly what he thought of his so-called god.

"No." Azeem held his hands out before him. "It is Mirra, goddess of fertility, who makes life in the desert possible."

"Mirra," Didryk repeated. He had not guessed that. With his line of attack stalled, he had nothing to do but retreat. "Thank you, Azeem." He went inside and shut the door.

CHAPTER FORTY-FOUR

MESEMA

Mesema sat in the rooftop garden in the lowering dark. In the west, she saw the river and the Holies, and beyond them, the western wall and the gathering of the Yrkmir army. Their campfires appeared, one by one, as pinpricks of light against the shadowed sands, like stars in the night sky. But stars were nothing compared to the conflagration in the north. There, arcane fires of blue and orange wove their threads across the front of the Great Storm, forming a tapestry that blazed against the horizon, five times higher than the walls and stretching far into the western sands. The wall, the water that ran through it and the northern dunes were lit as if by day—but the Yrkmen camped far enough to the south that darkness yet fell upon them.

Mesema had begun to lose confidence they would succeed. Sarmin had not found a way to heal the Storm, and though it appeared Govnan had bought them some time, there was precious little of it left. She had not forgotten the pale sickness, how it had drained Pelar—he had been so fragile, so weak. And what the high mage blocked for them was nothing compared to Mogyrk's Scar.

Now the only enemy who had ever captured the palace had returned. Mesema did not care to think of what might occur should the Yrkmen sack Nooria—what might happen to Sarmin, to herself . . . She wondered where Nessaket had gone, whether she was safe and could remain so. She sorely missed the Empire Mother's advice. Nessaket had warned her of Arigu and cautioned her to stay away from Banreh, and she had ignored her and made a mess of things. Besides the emperor, Arigu and Dinar were the most influential men at court. And together . . . she thought of the few men who remained in the city. While all of them might be relied upon to support Sarmin in other matters, this might drive half of them away—those who were military men and admired Arigu, and those too devout to oppose the high priest of Herzu. The pressure to put her aside would be strong, but Sarmin would refuse; she knew that. And his continued refusal would put him in a precarious position.

Surely the two would not make their play in a time of crisis? And yet it had happened before: it was during the height of the pattern-sickness that Tuvaini had manoeuvred his way to the throne. The soldiers had come to take Beyon's wives—she still dreamed of that night, the terror in the women's faces, how the blood had spilled across the floor. She glanced at her men who hovered by the stairs. If Arigu sent his soldiers after her, Sendhil and the others would be little protection against them. But with Pelar safely out of their reach there was nobody to put in Sarmin's place—unless they meant to use Daveed.

No. Nessaket would not allow it; she would never be part of such a plan again. This was a simple power play, nothing more, men jockeying for position and influence. Not another coup. She would be in a better position now if she had been able to find the slaves—but she had run out of time . . . all of Nooria had run out of time.

At least she did not feel Banreh's pain as she had before. Now it whispered behind her thoughts, like grief, and she was glad of it, for she needed a clear mind. She gazed up at the statue of Mirra that rose above the bench, Her finely carved eyes flickering in the light from the torches, and for the Empire Mother's sake Mesema said a prayer.

A whisper of footsteps came upon the stairs and the guards shifted to allow Grada, lithe and liquid, to step through their midst. She looked at each of the men in turn before stopping at the bench. She watched Mesema, the blunt features of her face lost in shadow, until finally she said, "Your Majesty."

Mesema inclined her head at the Knife in the way of her own people. "Grada."

"May I speak to you privately, my Empress?"

Mesema nodded and waved the guards back down the stairs, out of earshot, and the Knife waited, listening, until she was sure they were alone.

Then she bent down and in Mesema's ear whispered, "Do you trust each of those guardsmen with your life?"

"Of course!"

"Don't answer too quickly, Empress." Grada's dark eyes narrowed. "Think carefully on each one."

Mesema stood up and paced to the statue of Mirra and back again. The fire in the north cast the goddess' face in darkness. "I don't know," she admitted at last.

"One of them has told stories: he said you went out into the city to see Banreh before he came to the palace, and afterwards you went into the dungeon to see him again."

"But they couldn't know I went to the dungeon—I did not take them, or tell them." Mesema clutched her roiling stomach. "And you're the only one who knows I was in the city, and why—that was nothing to do with Banreh."

"Then how?"

Mesema shrugged. "Perhaps someone followed me? But you would have noticed, Grada."

"Meere has heard the rumours, and they are said to come from one of your men." Grada frowned. "That could be a lie, but I think they would not risk an untruth, not when their message is so important. They want to remove your influence over the emperor, and replace you with Arigu's niece. They find him too . . . soft . . . in your company."

"His niece, is it?" Mesema wiped sweat from her forehead. Arigu had helped Tuvaini against Beyon; he did not move without a powerful ally to cover him. He was a coward. Sarmin would face down all of Yrkmir by himself if need be, but men like Arigu and Dinar sneaked and whispered. It disgusted her. "Dinar is working with the general, and he has just caught me with the prisoner again."

"Your Majesty . . ." Grada seemed about to curse, but she held her tongue. Mesema knew she had made a mess of things; she needed no reminder. "Listen, do not be angry with me. It will not alter the situation."

Grada sighed and touched the twisted hilt of her Knife. "You must change your guard."

"No." When Grada frowned, she added, "If I do, they will know I am afraid. If I keep the same guard it will show I have no reason to be ashamed—and I will not provide them any further gossip."

"I am only concerned that this is more serious than it seems. Daveed—"

"That has occurred to me too," Mesema admitted in a low voice. "But I do not believe it. This can wait until after the battle . . . if we survive."

Grada gave a slight bow. "If that is your decision, Your Majesty. But know that the Knife of Heaven will serve the empire if required." Mesema did not know whether Grada meant by that she would kill Dinar, Arigu, or the child. The comfort she had felt with the Knife dropped away: Grada could kill even Sarmin, if she thought there was a call for it. She had been relaxed, as if confiding in a friend, but Grada was no friend, nor was Nessaket. Even Sarmin had to balance his affection for her with the demands of empire. She had no friends.

She returned to the bench and faced the great web of fire. It had grown, stretching its tendrils higher into the air, adding green and yellow to its mix of colours. She had heard those in Fryth and Yrkmir could sometimes see bright lights in the northern sky and now she wondered if the army camped before the walls saw any similarity here. But such curiosity no longer mattered; it would never come to anything. They had failed. *She* had failed.

The heat pressed against her skin; the Storm stood in the way of the mountain wind. And yet a small breeze picked up, blowing petals and dead leaves in a tiny whirlwind around her feet. They rose and blew through the hands of Mirra's statue, then drifted towards Mesema, settling all around her with gentle touches of rose-scent.

Mesema knelt before the stone goddess. Mirra had sent her a message, just as She had so many months ago, in a different garden, out in the desert. Mesema stood and studied the carved face, limned by the coloured lights of Govnan's fires. Healing, peace, the growing of things: that was Mirra's way—but it worked *after* wars, not during them. With soldiers camped outside the walls it did not seem to be Mirra's time, but perhaps that was the point—it was easy to follow one's beliefs when they were not being tested. It was always Mesema's impulse to look for peace, to love, and she thought she had failed—but Mirra had faith in her. Perhaps there was still something she could do. If this was the only sign she was to receive, then she would pay attention. "Thank you, Goddess," she said aloud, "I will honour you as best I can." Light played along Mirra's arms as if in answer.

CHAPTER FORTY-FIVE

MESEMA

Sarmin waited at her door, his eyes shadowed with fatigue. At first he leaned on the wall, his eyes on the rug, and she thought he was too tired even to meet her gaze. But then at last he found his way in, closed the door, and settled on her cushioned bench, facing away from the mirror. He leaned forwards and put his head in his hands. "We have found Adam, but not my mother or brother. He says he let my brother go. I fear the first austere's hand in this."

She went to him and put a hand on his shoulder.

"I regained my pattern-sight, but I can do nothing with it—it is like seeing the words, but not being able to read them. Neither Didryk nor Farid have the talent I once had. Yrkmir waits—the first austere waits—and Govnan cannot last forever. Mesema"—he reached up and took her hand—"I wish I had sent you south. I wish my mother—"

"I know."

"I think the duke regrets his alliance with me. The Yrkmen are strong, and their first austere has magics I cannot touch—not as I am. But I have both Adam and the duke, which is what they want. I could hand them over, say the words of love for Mogyrk . . . but would it save us?"

She thought of the Red Hooves her father had held captive, and the things they had preached to one another while she played in the grass. "No, it would not. Listen: they want to wipe the world clean so that when it dawns again, all will be new. To them we are nothing more than filth to be washed away."

"Adam claims to think differently."

"Some of them carry the light of their faith, others carry the sword." It was so with all things, not only gods. She knelt down before him and brushed a curl from his cheek. "Do not betray the trust of the duke."

"He nearly betrayed mine."

"But he did not, my love." He gave her a curious look and she blushed, because it was the first time she had ever said the words. She hid her embarrassment behind teasing. "Is it too soft to speak of love? Does this palace tolerate such emotion, or does Herzu keep a tight hand on us now?"

"I care nothing for Herzu." He leaned down and touched his forehead against hers. "I am looking for another god. I have been reading an old book that belonged to Satreth . . ."

She looked up at him in surprise. "Mirra touched me with her grace in Nessaket's garden. Perhaps it was a sign."

"Yes." He frowned.

She knew Mirra was the goddess of women and not easily embraced by men, but Mesema must follow through with the sign provided to her. "What is it?"

"The Megra said something to me before she died—she said healing the Storm would be Mirra's work."

"She did?" Mesema smiled and leaned in to kiss him. "Is Azeem waiting for you? General Lurish?"

"No."

She kissed him once more.

Sarmin pulled away. "I should—the generals . . ."

But she drew him close. The truce would last just a few days, and they had this time, so she would use it. He returned her kisses, his breaths heavier, his touches longer, and she stood, untied her dress, and let it fall. Now she stood naked before him. She had never done that before; she had always been too worried about how she might compare to the more beautiful concubines, what he might think of the loose skin on her stomach from when

Pelar had been born. But now she wanted him to see her, as she truly was. He stood and let his own robes fall, showing his thin body, his wide, bony shoulders narrowing into his hips, his pale legs. Together they moved to the bed. Though war waited not far away, they took their time, and when she finally trembled and shook above him the palace had gone quiet.

He put a hand on her stomach and smiled. She rolled to his side and put her head on his chest. "Dinar and Arigu will use me to move against you."

"Because you are Felt."

"Because I have seen Banreh, because I am Windreader, they will paint me as the enemy. But I do not know if they will move now, or after the war."

"They will not move against me if they are satisfied, if they believe victory is at hand."

She watched the wall and said nothing. Victory did not appear to be at hand. Banreh's death would have satisfied Arigu, but it had been Arigu himself who had advised Sarmin to keep the chief alive. She would not be surprised to learn that had been a trick, designed to make Sarmin look weak.

At last she said, "We need to talk about the worst. If Yrkmir breaks through, if they get to the palace, we need to talk about that."

He said nothing so she went on, "Your mother has pika seeds somewhere in her room. Probably hidden among her cosmetics. I would rather do that . . ." She rose up on an elbow. "Grada should go south to guard Pelar. He will be the true emperor."

"Emperor of what? If we lose, what is he?"

"Alive."

He caressed her hair. "Do not take the pika seeds unless you are sure there is no rescue for you—even then—" He kissed her forehead. "Even then, think carefully."

"I will." She sighed. "I am thinking of those slaves, taken from the Grass. I wonder if they are still alive, and whether they will live through this. I wish I had been able to find them."

"I wish so too." They lay in silence for a time, and then he said, "Show me that cut-up poem again." She sat up and reached for the book of poems, retrieved the bits of paper and scattered them over the sheets. Sarmin cocked his head one way and then the other. "Govnan is tricking the Storm because it can't see true fire. Mogyrk Named all things, giving them symbols, and in so doing, gave his followers patterns to work with. But I think he did not Name everything, for he did not know everything."

"How could a god not know everything?"

Sarmin sat up. "The Megra said something else to me before she died: 'Just a man'—that's what she said to me, and I thought she meant Helmar, but now I think she meant Mogyrk. He was not a god, but a man like Helmar—a man who thought he could remake the world and failed."

Mesema touched a ragged edge of paper. "And yet they worship him."

"A man can ascend to godhood—many of our emperors have done so. Except that Mogyrk never died. He is both dead and not dead." Sarmin frowned and looked towards the window. "Do you hear that? A buzzing sound, like a thousand bees, or a thousand people, talking far away."

She listened. "I don't hear anything." She rose from the bed and picked up her dress from the floor. "Dead and not dead," she repeated. "Here and not here." She pulled the silk over her body. "Come."

"Where?"

"To see someone." She tied the silk inexpertly; since Tarub and Willa had begun dressing her she had regressed to a childlike incompetence. She pulled up on the fabric as Sarmin rose and slipped into his robes. "It's not far," she promised, walking to the door in her bare feet.

She was surprised to find Grada waiting in the corridor. "Is there more news?" she asked, but Grada only looked at Sarmin.

"She is guarding me," Sarmin said. "Now, show me what you want me to see."

Mesema glanced at Grada before leading him down the hall. She would not ask why he needed the Knife at his side—she did not want to know. Inside Nessaket's room Rushes sat, singing a song to the child in the cradle.

Sarmin slowed and stopped before the doorway, shaking his head.

"Just look at him," she said. "One more time, look at him." Now that he had his pattern-sight, things might go differently.

He gathered himself. She knew he resented this boy, resented the affection everyone showed him, resented that he was the only person who still searched for Daveed. All of that showed on his face before he finally entered his mother's room.

Rushes leaped to her feet and he waved her off. "Sit down, Rushes. I am here only for a moment, to see the boy."

And yet he paused again, just inside the door. Mesema took his hand.

Finally he moved and Mesema walked with him, never letting go. And there he stood, looking down for a long time, until finally he gave a sob. "It is him," he said, letting go of her hand and lifting the boy from his silks. "It is my brother." He held Daveed against him, all chubby legs and curls and fists. "I didn't see him—I was looking at him the wrong way, like through a mirror, backwards. But it is him."

He turned to Mesema, wide-eyed, the boy squirming in his grasp. "Now I realise— The letter! I must go and look at it again too."

He meant the letter taken from Lord Nessen's courier, the one he had said meant nothing. She reached out to take Daveed from his hands, but he paused, pressing the boy against his chest and inhaling his scent. "My brother," he said, his voice filled with wonder. But his hesitation was brief; no sooner had Mesema taken Daveed from his hands than he was already at the door. "I will see you in the morning," he said, his eyes focused on her but also past her, towards the next thing he had to do.

"In the morning, my love," she called after him.

She replaced Daveed in his cradle and took a deep breath. "Rushes," she said, "I need to look for something among Nessaket's things. Some seeds . . ."

CHAPTER FORTY-SIX

SARMIN

Sarmin entered his room to find Azeem gone. He leafed through the papers on his desk, looking for the scroll from Lord Nessen's courier. Rahim had sent plans for war machines—too late for the upcoming battle. He glanced at the designs and put them aside. There were some communications regarding the provinces, others about the delivery of swords for the Blue Shields; all of these could wait. Again he heard the same buzzing sound he had heard in Mesema's quarters. He walked to the window, parchments in hand, but his view did not encompass the Scar. He felt it along his skin, prickling the fine hair of his arms.

He dropped the parchments on the desk, accidentally knocking free the scroll-tube he was looking for. It rolled along the wood and hit the rug with a soft whisper. He picked it up. Nothing had yet come of the surveillance on the man's estate, though they still believed him to be a Mogyrk sympathiser. Sarmin had been certain the manse had something to do with his troubles, but this scroll had offered no clue the last time he read it. Now, as he unwound it again, he remembered the awkward handwriting, the spilled ink, the touching letter from a mother to her daughter.

But now he looked at it in a different way, just as he had looked at Daveed and finally *seen* him.

He unrolled it the rest of the way and scanned it. It still read like a fond note, but the ink that appeared to be so carelessly spilled served to underline particular letters. The missive was long, and much ink had been spilled—but Sarmin traced each letter with his finger as he read them aloud, and finally he cracked the code. All this time it had been sitting on his desk and he had not realised.

ARIGU'S MAN BROUGHT ALLIED SLAVES. LORD N REFUSED SHELTER. POISONED? APPROACH EMPEROR? RECOMMEND.

Sarmin sat back in his chair, amazed by what he had seen with his new eyes.

Arigu's captain had prevailed upon the hospitality of a Fryth sympathiser, who had refused to let him enter with his bounty of illegal slaves. Lord Nessen had ended up dead. But where were the slaves? If the captain had left them at Lord Nessen's estate in the north, he thought that would have been in the letter. No, somehow the slaves had been brought to the city. Grada and the Grey Service had been watching Lord Nessen's estate in the Holies. She had told him she saw nothing but food go in.

Sarmin stood and paced. Of course—the slaves were there. That is why she had seen nobody come out. "Grada!" he called, "come! You will not believe what I found."

She entered. Her face was not curious; that was not one of her usual expressions, but what she did show was patient interest.

"You were right to watch that house and bring me this scroll. Mesema was right to investigate. The Fryth slaves are there."

Azeem entered behind her, his hands folded around a leatherbound ledger. "Azeem!" Sarmin beckoned him forwards. "Send a platoon of Blue Shields to Lord Nessen's manse in the Holies. There are a number of Felting prisoners there who must be freed."

As Grada took her place beside Sarmin and leaned down, examining the scroll, Sarmin looked up into the hall—and saw one of his sword-sons turn, place a hand on the hilt of his hachirah and begin to draw it.

"Grada," he said, but it was too late for her to help; the man had already drawn his weapon and clashed blades with someone in the corridor. He heard Ne-Seth give a shout of surprise; in an instant Grada was at the door, the Knife in her hand. He heard a thud as someone fell to the rug in the corridor.

A sword-son entered, a bloody hachirah in his hand, his eyes black as night. A pattern, dark and malicious, had been laid over him, greasy, iridescent half-moons and circles rising from the floor to infect him like rot.

"Ne-Seth!" Sarmin called out, his stomach turning with worry, "Ne-Seth!" He heard an answering groan from the corridor.

At the sight of Grada the infected sword-son slashed down at her, but hachirahs were heavy and slow to wield, and Grada was fast. She dodged away from his swing, spun, and got inside the reach of his sword before he had even lifted it again. She slid the blade between his ribs with a grating noise.

The sword-son's eyes cleared to brown as the pattern shrank away from him like a dying vine and disappeared into the floor. He blinked and looked at Sarmin, a question on his mouth, just as another sword-son came behind him and cut through his neck in a gleaming sweep of metal. His head toppled away and hit the floor with a thud, followed immediately by his body. Blood pooled around the man's severed neck. Sarmin knew the sword-son had been himself in that last moment. He had not known what had been done with his hands, just as Sarmin had not known his own hands had murdered Marke Kavic.

Sarmin felt ill. He pressed a hand against his mouth, stood, and turned to the window, taking deep breaths. To his right he could see Govnan's fires, rising over wall and building, blinding against the night. He knew the blankness lay beyond them, a void against the stars. He closed his eyes.

"Has the truce ended?" Azeem asked. Sarmin remembered Arigu's recommendation to attack first. Would anything have gone differently if he had?

"Azeem: go, do as I asked and send the Blue Shields to the Holies." He did not hear the grand vizier leave, but he knew that he had. The buzzing filled his ears again; he shook it off and ran into the hallway to check on Ne-Seth. The sword-son was alive: a line of red ran from his shoulder to his groin, but it was a shallow cut.

"Take him to Assar," he commanded, and the remaining sword-sons lifted him in their arms and carried him away.

He considered the spray of red on the wall. "Grada, I can no longer wait to question the prisoner." Didryk had said he did not know how to stop this kind of attack, and Sarmin believed him. But Adam was a second austere, and he might know secrets that were beyond the duke's rank. The leader of the Mogyrk church—the ruler of Yrkmir—might be testing the Tower, and only Sarmin knew enough to begin to answer the challenge. He would have to try to meet it with all the force the Tower might have had in a better time. If the first austere had known how few the mages were, and how helpless, he would not have held back, testing and evaluating their abilities with his small offensives. He would have attacked outright, and he would have won. But Govnan's fires in the north must give an entirely different impression of their power. Twice now the high mage had saved them.

Sarmin led his Knife to the dungeon, past the tapestries and mosaics and golden doorknobs, all of them two things now—what he saw, and the pattern that defined them—all the way to the servants' halls and the steps down to the dungeon. The steps were long and dark and cold, and he remembered waking to himself in one of the oubliettes, a skull in his hand.

The Blue Shield guard lifted two lanterns from the wall and guided him down a row of cells. "Same one as the last prisoner, Your Majesty," he said, hooking one lantern on the wall. It lit the inside of the small cell, and Sarmin recognised the dirty pallet and the slop-bucket against the wall. But Adam did not recline as Banreh had; he crouched against the floor like a cat, his eyes alert and wary.

Sarmin made no small talk. "Why did you let my brother go?"

"Because I could not allow him to be raised by Yrkmir as had been planned. The first austere is a heretic. He has no wish to bring souls to paradise, only to destroy them. He wants everything to end—all souls to be destroyed. I thought it better to let your brother go home, and to bring all of you to Mogyrk."

Sarmin gave no indication how he felt about that. "Tell me: how does the first austere send a pattern to take over a man's will?"

Adam cocked his head. "Don't you know how Helmar did it, Your Majesty?"

In fact, he did not. He had known only how to remove someone from the pattern, as he had done with Grada—and now he could not even do that. "But the first austere has no great pattern to work with, as Helmar did."

"No. He can take only one man at a time, and it requires all his concentration."

"So you do know."

"Only in theory. I have never seen it." Adam stood and brushed the dust from his red robes.

"Is there a ward against it?"

"Will you ward every man in the palace now a second time, with Yrkmir at the gate and the first austere sending his attacks?" Adam smiled. "I do not think you have the time. Your only choice is to kill him."

"Where is he?"

"Somewhere in the city."

That much Sarmin knew, and he hit the iron bars in frustration. "Where?"

"That I do not know—but perhaps you could draw him out. The emperor would be a tempting target for him."

"That is why he came, Your Majesty," Grada hissed. "He wants to trick you into being killed or captured."

"Do I?" Adam turned out his hands, palms up. "Or am I just seeing clearly? We will all die soon enough when the Scar takes us. The question is only how we will die. I would think an emperor of your quality would want to die well."

"There is no point to this, Your Majesty." Grada paced towards the iron bars, fingering the hilt of her twisted Knife.

"Very well," said Adam, crouching again, "but if you want to know more about Mogyrk—about how your death can be transformed into everlasting life—I will be happy to talk with you again, Magnificence."

Sarmin backed away. He thought the man sincere. That was what disturbed him.

CHAPTER FORTY-SEVEN

FARID

A courier had delivered a scroll-case full of parchments from Duke Didryk, and Farid took them to the Tower library to examine them. The duke had drawn as many symbols as he could on the ten sheets—likely the ones most used by pattern mages—and Farid set to memorising them: Stone, Fire, Air, Blood, Water, Wood, Bone, and more—two hundred and forty in all—spread out under his fingertips. He judged that it would take him a few hours to get to know them, but once he'd done that, he could start to analyse the patterns Govnan had shown him, including the one he had drawn on the wall while dreaming. Those shapes surrounded him, intrigued him, teased him, but though his fingers itched, he refused to put the spell into action—not until he knew what it was he had built, for it might do anything, even destroy the Tower.

Mura was still at the wall. Moreth had returned and was now in the depths somewhere beneath Farid, meditating and practising self-control. Farid wanted nothing to do with the rock-sworn. He sat on a wooden chair and kept his feet from the floor. Never before had he been so aware that the city was built of stone, with barely any bricks or wood. The Tower was magically wrought stone: its floors were stone, its courtyard, stone. He remembered the two men Rorswan had killed, and he shivered.

The sun had set, but Govnan's fire in the north gave Farid enough light to read by. He had only a short time before it was his turn at the wall, so he turned to the old parchments at last and began to translate them, using the duke's notations as a guide, his attention entirely taken by patterns until the shapes and lines began to swim before his eyes.

The pattern he had drawn along the walls fluttered and dimmed; the floor undulated with dark warning. He pulled his legs further up onto the chair. Had Moreth lost control? Would Rorswan eat him? But this was no rock-spirit. Black threads twined across the stone, adding obsidian pattern-shapes as it moved: triangle, oval, square. It gleamed with an oily resonance, creeping towards him, its tendrils testing the legs of his chair. He climbed onto the table and looked around at the rest of the furniture. He could go no higher.

The pattern picked up speed, sensing him now, rushing across the seat of the chair and reaching out over the table's surface. He edged away from it, concentrating on the shapes, on pulling them tight as the duke had taught him, but they seemed to slide out of his grasp, wiggling away from his intent like slippery fish. It touched the wood of the table and now it moved towards him in unhurried fashion, as if its wielder knew he had nowhere to go, until at last it hooked around his ankle. He hissed when it burned his skin. He could feel it winding up his leg and encircling his torso; it was cold now, colder than river water.

His sight went dim. His body relaxed from its fearful pose and his legs slipped from the table. These were not his movements; these were not his feet walking out of the door. "No," he said. "Let me go."

I cannot. There is work we must do. The voice whispered to him like a lover. "Who are you?"

I am the voice of Mogyrk. I am death and life. I am the promise of rebirth.

He moved down the stairs now, his steps sure and confident, his robes no longer a concern.

The traitor Didryk freed you from your fate, but I cannot allow that.

He reached the bottom of the stair and passed the rock-sworn statues.

Here my enemies lie already vanquished. But it is not finished. Not yet.

"You can't." He hoped the doors might offer a challenge to his captor, but his body was made to heave against it until the left-hand one stood far enough open that he could slip through. Ahead of him he could see the destructive pattern in the courtyard, its shapes twisted, its lines closed. It was all ready to be fixed and pulled loose. The guards, standing along the walls, would not think he was casting a pattern; he would look as if he was out for an evening stroll.

"No!" he shouted, but no sound came from him.

The voice laughed and he felt a *pull*.

Farid came to himself in the courtyard. "No," he whispered. He looked up at the curved wall of the Tower. Lights flashed up and down its length as ancient wards built into the stone were triggered. Farid felt sure the pattern mage had failed—but then he saw the stone shift, dust rolling from its edges. "No!" He reached for the other pattern, the one in the library. All he knew about that one was that it reached back in time, forwards and backwards. If it could stop this . . . He reached out with his mind and pulled that pattern too.

He heard the laughter again, fading into the distance. *Thank you.*

He had only accelerated the destruction. The smooth wall of the Tower crumbled downwards, its many windows collapsing like closing eyes. Moreth was in there, at the bottom, too far to warn, too late to save. The dust washed over Farid like a sandstorm and he scrambled backwards, coughing. A rumble sounded deep in the earth and the courtyard shook. But it was not just the courtyard; the whole city was shaking, reacting to the destruction of the Tower. The highest stones dissolved as they fell, transforming into a white cloud that hovered in the air, and the domed metal roof hit the courtyard floor with a great ringing crack. The bell separated from it and with a dull clang, fell over its collapsed ropes. The lintel around the great brass doors ran away like sand, and the doors fell into the dust without a sound.

All fell silent.

"Moreth!" Farid scrambled to the edge of where the Tower had been, but it was too dark to see anything. All the torches that had been lit inside had been snuffed out by the weight of the powdered stone.

"Moreth!" The same spell had been cast in the temple of Meksha, and the people inside it had suffocated. He scooped up the dust with his fingers, all the while knowing his efforts were futile.

"Moreth!" The Blue Shields ran towards him, shouting for ropes, shovels, wagons—Farid had blamed the rock-sworn for the death of those two thieves—and now he had killed Moreth. Now he knew what it was like to lose his will to another. They were the same, he and the mage, but it was too late to admit that in any way that mattered. He knelt by the pit of the ruined Tower and held his head in his hands. Time stayed still. He had been playing with the patterns as his sister once played with twine, even knowing they could destroy and kill—for they had killed his mother.

He might have sat there a minute, an hour, or an age, preparing the words he would say when he turned himself in to the Blue Shields who surrounded him.

But a plume of dust rose into the air, spurting like a fountain from the pit, spraying the eastern side of the courtyard, and he gave a great shout of delight. Of course: Moreth was *rock-sworn*. He could not be killed by stone.

"Moreth!" He leaned over the edge and looked at where the lower rooms of the Tower had once been. The dust continued to flow upwards, and slowly the edges of the pit took form. At last Farid caught side of the mage, pale as a ghost for all the dust that clung to his skin, standing in a pile of dissolved stone, wavering in exhaustion.

"Wait!" Farid shouted, and he ran to the bell. He started tugging on its ropes, but the enormous bell sat on top of them. At last, with the Blue Shields' help, he managed to untangle a length long enough to throw to Moreth. Moreth gripped the rope, secured by the bell's great weight, and puffing and panting, they pulled the mage up.

They all collapsed at the edge, coughing and thanking the gods, until Farid sat up again, a new awareness taking form. "What's down there?" he asked Moreth.

"The crack—where the portals were."

"The crack . . ." He looked over the edge. "Can you remove the rest of the dust?"

"Why?"

"Just—please?" Farid's heart beat against his chest. He knew it wasn't the crack; there was something else at the bottom of the pit now: something the ancient pattern had brought forth, either from the past or the future.

As the Blue Shields moved around them, looking for what might be salvaged, Moreth sighed and held out a hand, and once again the dust began to empty from the cavity. Farid watched until it was completely gone and Moreth collapsed against the flagstones.

With a jolt Farid realised he should not have overtaxed the mage—he could end up swallowed by stone—but Moreth was already recovering himself. His efforts had been successful. A circular pool was revealed at the bottom, yellow light dancing across its surface, but it was not water that rippled there. Power warmed Farid's skin, power that drew him like the smell of food after fasting, or the thrill of queenflower, or the touch of the right woman—all of those things together and more. He would go to it. He must go to it. He tugged on the rope to make sure it was still held firmly by the bell, then lowered himself into the pit. The hair on his arms stood on end and his breath caught in his throat.

Above him he heard voices—the Blue Shields asking what he might be doing, Moreth attempting some explanation. Farid held a hand out over the bright circle. This was not molten rock, nor water, nor anything of nature. This was of heaven, powerful and bright, sweet as honey and strong as wine. He heard a Blue Shield shouting down to him, heard Moreth calling his name, but he would answer them later. He stepped up on the copper rim of the pool and looked down into its depths. There he saw glints of green and copper, swimming like fish in the bright haze. He jumped in.

CHAPTER FORTY-EIGHT

GOVNAN

Govnan felt it, hot as a furnace, bright as the sun, and the efreet felt it too, leaving off their work a moment to turn their senses its way. The potent call of magic rose from the Tower's courtyard, strong as a river, ancient as a mountain, brighter and more sweet than the spells coiled into the walls of Nooria. He longed for it as a parched man longs for water, imagined filling himself with its light, wondered at the power he would have if he could only take hold of it. Metrishet let go of its work and flitted in that direction, but Govnan took hold of himself and willed the fire-spirit to stay.

Satreth's hidden magic has been found.

"The Reclaimer?" The emperor who had fought his way back into Nooria and forced the Yrkmen out was the last to see truly powerful mages. Had Yrkmir hidden this magic from the Tower? If so, it was his by right. He turned away again, the temptation biting at him.

We eat. Ashanagur's voice.

First Kirilatat, then Ashanagur turned from their tasks.

Hungry.

Govnan struggled against them, but his will wavered. . . . *Stay to our tasks. The magic will wait for us.* But Ashanagur was ancient and clever, and he whispered to the others, just below Govnan's hearing, urging them to let go, to follow their instincts, to search for the magic, to eat. He even began to whisper to Govnan about the flesh that waited for them to the west, and the bright magic for which he longed.

Desire shook the old man. He fell to his knees. *I will bind you again. I will . . .*

Eat?

Govnan ran his hands along Ashanagur's molten form, feeling its power and emptiness. *Yes. Eat.*

Ashanagur came closer, his colours shifting with longing, tendrils gleaming violet and green. *Yes. I eat.* The fire enveloped Govnan in a cascade of light and beauty that he did not have time to fully grasp before his thoughts began to burn away, one and then the next, like leaves in flame.

CHAPTER FORTY-NINE

SARMIN

They hurried through the dark, torches held high, the street-stones ragged and uneven under their feet. Grada kept an eye on those around them—any one of them could turn and become the tool of the first austere—and his sword-sons watched the roofs and high walls, wary of archers. They took too many risks in their breathless rush to the Tower, but Sarmin had insisted. He would see what the first austere had wrought.

Blue Shields waited for him at the entrance to the courtyard, more torches in hand. Between their flames and the fire in the north Sarmin could see very well. And there was another light, subtle but insistent, rising from where the Tower once had been.

Sarmin halted before a statue of Meksha. He saw no rubble or stone pieces; instead, piles of dust high as dunes, a domed roof big as a house and a great bell lay in the courtyard, surrounded by smaller debris—books, mirror-backs, cooking-pots. No longer did the gleaming roof pierce the sky. The great brass doors no longer warned of power within. The Tower no longer rose like a great pillar, commanding a view of the desert in every direction. Sarmin took a stumbling step forwards. News of this would travel the world swifter than a pigeon could fly, and soon every nation and people would know that Nooria's mighty Tower had been struck low.

A dust-covered, hulking man approached and he recognised Moreth, the young rock-sworn.

"It is gone, Your Majesty," he said. In one hand he held a child's ragdoll, covered with powdered stone.

Sarmin pressed his lips together. "What happened?"

Moreth was slow to speak, like the rock he had bound to him. "Farid might know."

"Farid is alive? Where is he?"

"He went down there, Magnificence." Moreth gestured towards the ruin and scratched his head, looking miserable. "He jumped into the . . . Rorswan says that he still lives."

"Jumped?" Sarmin looked at the hole where the Tower had been. "Show me." Moreth led him on, and he marvelled at the destruction. The first austere must have divined the state of Cerana's mages. Now there would be no avoiding open war, though he did not think the first austere had ever intended he could.

As he grew closer to the ruin a tingling lit upon his skin and his heart beat faster. There was magic here. Moreth stopped at the edge of the ragged pit and pointed. "He jumped into that old well."

Sarmin followed the line of his finger and saw a pool of scintillating light casting colours against the ragged walls of the pit. Around it several Blue Shields were struggling with a length of rope, presumably in an attempt to rescue Farid. Sarmin reached out a hand towards the magic, but it was too far away, fully half the diameter of the ruined Tower. "I will climb down."

"Your Majesty! Will you help with the rescue?"

He did not answer but took hold of the rope that was secured by the great bell and grasped it. He had never in his life slid down a rope, nor climbed up one, but he was the emperor and he must be assumed to be capable of everything. He lowered himself too quickly and the hemp burned the palms of his hands. His slippered feet hit the bottom too soon, shocking him, jarring his knees.

Grada slid down immediately after.

"Your Majesty!" A young soldier with green eyes made his obeisance; the others were still fussing with their rescue attempt.

"Rise," Sarmin said with a gesture, passed the Blue Shield and forgot him. He stood on the edge of the pool, his slippers balanced on the copper rim, and held out a hand to the light. It was the brilliance of it that amazed, the brightness that flowed into him from his suspended fingers, warm and pillow-soft. And when he opened his eyes he saw each man in designs: Didryk's ill-fitting ward laid over his surface, below that the person he presented to the world, and underneath that his true self, shown in a spectrum of colour. One of the soldiers was revealed to be twisted and malicious, but when Sarmin attempted to alter him, he found that nothing had changed in that way; he could not affect patterns, only see them for what they were. This was the wisdom Meksha had offered him.

Sarmin waved a hand at the soldiers. "Leave us."

One by one they made their way up the rope as Sarmin settled in the dust and dirt next to the pool and watched the colours dance over its surface. This was what the Yrkmen had hidden: they had buried Meksha's true blessing beneath the Tower. That explained the fading of their abilities, the dwindling number of mages: with less power there was less to send into every next generation. This was what had cracked the wall—the pool, paved over or blocked for many years, had finally pushed its way through the stone, causing the very earth to tremble.

But though they had gained, they had also lost: they no longer had the portals to the other realms. Those spells had been woven into the stone, and the stone was gone.

That was a worry for another time.

"Can you see the magic, Grada?" he asked.

"Only out of the corner of my eye," she said, and that seemed to him a very good answer. When he turned to her he saw her in many different ways: assassin, daughter, worker, even lover. Her colours were violet and yellow, showing a loving spirit crossed by brutality, and that did not surprise him.

"Farid will be well," he said. He stayed by the pool a while longer, absorbing its warmth. When it came time to rebuild the Tower he would put this pool in its centre, as Ghelen had before him in the days of the founding.

At last he stood and did his best to climb the rope, though in the end the soldiers had to haul him up. As he straightened, dusting the dirt from his robes, he said to Moreth, "You must descend and have a taste of Meksha's blessing."

Moreth looked at the pit with curiosity but said, "I dare not, for my control over Rorswan is weak, Your Majesty."

"As you will." The courtyard had fallen into darkness, even with the torches lining the walls, and with a start he looked to the north. Govnan's great net had fallen, replaced by a featureless, blank space, emitting no light, taking no form. "The Storm," he said, looking away from it, dread curdling in his stomach. Grada took her place beside him, but for the first time her presence offered no comfort.

The sound of running feet filled the silence, sandals slapping against the stone, and when he turned Azeem veered into view, his eyes wide, his robes in disarray. He reached Sarmin's side, put his hands on his knees, and took deep breaths. "Your Majesty," he said, puffing, "the fighting has begun."

CHAPTER FIFTY

SARMIN

"It was Govnan's fire, Your Majesty," said General Hazran, his bushy moustache drooping over his lips, his mind set on both duty and honour. "I believe it wrested control from him before it attacked the Yrkman army."

Sarmin slowed in his path to the throne room. That Govnan was dead had not occurred to him. He pressed his hand to his stomach, as if to push down the rising grief. There was no time to think of the old man, his bright eyes, his wise counsel. Right now there was a battle to fight, and the Storm approached.

"If I may, Your Majesty," said General Merkel, "the Yrkmen attacked first. I hear the first austere attempted to assassinate you with a pattern-spell—and let us not forget they have destroyed the Tower!"

"If that is what happened," said Arigu, his voice hinting at some deception. Sarmin gave him a sharp look.

"They have been attacking us from the beginning," said Lurish, waving a hand. "The marketplaces, the temple of Meksha—"

"In any case, Govnan's fire made a great commotion among the ranks of the Yrkmen, killing many and sending others running in fear." Arigu smiled, his spirit flashing a spectrum of colours. "But then the austeres trapped them—and now they act as no more than lanterns, casting light over the battle."

There was a sudden silence as everyone considered Govnan's likely death. It was Lurish who braved the quiet. "High Mage Govnan is gone—but what of our other mages?"

"The mages survived the destruction of the Tower," said Sarmin, finally moving to the dais. Grada took her place at his right. "They join the fight at the wall." He did not mention that Farid was still at the bottom of a well, leaving only two, but the paucity of the Tower mages would not be secret for long. The soldiers would remember that only two had ever come to fight with them. They would talk, and the talk would eventually spread throughout the empire: the Tower was gone, and Cerana's mages with it.

Mesema came in through the side door, followed by her guards, and walked to the bottom step of the dais. In his sight the essence of her was undivided. Her pattern, herself, and her soul were one and the same. There was no lie to her—and no lie to the love she gave him. He drew strength from that.

"Arigu." He turned to the general. "I want to hear your plan should Yrkmir breach our walls."

A hush fell over the gathered courtiers. Dinar took a step towards the throne, his eyes glinting in the lantern light, as the general gave a lengthy pause. After a moment Arigu leaned in, too close, almost rude in his proximity. Sarmin could feel the tension in the sword-sons behind him. "There is an issue to be addressed, Your Majesty."

"Then address it."

Arigu cleared his throat. "The worship of Mogyrk has been made legal and its priests spread its poison throughout our city. A Mogyrk duke who killed several of my White Hats sleeps comfortably in the guest wing. The Felting chief rests in the temple of Mirra, secure in his friendship with the empress. Even the austere is safe from harm in the dungeon. Consorting with our enemies has led to weakness." Arigu turned towards the small, rapt audience, indulging his sense of theatre. "Now our own Tower has been destroyed. The Tower, a pillar of Nooria, key to our defences, is gone."

Sarmin watched the face of each man in the room. Dinar and Arigu would have planned ahead; they would have spoken to every one of his courtiers, convinced them of the rightness of their complaint. "The duke has protected all of you from pattern-attacks." He did not mention Banreh. He realised Arigu had tricked him into keeping Banreh safe just for this display, and it was not something he wished to admit. "And my wife has proven her loyalty time and again. Did she not help me execute Helmar?" At the foot of the dais Mesema stood very still, like a mouse in the sight of a cat, her men nearly as still behind her.

Dinar gave a chilling smile. "Before that she helped Beyon, heaven and stars with him now."

Beyon had been buried with all honours and no citizen knew he had been marked; but the palace knew. They had deposed him for it. Now Dinar was skirting the issue of Pelar's parentage, so Sarmin spoke carefully. "My brother was never one of the Many." Azeem and Grada flanked him now, both silent, one out of consternation and the other out of rage.

Arigu raised his hands, palms up, to show his honesty. "When I brought her from the Grass, I saw the empress—then the princess—caught in a furtive embrace with the traitor. Long before today she plotted with the chief."

"And I caught her with him in the temple of Mirra, in an intimate tryst," said Dinar. "Assar will attest to it. She is led by this chief and has sympathy for the Mogyrk cause."

Assar backed away, his eyes shadowed. Arigu gestured at one of Mesema's guardsmen. "Sendhil, tell him."

"Your Majesty," said the guard, presenting a sorrowful face, "the empress disappears for long periods of time, out of our sight, and I fear her secrets will lead us to the traitor and his Mogyrk allies."

"You see," said Arigu.

"That is proof of nothing," said Grada. "I was with her—I am not Mogyrk."

"No. You are worse," said Dinar.

She took a half-step, gripping the hilt of her Knife, but Sarmin cut her off with a movement of his hand. "What is this about? The Yrkmen wait at the gate. The Tower has fallen. The Great Storm approaches and yet you are here, spreading rumours and division." A buzzing came to his ears and his skin tingled with the Scar's magic; he shook it off and focused on Arigu.

"My men won't give their lives for a corrupted empire. The city is rotting for the indulgences you give to traitors and Mogyrks, Magnificence!"

A shocked silence fell over the room.

"Give us the chief," Dinar said in a voice like smooth steel, "and put aside your wife. Then the men will fight. Your Majesty." To punctuate his demand Sendhil took Mesema's arm as if he meant to take her to the dungeon, or worse.

The sight filled Sarmin with cold rage and he snarled, "You would bring Nooria to ruin over this?" They knew he would never give up his wife— they would never allow them to take her—but they also knew that he could never abandon his city's defences. It was a trap, designed so he would fail, but what then? Would they install Daveed on the Petal Throne, with Arigu as his advisor? Or would they find Pelar and groom him to their purpose? Trying not to look at the rough hand clenching Mesema's skin he did a calculation: he had Grada and the four sword-sons. They had double that number—if no one switched sides.

Beyond Dinar's dark robes he saw Duke Didryk, standing at the great doors, waiting to be announced. He carried no sword and his guards were not with him.

Sarmin wondered if things might have gone better had he just killed Banreh when his mother told him to—or if he had allowed Dinar to carve the man to pieces. It had never felt like the right time, the right action. Was it Mirra's mercy, or Meksha's restraint—had he held Her gift even before he went to the pool?

He understood Arigu's fears: as a general, he depended on the strength of the emperor. Arigu saw no power in mercy; winning was all-important. Winning palace games, winning battles, winning wars: winning kept Nooria safe. And yet it was for Sarmin to shape the empire, for Sarmin to decide what things were worth killing for, what wars were worth fighting. *What kind of man am I? What kind of man do I want to be?*

Sarmin approached the high priest. "Dinar has been making his sacrifices regularly: a prisoner here, an innocent victim there, sand-cats, birds, jackals—has it helped our city? Has it helped our palace?"

"Herzu is displeased with you and with your love of Mogyrk. Sacrifices do little in such a circumstance."

Sarmin walked a slow circle around Dinar. He saw that the traitor guard still held Mesema in a tight grip and he clenched his fists. "You mean my curiosity, my wisdom, my love for Cerana. These are things you cannot understand. They disgust you." Grada moved closer, her hand ready on the hilt of her Knife.

Arigu waved a hand, uncertainty in his face. "What we are asking for is punishment for the transgressors, no more."

"And tearing the skin from a man is fair punishment?"

Dinar sneered and spat, "Herzu cares nothing for what is fair. Herzu is about power, and what can be done with it. Taking lives, taking thrones. If you are strong enough to do it, then it is yours to do. There is no fair."

"Thank you," said Sarmin, and plunged Tuvaini's dagger between the high priest's ribs as his brothers had shown him, as he had killed the Pattern Master. Behind him steel rang as all the sword-sons drew their hachirahs. Grada already held her twisted Knife and was scanning the men before her.

Dinar fell to the ground, his eyes dark and lifeless, and Sendhil after him, stabbed from behind by one of his own men. Mesema stumbled and sat down on the steps of the dais, her face pale.

Sarmin faced the assembled courtiers. He had decided who he wanted to be, and who should die and who should live. "I claim this palace for Mirra." Not one of them could look away. *What do they see?* he wondered. He turned to Arigu. To his credit the general did not even flinch. "I made an interesting discovery at Lord Nessen's manse," he said, "but you already know about it. You took the slaves from the Grass, violating our ancient agreement with the horse tribes. Banreh learned of it and rightly fought against you.

"Selling slaves who look like the empress and her family would bring you a great deal of money among certain nobles—but your man ran into trouble. He chose the wrong estate to shelter in. There was an altercation and Lord Nessen lost his life. Finally your captain brought the slaves here, only to find that the buying and selling of slaves is barred until my *Code* is finished. He knew Lord Nessen would not come to town, being dead, so he hid them in his manse in the Holies."

Arigu swallowed. "They are Mogyrk—rebels—"

Grada held her Knife to his throat, and he fell silent.

"Duke Didryk treated you well." Sarmin motioned to the tall man standing motionless at the door. "How have the Felting slaves been treated, I wonder? I will find out shortly." Sarmin backed away. "You are guilty of prosecuting a war against my wishes, of making slaves of our allies, and telling untruths before the throne. But you may still go free if you pledge your loyalty to me."

Azeem made a strangled noise in his throat; Grada glanced at Sarmin in amazement.

Sarmin held his breath. The war, the throne, the very survival of Nooria depended on Arigu's decision.

Arigu stood motionless for a moment, then slowly lowered himself to his knees beside Dinar's body, laying his sword crosswise before him. He laid his forehead upon it and spoke. "I pledge all of my loyalty, my breath, my vitality, and all of my words to you, my Emperor."

Sarmin let him wait. He met the eye of every man in the room until, satisfied they were cowed, at last he said, "Rise, Arigu." He climbed the steps to the dais and sat on the Petal Throne. "Lord High Vizier, let it be known that Chief Banreh is to be freed of all constraints and punishments. The Felting people will be given shelter in the guest wing, and he may join them there." He looked at the shaken general. "Now we may speak of the war."

The men looked at one another and at the dead bodies on the floor. Nobody spoke, not even Azeem, though he was clearly struggling to find the right words.

The gong sounded, breaking the moment; the herald rushed forwards, unusually flustered. "The Empire Mother, Your Majesty," he said.

Ice washed over Sarmin's skin. *Something is wrong.* The timing of her return, the fact that she would make her first appearance here, in the throne room, where all the generals had gathered . . . it was the first austere who had decided these things, not his mother.

His fears were quickly confirmed. When she came to the door, passing Didryk without a glance, he saw her black eyes, her expressionless face, and beneath it, the hatred and malice of Yrkmir. "Mesema," he said over his shoulder, "hide!"

Nessaket opened her mouth and from it poured a stream of lines and symbols—triangle, crescent, half-moon, line, triangle again—a bright ribbon of pattern-work that cut through General Merkel like a sword. She lifted both hands and patterns ran from them too, red and liquid, harm at the core of them, cutting through Hazran's cheek before he dodged behind a pillar. The sword-sons ran forwards and she caught one through the neck, his blood and the sharp pattern running together. Boneless he fell to the floor with a clatter of steel. Didryk crept up behind her, his eyes intent, as the patterns flew across the room like blades, cutting gashes in the walls, ripping through cushions and skin with equal ease. Through it all Sarmin stood before the throne, unmoving, and her patterns did not touch him.

Another sword-son neared Nessaket, with Grada close behind. He lifted his hachirah to strike. "No!" Sarmin cried, and the sword-son dropped his weapon and grabbed her wrist instead. The pattern-thread cut his hand and shoulder and his blood rose in a crimson arc. Didryk wrapped an arm around her from behind, putting a hand over her mouth, and Grada and the sword-son managed to push her palms behind her. Blood rushed between Grada's fingers—hers, or Nessaket's?

Sarmin made a quick assessment of the damage. Mesema had hidden behind the Petal Throne and was safe, but she had now lost two guards: Sendhil, and the man who lay across the steps with his throat cut open. General Merkel was dead. Others pressed hands over deep cuts.

He ran to his mother, still struggling in Didryk's arms, her eyes blank and wild. He could see the black pattern that controlled her, rising from the floor and wrapping itself into her mind and her skin. But he could not purge her of it.

He hit his fist against a pillar. "Can you help her, Didryk?"

Didryk frowned and pressed a hand against Nessaket's forehead. "She has been with the first austere for some time," he said, "and the patterns run deep. Still . . ." He drew his thumb across her skin, up, down, around and across, and waited. "No," he said with a frown, "my work is too simple."

Sarmin crouched down before his mother. Behind the web that trapped her, behind her skin, he searched for her, his mother, the woman he remembered from soft nights and song, from garden sunshine and laughter, and from hardship, loneliness, loss. He searched for her grief, for her love, for her anger—and found her at last, buried deep, a flame flickering against the storm that was the first austere's lunacy. "Mother," he called, and she stirred, the flame growing brighter. He pressed his hand against her heart, and her arms thrashed; her head moved from side to side as she tried to free her mouth and loose the pattern upon him. But Didryk and Grada held her firm, and the mother who existed inside the body grew stronger, pushing back at the darkness.

Mesema knelt beside him, adding her hand to his. "Mother," he said, "I know you are there, because you took care not to kill me." In this world there were three people who could never be persuaded to harm him, no matter how powerful the magic: his mother was one, Grada and Mesema the others.

Nessaket opened her brown eyes and looked at him. "Sarmin!" she breathed, and Didryk let her go and stepped back. Sarmin watched the webs that had trapped her die away and shrivel into the floor.

It was not over; the first austere was seeking more people to entrap. But Sarmin could see the path of the first austere's intent, dark against the tiles, and he knew now that he could find him.

"That is twice the first austere has tried to kill you, Your Majesty," said Azeem, his voice straining for his usual calm.

Only twice? But he had failed. Sarmin could not deny feeling disappointment. The first austere was nowhere near as powerful as he had thought. Yes, he had some unusual tricks, but that was the whole of it. Of all the mages in the desert and the city there was nobody who came close to what Sarmin once had been. Only Mogyrk could match him, and Mogyrk lay in the Scar, caught between life and death. But, as weak as the first austere might be, Sarmin could not defeat him alone. He needed a working of many parts, pieces of a design, but not the Many. He needed allies.

He looked over his shoulder for someone to command and found one, a guard standing wide-eyed over Dinar's body. "You: get Austere Adam from the dungeon. We will need his help." No sooner had he spoken than he saw the pattern-ward flash blue on the guard's forehead. When the guard turned, unharmed, to retrieve Adam, Sarmin breathed with relief. The court was protected from pattern-work, just as he had planned. But then the ward flashed red on the forehead of an old captain and he exploded in a spray of blood and bone, the buttons of his uniform falling against the floor like Settu tiles. With another flash, yellow, a palace slave fell upon the cushions, holding his neck, unable to breathe. The first austere was searching for a way past their wards and succeeding—but not completely. Not yet.

Sarmin stood, helping his mother up with him. The first austere must not be allowed to pick off his courtiers one by one. He must be killed, and it would be Sarmin who killed him.

CHAPTER FIFTY-ONE

DIDRYK

Didryk let go of the Empire Mother and stepped into the corridor. Now that she was recovered she would not want to find a Fryth man grasping at her. He did not know the spells the first austere had used—he had never used such things in Fryth; he had not needed to. The surprise, Yrkmir's advantage, had been complete. The first austere did not care about killing his fellow Mogyrks, and he certainly would not hesitate to kill every Cerani if he could find more ways around their wards. Didryk found that he did not want that to happen.

He heard a sound to his left, and turned to see three Blue Shields leading a host of men and women into the corridor, blond of hair and wearing woollen tunics. They must be the Felting slaves who had caused so much trouble. The emperor had found them at last. They were being led towards the throne room.

But cold air rushed against his skin; the hair stood up on his arms and a ringing pierced his ears and sent his teeth to vibrating. He stumbled. This was the familiar power and dread that came from pattern-work, except this time greater than any he had felt before: the first austere was preparing a master working.

285

In a panic Didryk looked around at the Felting slaves. *Let me save at least one . . . at least one this time.*

And then he found the boy, all blond curls and green eyes, and Didryk knew who the child must be, knew what Banreh had not told him, understood at last what had driven his friend to Nooria. Quickly he crouched and drew a ward upon the boy's forehead. No sooner had he finished than the pattern-work pushed over Didryk like a wave and he held the boy's head against his jacket, hiding his eyes.

All around him the Felt flew apart, blood and bone slicing through the skin, their bodies opening like flowers, showing organs and glistening muscle. His jacket was soaked with blood and he tasted something foul on his lips. He felt the same rage he had felt the day his city had been destroyed. *Why?* The first austere would die. Didryk would live long enough to ensure that.

But the boy was safe. "Don't look," he admonished, carrying the boy away, into the throne room. "Come, you will see your father soon."

CHAPTER FIFTY-TWO

MESEMA

Mesema took Nessaket's arm. "Come, Mother. I will take you to your room."

Sarmin watched them, a grave look on his face. He would send High Priest Assar to the women's wing; she did not need to ask him. As she moved towards the corridor a guard caught her eye and shook his head: *no*, something bad waited for her there. Always something bad. And from behind him Duke Didryk pushed his way into the throne room, a boy in his arms, blood on his robes.

Banreh's boy: she could not mistake him. His grass-child, the one he said he had wished he had made with her. She paused, Nessaket leaning against her, and looked at him, so much like the man she had loved that she felt a tear in her eye. *Had loved.*

She had been right about the slaves. She had been right about Lord Nessen's manse, about Arigu, about everything. And in all that time she had doubted herself. Closed in by the palace, closed in by the generals and priests as much as the ancient table at which they sat, she had doubted herself: she, who had found a way through Helmar's pattern, who had freed Sarmin from the torment of his old room. Only Sarmin had ever listened to her. Sarmin had taught her to read, had listened to her words, had fought the Pattern-Master at her side. She turned towards the service door, but Arigu blocked her path.

"The chief didn't tell you, did he?" Arigu inclined his head in the boy's direction. "There is always something he's not telling, something he wants you to do for him. You might have lost everything for that slave boy. The duke, too. Did your Chief Banreh care?"

"But you knew." Mesema spoke with sudden understanding. "You knew the boy was Banreh's son when you took him for a slave." She paused. "And it was you who put me at risk, not him."

Nessaket spoke in a hoarse voice. "That is how Arigu intended to control him—the same way I once sought to control Beyon through keeping Sarmin. But the horse chief is no Beyon, to wait and to hope and to despair."

Shocked, Mesema glanced at Nessaket's face. Her eyes were focused far away. She was not well.

Arigu's hand gripped his sword-hilt, but he did not draw. It was only a dark memory that had moved his hand.

Without another word Mesema pulled Nessaket through the side door. Everyone in the palace sought to control everyone else. And Banreh had sought to control her: he had brought her here and convinced her to accept Arigu's treachery, only to try to persuade her to return with him once it all went sour. His friend Didryk had marked her arm to force her actions. But she was not important, not really; only the sons she might bear. Sons they would also try to control.

Only Sarmin valued her for who she was.

The stairs were difficult for Nessaket, but the guards offered their assistance, and at last Mesema steered the Empire Mother into her bedchamber and sat her down upon a bench.

"It is over for me," Nessaket said.

"All you need is sleep," Mesema said, plumping the cushions.

"I did not mean that I would die," said Nessaket, sounding more like herself. "Only that I am finished with the palace. I am finished with its whispers and its daggers and its love of war. Once I wanted it all for myself, but I am done with that. It no longer has value for me. After I have rested I will sail south with Daveed."

Mesema straightened and looked out the window. There was no view of the Blessing from here; for that she would need to go back to the garden over the old women's wing. "What was he like?" she asked. "The first austere?"

"Like every other man," Nessaket said. "Will you come with me?" Mesema turned the question over in her mind. To be with Pelar, to find safety in the forests of the south . . . but how long would that safety last? How long before the emptiness of Mogyrk sought them there?

"No," she said. "My place is with Sarmin." There would be no pika seeds for her. She would fight by his side as before.

Nessaket nodded, leaned back and closed her eyes.

Mesema passed High Priest Assar as she left the room. He gave her a curt nod as he hurried in to attend the Empire Mother. Mesema made her way back towards the throne room, then stopped at the Great Hall and turned towards the temple wing. If they were all to die here, then she would see Banreh one last time.

No one stopped her as she walked through the curtain of vines. Behind it, he lay as before, except that his wounds looked less severe, his breathing was less ragged. She crossed to him and ran a finger down his cheek. He was still so handsome; his face could still make a traitor of her. But when he opened his eyes she stepped away. "Your son is safe."

"Thank the Hidden God." He moved to sit upright, but thought better of it and settled back against his pillow. "Mesema—listen. Didryk will bring this place down. We have a plan. Afterwards he and I and you and the boy—we will go north. We will be free."

"You are already free: Sarmin has made it so. But Ykrmir stands outside the walls. How did you plan to escape them?"

"Didryk," he said, as if remembering.

She gave a sad laugh. "Only Sarmin thinks things through properly. You should thank him, when this is all over."

He looked at her then—truly looked at her. "So you will not come with me?"

"No," she said, resisting the temptation to touch his face one last time, to feel his lips against hers. She had made her choice long ago, when Beyon still lived. "My place is not with you, not any more. Goodbye, Banreh."

The scent of roses followed her from the temple.

CHAPTER FIFTY-THREE

FARID

Farid ran to the wall, all the way from the Tower courtyard, after finding himself on his back in the early morning light. Govnan's fires in the north were gone. Moreth was no longer with him. Mura had never returned. He guessed the fighting must have begun, and as he drew closer to the Storm Gate he knew he was right. He heard no swordwork, no swinging of maces and chains as in the old stories, but archers moved along the wall, firing their bows, their officers behind them shouting orders. Catapults were loaded and fired and soldiers ran back and forth, relaying messages between their superiors. Farid slowed and watched the unusual activity; he had grown used to an empty city. The wounded sat with their backs against the western wall, cradling their injuries, and he saw Duke Didryk among the physicians.

He did not speak to the duke—he no longer needed his lessons since Meksha had blessed him. Now he understood patterns the way he needed to, down to the heart of them, and he could turn them to his will. But he also recognised their uselessness in the face of what was truly important: his love for his father, loyalty, the trust of his fellow mages. He climbed the steps and found the mages crouched beside a barrel full of arrows. In front of the wall was the Yrkman army, a sea of men and sharp metal, all blond heads and red coats, each one of them bent on getting through the wall.

Moreth held his hands to the stone, his eyes closed. Mura held her hands before her, sending a contrary wind against their archers—but only the ones before the Storm Gate. They did not have enough mages to cover the whole of the battlefield—surely Yrkmir could see that and would take advantage?

The fire-spirits he had seen with Govnan in the north quarter were now gathered into a tight circle, struggling against invisible bonds, surrounded by the charred bodies they had managed to consume before the Yrkmen trapped them. Farid had an idea what to do about that, but first he had to ensure the safety of the Storm Gate.

He ducked down before he became a target himself and Mura, sensing him, touched his arm.

"Look," she said, and Farid raised his head again. An arc of Yrkmen soldiers approached with their shields out, protecting a group of austeres aiming for the wall. They raised their shields higher and higher again to protect the pattern-workers from the arrows and stones being thrown at them, and now Moreth joined in the effort, sweeping sand up into their faces and causing the ground to shift beneath their feet. The rock-sworn did not use as much force as he could have, fearful of losing control of his spirit. But if they made a hole in the stone, then Rorswan could repair it. Five Yrkmen soldiers fell and three austeres with them—but the remainder reached the thick wall. Farid did not try to see beyond the shields at the pattern-workers' fingers. He knew what pattern they would shape.

"Moreth," he said, crouching next to the rock-sworn who was still covered in dust.

"I will make sure the wall remains whole." Moreth spoke in Rorswan's voice.

Farid laid his own hand on the stone. He could sense the shapes the austeres were drawing and he found that by concentrating, he could break their lines even as they were still being formed. He spread his senses out across the entire western wall and felt them all—a dozen patterns, two dozen of them—and lifted the shapes from their webs.

He felt all of the patterns that were laid out in front of him: warding patterns, patterns to call water, and patterns intended for destruction should the Cerani army leave the city and attack them on the sands. Farid concentrated on the wards first, twisting their shapes and dragging lines out of their structures, stripping them of meaning.

Though he focused on the wards, other things sparkled at the edge of his awareness, greater things, and in a breathless rush his sight expanded out to them. He saw the whole city: the life rising from its soldiers, the magic in the charms and prayerbeads they carried, and the power in Meksha's river and well. The wall itself held ancient wards and spells that he could not fathom, even with the power that had been given to him. They twisted and pulsed around the very stones and he knew that Cerana was more powerful than he could ever have believed. Just as the first austere could not have destroyed the Tower without his help, so the Yrkmen could not break through the wall with a simple pattern designed to powder stone.

Beyond the wall he felt the souls that pulsed in every Yrkman, their fears and doubts, their loyalties and brave impulses. Every one of them was as loved and connected to the world as the men who stood on the wall—and that was the evil of this war, of Yrkmir, and of Cerana too.

His senses faded when he turned his mind north, as if a fog had cut them off, and when he turned he saw the Storm bearing down on them, a blank wall as high as the mountains, as if that part of the world had been erased. It had grown so large that he had failed to see it, like the sky. He reached out for the emptiness and tried to sense something in it that he could alter, but he found nothing. It was as if he were blind.

A pattern moved towards him from inside the city—a line, a direction, a stream of dark shapes and letters meant to command—and he recognised the same spell that had been used against him in the Tower. He knew this mage and his madness, and knew his bent towards chaos. It diverged upon the wall, splitting into five, rising up through the stone and winding around the legs of White Hats, sinuous and malevolent. In the space of a moment the soldiers had turned and begun firing at their fellow Cerani. The struggles were short but deadly, and Farid felt the lives go out, five, six, seven. A solemn minute later, the White Hat bodies were thrown over the wall.

Farid watched in horror. He had been luckier when the pattern had taken his body.

"Mogyrk spells," said the man next to him, a captain, by his insignia.

Farid could still feel the edge of the pattern-command, sharp and full of harm, cutting through the soldiers' will. Now he knew how to find the man who had cast it—but there was something he must do first. He glanced at the battle—the Yrkmen had lost their wards and red-robed austeres were struggling to replace them under a hail of stones and arrows. But they were undeterred, as were their archers, focused on their duty.

Farid sensed the pattern that trapped Govnan's fire-spirits, its signs and strokes, and knew it to be the same kind of barrier that the high mage had used against the Storm. The spirits could not sense it and therefore could not break it. He wondered if that was what had kept Meksha's well hidden for so many years. He saved the pattern to his memory before twisting it, lifting the lines from their places in the sand and freeing the efreet.

At once a green and violet fireball spun into a group of Yrkmen archers and they screamed as the conflagration exploded outwards, consuming them. Farid stared in shock: those men had died because of him. He felt the light of their lives leave the world. Four more efreet followed the first, three moving quickly and the other slow, taking a human form. The fire moved among austeres, swordsmen, and archers—it did not matter; it took them all, one and then the next, and the next, and he stood in horror, careless of the arrows aimed towards the wall, towards him. He had seen that a bound mage felt pleasure in his spirit's kill, but he felt only sickness.

The Yrkmen began to run in confusion, but only in the confined area before the gate. The battle was larger than that, spreading beyond Farid's view. He would have to leave the rest of it to the soldiers who were trained to battle, greater in number and less sensitive to death. He turned away from the fighting and followed the line of pattern-casting. He would find the mage who had destroyed the Tower.

CHAPTER FIFTY-FOUR

SARMIN

Their carriages rumbled along the streets, bumping over stones and against wall in their rush, barely slowing for the turns, then rushing onwards again. Sarmin rode in the first; his remaining sword-sons were in the second. Grada sat opposite him in the gloom, still clenching Adam's arm. Since he had been released from the prison she had not let go of him, as if given only half a second the man would betray them. Adam looked comfortable nevertheless, leaning back in his seat with a resigned air. Sarmin squinted at him in the dim light. He saw in the austere a willingness to cause harm, but only to satisfy the zealotry that outweighed every other trait in him.

"I hope that through my cooperation, you will see the greatness and mercy of Mogyrk before it is too late," Adam said to him.

Sarmin did not reply.

The carriage slowed and Grada poked her head out, looking for danger. In a moment she drew back inside and said, "It's Farid, the pattern mage."

"Farid? What is he doing here?" So he had found his way out of the well.

Grada opened the door and the young mage peered in, saw the emperor, and began to kneel on the road. Sarmin waved a hand. "Speak."

"I am following the trail of pattern-work," said Farid.

"And so are we. We will fight this man and end this battle," said Sarmin, projecting more confidence than he felt. Both Didryk and Adam had said the first austere knew secrets no other pattern mage had access to—but so had Helmar, and he had beaten Helmar. Farid climbed in beside him and the carriage continued towards the southern quarter, where middling merchants kept fine houses. Sarmin checked the street and hit the carriage roof. "Stop—stop," he ordered. The horses were making too much noise. They would walk the rest of the way. Grada climbed out first, checking the road for dangers, and the sword-sons had surrounded Sarmin's carriage before he had even placed a hand on the door. Adam climbed out last, struggling without the use of his hands.

"Untie him," Sarmin ordered, and Grada obeyed without comment.

They moved forwards, Grada and the sword-sons listening while he, the mage and the austere used a different sense, reaching out for pattern-work, for its movement and colour, until they came to the wall enclosing a square three-storey house.

"In there," Sarmin hissed.

Farid came to a sudden stop. "No . . ." He looked down at the street, and Sarmin saw rising to the surface glowing triangles, circles, and lines in shades of blue and yellow. In seconds a glimmering circle the length of three men had encompassed them all.

"How could he hide such a pattern from us?" he asked as Farid knelt down, his eyes fixed on the bright shapes.

"The first austere holds Mogyrk's secrets," said Adam in a monotone: words he had likely memorised long ago and now repeated by rote. But Sarmin watched him with concern, wondering whether he might yet betray them.

Farid breathed out, and the pattern's triangles drifted away like petals on the wind.

Sarmin had never seen it done before, the breaking of a pattern, and he breathed a sigh of relief. The first austere's designs were not unstoppable.

"Look," said Grada. Through the gate was a courtyard surrounded by high walls, with a statue of Mirra in the centre. It looked empty, but he blinked and made out a hint of movement. The first austere, dressed in a mix of dull colours, had camouflaged himself against the stones like a moth. Now he stepped before them and Sarmin's vision resolved, showing a muscular, grey-haired man just past his prime. He had expected another austere like Harrol, white and chilling.

He held out a hand to keep his sword-sons from attacking.

Not yet.

The first austere smiled, holding his arms out to either side. His grey hair was still difficult to see against the street-stones, and Sarmin wondered whether that was even his true colour. It struck him that although he could see into men's souls, he could see nothing in the first austere.

The man's pale eyes swept over their group. "Adam. Come to me."

But Adam did not move; he was frozen in place, as if torn between kneeling to his superior and killing him.

Sarmin felt a shift in the street, a tug along his consciousness. "No!" There was yet another pattern hidden beneath them—but the first austere gritted his teeth with effort, for Farid was working against the pattern even as he attempted to loose its destructive power. The newly risen symbols wavered and crumpled.

The first austere lifted a hand, and from it flowed a torrent of lines and shapes, red and menacing, sharp as razors. Sarmin dodged out the way, but the pattern grazed his shoulder, drawing blood.

Finally Adam reacted, spreading his fingers and causing a circle of shapes and lines to appear around them, though he had drawn nothing. He stumbled; it had not been easy.

Their attacker renewed his efforts, lifting his other hand and beating against the ward with a sickly-yellow stream of shapes, and Adam fell to his knees, beaten back by the onslaught. The austere had not yet been able to harm them, but neither could they harm him, stuck as they were within Adam's hastily constructed circle.

"I will kill him," Grada murmured and stepped forwards, her Knife held out in front of her like a shield. But she had put too much faith in the spells wound into that ancient blade, for as she stepped past Adam's shapes, the yellow pattern-stream lashed out at her. She dodged, jumping sideways to avoid the worst of it, but it a crimson line appeared above her sash and spread rapidly, staining the grey linen of her robes. She fell, a stunned look on her face.

"No!" Sarmin cried, and drew Tuvaini's dacarba from its sheath, but Grada shook her head at him from where she lay on the street-stones, trying to stop him from running towards the first austere and being killed. He knew he could not send his sword-sons either.

But Farid stepped out before Sarmin could stop him, his eyes narrowed in concentration. The enemy focused his attacks on the young mage, the yellow and red patterns melding together, but the shapes fell away, bent and broke apart before they could harm him.

Farid could not last long; sweat had already broken out on his brow and his whole body was trembling.

"Now!" Sarmin shouted, and the sword-sons rushed as one, their weapons raised, and Adam rushed forwards too, though he held no weapon, and his green and blue shapes scattered apart across the stone. But the first austere's skin mottled brown and grey and his pale blue eyes changed to rusty pebbles. Half a moment later he had faded into the walls and road behind him. When the men reached where he had been standing, they found nothing but street-stones.

The sword-sons turned in a slow circle, looking for a sign of movement, listening for a footfall. But after a time they lowered their swords. The first austere was gone.

CHAPTER FIFTY-FIVE

FARID

Nobody spoke when they re-entered their carriage. The emperor was lost in thought, his copper eyes shining with frustration as he helped Grada into her seat. She pressed a hand against her stomach. The bleeding had slowed, but she looked pale. Adam appeared shaken, and for the first time Farid felt some sympathy for him. Attacking the first austere must have been to Adam what attacking the emperor would be to him.

Before climbing up into the carriage Farid looked north—and he drew in his breath; all the pattern-work of war had drawn the Storm over the northern wall. It now stretched out over a third of the city and west across the dunes, taking up half of the world, and he realised it did not matter if they won, for the emptiness would take them all, just as Adam had predicted. He entered the carriage still staring at the wall, lost in the realisation that his life was likely over.

"You must pledge yourself to Mogyrk now," Adam said, addressing no one and everyone. "The end is near."

The emperor ignored him and directed the driver towards the Storm Gate.

They travelled in silence. Farid told himself to be brave. He had faced down the first austere, but the advancing void frightened him even more, and now they were heading straight for it.

At long last the carriages stopped. Farid was nearest the door. He did not know the protocol when travelling with the emperor, but he thought that on this day it did not matter. He let himself out into a group of wounded soldiers being tended to by a round priest. The emperor climbed down beside him. Farid bowed and said, "With your permission, Your Majesty, I will join my fellows on the wall."

Sarmin dismissed him with a wave and he ran up the stairs, dreading what he might see. Before he had reached the top he heard screams, high and desperate, and several men ran past him down the stairs, their eyes wild, running in fear. His stomach clenched in terror, but he continued to the top and looked out over the parapet. As he expected, there were no heroic soldiers standing out on the dunes; no flags had been planted in victory. But the Yrkmen were moving away—whether from the Storm or from the walls, he could not tell. Charred corpses, bloody corpses, and patches of sand melted to glass covered the land beyond the wall. He saw the white-clad austere with whom the emperor had spoken; an arrow was sprouting from his chest. In the distance, the larger elementals rested on the dunes as if sated, ignoring those retreating soldiers forced to pass nearby. Farid looked away from the one that had taken the form of a shapely woman; it disturbed him.

But the smaller efreet were not resting; they were making a meal of the Cerani on the wall. He heard a crackle to his right and ducked just as a ball of flame, bright as a tiny sun, darted over him. The elementals took a running archer here, a crouching captain there, their movements teasing and malicious. Soldiers scattered before the grasping fires.

Farid crawled over a charred patch of stone, his mind coiling with dread as he wondered who had been standing there—the captain who had spoken to him? An archer collecting arrows? Mura or Moreth?

With relief he saw his fellow mages standing unharmed beside the barrel, now empty. The arrows had been used up and there had been no one to replace them. As he quickened his steps he saw the rock-sworn press one hand into the stone. Mura held Moreth's other hand, and together they brought forth a churning wall of sand towering high over the parapet, running so far north that it nearly intersected with the Storm and so far to the south that Farid could not see the end of it. Grit stung his face and he covered his eyes with both hands. But the fire was on the other side, giving their soldiers a reprieve.

"I can trap them," Farid shouted. "I remember the pattern the Yrkmen used."

"I can trap them." It was not Moreth's voice but Rorswan's.

"Moreth," said Mura, looking down at the rock-sworn. "let me talk to Moreth."

But the sandstorm shifted, concentrating around the forms of the small efreet, and denser and denser it churned, hissing as it adhered to their shapes, trapping them inside spinning cages. The sand turned to molten glass, gleaming violet, green, and orange, the colours of the fire inside, and with a pop the glass turned into stone and fell to the sand.

Moreth sighed with delight, his spirit pleased with its meal, but the two larger spirits now stirred, their attention focused on the wall, and the protective sandstorm was gone.

"Moreth," said Farid, "I can trap these two." But sand rose up in a rush around the burning forms of the efreet, shifting and falling upwards until the fires were no longer visible, not the green-and-black of the eldest, nor the molten brass of the other. Farid wondered how something so changeable as sand could hold the ancient efreet, but with a loud snick it solidified, became smooth, reflecting the light of the sun in its gleaming, pink-brown surface. Moreth made a grating sound deep in his throat, like two rocks rubbing together, and when Farid turned to look at him he had gone still.

"Moreth?"

Mura turned as well, and shook the rock-sworn's shoulder. "Moreth!"

His colour faded, and at first Farid believed it to be the pale sickness, but it was a different hue: the colour of his stone, the colour of Kobar and the other statues that had once graced the Tower's hall. Moreth had been taken by his elemental.

Mura fell to her knees.

Farid kept a hand on the rock-sworn's shoulder as if comforting him. Perhaps he was still aware, trapped inside the rock as the rock had been trapped inside him. "He saved us from the flame," he said through numb lips.

Mura nodded and took Moreth's stony hand in hers. "He didn't have long enough—he never learned . . ."

Farid put his other hand on her shoulder. "What will we do?" But Mura had no answer for him. Even if they fought off Yrkmir and stopped the Storm there would be no Tower, and only two mages remaining. With the fire gone the soldiers on the wall resumed their business with a disturbing calm, returning the odd shot from persistent Yrkmen archers or preparing their stations for the next attack.

Farid sighed. They had not defeated the first austere, but his army was broken, at least for now. Bodies burnt almost to cinders were scattered across the sands, but he knew the morning had been won by more than just fire; it had also been the archers, Moreth and Mura, and the overall hard work of Cerana's army. He had helped too, by destroying their wards. But most of all there was the Storm, obscuring the sky and rushing forwards at each use of the pattern. Surely that had affected Yrkmir's morale and made them hesitate to use their main strength—their patterns—against Cerana. Whatever they believed, the austeres were only human.

He took Mura's elbow and helped her up. Their work was not yet done.

CHAPTER FIFTY-SIX

DIDRYK

Didryk had set up his station by the Storm Gate, where he had been busy wrapping wounds and setting minor patterns to start the soldiers' own bodies healing, but every time he glanced over his shoulder, the Storm looked closer. Now he helped to load the men onto wagons and move them further south, though he knew they could not outrun it forever. His hands shook as he gathered up his bandages and pushed them into the chest High Priest Assar had brought him. It also contained needles and thread, herbs and queenflower for pain. Just as he shut the lid someone pulled at his arm, and he turned to see the emperor. "Your Majesty!" He looked past him for Azeem, but saw only his sword-sons, each one of them nearly tall as himself and more muscled. Even the woman who normally followed Sarmin like a ghost was not there.

"You are a physician, Didryk."

"Not . . ."

"I need you to heal Grada." Sarmin motioned to the carriage.

"What has happened?" Didryk stuck his head inside and saw the woman laid out across a bench, her robes stained with blood, a hand pressed to her abdomen. She blinked at him, her eyes dull.

Sarmin jostled his arm as he too pushed his head in to look at Grada. It struck Didryk that he cared for her more than an emperor should care for a guard or an assassin. "The first austere cut her," Sarmin said, his own face pale. "We did not defeat him."

Didryk felt a twinge of fear: so the first austere still walked the city, laying his patterns . . . he could take one of them at any moment, or worse.

Instead, he concentrated on the task at hand. "Get her into the light." Ignoring the approaching Storm, he allowed the sword-sons to pull Grada from the carriage and lay her out upon the stones. Gingerly he opened her robes and examined the cut, then looked up at one of the guards, a brown-eyed, thin-nosed young man. "Get me needle and thread from that chest."

"Do you not have a pattern that will fix it? I would have—" Sarmin stopped, biting his lip.

"It does not work that way. It takes time."

The sword-son handed Didryk his tools and he probed the wound, checking to make sure nothing vital had been damaged. "Our main concern here is keeping the wound from turning foul. I will lay what patterns I can—"

"I could have done it before I lost my ability. I need you to try." Sarmin took a stone from his pocket and pressed it into Didryk's hand.

Didryk turned it in his palm. Set into the stone in tiny crystals was a butterfly, rendered in a rainbow of colours, the patterns of its wings in perfect, patterned detail. Someone had spent months, perhaps years, making this. "What—?"

"It's the key—the key to healing the wound. All wounds. Show her how to be whole."

Show her how to be whole. That was what Didryk did whenever he healed. "Yes," he said, "I know how to hold an injury on one side and the healed image on the other."

"The truth of destruction and the lie of being healed."

"Yes." All of this Didryk had learned years ago from his stolen books, though not in those words. He wiped the sweat from his forehead. It dripped down his back and chest and filled his palm where he held the butterfly-stone. The Great Storm had not stopped the heat of the sun, though it obscured the northern sky.

Sarmin tapped the stone again. "Try." And then, in a lower voice, "Please." His men looked up and down the street and at one another, hands on the hilts of their weapons, eyes sharp and wary.

Didryk closed his eyes and sent his pattern-sense into the wound, a neat-edged cut across the flesh. If it had been any deeper she would be dead already. He clasped the stone in his hand and imagined her stomach healed—no, smooth and undamaged, as if she had never met the first austere. He looked at the skin around the wound and imagined it whole, imagined how she had looked to him in the throne room, athletic and full of health. But he felt nothing, only the street-stones beneath his feet, leading into those now gone, lost in another, greater wound, their constituent parts of rock and gem and iron unwound and fading into the Storm.

It was all wrong, the coming apart of things. Mogyrk offered on one hand the power to transform and heal, and on the other, destruction and rot. Didryk held them together, the emptiness before him and the street-stones that should exist in its place, and he envisioned the lost houses, the lost carts and boats, the window-screens and bed-ropes, everything he sensed within the void, the scattered pattern-pieces without the lines to anchor them, drifting away towards the Scar. And in the Scar was Mogyrk, caught in the moment of death, His power deep and whole, not described by any pattern but giving life to every one, and every one lashing Him to the earth. In Him lay a riot of colours and thoughts, frayed but alive, sorrow sharp enough to cut. *Madness.* Shaken Didryk withdrew from the Scar and stilled his thoughts.

Sarmin gripped his arm. "It is done."

Didryk opened his eyes. Grada lay before him, her skin unmarked, undamaged. And he looked north, beyond a long street lined with houses, ovens, carts, and temples, to the horizon, where mountains rose up into the heavens. The Storm had cleared. He saw the distant peaks and his heart lurched. He had missed looking north towards his home. *Home.* Mogyrk had no home besides the Scar.

"With the Storm gone the Yrkmen will regroup," said Sarmin, standing. "We must hurry."

Didryk blinked. He tried to stand. Then darkness took him.

CHAPTER FIFTY-SEVEN

FARID

"**N**ow that the wound in the north is healed, Yrkmir will attack again," said Adam. "They are bent on destruction and not so easily discouraged as this."

Emperor Sarmin agreed. "There are other wounds they might call near; they seek to encourage the Storm. They left one in their own lands to fester there—the Megra told me so. They want it to be the end of everything . . . only their soldiers might disagree."

Farid leaned forwards. "And so what do we do, Your Majesty?" The carriage began moving with a jerk, the horses' hooves clattering along the street-stones. Farid could not help but cling to the edge of the window. This was only his third time in a carriage.

"Our task is to face the first austere," said the emperor, his face grim. "We go to the Scar."

Austere Adam rubbed his chin as he considered it. "Of course he has gone there. He would want to be close to Mogyrk." Farid watched him warily. His hands had been tied before; now he was free. He was not sure whether the man was a prisoner or a trusted ally.

"We know that it is possible to walk through the Storm," said the emperor. "We need only to trick Mogyrk's eye."

"You cannot walk through the Scar as through the Storm," said Duke Didryk, slumped against the wall and speaking with care, "for the two are very different. It is the difference between the river that feeds the ocean and the ocean itself. Everything the Storm takes ends up there—streets, trees, thoughts, emotions. I felt them flowing into the Scar when I healed Grada. But we must find a way. Mogyrk must be killed."

The austere sat up on his bench. "He cannot be killed, neither can He be brought to life."

"It is He who is causing this," the duke said. "We tie Him to the earth with our spells, bringing His death to all of us. You have felt it, Adam: His vitality that lends power to our spells. Whenever we draw away His life, He searches after it."

"But it is foretold!"

Silence fell in the carriage as it twisted and turned. "The battle . . ." Mura began. Tears for Moreth still wet her cheeks.

Grada, next to her, shifted on the bench seat. "It is in Arigu's hands now. We have strong protections—and killing the first austere will advance our cause. We bring Blue Shields with us."

The carriage slowed. "A quick stop at the palace," said the emperor, opening the door and climbing out. "I need all of you working together if we are to prevail, and here is our path through the patterns."

Farid looked past him to the courtyard beyond and saw Rushes, standing with a dark-haired older woman. He smiled, and she caught sight of him and smiled and waved, and he wondered if she knew who he was without hearing his voice: she was well—she could see. His heart felt lighter. He may have made too many mistakes in the last few days, but at least he had helped Rushes. He waved back at her. He would do what he could to keep her safe. That was what it meant, to be of the Tower.

The dark-haired woman stepped forwards and took Emperor Sarmin's hands. "Remember, my son: you are the emperor. The desert is yours. Nobody can defeat Cerana on the sands." The emperor squeezed her hands and let them fall. The fair-haired woman Farid had met before climbed into the carriage together with the emperor. With a jerk they set off again.

"Empress," said the duke, bowing as best he could in the close space.

Farid concealed his surprise. *The empress!* A week ago he might have questioned the wisdom of bringing a woman on such a dangerous mission, but
he knew Grada and he knew Mura—he knew much more about women
now. He would not want to fight without them.

"The Scar is close," said Duke Didryk. "I can feel it."

They rode southwards in silence and passed through the Low Gate. The
roads east were unused and often covered by sand, slowing the carriage.
They waited, rocking in the darkness. Farid could feel a buzzing against his
skin. After a time, against all expectations, he fell asleep.

He woke to Austere Adam's voice. "Here—here. I can feel him." Someone
hit the roof of the carriage and they stopped moving. Farid sat up, trying
to get his bearings. The inside of the box was as hot as an oven, but the air
outside promised no relief. Everyone moved sluggishly, stretching arms and
legs; somehow the urgency of their mission had left them during the long
journey.

The door was opened by the coachman and Grada climbed out first, her
eyes scouring the sands for enemies. Mura followed her, then the duke, until
all of them were standing under the heat of the sun. The sweat evaporated
from Farid's skin in seconds. He turned and looked all around. Behind
them flowed a train of carriages, one for the sword-sons and Azeem, the
rest full of Blue Shields.

He looked east and saw it: the Scar rose before them, a wall of scintillating colour and motion. While the wound at the northern wall had been
blank and featureless, the Scar showed energy and light. It was so large that
he could not determine its distance. It took up the whole of his vision, and
yet he could see the dunes in front of it, far enough away to make it a day's
travel. He tried to make sense of what he was seeing, feeling the magic
prickle against his skin.

"Here!" A strangled cry from Adam.

The first austere rose before them, sand still sliding away from his form.
Farid had seen Adam's ward in the southern courtyard; he could easily remake it. As he worked, a wind flowed from Mura, brushing against his
cheek. Duke Didryk scuffed at the sand and knelt, undoing a pattern hidden there. Emperor Sarmin stood in the midst of them all, not moving,

and neither did the empress at his side, though her golden hair wafted in Yomawa's wind.

Behind him Farid could hear sand scattering from running feet: likely Blue Shields running from their carriages. "Stay back!" he shouted over his shoulder, not knowing whether his words would have any effect.

Mura held out one arm, her palm flexed outwards, as she moved in front and set the full force of Yomawa against the austere. Sand rushed from the ground with a loud hiss, flying against her enemy, each grain carrying the force of a dagger, but warding symbols flared and the sand fell harmlessly to either side.

The first austere lifted his own hands, palms facing out, and from one came a ribbon of indigo shapes and lines, hastily constructed but deadly nevertheless, cutting through Adam's cheek like the edge of a sword. The man had learned how to bypass the shapes Farid had put together. Blood splattered over his robes as confirmation, and a line of bright yellow, looking sickly beneath the sun, came from the first austere's other hand.

Farid raised no hand. No movement was required, no drawing of circles. It was his mind—his will—that unravelled that thread before it could cut again.

Mura raised her hands against the first austere a second time and sand swirled around Farid, obscuring his vision, ending his work. He could not protect himself. The austere's pattern came across the fingers of his outstretched hand and snapped them. He screamed as bones punctured skin and he fell back. The sand blowing against his wound was an agony of tiny blades, and the knowledge that he was about to die settled inside of him—but the austere could not see either, and the stream of pattern-shapes flowed over Farid's head and beyond him into the desert.

"Concentrate!" Adam snarled at him. "Forget the pain." Farid got to his knees and saw the duke caught in a whirlwind, his dark hair blowing like a cloud around his face. He looked uninjured, but his hands were pinned to his side and his eyes and mouth were squeezed shut against the sand.

"Kill him," said Didryk, his voice tight with concentration, though what he was doing, Farid could not tell.

"Hurry!" Mura said. "I can't hold him long." The whirlwind faltered and the austere began to smile.

Grada started to move towards the first austere, but the emperor stopped her.

"No, Grada," he said, taking the Knife from her hand. "This is our work now." With his left hand he took his wife the empress' arm and together they stepped into the biting sand.

"Magnificence!" Grada fell to her knees. "No—!"

The austere fought to lift one arm and pointed at Mura, a river of molten silver shapes flowing from his fingers, its course unaffected by wind or sand. Farid caught the pattern in his mind and struggled to undo it, but it felt sticky, as if strung together by honey. Adam joined with him, and the shapes rippled under the force of both their efforts, but still Mura screamed and clutched her throat, falling to her knees, choking.

The first austere lifted his other arm and pointed at the emperor.

CHAPTER FIFTY-EIGHT

Mesema clutched Sarmin's hand and with their eyes closed, they pushed through the wind and sand. She remembered the path through Helmar's pattern as well as her own corridors, and this pattern was a simpler, rougher one: half-moon, line, circle, dot, square. Her path lay clear. She stepped around the shapes and Sarmin moved with her. A second later the sand that had been scouring her cheeks and neck fell away. *Mura is hurt, or dead.* She could not stop and look. She paused, searching for more patterns to come against them and saw the first, red against her eyelids. Circle, square, half-moon again. She sidestepped, pulling Sarmin along with her.

Sarmin let Mesema lead him. He felt Mura's attack fall away and wondered whether his wind-sworn mage had died. His hand sweated around the twisted hilt of Grada's Knife. The last time he had used it, his brothers had spoken to him, guiding his hand; but today the Knife was silent. Heat seared his cheek—an attack from the first austere, barely avoided by Mesema's sidestep. He knew he was drawing closer to his enemy; he could smell the man's sweat and the stink of his wool, fabric for the mountains,

310

not for Cerana. The man did not belong here. The conviction strengthened him and he gripped the Knife harder.

Mesema took two more steps and sidestepped again. "Pass through the diamond," she said, pulling him to his left. Then she stopped. He listened to her breathing. "We are there," she said at last.

Didryk knelt beside the wind-sworn mage while Farid and Adam focused on protecting them. Mura's neck swelled and her face began to turn blue. She had stopped struggling. He touched her clammy skin. The pattern had polluted her with disease and infection. He moved his fingers, beginning to undo what had been done.

"Save her!" shouted Farid, his emotion clear in his voice.

Yes, I know. I will try. Didryk remembered the slaves in the corridor, remembered lifting Banreh's son from the carpet of their dead flesh. *But not everyone can be saved.*

Mura's back arched; her body convulsed. *Not yet—not yet.* He began another pattern, one that would open up her airway so that she could breathe. He had done it only once before, and he did not have Farid's memory—but the mage took a gasping breath, and then another, and he wiped his eyes. "Thank Mogyrk," he whispered, lifting his head for the first time, and saw the emperor and his wife.

Sarmin and Mesema walked towards the first austere, hand in hand, and the grey-haired Yrkman held out his palms to them. From his left spiralled a stream of shapes and lines glowing in reds and blues, and from his right came the same silver pattern that had nearly killed Mura. But the emperor and empress walked unharmed through the attacks. The empress was leading, sometimes stepping to the side, sometimes walking straight ahead, but never hesitating. They drew closer to their enemy, until at last the austere's eyes grew wide.

"We are there," said Mesema.

She dropped his hand and Sarmin opened his eyes to look into the pale gaze of the first austere.

"You cannot stop this," said the first austere, gesturing at the Scar. "It is foretold: all of the world will be dust."

"That is your desire?" said Sarmin, raising Grada's Knife.

"My desire is irrelevant," said the austere. "It is Mogyrk's will that all who are part of His design will go into the light and the rest will be destroyed."

Sarmin pressed the blade against the austere's chest. To his credit, the austere did not flinch away. Curiosity made him ask, "Was it foretold that I would kill you?"

"I am ready to join Mogyrk in paradise," said the austere. "But you will die after me, and go to dust."

"So be it," said Sarmin, and drove the blade home. The Knife vibrated against one of the man's ribs, and blood flowed out over his hand. The austere's mouth opened as if to say one more thing, but instead he crumpled. Sarmin knelt over him and grasped the hilt of the Knife to pull it free. The wind blew soft against his cheek and he heard a whisper: *Well done, my brother*. Pelar spoke through the Knife that had killed him.

My brother! Sarmin knelt over the dead austere, tears filling his eyes, but he heard nothing more. He had another brother now, Daveed, all soft flesh and curls and smiles. A brother to fight for. After a moment he pulled Grada's Knife free, stood up, and turned back to the mages.

Didryk knelt by Mura, who sat up, coughing and clutching at her neck. Adam's cheek had been sliced open and blood streamed down his face and robes, but he did not appear to have noticed; his blue gaze was blank as it met with Sarmin's. Farid clutched broken fingers. And Grada—Grada watched him, relief in her eyes. He resisted the impulse to go to her and instead took Mesema's hand.

"Didryk, can you heal Adam and Farid as much as possible?" he asked. "We are not yet done: the pattern-work he used will have the Scar upon us shortly." He turned to Grada. "You must guard Azeem and the others. Do not approach the Scar again—if things go wrong, you must follow Pelar south and guard him, for he will be the emperor after me." Grada opened her mouth as if to protest, but then she bowed and turned away.

Sarmin crouched in the sand and took a breath. They could be afforded only the shortest of breaks before the real work began: the work of healing the Scar.

CHAPTER FIFTY-NINE

"We're ready." Sarmin took Mesema's hand and squeezed it. He motioned to the mages and they gathered into a group. Each one of them knew their task. Each one of them was to apply their own talent: Didryk, to make things whole, and Farid, to keep them from unravelling; Mura with her wind-spirit to hide them, and Adam to lend his strength. The Scar had reached towards them and its wall was now just a few yards away, as if in welcome.

Farid took Mura's arm and marked it with a binding symbol for air. "If this works, Yomawa is no longer bound, just chained. I think this is what Govnan did in the other plane. Then it can surround us." In response to his words the wind whipped up around them, hurling sand into Farid's face. He lifted a hand to protect his eyes.

The sand did not blow at Mura. She looked into the sky. "Yes. I feel it."

Sarmin did not ask Mesema whether she was ready. She clenched her hands to keep them from trembling. "It is time," he said, "Let us begin."

Duke Didryk walked behind Mage Mura. As he approached the Scar he felt a shedding, a falling-away of things he no longer required—grief, despair, fear—and the emptiness tingled along his skin. He could let it all go; he could fall into pieces, let Mogyrk pull him apart looking for Names and meanings and misunderstand it all. It would be a relief. But then he remembered himself and what he was here to accomplish. He shook off the temptation offered by the void and kept on, Yomawa's wind blowing wildly through his hair.

A flower trembled into view, shaking into existence, its Names and parts winding together for the briefest moment, holding onto the lie that was the pattern—but the lie could not sustain it and it began to crumble. *The truth and the lie together,* Sarmin had told him when he handed him the butterfly-stone. Didryk held it together, let it see itself as a whole flower, reflecting his own vision of it, before he moved on, catching an entire tree in its instant of wholeness. His steps were slow and he held on to Mura's robe to keep her from going too quickly. His fingers began to snap apart, flesh from bone, but he felt Farid's hand on his shoulder, repairing the pattern that was Didryk. Mogyrk could not see him for the whole person he was; Mogyrk saw only skin, flesh, blood, bone; without the idea to bind them the separated symbols would drift into the chaos that was the Great Storm.

They walked in a line, Yomawa first, then Mura, then Didryk, followed by Farid and Adam, and the emperor and his wife. Time and distance warped and curved so that the duke did not know how far they walked or how long they had been there. He caught and made whole whatever he could—grass, leaves, birds, toads—though he was never sure if he made them what they had been or only what he could summon from broken shapes and twisted lines. It mattered only that they left the chaos and made themselves solid and real. He did not know how long he walked, with tiny steps pushing against Yomawa's fierce wind, fixing all that he saw, but he did know the exhaustion that rose within him. Had it been a day? Two? Longer? Time had no meaning in the Storm.

When Didryk did not think he could take another step Mura said, "We are there." They had reached the centre of the Scar, where Mogyrk both died and did not die. Didryk stumbled to his knees at the foot of a large rock, one that before the death of Mogyrk and before the Scar would have offered shade and comfort to a traveller. It had always existed there, at the centre, unaffected by the flickering of the pattern. It was said only the most blessed and holy were allowed to approach the place of his god's death; he, apostate though he was, now reached out and touched the rough surface. Here at the centre the Storm did not exist, and yet the stone was crumbling. Dust came away on his fingers.

Sarmin touched the grey stone. Here was the god's true wound, the focus of the confusion in the Storm. He had no plan for this moment; he had planned only to reach the centre, and once there he had hoped the solution would be obvious. But now he hesitated.

He did not think the others had noticed they were standing in a meadow. The mages' concentration had been so hard and their exhaustion was now so complete that the great rock at the centre commanded all their senses. But green grass sprinkled with wide-topped flowers surrounded them. He had never seen anything green except for gardens grown in pots, such as Assar and his mother kept. Sarmin looked with amazement at each blade of grass and each flower; they numbered in the thousands. Didryk had put together every one from the spinning chaos. Now the duke knelt, his face grey, and Adam prayed beside him. Farid and Mura stood together, both pale and shaken. But they were alive—everyone was alive. So far.

The grass tossed under Yomawa's hand and Mesema turned her face to the meadow. "The wind will show me what to do," she said quietly. She pressed his palm against the stone and he felt it, squirming and spinning within the flesh: the god. The man.

Mesema watched the images form in the grass. She saw Him, the Mogyrk god, in the lashing wind. He had torn the world apart to learn what it was made of, given everything a name, and then tried to build it up again. But as Sarmin had told her, the pattern was a lie; it could not reproduce life in full. It had failed with Beyon, and likewise the god had failed, for he had created an approximation of life, not real water, not real fire, not real people. Finding himself alone, he tore it all apart again, looking for the missing essence, trying to learn what he had done wrong, but in his growing madness he could no longer distinguish one thing from another, not even himself.

The desert grew and though the pattern had become a chaotic blur to him, still he reached for it. When Helmar used it, when Sarmin used it, when Yrkmir used it, he reached for it and tried to understand it again, but he could not. He was unable to see life, but he could not see death either, and so he waited.

Now she felt him beneath her hands, writhing in pain and loneliness. For a thousand years the pattern had been his only company: the pattern of lies and misdirection. If his body truly made a bridge to another world, it was sustained only through his agony.

Sarmin took her other hand, and together they embraced the great rock. "We have brought back your meadow," he said, "and your birds and butterflies." He had to shout to be heard above the wind.

"Remember yourself," Mesema said. "You are a man of great power. You created the pattern, and then you broke it. We fixed it for you—come and see."

The god stilled, listening, but she knew their words danced around him like fireflies, detached from their meaning. She stroked the hard stone and imagined a man of Yrkmir, tall, blond, wrapped in woollen robes. "Remember yourself," she repeated. She tried to show him what the wind had shown her. A scream rent the rock in two; a great crack sounded and Adam and Didryk dived out of the way as the two pieces of stone fell apart. Inside stood a sculpture of a tree, each part from the roots to the leaves above rendered with lifelike movement. A tree could not live without each of its parts: the leaves to draw in sunlight, the branches to carry water, the roots to drink. Mesema touched the bark, cold from its time inside the stone. "We must become part of him."

Sarmin did not question her. "What is the symbol for Mogyrk?" he demanded of Adam.

Adam stood and frowned at the rich soil that clung to his robes. Though he was the priest of the god who lived here, he seemed the most confused by the Scar. He drew a symbol in the air. "Draw it on the tree," said Sarmin, and Mesema watched the austere's fingers as the symbol was constructed. All this time the god was quiet, though Mesema reached out with all her senses trying to find him. And then he reached back, his mental fingers exploring, and she felt her skin pulling away like wet clothes. It did not hurt; it felt as if she became two things—Mesema's blood and bone, and Mesema's skin. But then she felt Farid's hand on her and she became just Mesema once more.

"Thank you," she murmured. *You see?* She directed her thought at the tree. *I am human like you.* "Farid," she said, shouting over the wind, "bind me to the tree. Use the Mogyrk symbol and bind me."

The mage looked to Sarmin first, but she grabbed his arm. "Bind me."

"Bind her," Sarmin said. "Bind *us.*"

Farid drew on their wrists with his finger and Mesema felt Sarmin flow into her, felt his love and his determination. Then Farid drew the same mark on the tree and together they plunged into the mind of the god, clasping hands to keep hold of themselves in the presence of such power. And madness.

All alone. Leaf wing wine sand song hair. What petal thorn am oil berry taste. I. Twist string wind warmth drink failure. Cannot tree six. See. Alone. The god shrieked and writhed like a baby.

This Mesema understood. This she knew. *Shhh now. You are safe. We have you.*

One two petal me. What—what am I?

You are a man. You are a mage. A god. In her mind she wrapped him in her arms, cradled him as she would cradle Pelar. *We have come to help you.*

A pause. *I remember.*

Sarmin joined them, his voice resonant and soothing along the bond-marks. *Do you remember the pattern?*

I remember I cannot die.

You can die now. We have you. You are safe. Your meadow—can you see it?

Yes. I see it. I see you. Both. I see . . . Mogyrk's mind faded. *Love.*

When the god died there was no fire, no trembling of the earth, no parting of the heavens. The wind blew over the meadow, and the flowers scattered their petals.

Mesema leaned back from the stony tree.

Adam fell down on his knees and wept, and Didryk stood to his side, looking lost. Farid and Mura embraced one another; he ran a finger along her wrist and the wind died down. Through all of it Sarmin held Mesema's hand and used their bond to stay with her. She liked that. She had been linked to Beyon and then to Banreh, but never before to her husband.

She stepped closer and laid her cheek against his robes and he wrapped his arms around her.

"Is it over?" she asked.

"It is." Sarmin raised his voice so the others could hear. "It is over." His gaze swept back towards his city. "And it is just beginning."

Grada found Sarmin a while later and asked for her Knife. He gave it to her with no argument and they stood together, watching the grass bend in the wind. "Do my brothers ever talk to you from the Knife?" he asked.

"No."

"How long were we in the Scar?"

"Days." She smiled. "Arigu was here with news of Cerana. We have won the battle. They did not wish to fight once the austeres sensed their leader was gone."

He had won this war, if one could call it that; but there would be other enemies, other battles, and his empire had much work to do before that. Sarmin watched the grass, enjoying Grada's quiet company, not wishing to end it just yet.

She stretched and looked to the south. "I should make my way downriver to find Pelar and the other wind-sworn, Hashi," she said, "and bring them back to Nooria."

"Yes," he said, his heart heavy. But Grada would return, and she would bring him his son. He had said too many goodbyes, but this would not be one of them.

"You were brave," she said, and he inclined his head in thanks. They fell silent again, and he wondered that the two of them, who had once been so close, had so little to say—but perhaps that came through knowing one another well enough that words were unnecessary.

At last she moved off, towards the Blue Shields and their conical tents, the banners flying in the breeze.

That night Mesema found him standing in the grass, staring out towards Nooria. He felt her approach and turned, reaching out his hand. She clasped it and stood by his side. The sun had already set, but in the dark the city remained visible, a massive beast of light-coloured stone rising from the sands and cutting across their view of the mountains.

"It is not so destroyed that we cannot rebuild it," he said.

Along their bond she felt hope and determination.

"No." She shivered, and he wrapped an arm around her. "The question is, will the desert take over the meadow, or the meadow the desert?"

"We will find out," he replied. "My plan for the city will not change either way. Between the Tower courtyard and the ruined temple of Meksha I will create something new, a place for learned men to gather and share their inventions. The temple scholars will be the first to establish their workshops there, but we will invite curious men from all over the world."

"And the Tower?"

"We have yet to explore the magic that Meksha left for Uthman. We don't know all the things it can do, or its dangers. When we know more we will know what to build."

Mesema squeezed his hand and looked back towards the others. Azeem, Didryk, and Adam sat around the fire, talking. Adam kept his head bowed and his words short.

"You didn't ask about the palace." Sarmin wrapped his arm around her shoulders. "The palace will be rebuilt too, with apartments for the empress close to mine. And there will be no temple of Herzu, and no slaves."

She said nothing, only listened. He continued, "Since we are rebuilding, why not rebuild the very ways of the empire? I can start with the palace, as it belongs to me. The palace will establish the ideal for everyone. In all my years living in the palace its ways have never suited me."

"Nor mine," she agreed.

"We shall make it more Windreader."

Smiling she tugged him away from the fire, further into the dark.

"Where are you taking me?"

"On nights like this, the young Windreader women may choose a man to take into the grass with them. And here is grass. And I choose you."

He followed her until the men's voices grew faint and the darkness covered their movements. Mesema dropped into the grass and he sat down next to her. Singing drifted from the campfire and he leaned forwards, listening, surprise on his face. "Can Azeem sing?"

She caught the distant melody and laughed. "You know, I think he can."

"And I can hear it." Sarmin smiled and put a hand against her cheek. "It is a good tune. There is so much more for me to learn: how music works, how to make machines, how to build a dome—and all about you."

"You know all about me."

"But I don't." He lay back and looked up at the stars. "I have never been so far from the palace, and yet I feel that I am home."

"You are home. All of this is yours." Mesema leaned back on her hands and watched the moon. His fingers curled around her shoulder and she turned back to him.

"Ours," he said. "Ours."

ACKNOWLEDGEMENTS

This is for everyone who was there, in the middle of the day or the middle of the night, to offer encouragement: John Anderson, Will Carlson, Teresa Frohock, Lorin Manley, Phil Mazarakis, Keith Rodwell, Vincent Russo, Courtney Schafer, Marie Semensi, Fred Swart, Gillian Swart, Sarah Swart, and many others. Also thanks to all the BookSworn and Night Shade authors who share their wisdom without hesitation. Finally, to everyone who buys books and recommends them to friends: you are the best! Thank you.